Chapter One

"I am an orphan," she whispered.

Cassie Belanger watched as her mother's casket was lowered into the sandy desert soil. The sky was blue, bright and sharp at noon; already it was nearly seventy degrees and still February in Bowie, Arizona. By June, Cassie knew, the heat at midday would be unbearable.

A dry north wind whispered sand over the toes of her shoes, carrying the faintest scents of juniper and sage. It seemed very quiet, standing there on the wide marble-pocked lawn listening to the squeak of the pulleys as they brought the body of forty-two year old Kathy Belanger, clad in her best purple only-for-church dress, to her final resting place.

A single blue carnation, from the high pile of flowers heaped atop, slipped from the casket lid and fell softly into the concrete lined grave below. Cassie watched as it tumbled end over end into the darkness that waited to receive her mother's body. Her mind was still in free fall, her world had changed so suddenly, so dramatically, and she couldn't, at least she hadn't yet, been able to grasp the enormity of it.

The service had been brief; Pastor Williams intoning the Lord's blessing on Katherine Belanger, his voice echoing flatly in the thin desert air. He spoke of her mother's life, of her faith and her sudden tragic end.

A step from a dark curb; from the same corner of the same street that she crossed five nights out of seven, coming home in the early morning hours, her heavy wool jacket hiding starched nurse's whites. A mile-long walk from Bowie's Adventist Hospital to the Desert Rose trailer park where a dozen and a half decaying trailers housed the most desperate rung of Bowie's dwindling population.

"A step from the curb and into the arms of God," Guy Williams had said, as he stood at the pulpit and addressed the handful of somber clad co-workers, neighbors and friends.

Cassie had cringed at this; it wasn't the arms of God that had awaited her mother as she stepped into the street, not by a long shot. She heard again squealing tires and the sickening crumple of metal on flesh, the sounds that haunted her dreams.

She'd listened, dry-eyed. Her heart aching, her eyes burning to weep, but it wouldn't happen.

Sheriff Pranger had knocked on the tin door of the old singlewide that she and her mother shared. Cassie had opened the door and there he'd stood, in the predawn darkness, nervous hands turning his hat over and over, his eyes never meeting her own as he mumbled an uncomfortable greeting.

"Better go get your coat, Honey," he'd said, fighting the urge to look away, "and come with us."

Over his shoulder Cassie had seen Guy and Grace Williams in the shadows, clothing rumpled as though thrown on in haste. Pastor Williams stood, tight-lipped and pale, as his wife pressed her face into his shoulder and wept.

Cassie had known, as she turned to find a coat and shoes, that her mother was dead. She had shed her tears, weeping silently into her pillow, as she lay awake on the twin bed in the Williams's spare room. Then, this morning, she'd dashed from the arrangement office of the mortuary and into the ladies room, overcome by a storm of tears. She'd sat on the cushioned bench, her head lain against the cool wall of the restroom, her small frame wracked with sobs, and her face burning with tears until she felt as though she were choking on them, drowning in her grief.

She was an orphan.

Could it have been only a week earlier that she and her mother had been shopping together, chatting and laughing as they searched for a new school outfit; the one that Cassie would wear to her college orientation?

Portland, Oregon seemed a world away; a cool, forested, rainy place far to the west. It was there that Cassie had sent her transcripts, hoping to begin her dream of writing at the university. Only a week before, she and her mother had laughed and cried together at the thought of her leaving.

She had hoped to begin school with the spring term, and orientation was just two weeks away, a frenzied handful of days to pack and say goodbyes. Only a week before....

The days leading up to the service had been a blur. Even in her grief, Cassie knew that if she stayed, if she didn't catch a bus, right now, and escape the confines of this dusty little town, she might never escape at all. Her writing might forever remain a dream.

So she had talked to their pastor, Guy, and to her mother's best friend, his

Just Past Oysterville

Shoalwater Book One

Perry P. Perkins

PublishAmerica
Baltimore

First printing

ISBN: 1-4137-0914-1
PUBLISHED BY PUBLISHAMERICA, LLLP
www.publishamerica.com
Baltimore

Printed in the United States of America

For Victoria...always my inspiration.

Acknowledgments

Far more family and friends helped, encouraged and challenged than I could ever thank in a single page.
Here's the top of the list:

Diane Anderson, Elizabeth Kirkham, Heather Friesen,
Jeni Bullis, & Melanie Zallee –
my extra eyes

Pastor Doug Farrington – my friend and compass,

&

"The real Cassie" Geisert, even if
she won't eat oysters…

"Ointment and perfume rejoice the heart: so doth the sweetness of a man's friend by hearty counsel."
~Proverbs 27:9~

A child abandoned
A life destroyed
Two hearts, unable to forgive…

Prologue

In the darkness he feels the chilly water seeping through his boots with the rising tide. Frigid rain, peppered with sleet, stings his face, numbing his fingers until he can no longer feel the bottle as it slips from his grasp, draining its last inch of bourbon into the sand. He stares, unseeing, into the blackness, weeping in the bitter, salty air.

Thunder crashes, mingling with the distant roar of the surf. The revolver comes from his pocket warm and heavy in his hand, like a living thing. The man sways drunkenly in the wind, caressing his cheek with the pistol. He curses, sobbing her name into the wind as the barrel comes to rest against his temple.

Then, with a sigh, he squeezes the trigger, the shot echoing with the thunder as the hammer falls.

wife, Grace. Guy had listened as Cassie poured out her hopes and dreams, her fears and reasonings, nodding silently throughout, and then assured her that she *must*; in fact, that she *would* be on that bus. Then they'd packed up the Belangers' few belongings, loading them into the church van and hauling them to the Williams' to be stored, as Cassie filled a duffel bag with the few items she would need for her trip.

ত

The night before, after clearing the dishes from the Williams' dining table, Grace had privately tried to talk her out of going so soon. She'd begged her to wait until the summer, or better, the fall, to give her grief some time to heal. Cassie sat, listening to the length and breadth of Grace's argument, but not for a moment considering it.

As she'd glanced around the warmth of the Williams' home, her mind had flooded with the memories of better times. How many nights had she and her mother eaten dinner at that same table? Or played board games, roaring with laughter at Guy's flagrant attempts to cheat? Or sat and watched movies, piled onto the big, faded sectional in the living room, scattering popcorn across the carpet?

How many times had the five of them just sat and talked? Talked about what was happening in their little town, about Guy's latest sermon, who had listened and who hadn't, or just about life, and what hand it was dealing each of them?

Cassie had slept poorly that night, waiting for her exhaustion to overwhelm her. The spare room had been Kenneth's, Guy and Grace's son, before he had joined the Air Force, as evidenced by the posters of fighter jets and rock stars taped to the walls. A battered stereo sat atop a child-sized rolltop desk, paperback novels and compact discs were scattered across the rest. The room had been aired and carried just the hint of Kenny's cologne. Cassie stared out the window at a great, yellow, harvest moon and thought about the Williams family, who had been her surrogate aunt and uncle and cousin since before she could remember.

Grace had offered her home and heart, permanently, and as much as it had hurt Cassie to do so, she'd been forced to turn her down. It wasn't just for fear of missing her opportunity, though that was real enough. She knew she must leave because of what she had found in the bottom drawer of her mother's dresser.

A faded manila envelope, buried beneath a pile of faded sweaters, had contained an old, yellowing marriage certificate.

The single page, heavily creased and water stained, had been legible enough to decipher as being the record of her parents' marriage. It looked to be the original and included their places and dates of birth, and occupations.

Cassie felt her eyes stinging as she read her father's name in print for the first time. *William Alfred Beckman.*

The second item nestled beneath her mother's sweaters, shocked her even more. The handgun was a large caliber, maybe a .38, or a .357; Cassie wasn't familiar enough with pistols to tell the difference.

The hole at the end of the short, blued barrel seemed enormous, as she gingerly set the gun on the bed beside her. She could see that it was loaded and a curious little padlock filled the trigger space. The lock had a keyhole in the center of it, but there was no key with the gun. Cassie was certain the ring of keys that the hospital nurse had given her, the ones from her mother's pocket, would have a key to fit that lock.

She had never known her mother to use a handgun, and she had never touched one.

There was a small, framed certificate on Cassie's bureau that she had earned years before at Girl Scout camp. The NRA Marksman award had been given her after proving her competency with a .22 rifle on the camp's shooting range. In an area with as many rattlesnakes as Bowie, it was wise to know how to shoot a rifle safely. Cassie stared at the carved wooden grips of the big pistol, and then called for Guy.

He had recognized the pistol right away, and smiled, carefully pointing the barrel at the floor and unloading the fat cartridges from the cylinder.

"I helped your mom pick out this gun," he had said. "I tried to talk her into something a little smaller, like a .22 magnum, or a .380, but she wanted this one," Guy laughed suddenly, "and boy-oh-boy could she shoot it! We must have killed a thousand pop cans out past the quarry, your mother, Grace, and I."

Cassie was shocked.

"*My* mom," she asked incredulously, "shot *this* gun?"

"Sure," replied Guy, "she was an ace, I never understood how she could shoot a big .357 like that with those thin wrists of hers, but she did. Not long after she moved here, we went up to Tucson and took a handgun class, got verified and everything," the pastor sighed.

"We used to go out to the quarry 'most every weekend and target shoot," he said, "it was cheap entertainment back then."

Cassie had stared at the pistol a little fearfully.

"I guess," Guy continued, "that this old hand-cannon is yours now, but I'm going to lock it up for safekeeping. If you decide you want to shoot it let me know and we'll go out to the quarry with Grace. If you like, sometime when you're back from school, we can go up to Tucson and you can take that safety course. After that, if you want it, it's yours to take."

"Well," Cassie said, still dazed at this side of her mother that she had never known, "let me think about it, I'm sure I'll want it eventually, maybe after I get out of school."

"That'll be just fine," Guy said, picking up the now-empty weapon and slipping it into the pocket of his jacket. He gathered the shells and put them in the other pocket.

"I'll get it cleaned up and oiled before I put it away," he said, "looks like your mom kinda let it go the last few years…"

Guy's voice faltered and the room filled with silence, and she realized that her pastor and his wife must have been suffering almost as much as she, having been her mother's best friends since before Cassie could remember.

Finally, Guy slapped his knees with his palms and stood.

"Well," he said, "these boxes aren't going to pack themselves…"

"Guy," Cassie had whispered, unable to look up and meet his eyes, "why did Mom want a gun like that?"

There was a long pause and after a few moments Cassie thought he wasn't going to answer. Finally, clearing his throat, he'd spoken.

"Well Cass," he'd said, "sometimes it can be scary living on your own, especially with a little one in the house. Way out here on the edge of town, you want to feel safe…"

There was another long pause, but he left the sentence hanging, slowly walking out of the bedroom. Cassie could hear the quiet, unintelligible murmur, as Guy spoke to his wife. Then the sound of moving and taping boxes resumed. Cassie wasn't sure how she felt about Guy's answer, but she knew this; there was more to it than he'd told her.

Sitting there, Cassie had pulled the marriage certificate back out of her pocket. For some reason she hadn't wanted Guy or Grace to see it. She unfolded it once more and studied her father's handwriting on the faded page, listening to the windy scratch of sand, like cat fur, whispering past the aluminum walls.

William Beckman, she read again, a man she had never met and of whom her mother refused to speak. His date of birth didn't mean much to her, nor did the listing of his occupation as a fisherman; what started her heart beating hard was the cryptic entry for his place of birth. There, in what Cassie assumed was her father's own rough script, were the words *Just past Oysterville, WA*.

The strange phrase had stuck in her consciousness like a burr, and she read the line over and over, sitting on the edge of her mother's bed as their meager belongings were loaded into apple boxes from the Bowie Grocery.

Just past Oysterville, did it mean that William Beckman had been born someplace called Oysterville? If so, why not just write that? If he had been born in the next town, why not put the name of *that* town? Cassie rescued her mother's atlas of the world from a box full of books and had found Oysterville at the very tip of the Long Beach Peninsula in Washington State. Her discovery, however, only added to the confusion, there was *nothing* past Oysterville except for the Pacific Ocean to the west and Willapa Bay to the east.

As Cassie sat, the tattered atlas across her knees and a numb void of loss shadowing her heart, a sudden need, dark and simmering, flickered within her.

What if she went to this place, this Oysterville, and found somebody there who had known her parents, maybe even knew her father's whereabouts? Could she find him? Could she track this William Beckman down and let him know the wife he had abandoned had lived and breathed and struggled and sacrificed to raise his child? That she had worked three jobs to put food in the belly of the daughter he had walked away from, and carved out a life in a run-down old trailer on the edge of the desert?

She could, no, she *would* tell him!

For her mother and for herself she would find this man and tell him that Katherine Belanger was dead. He would ask how, and what would she tell him?

Alone, in the cold early hours of morning, she had been struck by a drunk driver and left lying, broken and bleeding, in the street. A drunk driver who had, himself, been found dead an hour later, hopelessly crushed beneath the crumpled remains of his Cadillac, in a ditch along Interstate 10.

The fine white pages of the atlas had crumpled unconsciously in her fists.

No, she thought fiercely, *I won't tell him anything, except that she's dead.* She would tell him this and then turn and walk away, as he had walked away.

When Cassie had closed and locked the door of that shabby, rented trailer for the last time, it was with a burning sense of purpose. That purpose had warmed her as she walked through the cold night to her borrowed room at the Williams' house.

She would find out, for herself, who and what was just past Oysterville.

* * *

Cassie had made her plans, even as those around her took care of the details of her mother's funeral. As much as she disliked the idea of lying to the Williamses, she would do so, cashing in her ticket at the bus station and thumbing rides all the way to the West Coast.

The small amount of money she had saved for college (this she had already transferred to a Portland bank) now included the few hundred dollars that had remained in her mother's savings account. With the cash from the bus ticket, she was sure she could spend the next several months searching for her father.

She had called the university and, despite what she had told Grace, there would be no problem holding her loan, and enrolling in the later, fall courses.

But now, just a day later, as she stood under the bright blue awning that shielded her mother's casket from the sun, Cassie began to doubt. She wondered what she'd really say when she found him, if she found him.

Guy had often said, while standing behind the pulpit of the Bowie Baptist Church, that there was a place within each of us designed for love. That nothing else, not money, or fame or power, would fill that void. Most of the bad that was in the world, he said, came about from the futile attempt to fill that place with something besides love.

Cassie suspected that hating her father wouldn't fill it either, but could there be more? She shook her head as the last blue flowers disappeared into the darkness of the grave. She didn't know, and she didn't want to know. For now, hate would have to be enough. As her life in Bowie, Arizona ended, she felt in her pocket for the folded copy of the marriage certificate, her first step, her only clue to finding her father.

And as for what she would do when she found him, she would, as Kathy Belanger had been fond of saying, burn that bridge when she came to it.

* * *

Those who had words to say said them and the graveside memorial ended.

Guy saw Cassie standing near the edge of the canopy, next to his old station wagon, nodding absently as the line of well-wishers slowly passed, murmuring their condolences.

She looked, to him, like one of those dogs with the bobbing heads that you put in the back window of your car. Just nodding and nodding, eyes glassy and vacant, the lights are on, the power's running, but the folks have gone to Florida, thank you and please leave a message.

Guy ran an unsteady hand through his hair; it had been a long week, and he was feeling his years more and more as each hour passed.

It's not, he thought, *like we haven't lost friends before*.

But he knew this was different; the Belangers were family, Kathy had become the sister he'd never had, and Cassie was almost a daughter. Hadn't he watched her take her first steps across the faded linoleum of his kitchen? Hadn't he been the one sitting where her father should have sat for a hundred soccer games and dance recitals? He sighed, feeling a cold churning in his belly at the thought of Kathy's absence, the bone-weary sadness at the pain his wife was facing, losing her oldest and dearest friend.

Grace was being brave, of course, keeping strong for Cassie, but a husband, a good husband anyway, was the one on whose shoulder you cried after the lights were turned off and no one else could see.

Cassie.

Guy watched her accepting hugs, condolences, and murmured kindnesses that she would never remember. He watched her eyes, and saw her mind awhirl behind them, as though all of this were already a memory.

He knew she was planning something, but what? She was too smart to not be subtle, but he had watched this young woman grow up from an infant, almost as much in his own home as her mother's. As a father himself, Guy recognized a whitewash when he saw one. Cassie had given up on her hitchhiking plans much too quickly for his liking. He knew the girl, and her sudden and unquestioning submission was out of character. The Cassie he knew would have fought, setting her jaw and refusing to budge. She could be a pit bull when it came to getting her own way, and when she suddenly became a poodle, something was wrong.

Cassie looked up and caught his eye, and Guy produced a weary smile as he came up to her, placing his hands on her shoulders.

"You hanging in there, Cass?" he asked, and Cassie nodded, smiling as best she could.

"You, um..." Guy continued, looking over the tops if his wire rimmed glasses and into her eyes, "you take care of yourself, Kiddo. Call us as soon as you get to Portland. I…I hope you find what you're looking for."

He looked in her eyes as his mind raced.

What are you thinking, Cassie Belanger? Guy wondered to himself. *What are you up to? And more importantly, what can I do about it?*

Guy smiled again and bent to kiss her forehead, then turned and walked away.

Grace Williams came and took her hand.

"How are you doing, Honey?" she asked.

"I'll be okay," Cassie answered, taking a deep breath.

"Are you sure you have to go so soon? Maybe you could just take a week or two, let things settle and then—"

"No," Cassie interrupted, "the bus tickets are nonrefundable. Besides, I want to get there early and have a look around the campus on my own."

Grace sighed. "Oh Cassie," she said, "all the way to Oregon? You must be able to find a school closer to home? There has to be *one* college in Arizona with a writing department!"

Cassie smiled. "Portland State University is one of the best writing colleges in the country, besides, they've already accepted my transcripts."

"It's just—"

"I know," Cassie said, "I know, it's so far, you keep telling me. I just feel like I have to get away. I need a new place, someplace unexpected where I don't recognize every rock and tree. I can't write here, it's too familiar, especially now…."

Cassie paused, and took another deep breath, fighting the tears that threatened to well and overflow. How could she tell Grace how she felt? How could she explain the way that her soul turned cold whenever she passed the street where her mother had died, hearing the screech of rubber and the crush of metal? How she pictured her lying there in the darkness, crying for help? How many times now had she woken up, trembling and gasping for air, with this vision seared into her nightmares?

"I know," Grace whispered, "I know. Maybe you're right, sometimes change is the only way to heal."

Cassie squeezed her hand gratefully, unable to look in her eyes.

"Now," Grace continued, "tell me the truth. You've given up this silly notion of hitchhiking and bought a bus ticket, right?"

Cassie hesitated, "Yes…" It was the truth, *technically*, she had, at one point given up on the idea, and she *had* bought a ticket.

Grace squared her shoulders and stepped back, all business. "Let me see it…."

As she dug through her pockets, Cassie grimaced.

"Thanks for the trust," she muttered, "it's a real vote of confidence."

Pastor William's wife smiled at that.

"Oh, I trust you dear, but I was young once myself, and I remember how hard it can be to let go of a good idea."

Cassie found the blue and red striped Greyhound envelope and handed it to Grace, who opened it and quickly scanned the ticket inside.

"Gracious," she exclaimed, "two hundred and fifty-eight dollars! You should be able to fly there for that!"

"Not both ways."

"Cassie!" Grace cried. "This bus leaves at three, that's less than an hour away!"

"Don't worry," Cassie replied, "Frank is going to pick me up in the taxi, and he should be here any minute."

As though on queue, a horn honked from the street as a faded yellow cab pulled up to the curb. Cassie reached into the backseat of the Williams' station wagon and grabbed her faded duffel bag and jacket.

"Well," Grace said, taking a deep breath, "if you're determined to go, then give me a hug and walk away before I cry."

Cassie felt tears well once more in her own eyes.

"Thank you so much," she said, "for everything. Thank Guy too, for helping with the funeral, and with Mom's stuff."

Grace Williams dismissed this with a quick wave of her hand, "Oh, it's just a few boxes. The Williams clan has lived on that farm for eighty years, I can't imagine the attic will be going anywhere in the next two or three."

Then she stepped forward and pulled the girl close, hugging her fiercely, as Cassie whispered into her ear.

"Please keep flowers on her grave, she likes—"

"Blue carnations, of course," Grace answered, tears now flowing down her cheeks, "I loved her almost as much as you, remember? Now go on, your taxi is waiting…."

Cassie drew a deep, shuddering breath as she backed away toward the waiting cab. "I love you, Grace…" she said.

"I know," her pastor's wife replied, "make sure you call me as soon as you reach Portland…and go straight to the college…and stay on campus."

The young woman laughed through her tears, "I will, I will…I'll be fine."

Then Cassie climbed into the passenger seat of the taxi and quickly closed the door. She kept her eyes forward as the car pulled away, heading towards the bus station, and bit her lip fiercely as the tears ran down her cheeks, clutching desperately at the folded scrap of paper in her pocket, her talisman.

She watched through the dusty windshield as they started through town.

As much as she yearned for escape from the constant, painful reminders of her mother's death, for the excitement of college, and most of all for the possibility of confronting her father, Bowie was still the only home she had ever known. She etched the images before her into her memory as though it were the last time she would see them.

Passing the library, which sat like a squat brick pyramid, Frank turned onto Main Street. From there Cassie could see the Yucca Lodge Motel, where she had worked the last three summers as a room attendant. Mrs. Miller, her supervisor, was eighty-six now and pretty much just loaded the supply cart each morning and spent the rest of the day sitting in one of the empty rooms watching her soap operas and smoking long, thin cigarettes.

Past the motel, Cassie could see the conical roof of another Bowie landmark, the teepee tavern. She rolled her eyes.

Shaped to resemble an Indian teepee, the tavern's great beige cone rose above the landscape like a beacon for the thirsty folk of Bowie. Both signs, in four foot blazing neon, were currently fired up and blinking the word *Beer* on either side of the building.

A lone blue mailbox sat beside the post office, available for those who couldn't stop by between the convenient hours of ten and two. Cassie pictured Mr. Tolstrom, Bowie's postman, sitting in the sorting room, his establishment's doors securely locked, casually reading the townsfolk's magazines (and the occasional personal letter) before slipping them into the outgoing bins.

The cab wheezed to a rattling stop as a flashing bar came down across Main Street and the iron clang of bells rang painfully in their ears. Frank snorted in disgust and rolled up the windows to block out as much of the noise as possible. The small cab grew warm quickly as they waited for the Union Pacific to make its slow pass through town.

Once the bar lifted and the cab was underway again, they passed Welker-Scott Memorial Park, its swing-sets and chain-link backstop lonely and forlorn amid the swath of dry, russet grass, as dead in winter as it would be in July.

Cassie smiled, and in her mind's-eye she saw herself and her various school chums through the years, swinging gleefully on the rusty swings, braids flying, their scab covered knees bared to the world. Years would pass and find them clustered together along the fence, whispering and giggling, pointing proprietary fingers at the boys who played baseball, spit in the dirt, and strove mightily to pretend that they were blissfully unaware of their female admirers.

A few years further and they would sit on the brief spring grasses in small groups of twos and fours, holding hands with those same boys, heads bent in impassioned whispers. She smiled again; wondering how many times this cycle had repeated itself, while the park remained unchanged.

Cassie wiped fresh tears from her burning cheeks as her only world slipped slowly past her and was gone.

Chapter Two

Twenty minutes later, just outside Bowie, Cassie stepped off the highway and onto a narrow dirt track that meandered its way across the desert. It skirted the equally small town of Luzena, and headed toward Willcox, which couldn't even be considered a small town.

Luzena was too close to Bowie and Cassie wasn't about to risk being seen walking down the highway with her thumb out when she should be on the three o'clock bus to Tucson. The chances of being spotted by someone she knew, or worse, someone Grace knew, were just too high.

Again she felt a stab of guilt for the lies she had told to the family that had shown her so much kindness.

Cassie squared her shoulders and tugged the strap of her duffel bag tighter.

It was done, and she couldn't change it.

She had let Frank the cabbie take her as far as the bus station, and then waived off his offer to wait with her.

"My bus is leaving in ten minutes," she had told him, running for the door. "Go get yourself a fare back to town!"

"Yeah, right." Frank had laughed, as he pulled away.

Once inside the station, Cassie had watched through the window until the taxi was out of sight, then pulled out her bus ticket and walked up to the cashier's desk. The attendant was a graying matron with blue-shadowed eyes and impossibly long lashes.

"One moment," she had said, as Cassie had opened her mouth to speak, "I'll be right with you."

The woman made a show of counting through a thick stack of tickets, then recounting, and finally, with a smirk playing at the corners of her lips, counting them a third and final time. With a sigh, she set the stack down and turned to Cassie, whose own eyes had begun to flash dangerously.

"May I help you?"

"Yes please," Cassie said, "I need to cash in my bus ticket."

The woman stared at Cassie with frank disapproval, studying the girl over the top of her black-framed reading glasses, before taking the ticket from her with two fingers as though she suspected that it might be soiled.

"Reason?" she asked.

"No reason," Cassie replied, her eyes suddenly glazing over and her smile becoming vapid.

"I just need to cash it in, and it's refundable, that's what this word here is," Cassie pointed to the ticket's large, red lettering, her voice dripping with sincerity, "right?"

The impossible lashes blinked once, then twice; the woman's scowl deepening the crevasses of her face.

Katherine Belanger had been known to say that her daughter had a gift for finding the one thing that could drive a person absolutely crazy.

"It's like she can see this big invisible button, and Lord help you if you give her reason to push it." Kathy would laugh, *"That girl can make you yank your hair out, and her smiling that sweet smile the whole time!"*

The ticket attendant at the Bowie Greyhound station was no exception, and her eyes narrowed dangerously as she glanced back and forth from the ticket in her hand to Cassie.

"Well," she replied, "It *is* refundable, yes, but—"

"Great!" Cassie cried, clapping her hands, "That's what I want to do, exactly!"

The woman's face was a thundercloud as she jammed a small key into the desk drawer in front of her and began savagely counting out fifty-dollar bills. Cassie waited until she had almost reached two hundred and fifty dollars.

"Oh wait! I'm sorry," she said, with an insipid giggle, "I needed that in tens and twenties...."

The woman didn't even look up at she stuffed the fifties back into the drawer and counted out the money, pushing the stack across the counter and under the window toward the girl.

"Thanks so much," Cassie gushed, "and have a great day!"

Turning to go, she heard the attendant's *Window Closed* sign come slamming down on the counter as the older woman stormed away. Picking up her duffel bag, Cassie started across town towards the highway, whistling as she went.

She was still chuckling as she hiked out past the bluff and turned south, away from Interstate 10 and towards Buckeye Mill.

Two miles further, the trail ended at an intersection with a seldom-used dirt road. It was a single lane of deep ruts, torn up by the fat tires of four-wheel drive trucks, winding around scruffy junipers and islands of sage. To the west the road led far across the desert, disappearing over the next arid rise. Cassie followed it, sipping sparingly from the first of her two water bottles. As she hiked, she recorded her thoughts on a small dictation machine that her mother had bought her for Christmas.

"Well Kiddo," Kathy had said, as Cassie squealed with delight at the gift, *"A writer has to be able to put their thoughts down, whenever and wherever they are."*

In the bag on her back Cassie had a case of twenty miniature cassettes that fit the recorder, as well as two spare sets of batteries. Five of the thirty-minute tapes were already filled with ramblings about school and leaving home. She knew she would have to put down her thoughts and feelings about her mother's death, but it was still too soon for that. She hoped to get some good material on her trip west; who knew what might come of it?

Several hours later, the rutted track ended at the steep shouldered edge of Interstate 10. Cassie scooted down the dusty embankment and squinted at the sign fifty yards up the highway.

Bowie, 20 Miles.

She had come out four miles short of Willcox, still a little too close to home for her taste. Nothing to do about it now but keep walking and try to make herself scarce when traffic came along. Cassie had looked at her Arizona map and decided that once she neared Benson, fifty miles to the west, she should be safe from the chance of any accidental sighting by a nosy neighbor. Sixty miles was the far-off big city for most of the residents of her little town. The traffic on the Interstate was light, in fact it was nearly nonexistent, and Cassie smirked into her recorder,

"That's right folks," she said, "be sure to watch out for the rush-hour traffic to the thriving metropolis of Bowie!"

Occasionally a lone pickup would come barreling across the flats, headed for Willcox or Tucson, but they were no great threat. The thin air and flat terrain made for wonderful acoustics, and Cassie had plenty of warning to scramble off the shoulder of the highway and duck behind the nearest cluster of juniper trees. The heat of the day began to fade as the sun turned orange on the western horizon, and Cassie tugged a worn denim jacket from her bag and slipped it on. She was suddenly overwhelmed with memories. She had begged for this jacket as it hung in her mother's closet.

The copper buttons were tarnished and the hems and cuffs were beginning to fray. The scent of her mother's perfume still lingered and the memories broke loose within her. Cassie climbed, sobbing, to the top of the embankment and sat, legs dangling over the precipice. There she buried her face in her folded arms and breathed in the faint smell of roses that had been a small part of the mother she had lost.

&

The funeral had been held at the Sunset Chapel, across the street from Bowie's high school. Built in the early 1930s, the chapel had seen better days. Its pitted rose-colored stucco walls were beginning to crumble at the corners. Equally worn, but meticulously clean, the interior's faded beige carpets were permeated with the scents of flowers and wood polish. Cassie had been escorted to the family room, alongside the chapel itself, and from there she could see the casket that held her mother's body. Covered in fine blue fabric and edged in gleaming dark cherry, it rested on the draped bier, and beside it stood a small oak table topped with a dozen blue carnations and a framed picture of Katherine Belanger. Soon the casket would lie in the shadow of the small marker that would identify to all that Katherine Belanger had been Cassie's beloved mother. Guy and Grace had insisted on paying for the marker and having it in place as soon as possible following the service, knowing that Cassie couldn't afford to. She had thanked them tearfully, insisting amid their protests that she would pay them back. Grace Williams had sat beside her in the small curtained area, squeezing her hand as Guy had stepped up to the podium and opened his Bible.

"Katherine Belanger," he began, "if she were here, would thank each of you for your presence today to celebrate her graduation into glorious everlasting life. I've known Kathy for many years, and as I prayed about what I would share today, the word that kept coming to my mind, was love." Guy slipped his reading glasses on and bent slightly to read from the Bible.

"So, I thought we'd start today by defining love. In his letter to the Corinthians, Paul tells us that love is patient..."

Guy had continued to speak, giving each definition of love, followed by an example from Katherine Belanger's life, but Cassie heard little of it, and barely felt Grace's rhythmic squeezing of her hand. In her mind, she was ten years old again, and she and her mother were sitting in the shade of the willows, along the edge of the river. Kathy was reading to her daughter from that same letter to the headstrong people of Corinth.

"This is the Bible in a nutshell, Baby," her mother had said, *"love is something we are, not just something we do. Love Jesus, remember what love is, and try to be that every day; everything else will work itself out."*

❧

Cassie couldn't say how long she sat there, looking down on Interstate 10. She was still rocking gently as the sun disappeared and long, purple fingers of night began to stretch across the desert, her face hidden from the world and her mind enveloped in memories. Her mother's smell, the touch of her hand on Cassie's face as she brushed her hair, the strength of her arms as she held her daughter.

When Cassie's tear-stained face did finally rise, her cheeks damp and puffy with crying, she was able to take a deep breath of the cool desert air, the scent of hot asphalt and bitter junipers mingling in her nostrils. Her heart ached, and she longed to wake up and have the last week be nothing more than a terrible nightmare. Wiping her eyes, Cassie shouldered her duffel bag and resumed her hike in the fading amber glow of sunset.

The temperature in the desert drops quickly with the setting sun. Luckily, for Cassie, there was a great, glowing full moon rising, so she could leave her flashlight in her bag, following the highway in the strange, shadowed monochrome that washed across the plain as far as she could see. Soon she was shivering as she buttoned the jacket to the collar and stuffed her hands deep into the pockets of her jeans. Just as she was debating pulling more clothes from her bag, Cassie topped a small rise and saw a broken-down pole barn, slowly collapsing into ruin a dozen yards north of the highway. Growing up on the outskirts of civilization, she knew better than to sneak silently up to the building. Cassie whistled and scuffed her feet as she approached the sagging door, kicking up a few rocks that bounced noisily off the side of the nearest wall. This would alert anything on more than two legs to her presence and, if it hadn't already caught her scent and done so, it would turn tail at the sound of her approach.

Either the barn was vacant or whatever had been living there fled unseen, as the interior was stark and empty in the beam of Cassie's flashlight. The floor was the same hard packed dirt as the desert outside; drifts of dust had blown up one wall from the nightly east wind, partially burying the tumbled remains of a couple of stalls.

Beneath the rotting wood rails, Cassie found several long forgotten bales of hay. These she eyed suspiciously, poking and prodding with a stick until she was satisfied there were no mice or rats hiding inside.

Taking a small multitool from her pocket, Cassie clipped the brittle twine of the first bale and began to spread the hay around for a bed to lay her sleeping bag on.

Gathering another handful of dusty straw and kicking one of the weathered boards to pieces, she used an old Zippo lighter that had been her mother's (and, she suspected, her father's before that) to start a small fire in the center of the dirt floor, well away from the walls and her bedding. Stars twinkled brightly through the cracks in the roof, the weather-beaten timbers having warped and shrunk with time.

Exhausted, Cassie pulled her sleeping bag from the depths of the duffel and rolled out her bed, lying just within the circle of warmth, and munched on her meager supply of granola and venison jerky.

The jerky was a gift from a co-worker of her mother's, whose husband went deer hunting in Texas each fall. The salty meat was firm and tough, but tasty and her mother's friend had sworn that it would keep for a year or more in an airtight bag.

The meat was filling, but it made her thirsty. As much as she wanted to cool her throat with the remains of her second water bottle, she knew that it would doom her to a dry, miserable morning before she reached Vail, twenty miles short of Tucson. So, after taking two small sips, she screwed the cap on and stowed the bottle back in her bag. She sat, looking into the tiny fire for a while.

"You take care of yourself, Kiddo. I hope you find what you're looking for."

Guy's words drifted through her mind. Had he known what she was planning? If anyone in the world could have second-guessed her, it would have been Guy Williams, but no, surely he would have stopped her if he had.

Cassie slipped the small recorder from her pocket and pressed the record button, watching the tiny red light pop on as the tape began to roll.

February 11th

"I'm spending my first night on the road in an old barn off Highway 10. Guy and Grace think I caught the bus and I'm on my way to Portland by now. I feel so bad, lying to them. I'll have to call them in a couple of days to let them know I'm okay. I don't know if I have a chance of finding my father, but I have to try. I have plenty of time before fall classes start. I don't have much money, but I can dip into my college account if I have to. I want to look him in the eye; I want him to know what he lost when he walked away from us. Guy says that healing only comes when we forgive. That's probably true, but I don't feel any forgiveness for William Beckman. Maybe it'd be better if I don't find him. I miss Mom. I'm tired of crying; it feels like I cry all the time. Anyway, I'm sleepy and my fire is dying, I'd better call it a night."

Before putting the little recorder away, Cassie slipped the half-used tape from the machine and replaced it with a tape from her shirt pocket. Penned on the label in red ink was a small heart; Cassie closed her eyes as her mother's voice murmured through the tiny speaker.

"*Trust in the Lord with all of your heart and lean not unto your own understanding. In all your ways acknowledge him, and he will direct your path. Merry Christmas, baby.*"

Too exhausted to think anymore, Cassie said a quick mechanical prayer, asking for God's blessing on the Williams family and safety for herself, then she climbed, fully dressed, into her sleeping bag.

She pulled the thin, flannel-lined bag up over her head, zipping it to the top and, with the dry smell of straw and wood smoke surrounding her, listened to the soft whisper of the desert wind and fell asleep. She was too exhausted to notice the dryness of her prayers, or the feeling that when she had spoken them, they went no further than the ramshackle walls of the barn.

❧

Eleanor Young sighed as she locked the front doors of the Bowie Greyhound station. Her dogs were barking something fierce tonight, and even the new orthopedic inserts that Dr. Manadrell had given her were doing little to ease the throbbing toothache in her feet.

"Getting old Elli," she sighed, flipping the plastic door shutter from open to closed, and switching off the neon bus sign and awning lights. She had laundry to do tonight and a pot roast to get into the oven and, more than anything, she'd like to forget both and curl up on the couch with a thick Jean Auel caveman epic, or maybe a hunky action movie, and one of Joe's beers.

As she passed back around the counter she paused to sit a minute, removing her thick-soled shoes and rubbing her aching arches. Elli Young's eye caught the creased boarding slip resting at her station, the word CANCELED stamped across it in crimson capitals.

That little snippet hadn't improved her mood today either, with her wide eyes and snotty little smile. The old woman grimaced as she picked up the slip with one hand, the other still kneading relief into her arthritic extremities.

Cassie Belanger, she thought, *where have I heard that name?*

Who cares?

Maybe she'd swing through *Quick Time Video* on the way home and grab a pizza and a couple of movies. If Joe didn't like it he could fix his own pot roast. She almost laughed out loud in the empty office. The day that Joe Young marched his clodhoppers into the kitchen and fixed himself a meal was the day that they'd buried his old ball and chain!

Cassie Belanger.

Dropping the ticket back on the worn counter, Elli picked up the heavy, black receiver of the old rotary phone and dialed a number from memory, scowling once more as the young woman's voice echoed in her memory.

Have a great day!

The line was picked up after two rings.

"Hello?" A woman's voice said.

"Hello, Gracie?" the older woman replied, her mind already drifting to a mushroom and pepperoni pizza and a good ninety minutes of Mel Gibson's flexing muscles. Now *that* would be a nice end to a long and lousy day, "it's Eleanor Young, down at the bus station." She glanced over the top of her glasses at the ticket again, "Say, aren't you friends with a 'Belanger'?"

❧

After a long and restless night, Cassie woke up to a chilly gray morning. Sometime before dawn, a heavy dew had fallen, descending through the gaps in the barn roof and seeping through cracks in the walls. For a few moments she lay still, looking out through the sagging barn door. The building had been abandoned longer than she had thought when she'd stumbled across it the night before. The roof and east wall were just a skeleton of thin sticks, cracked and gray with age, and Cassie could see scarlet holes in the boards where the old iron nails had long since rusted away.

Cassie shivered as she climbed from her damp bedroll and, with shaking fingers, pulled dry straw from the middle of the remaining bale to start a fire. Luckily, she had tossed her duffel bag into the corner and covered several shattered pieces of board, which had stayed dry enough to light. Returning the battered Zippo to her pocket, Cassie hunched low over her work, rubbing circulation into her arms and legs, as tiny flames licked at the dry straw and wood. She fanned the flames with her hands, as it fed and smoked, until a small fire was snapping cheerfully at her feet.

After a sip or two of her dwindling water supply, and a handful of granola, Cassie rolled up her clammy sleeping bag, promising herself that she would let it air-dry after the sun was fully up. She ran her fingers through her short dark hair, wincing at the tangles, and brushed away the larger pieces of hay that clung to her clothes.

"Well," she said to the sagging walls, "I must be a real beauty this morning!"

Without running water, her soap and toiletries were useless. She packed them back up and made a mental note to find a gas station up the road with a rest room for her morning ablutions. For the moment, she settled for a quick and merciless brushing of her tangled black locks.

Half an hour later, she still wasn't warm, but at least she had stopped shivering as, pulling her bag onto her shoulders, Cassie crushed her fire, kicking sand over the smoking remains. Then, squeezing out through the broken door, she hiked back to the highway, breathing deeply the cool morning air. The sun was just peeking over the edge of a gray-blue cloudless sky, promising another hot day.

Following the highway, which was all but deserted at this hour of the morning, Cassie turned west again, crossing the featureless plain in a mile-eating gait that warmed her quickly. Her watch read eight o'clock when the sun and the hiking had been enough that she stopped to remove her jacket.

She considered unrolling her sleeping bag to dry, but decided to wait until she was tired enough to need the rest.

❧

By ten, Cassie had skirted the town of Willcox. Finding her way back to Interstate 10, she topped a rise and saw, a half-mile up the road, a small gas station and grocery store. Stepping off the highway and behind a cluster of brush, she unlaced one of her hiking boots. From the back of the boot, just above her heel, she removed a plastic sandwich bag filled with cash. Cassie had read a story in junior high about an old hobo who befriended a young boy while riding the rails. The hobo, wise to life on the road, told the boy to always split up his money, keeping a few dollars in his pocket and the balance divided and hidden in his shoes. This way, if robbed, chances were that you wouldn't lose all your money. This had seemed like sound reasoning to Cassie, as well as adding a little spice to the adventure. Now, however, after removing a ten dollar bill and replacing her insole, she felt a little foolish, teetering as she laced up her boot, hiding behind a bush in the middle of the empty desert.

With cash in her pocket, Cassie hiked to the little market where she bought a loaf of bread, a package of bologna and a couple of candy bars. She stopped at the hotdog bar and slipped a handful of mustard packets into the pocket of her shirt, the cashier didn't notice. After she had paid for her groceries, the old man behind the counter directed her around to the back of the store for a water hose to refill her bottles. There was no rest room.

"Employees only," the manager had grunted in reply to her question, still not looking up from his fishing magazine.

Cassie used the hose to wash her face and arms, letting the cool stream flow over the back of her neck until she felt refreshed. The rivulets of water were already disappearing into the parched soil when she coiled the hose back up and, munching on a thick sandwich, started back toward the road.

Cassie had worried the cashier might ask her who she was or where she was headed, but he hadn't. She felt secure that he wasn't a very gregarious fellow and that her passing would be quickly forgotten.

As she started back down the highway, a semi truck pulled out of the westbound lane to stop, in a cloud of dust and the squeal of air brakes, in front of the gas pumps. A middle-aged man wearing a bright red baseball cap over his long, blond hair climbed down from the cab and, after stretching a bit, walked into the store. A thought struck Cassie, as she stood there looking at the dusty blue cab, and she turned and walked back toward the truck. She was standing near the bumper when the driver returned, holding a paper grocery bag in one hand and fishing in his pocket for his keys with the other.

"Excuse me," Cassie whispered, then louder, "Excuse me!" The driver stopped and looked up, seeing her standing there for the first time.

"What'cha want, kid?" he asked, still searching for his keys.

"Are you headed to Phoenix?" Cassie asked, trying to sound nonchalant.

"Yup."

"Could I catch a ride with you?"

The driver shook his head, "Nope, sorry."

"Maybe just to Tucson?"

"Can't do it, kid," he said, pointing to a small sign on the door of the truck, "company rules." The metal plate read *Employees Only!*

"I'd give ya a lift if I could, but I'm not going to risk losing my job."

Cassie was stunned; her master plan for crossing the distance between here and Long Beach was crumbling before her eyes.

"Do all trucks have that rule?" she asked, her voice starting to waver again, as the man pulled a rattling ring of keys from his pocket.

"Most of 'em," the driver called back, climbing into the cab and slamming the door. "You might try to find an independent, a fella who drives his own truck, but most companies are pretty strict, insurance rates and all. Really not a very safe way to travel anyway."

"Thanks heaps!" Cassie muttered, but returned the driver's wave as he pulled away.

This could be a problem. She had been depending on being able to hitchhike so her money would last through the spring. If she had to buy a bus ticket now, she'd never make it to summer term, much less September! Turning back towards the highway, Cassie swallowed the last bite of her sandwich and started walking again, her mind whirling. How could she tell which drivers were independents? Cassie thought about this as she walked along, and finally determined the only way would be to find a truck stop in Tucson or Phoenix and watch the rigs as they entered, looking for the telltale *employees only* signs.

This could take longer than she had expected.

Chapter Three

The day passed slowly as Cassie marched, doggedly, through the heat.

Around two o'clock, the hottest part of the day, she took a break to rest in the shade of a highway sign, spreading out her sleeping bag to finish drying. Her feet had started to hurt an hour earlier as blisters began to rise within her sweltering boots. Now, as the blisters had begun to break, her feet had become a raw, burning ache at the end of her legs. As soon as she had sat down, Cassie pulled a clean pair of socks from her bag and then removed her boots and blood spotted socks to let her feet air and dry. This was a lesson she had learned hiking through the hills around Bowie as a Girl Scout.

"Change your socks when you stop to rest," Mrs. Dillard (who some of the girls called *Kong* because of her hairy legs) had told them, "and you'll get a lot more mileage with a lot less pain."

Cassie mentally scolded herself, as she rubbed her sore, burning feet, for not stopping an hour before when the blisters had began to form.

She ate another sandwich and one of her candy bars, which had gone so soft in the heat of her pocket that she had to lick the chocolate first from the wrapper and then her fingers. Taking a long swallow of water, tepid and plasticy, she leaned back, closed her eyes, and began to relate the events of the morning onto her tape machine.

The heat of the afternoon sun made her drowsy. After putting on clean socks and lacing up her boots (the last thing she wanted was sunburned feet), Cassie leaned her duffel bag in the shade of a rock and closed her eyes. She had meant to take just a quick nap, waiting out the hottest part of the day. But her long hike, coupled with lack of sleep the night before, took their toll and she fell into a deep dreamless slumber almost as soon as she closed her eyes.

Cassie awoke with a start, hours later, to the piercing sound of brakes squealing to a stop nearby. Quietly, she peeked around the corner of the sign and saw a rusty old flatbed pickup parked on the far shoulder. Beyond it she could see an old man, walking off across the desert toward a rocky outcropping some yards off the road. The truck, at least forty years old, had tall wood rail sides and a heavy green canvas tarp, which covered the bed and had been tucked into the tailgate.

Before Cassie could think about what she was doing, she half limped, half ran across the highway to the truck, where she pulled up the tarp and looked inside. The rusty remains of a motorcycle, older even than the truck, were strapped firmly to the rails over one wheel well, the stylized figure of an Indian head, complete with headdress, surmounted the dented front fender of the bike. Several boxes of machine tools and parts lay in the back of the truck as well.

Cassie threw one last hurried glance at the truck's owner, who was just disappearing behind the rocks, a telltale roll of flapping white paper in his hand. She swallowed hard, her mouth going dry at the sight of a pump-action shotgun hanging on the back window of the cab. Desperation struggled with fear and prevailed as Cassie quickly tossed her bag over the tailgate and then scrambled in after it, tucking the tarp back in behind her. Climbing over the crates, she settled against the back of the cab, her duffel behind her, and tried to calm her beating heart.

At some point in the recent past, someone had spilled a bottle of beer, or several by the smell of it, in the bed of the truck. The fading, sour-sweet smell of hops nearly gagged her in the heat beneath the tarp.

The thick yeasty smell kindled the memory of her one and only experiment with drinking. She'd been fifteen and spending the night at a girlfriend's house after a birthday party. Her host's boyfriend, with most of the rest of the football team, pulled up to the back of the house after midnight and, after some quick and merciless peer-pressure, Cassie had climbed out the bedroom window and shimmied down to the porch behind her friend. They had ended up at the reservoir, parked back behind the trees and away from prying eyes. Her first beer had been awful and the others had roared with laughter as her face squinched at the bitter liquid.

One of the boys had passed her a half-full mason jar of amber colored liquid and told her to take a drink; it would take the taste away.

If the beer had been bad, the whiskey was worse by far. The dry bitterness burned across her tongue and roared up her sinuses at the same time, pinching painfully at the back of her throat and leaving her choking and breathless.

Teddy Waski, a hulking linebacker with a body like a dump truck and a brain to match, had laughed uproariously and slapped her on the back as she drank. A fair amount of the moonshine had splashed down the front of her shirt. All in all, Cassie had found the drinks, much like the company, to be uninspiring and was grateful when the others finally clambered back into the pickup and headed home. Her head had begun spinning unpleasantly, and half an hour of twists and turns along the rutted gravel road, left her sweating and sick.

Her stomach churning, Cassie had asked to be dropped off as they passed the narrow road leading to the Belangers' trailer. Stumbling though the door an hour before dawn, she had barely staggered to the bathroom in time to empty the contents of her roiling stomach into the toilet. Resting her head against the cool porcelain of the bowl, and wincing at the sound of footsteps in the hallway and the bright blinding light of the overhead bulb, she had looked up miserably at the sound of her mother's voice.

"Cassie, honey, what in the world..."

Her mother's voice trailed off suddenly as the smell of alcohol struck her. Cassie, with great effort, forced herself to her feet, and stood, weaving, trying to explain.

"Mom, I..."

The sound of Kathy's open palm striking her daughter's face was as sharp as it was unexpected, and Cassie reeled, striking the thin wall of the bathroom and clutching her burning cheek, her eyes wide and shocked. Her mother's face was like that of a stranger, pale and furious, eyes blazing, her lips pulled back in disgust and fury, baring her teeth in a feral snarl. Her hand was still raised as though she intended to strike again or had simply forgotten to lower it.

It was the first and only time that her mother had ever hit her. Kathy Belanger had always shied away from spankings, even when her daughter was young. Cassie felt tears began to spill down her cheeks; less from pain and surprise, as from the hazy understanding that something had taken place between them that could never be taken back.

After a long, tense moment, Kathy's gaze shifted from her daughter to her own upturned hand and she shuddered visibly. Cassie watched as her mother's shoulders sagged and her face became a hurt and weary version of the woman Cassie knew. Her hand had dropped to her side like a deadweight.

"Go to bed, Cassie, go sleep it off. I'll clean up in here."

Cassie had drawn a hitching breath to apologize, her young body quaking with shame at the disappointment in her mother's eyes.

"Go," she repeated. "We'll talk about this tomorrow."

As she turned the corner towards her room, she heard her mother's voice mutter to herself.

"I've cleaned up after drunks before."

Cassie had fled, weeping, to the guilty darkness of her room.

True to her word Kathy had sat down at the table with her daughter the next afternoon and listened to the whole story.

She had apologized for slapping her, and Cassie had asked her forgiveness again and again. Both had cried, and then laughed, and life had moved on. It was the first and last drink that Cassie had ever taken. Over the years she had been teased by her classmates, as bottles were passed, and she had shook her head. It wasn't a temptation. Each time the bottle was offered she would see, reflected in the sloshing contents, the disappointment in her mother's eyes.

All of this flashed through Cassie's mind in an instant, as she stowed away quietly among the debris that littered the bed of the old pick-up.

"Cassie Belanger," she scolded herself in a shocked whisper, "have you gone completely insane? How do you know this truck is going to Tucson? How do you know this guy won't shoot you and leave you in a ditch when he finds you in the back of his truck?"

As she huddled in the dim heat beneath the canopy, no answers came. All she knew for sure was that her sore, tired feet didn't have much hiking left in them, and that she was nearly out of water again. Wherever this truck was headed it was in the right direction for now. An old gas-guzzler like this couldn't go too long between fill-ups, and when it stopped, she could hop out the back and run like a rabbit.

"Well," she whispered to herself, as the image of the shotgun rose in her mind, "maybe not like a *rabbit*."

Cassie had nearly nodded off again when the driver's door suddenly creaked open, and she bit her lip to stifle a startled scream. There was a long pause and Cassie began to shake, certain that she had been heard. Then the door slammed shut and the truck rumbled to life, belching smoke. Whatever springs the pickup may once have had, had long since expired, and Cassie rattled and bounced along amid the clatter of loose tools and the staccato thunder of the rippling tarp.

Amid this din, Cassie drifted off to sleep once more. It would be many hours later before she remembered that her battered old sleeping bag had been left, draped over the rocks to dry, somewhere along Interstate 10.

The screeching of the pickup's tired brakes roused her from her sleep and Cassie blinked in the darkness, disoriented, until she remembered where she was and why. Panic clutched at her as she realized that her legs had gone completely asleep, folded under her on the hard metal truck bed. Not much chance to run like a rabbit, or anything else for that matter. The door creaked open, then banged shut again and, for one terrified moment, Cassie thought she heard the man coming around toward the back of the truck. As she held her breath and listened, Cassie heard diminishing footsteps along with a momentary blast of twangy country music as another door opened and closed.

Silence resumed, broken only by the sound of her own breathing and the slow *tink, tink, tink*, of the cooling engine. Cassie rubbed life back into her legs, wincing at the pins and needles as circulation returned to her feet. Slowly and quietly she pulled her duffel bag out from behind her and crawled over the crates to the tailgate, pausing to listen for any sound beyond. Hearing nothing, Cassie slowly untucked the heavy cover, and poked her head out, like a wary turtle, from under the tarp.

The parking lot was dim, lit by a single amber streetlamp, and mostly deserted, with only a handful of cars lined up in front of a low, dark building.

Somewhere nearby Cassie could hear the rush of freeway traffic and see the glow of streetlights beyond the tall hedge at the back of the parking lot, that and the muffled country music that seeped out under the building's door. Climbing quickly, if stiffly, from the pickup, she pulled her bag after her and jogged around the back of the building, a shabby tavern whose flashing neon sign identified it as *The Spur*. Rubbing sleep from her eyes, Cassie realized that, except for her sore back and feet, she felt better and more rested than she had in a week. The weather was pleasant, just cool enough to be comfortable in her jacket as she walked through the twilight towards the sound of evening traffic.

Now if only I knew where I was. Cassie thought. *I wonder how long I slept?* Long enough for the sun to set that much was clear. What if the driver had taken an off-ramp to another highway? She could be in California by now, or worse, in any one of the many tiny settlements that dotted the Arizona desert.

The tavern was in a low-rent district, and Cassie passed through two or three neighborhoods full of shabby box houses, mostly built just after World War Two for the soldiers returning home from overseas. She breathed a somewhat reserved sigh of relief, the little flyspecks on the Arizona map didn't have neighborhoods this big or streets this well maintained. The houses, however, were another story. Fifty years of wear and neglect showed in the sagging porches and peeling paint. Many had the junked remains of old cars and trucks, rusting into oblivion, on cement blocks in their yards. Occasionally, a motorcycle, or several, would be parked on the dirt-packed driveways.

Once or twice Cassie jumped as dogs ran out from under houses to bark at her as she passed. None left the confines of their yards, however, and after they saw that Cassie didn't seem interested in invading their territory the dogs quickly grew bored and returned to the confines of their subterranean stations.

An hour later she came to an intersection with a sign directing her to the on-ramp for Interstate 10. The street sign at the corner put her at the intersection of Buckeye Road and South 16th. The large green sign hanging above the intersection also stated that it was one-half mile to the Phoenix City Center Bypass. She was in Phoenix! She must have slept almost three hours in the back of that truck; this was an unexpected stroke of good luck, and Cassie breathed a quick prayer of thanks. Her first try as a stowaway had saved her at least one full day of hard walking, maybe two.

She sat down on the curb, in the pool of overhead light, and pulled a map from the inside pocket of her jacket. It was a huge Rand-McNally driving map with all of Arizona on one side and Phoenix on the other. She had a similar map of Washington State in her bag as well, along with computer-printed maps of Portland and Long Beach. She carefully unfolded the Phoenix side and, after several minutes of searching, she pinpointed her exact location.

A dimly lit bus snored past her, going the opposite direction. Tracing her finger back along the red line of Interstate 10, Cassie found the City Center exit listed on the sign above her head, then followed that a half mile south to its junction with Interstate 17. If she were going to find a truck stop, that was the place to do it!

She folded the map and stowed it back in her pocket. Her watch read nine forty-five and Cassie knew that she wouldn't be ready to sleep again until morning. So, after eating her remaining chocolate bar and finishing off the last of her water, Cassie repacked her duffel bag and headed east on Buckeye towards Interstate 10. With a little luck, she would find a road that paralleled the highway back to Interstate 17. She briefly considered refilling her water bottles from a hose lying in the yard of a nearby house. Her sojourn across the desert had left her very aware of her provisions. Still, after a moment's hesitation, Cassie decided against it, unwilling to risk having to explain herself to the homeowner should a light come on in the darkened windows at the sound of the hose.

Twenty minutes on shanks mare, as Mrs. Miller had been fond of saying, brought Cassie to the on-ramp for Interstate 10, where she found a blocked alley that followed the same general path as the freeway.

Cassie could see the streetlamps here and there down the long, narrow path and, from where she stood, the stretches of darkness between each bright oasis seemed forbidding. Standing alone in the shadows, she suddenly realized that she hadn't considered, in her hasty planning, any means of defending herself. The very idea, in fact, hadn't occurred to her until she found herself at the mouth of the long, dark alley. Cassie scanned the weed littered concrete but the best she could come up with was a short, bent pipe crusted with concrete. She hefted the crude cudgel and after a couple of experimental swings, started down the narrow road.

"Okay," she muttered to herself, "now if I can keep from hitting myself in the head with this thing..."

Her fears proved for naught and, except for one heart stopping moment when she spooked an alley cat and *did* nearly succeed in smacking herself, the way proved to be safe and uneventful. The terrified calico scooted across the path and to the top of the fence. It paused there to look back, appraising the threat and, determining Cassie to be a false alarm, it sauntered indignantly, tail high in the air, down the length of the fence and back into the darkness.

"Stupid cat!" Cassie hissed after it, taking a deep breath and waiting for the machine-gun beat of her heart to slow.

Knee-high weeds forced themselves up through the broken concrete, brushing at Cassie's legs as she passed, long skinny tendrils of bramble tugged at the hem of her jeans. A faint, cool breeze rose, tumbling a candy-bar wrapper down the path towards her.

Reaching the end of the alley revealed the highest of her hopes as Cassie saw, on the far corner of the intersection, a huge parking lot dotted with trucks of all shapes and sizes. Smack in the center of these, shining like a beacon to the freeways running on either side was the Flying T Truck Stop.

Cassie waited at the corner for the traffic lights to change and then hurried across the busy street. She wandered through the parking lot, growing disheartened at the number of *Employees Only* signs she found affixed to the big trucks. There were several smaller trucks and a few cars on the lot as well but, checking the license plates, Montana was the furthest west that she could find. She had a sinking feeling that it wouldn't be too long before she would be willing to hop a ride with anyone headed even remotely in the direction of the West Coast.

Cassie ate the last of her bread and lunchmeat, washing it down with a diet soda from a bright, humming vending machine near the gas pumps. The pungent smell of diesel fuel was thick around the pumps, and she took a deep breath as she walked past with her cola. Cassie had always liked the smell of diesel, an enjoyment that had caused her mother to roll her eyes. In the near corner of the parking lot she found a covered bus stop beneath a bright overhead streetlamp. The bus stop sat at the main entrance to the lot and seemed like a strategic spot to watch the incoming traffic. After digging out her recorder and her Bible, Cassie dropped her bag against the hard plastic wall of the shelter and sat with her back resting against the wall.

She related her thoughts and feelings on stowing away in the back of the pickup and her encounter with the cat in the alley. Then, after carefully packing the tiny machine back in her bag, she picked up the worn, leather-bound Bible with the fading gold initials, her mother's initials, on the cover. Inside the flyleaf was a brief, smudged inscription in a neat flowing script that read:

Trust in the Lord with all your heart and lean not unto thine own understanding, in all thy ways acknowledge Him, and He will direct your path. Proverbs 3:5-6

Cassie murmured the words aloud, laying the Bible back in her lap. She knew this verse, as well as the rest of the chapter by heart. This had been her favorite scripture growing up, one that her mother prayed along with her each night as she tucked her in to bed. For years Cassie had thought that her father might have written that verse in his young wife's Bible, maybe as a wedding or anniversary gift. The rough penmanship on the tattered marriage certificate in her pocket, however, was nothing like the small clean lettering on the Bible's flyleaf.

Marking her place, midway through the book of Psalms, was a photograph of a young woman standing waist-deep in pool of water. In her arms was a small, pink wrapped bundle, and standing beside her, with one hand on her shoulder and his other holding an open Bible, was a much younger Guy Williams. The picture, she knew, had been taken soon after her birth, the year that Kathy Belanger had moved to Bowie. Her mother looked so young, her long dark hair pulled back in a ponytail, wearing jeans and a white cotton shirt, knotted at her waist. She looked, in fact, very much like Cassie did now, eighteen years later. The picture had been taken with a zoom lens and the three of them filled much of the frame. She had always laughed at the long, feathered hairstyle that Guy had worn in the early eighties and she would tease him and ask if he still carried a banana-comb in his back pocket.

Her pastor would shake his finger at her with a mock frown and say that if he had, he would paddle her with it.

In the photograph, her mother was smiling as she held her newborn daughter for dedication, but Cassie could see the smile on her lips didn't reach her eyes. Her gaze held a sad, scared, far-off look. The arms that held her baby clutched protectively, not only from the river that swirled around them, but also from something else, some secret fear. Cassie had seen this look, off and on, her whole life, usually in those rare times when she pressed Kathy for information about her father.

"He's not someone you want to know, Cass," she would say softly, "best to leave it alone."

Her voice would be soft, but there was steel in her tone that warned Cassie to drop the subject. Once, when her mother had spent weeks deathly ill with pneumonia, fading in and out of delirium from the fever and medications, she had turned her head on her pillow one evening and, and looked strangely at Cassie.

"I was all alone, Baby," she had said. "I was young and scared and I didn't have anywhere to go. He was handsome and funny, and he said that he loved me; that he'd take care of me."

Tears had trickled unnoticed down her scarlet cheeks.

"You may be the only good thing that Bill Beckman's done in his whole life…"

Cassie had been ten years old at the time. She was alone with her mother while Grace had run to the store to fill a prescription for antibiotics. The girl had sat, terrified, by her mother's bedside, wiping her face over and over with a faded washcloth as the woman tossed and thrashed. She wasn't even sure that her mother had known she was in the room, and Kathy's words were never mentioned again after she recovered.

Cassie had looked long and hard in the mirror that night, trying to imagine what her father might look like. She definitely had her mother's dark, almost black hair, but her complexion was ruddy where her mother was very fair, almost pale. She had her mother's high cheekbones, but fuller lips and upturned knob of a chin that gave her face a heart-shaped, impish look.

Cassie had cried herself to sleep that night, quietly under the covers so Grace, who was sleeping on the living room couch, wouldn't hear. Beneath her pillow was the small pink diary her mother had given her for her birthday that August. Before turning out the light, Cassie had carefully printed, "Bill Beckman, my daddy" on the inside cover. She had underlined the name twice and then locked the little book back up with a tiny brass key. Somewhere in the Williams' attic, back in Bowie, that little pink and white diary rested in a cardboard box with Cassie's name on it.

The photo was starting to fade around the edges. It was her favorite picture of her mother who, though sad, had been so young and beautiful, holding her baby safe, as she was dedicated to God.

Cassie closed her eyes, fighting off the nagging voices of fear and doubt, and prayed.

"Okay Lord," she whispered, "I'm trying to trust with all my heart; I hope I'm not doing something really stupid here." Cassie clenched her fists in her lap, fighting tears, "Tell me what to say when I find him, show me what you want me to do…" She paused for a long moment, unsure of what else to say.

"Please keep me safe and direct my path, amen." She sighed, repeating the words her mother had used each night, and felt little satisfaction from her prayers.

Chapter Four

Cassie opened her eyes as a great, lumbering truck rounded the corner slowing and passed her in a cloud of exhaust, the license plate read Georgia.

She picked up her Bible once more and, after carefully removing her photograph-bookmark, continued to read. An hour later, Cassie closed the book and stood to stretch. A half-dozen vehicles had pulled into the truck stop parking lot since she had sat down, but none of them had plates from any western states.

She was just considering a cup of coffee in the café when a dusty blue cargo van pulled off the road and into the lot, washing her in the beams of its headlights as it passed.

Cassie blinked, looked at the rear of the van, and then blinked again. There, on the bumper, half hidden under at thick patina of dust was a yellow bumper sticker that read, *Water Music Festival 1997, Long Beach, Washington.*

Cassie forgot, for a moment, just how to breathe, as her heart began to hammer against her ribs. She gave her old Bible a quick squeeze as she stowed it back in her bag and, glancing upward, whispered, "Thank you!"

The van had pulled into the darkened lot to the rear of the café, between two big semi-trucks. Cassie watched, from the safety of the shadows as a tall, bulky man with close-cropped white hair, stepped from the van, stretched for a moment and crossed the parking lot towards the truck stop.

Cassie watched him as he walked away, noting that he wore a faded brown bomber jacket with a white turtleneck underneath, so she could find him again once he was inside. Once the man was gone and the door had swung closed behind him, Cassie crept across the lot to the van. Passing behind several of the towering semis, some with extended living quarters that had lights shining through the tiny curtained windows, she stopped behind a carrier full of new Toyotas and listened for the sound of footsteps. She could hear nothing but the soft stomping and lowing from the cattle-truck to her left and the bass hum of a huge refrigeration unit to her right.

Realizing that she would probably draw more suspicion, were she to be seen skulking, Cassie straightened up and walked quickly to the faded blue Chevy. Up close, it looked like it had seen more than its share of the open road.

Both the front and rear bumpers were pitted with small dents and the blue passenger-side front fender had been replaced with one painted primer-gray. All four tires, though, appeared to be fairly new and the van didn't have that miasma of burning oil that surrounded poorly kept vehicles after a long drive.

Coming around the far side, she could see the sliding door had been replaced as well, matching the gray fender. Through the dusty glass Cassie could see the dashboard was littered with maps, magazines, and what appeared to be several days worth of fast-food wrappers. She double-checked the bumper sticker and, sure enough, it still read Long Beach, WA. From her new vantage point, she could see what she hadn't been able to make out as the van had passed her. The grime-coated license plate was from Washington as well!

Cassie took a deep breath and leaned against the back of the van for a moment. *Planning* to ask someone if, oh by the way, did they mind driving her halfway across the country, had been one thing. Now, faced with the reality of the moment, she actually had to walk up to a total stranger who, oh by the way, hopefully wasn't a serial killer, and *ask for a ride*.

Once she had gathered her courage, Cassie glanced at the rear window and, after wiping some of the dirt off with her sleeve, peered into the back of the van.

In the darkness she could make out several closed cardboard boxes, a couple of sleeping bags and an even larger collection of drive-thru refuse. Stepping away, Cassie glanced around and, seeing no one, stashed her duffel bag under the dumpster behind the café. After pulling some flattened cardboard over the top of it and checking from several angles, Cassie nodded, satisfied that it would remain hidden for the short time she was inside.

Continuing around the side of the building to the front door, Cassie passed though the tiled entryway, lined with newspaper boxes and penny-candy machines, around the *Please Wait to be Seated* sign, and into the restaurant.

Most of the coffee bar and many of the booths were taken by lone occupants. Truckers, who read their books or magazines, ate in silence, or just dozed over their coffee cups. Near the end of the aisle, Cassie could see the back of a white-haired head above the seat cushions and the empty arm of a brown leather jacket hanging off the bench on the far side of the table.

She took a deep breath as she walked tremulously toward the man. The smell of french fries and strong coffee dominated the room. Cassie tried to focus on these observations and not on the knot that was developing in her stomach. She reached the table, turned to face the driver of the van and, suddenly, found herself unable to speak. The man looked to be in his early fifties, his face weather-lined and tanned. He kept reading his book for a moment or two and then, after slowly slipping a finger between the pages, he glanced up at Cassie over his reading glasses.

As soon as his gaze met hers he seemed to jerk slightly in his seat, his eyes grew wide and his face pale, then he blinked and whatever had come over him passed. Head to toe, his eyes took her in for a long moment and, under any other circumstances, Cassie would have blushed, but something in his manner made it clear that his stare was nothing inappropriate.

"Did you forget your uniform," he asked, in a soft baritone, "and my coffee?"

Cassie stood, blinking and dumbfounded, for a moment, trying to decipher what the man was talking about.

"No," Cassie stammered, "I'm not here…I mean, I don't work here. I'm not a waitress!"

"Oh?"

"No, I'm not. I was just wondering if you minded, I mean if I could…is that your blue van out there?" Cassie spluttered.

"It is," he replied, still looking directly into her eyes. His expression was serious, his voice flat, but his eyes had begun to twinkle with amusement.

"Okay," Cassie began, taking a deep breath, "let me try again. I saw that your van has Washington plates, are you from Long Beach?"

"I am."

Okay," she repeated, "um…are you heading back that way?"

"Eventually," he said, his eyes twinkling even more.

Pausing, Cassie tried to collect her thoughts before asking the next question. This was quickly becoming a most frustrating conversation. If only the man would stop staring at her and start answering her questions with more than just monosyllabic responses. Cassie decided to try another route.

"Can I…do you mind if I sit down?" she asked.

At this the man's stony expression finally broke and the corners of his mouth curled into a slight, sardonic, smile.

"Aren't I a little old for you, kid?"

Cassie felt her cheeks grow hot as she both sputtered and stammered, in an attempt to reply.

"No!" she almost shouted, lowering her voice quickly when heads at the nearest tables turned their way, "I mean yes! I mean…that's not what I mean. I just need to get to Washington!"

Cassie felt herself on the verge of tears. Her head was spinning from the convoluted dialog, and the knot in her stomach had tightened into a hard, solid ball that threatened even further unpleasantries if she didn't find herself in a less stressful situation soon. It was such a simple question, why couldn't she just ask it?

"The lady doth protest too much, methinks…" he said softly.

"Huh?" she replied, wondering if she could possibly sound as stupid to this stranger as she did to herself; she was fairly certain that she must.

"*Hamlet*."

"I…uh…" *Another brilliant response, would this never end?* She would happily walk all the way to Oysterville, barefoot, if it meant that she could just get away from this table and hide her crimson, burning face.

"You *do* know who Shakespeare was?" he asked, closing his book and seeming genuinely interested in her for the first time. Cassie was able to keep her mouth shut this time, and was grateful for that small blessing.

"Well," the man said at last, "if you've never heard of Shakespeare, I don't want to know. Have a seat."

Cassie sat.

A moment of silence stretched into two and finally the man leaned forward and, waving a hand in front of her eyes, asked in that same low voice, "Well?"

"Um…" Cassie groped for an answer, "Thank you?"

He laid a weary hand over his eyes and sighed.

"Okay," he said, looking up and smiling for the first time. "Let's try rowing this boat in another direction, shall we? Can you give me one good reason why a pretty young gal like yourself would be doing something as stupendously idiotic as asking to ride halfway across creation with a strange man?"

At last Cassie's embarrassment had found its limit and, unable to become any more humiliated, she found herself growing annoyed at the man's seemingly unending sarcasm.

"And are you?" she asked, her eyes starting to spark.

Now it was the stranger's turn to look confused. "Am I what?" he asked.

"A strange man?" Cassie answered sweetly, with the same smile that had driven the cashier at the Greyhound ticket desk nearly to distraction. Two could play this little game!

The man across the table merely looked amused. "The tales I could tell you kid!" Cassie knew she shouldn't, but the haughty way he had quoted *Hamlet*, like she was some ignorant country bumpkin who had never read a book, had stung. Cassie Belanger, as any number of the fine folk in Bowie, Arizona could tell you, didn't like to be stung.

"Tales told by an idiot?" she quoted, in that same sweet voice, "full of sound and fury, signifying nothing?"

That caught the man off guard. "Wha…," he started.

"*Macbeth*?"

He gaped at her.

"You *do* know who Shakespeare was?" she finished innocently.

Silence descended on the table, and Cassie was sure that she would soon resume her wait at the bus stop. Suddenly the man slammed both hands down on the tabletop, threw back his head and roared with laughter. This went on for some time until, finally, Cassie began to giggle herself as the older man's face turned bright red and he pounded the table, snorting for air.

Soon, despite the curious glances from the diners around them, both were doubled over, laughing uproariously, tears streaming down their faces. Cassie laughed and cried at the same time, her sides aching and her breath coming in short hitching gasps. The knot in her stomach loosened as some measure of the tension of the last week began to ease. It felt as though a small hole had pierced the dam within her as the pressure that had begun to leak out through the cracks and fissures of her spirit dissipated.

Their laughter was finally interrupted by the waitress who quickly set a cup of black coffee and a piece of apple-pie in front of the red-faced man, slipping the bill under the edge of his plate. She raised a questioning eyebrow, glancing back and forth between the two of them as they tried to regain their composure, shrugging, she turned and began to walk away.

"Miss," he said, "I'm sorry…" He snorted again and wiped his streaming eyes, "I think we're going to need another piece of pie here."

Turning to Cassie, he asked, "What's your poison? Dessert's on me."

Cassie sniffled, trying to stop the giggle in her voice.

"Apple would be great, thanks!"

The waitress gave them one more long look and then hurried away. He let out an explosive breath, mopping his face with his napkin. "Well," he said, still chuckling, "I guess I deserved that; I was starting to get a little full of myself there…"

Cassie decided to strike, as her mother would say, while the iron was hot.

"So?" she asked.

"What?" he answered, this time seeming to have genuinely forgotten the original question.

"So," she repeated, "are you heading back to Long Beach?"

"You first," he said, "why would you be doing something as dangerous as bumming rides at a truck stop?"

"No choice, I have to get to Long Beach and—"

"Why?"

Cassie paused, "That's my…"

He dismissed her with a wave of his hand, "If you're asking me to let you ride along all the way to Washington, then it's my business as well. Now let's hear it."

Luckily, Cassie had taken the time, during her long wait at the bus stop, to come up with a story that validated her trip.

"I'm writing a book," she said quickly.

Now it was his turn to raise an eyebrow. "Oh?"

Cassie rushed ahead, "Yeah, I'm working on a book about the histories of small towns on the Washington coast. It's for school. I need to spend a couple of weeks there before spring term starts, to do research." She held her breath; waiting for him to ask what school she attended. Instead, after studying her for another moment he just said, "Well, that's ironic, but okay," and took a sip of his streaming coffee. Cassie was almost disappointed that she hadn't been able to use the rest of her story.

"So," he went on, "what's your name?"

"Huh?"

"Well, unless you just want me to call you *hey you*…"

"Cassia," she replied, and then under some compulsion she didn't even understand, she lied. "Cassia um… Williams, but everyone calls me Cassie."

"Never met anyone whose middle name was *Um* before."

"It's just Cassie Williams, no um."

The man's eyebrow had inched back up, but he said nothing, chewing a bite of his pie instead. Then, after another sip of coffee, he murmured, "A rose by any other name, I guess. Names are like clothes, different suits for different occasions, that's what I say." The man offered his hand across the table, and Cassie shook it.

"Jack," he said.

Cassie smiled, "Never met anyone named just *Jack* before."

"Touché," he laughed, "I'm Jack Leland. Nice to meet you, Cassie. You're quick, I like that."

"Thanks," Cassie replied. "So, what's with quoting all the Shakespeare, Jack Leland?"

"Oh that," he said, "well, first off I'm not particularly stuck on the Bard, he just happened to be fitting in this case. Occupational hazard, I guess."

"Are you an actor?"

"Hardly," Jack snorted, choking on a swallow of coffee, spraying it back into the thick ceramic mug with a gargling laugh, "I own a bookstore just outside Long Beach."

There was a pause, and when Cassie looked at him she noticed something strange. Jack had stopped eating and was staring at something over her left shoulder. Cassie started to turn, when Jack quietly said, "Don't."

He spoke the single word with such command that she froze in her seat.

Jack began to tell Cassie about how he was on his way back from a book auction in Texas, and had just stopped off to get a break from the highway and a couple of cups of coffee. While he was talking to her, Jack's eyes never moved from whatever, or whoever, he was watching. Slowly and casually, he reached into his jacket, lying on the seat next to him, and pulled out an apple and an odd, wood handled knife. The short, crescent shaped blade was covered with a leather sheath, which Jack removed, and though the pine handle looked old and worn the blade was bright. Its concave edge looked razor sharp as Jack held it in front of his face and slowly began to peel the apple.

Jack kept talking, telling her how this was sort of a working vacation and he was planning on taking Interstate 8 down to San Diego, then follow Highway 101 all the way up the coast to Long Beach.

Finally, whoever had gotten his attention must have looked away, and Jack glanced back to Cassie, laying the knife down beside his plate, in plain sight. Cassie glanced from the knife to Jack and back, before leaning over the table and whispering, "What was that all about?" Jack gave a slight shake of his head, looking back up and Cassie realized that whoever it was, was coming towards them. She could smell the flat stink of stale cigarette smoke before he passed. From her vantage point all she saw was the back of a lanky frame, a dirty leather biker jacket, and a long, greasy ponytail, as the figure quickly passed their table and headed for the door. The other thing that caught her eye were the dark green tattoos scrolling out from under each sleeve and across the backs of his hands.

Then the stranger was gone.

Cassie looked questioningly at Jack, who had wiped the blade of his knife clean and was returning it to his pocket.

"He seemed to have taken an unhealthy interest in our conversation," Jack replied to her unspoken question. "I'm sure he was willing to offer you a ride if I had turned you down."

Cassie felt her mouth go dry at the thought. She tried to imagine being alone in the cab of one of those big trucks, surrounded by that stink, those tattooed hands somewhere nearby in the dark, and shuddered.

Jack reached for his pie once more as the waitress returned with another piece for Cassie.

Without thinking, she clasped her hands against the edge of the table and, bowing her head, said a quick prayer for the food. Jack watched, amused by the complete lack of self-consciousness the young woman showed, praying in front of a room full of truck drivers.

Cassie glanced up and caught Jack's gaze, misunderstanding his look.

"Do you have something against praying?" she asked.

"Nope," he replied, unruffled. "Stick with what works for ya, that's what I say. I've just never had it do me much good is all."

Cassie frowned but couldn't think of anything to say to that, so they ate together in silence for a few moments.

Finishing her pie, which wasn't a shadow of Grace William's apple creations, she glanced up at Jack, who was once again watching her with a speculative look on his face.

"Well," he said, at last, "I guess I could move some boxes around and make some space."

Cassie held her breath.

"Problem is," he continued, "I'm not headed straight across. Like I said, I'm planning on heading back up 101, the long way."

"That's fine," Cassie said quickly, "I don't mind..."

Jack's eyes narrowed slightly, "I thought you were in a big, all-fired hurry?"

"A bird in the hand, and all that," she replied. "Who knows how long I'd have to wait for someone else headed that way? It's taken me the better part of two days just to get here. I'm willing to change the plan if it means riding instead of walking, and I can pay for gas..."

"Nah," Jack shook his head, "keep your money, I was driving anyway. Pay for your own grub and that'll be enough. You're set on this, aren't you?"

Cassie nodded.

"Awfully foolish, if you ask me," he grumbled. "The next guy you asked might not have been the harmless old fool that I am. Might just be safer all around if you don't have to ask again."

"So, you'll give me a ride?" she asked.

Jack paused, chewing on his lip, then sighed, "Well, I guess we can give it a try. I suppose if you start getting under my skin I can always leave you on the side of the road somewhere."

Cassie nodded enthusiastically, "That sounds fair!"

"Just one thing," Jack said, pointing a finger at her across the table. "No drugs or any of that nonsense. I mean it! I think anything funny is going on, I pull over and you're walking again, we understand each other?"

Cassie nodded again. "Don't worry, I don't do drugs."

"Good girl," Jack said, "I didn't think you seemed like the type, but it's just best to have the understanding out in the open, just in case."

"Understood," Cassie replied quickly.

Jack continued. "I'm warning you too, right up front, I'm a grouchy old bear when I'm tired. I don't like people chattering away at me all day long," Jack paused, swallowing the last of his coffee, "and I have it on the best of authority that I can be a pain in the posterior on a long drive."

Cassie grinned in spite of herself. "Wife?" she asked.

"Good Lord, no!" Jack exclaimed. "Just a friend."

"A girl though?" Cassie pressed.

"You're startin' already…" Jack growled.

"So," Cassie asked brightly, "how's your pie?"

At that, Jack chuckled and dug back in. Soon the pie was gone, along with another cup of coffee. "The road isn't getting any shorter just sitting here," Jack said, gathering his coat. "Let me settle this bill and we'll go."

Cassie dug quickly into her pocket and pulled out a couple of dollar bills. "I'll leave a tip," she said.

"Fair enough and good manners," he answered, nodding. "Why don't you meet me out front? I need to talk to a man about a horse." Cassie stared at him, not having the slightest idea what he was talking about.

Jack shook his head and jerked a finger towards an overhead sign that read, *Men's Room*.

"Oh," said Cassie, blushing, "okay."

Jacked walked toward the cash register, chuckling, as Cassie escaped into the lobby.

Chapter Five

Cassie glanced through the scarred plastic windows of the newspaper boxes, but the headlines held nothing that caught her interest. Bored, she decided to meet Jack at the van and, stepping back out into the cooling night air, she started across the parking lot.

Recovering her duffel bag and whistling tunelessly, she headed for the van. Cassie was thinking of what an answer to prayer it was, meeting Jack like this, when from the shadow of a big semi, a hand suddenly clamped down on her arm. Cassie uttered a brief shriek, and then froze. Dark, scrolling tattoos covered the hand that held her upper arm in a viselike grip.

"Don't be scared, sweetheart," a soft voice drawled from the darkness. "I heard you asking that old fella for a ride. Just happens that I'm headed that way myself."

Cassie was suddenly cold and numb with fear; she could feel herself starting to shake, as the pressure of the man's hand on her arm slowly pulled her back into the shadows.

"It's…uh…it's okay," Cassie stammered, "I've got a ride already, thanks."

"Oh?" the stranger replied in a whispering sneer, the stench of stale smoke clinging to him like a thick, bitter smog, forcing Cassie to fight to keep from gagging.

"Don't you worry honey, my truck is *much* more comfortable than his and I promise ya, I'm better company…"

She felt panic beginning to gnaw at the edges of her mind, as the hand pulled her further back into the dark canyon between the trailers. Cassie knew she should fight, she should cry out, but she couldn't make her limbs move or will her mouth to open, all she could think of was the blackness of the shadows behind her.

As those shadows closed in, she bit down on her lip, hard enough to draw blood, and the sudden pain helped her pull her whirling mind back under control.

Cassie tensed herself, ready to spin and lash out; planting a knee where she thought it would do the most damage.

She drew a great breath of air to scream as she felt the man behind her fumbling with the driver's door of the cab. Suddenly he stiffened and Cassie heard a hissing gasp of surprise and then the clutching hand was gone and, with it, her terrified paralysis.

With a sob of relief she leaped forward, out of that horrible shadow and smell and toward the light. She started for the café, but something made her turn, some curiosity that would not be satisfied until she had seen what was happening there in the shadows.

In the dim place between the two trucks, Cassie could just make out the lean, frozen form of her attacker, just behind him stood another figure, slightly shorter and stockier.

As her eyes adjusted, she saw that it was Jack standing behind the malodorous stranger. One arm curled across the taller man's chest and the other…Cassie saw a dull glint at the man's throat and realized that Jack's other hand held that oddly shaped knife that he had used to peel the apple.

Now, though, it rested firmly beneath the trucker's left jaw.

Above the soft hum of the overhead lamps, Cassie could hear Jack whispering softly into the man's ear. There was a pause and the stranger suddenly flinched and with a gasp, began to nod his head rapidly.

Jack began to whisper again, through clenched teeth, and her attacker stuttered something in reply. Jack lowered the arm that was crossing the taller man's chest and reached his hand beneath the leather jacket, pulling a small automatic pistol from the man's belt. After another brief whisper, the trucker reached slowly into his pocket and retrieved a ring of keys, which jingled sharply in his quaking grip. These he tossed toward Cassie, who jumped back in surprise as the rattling keys hit the pavement at her feet.

"Kid," Jack called softly, "are you okay?"

"I think so…" Cassie replied, her voice quavering a bit.

"Good girl, here's what I want you to do. Pick up those keys and go around the far side of this truck, the one to your right. We're going to meet you at the back end of the trailer. Can you do that?"

"I think so…yeah."

"Good girl," he said again, his soothing voice belying the tension in the air, "hurry up now, kid."

Cassie bent and picked up the keys, almost pitching forward as her head swam with vertigo. On the third try her sweeping fingers managed to catch the heavy silver ring and she scooped up the keys and straightened, taking a deep ragged breath. When Cassie reached the far end of the trailer, Jack was standing there waiting. In his hand was the shiny automatic he had pulled from the stranger's belt. The trucker was leaning against the huge double-doors, his bony, tattooed arms sticking out from the sleeves of his jacket and his hands resting against the dusty back of the trailer.

Cassie saw that he wore a greasy pair of blue jeans and worn black cowboy boots as well. Jack stood several feet behind the man, with the pistol aimed at his back; he took the key ring from Cassie and tossed it onto the wide bumper of the trailer.

Wordlessly the truck driver picked up the keys and, selecting one, reached up with a shaking hand and opened the heavy padlock that held the door.

This done he swung the door wide and climbed up inside. As soon as he was in the back of the empty trailer, Jack stepped up and quickly relocked the padlock, sealing the driver inside his own trailer.

Jack turned to Cassie, searching her eyes for panic, then nodded crisply.

"Okay," he said, "time to move along."

They walked quickly to the van, where Jack unlocked Cassie's door and then climbed into the driver's seat. The engine started easily, idling into a soft smooth hum confirming Cassie's first assessment that, despite the van's road-weary appearance, it was well-maintained.

Jack pulled out of the parking spot and drove slowly back towards the café.

"First things first," he said, and removed the trucker's pistol from his pocket. Pressing a small button on the grip, he popped the magazine out into his hand. Then, pulling back on the slide, Jack checked the chamber thoroughly to be sure the gun was unloaded.

Setting the pistol down carefully between the seats he quickly unloaded the clip, stuffing the bullets into his jacket pocket. Then, with rapid efficiency he disassembled the slide, spring and barrel until he held an awkward handful of gun parts in his lap. These he slipped into an empty burger bag from the floor.

Next, he pulled a battered denim wallet from another pocket and showed it to Cassie.

"*Let's see*," he growled, grinning evilly in the dimness, "*what the Baggins had in his nasty little pocketses*!" He opened the wallet, thumbing through it and slipping the driver's license out. A small wad of cash was folded into one corner, and Jack left it there, sliding the license into his shirt pocket. The wallet then joined the gun parts in the bag.

"Be right back," Jack said, opening the door.

Cassie watched him walk over to a mailbox on the sidewalk next to the café. Looking quickly to his right and left, Jack opened the slot and dumped the contents of the bag down into the box. The bag he crumpled and tossed in a nearby trashcan. Starting back toward the van, he paused and, kneeling over a rusty gutter grate, he dumped the handful of ammunition down the sewer. Moments later they were heading west with the flow of traffic on Interstate 10. Jack checked his mirrors periodically and finally leaned back in the driver's seat and sighed heavily.

"Well," he said, "that was a little more than the pie and coffee I had bargained for."

Cassie started to speak, but felt her throat constrict, she could still feel the iron grip of the trucker's hand on her arm, and smell his stink in her nostrils, she began to shake once more.

Jack, his voice still soft and reassuring, sounded concerned, "Are you going to be okay?" Cassie nodded, and in a hitching teary voice replied, "Yeah, it's getting better…"

"You're starting to get some color back, anyway," he said, "I thought we were going to lose you for a minute there."

"It was pretty close," Cassie replied, her breathing returning to normal as her reaction to the stress of the last few minutes began to pass. "If I could just stop shaking."

"Adrenaline. Fight or flight response. You'll be okay in a few minutes. You did good."

"I did?"

"Yup. Tell me something, if I hadn't shown up what were you going to do next?"

"I'm not sure," Cassie said, closing her eyes and then quickly snapping them back open as the image of those tattooed hands floated before her.

"I was so scared I couldn't move," she said, "all I could think of was if he got me back into those shadows I was going to start screaming and kicking."

"Good girl, where?"

"Where?"

"Where were you going to kick him?"

Cassie blushed and glanced away, looking at the rush of nighttime traffic along the interstate.

"Good," Jack nodded, "that's *exactly* where. Don't let anyone fool you, kid, there's no such thing as a fair fight!"

There was a long pause as the traffic hummed around them and they flashed from one circle of light to the next along the thoroughfare. Finally, when Cassie could stand the silence no longer, she glanced back over at Jack.

"Would you..." she asked, swallowing hard, "would you have cut him, or...or..."

"Or shot him, if he'd turned on us?" Jack finished.

"Yeah," she whispered.

There was another long pause and Cassie began to think that Jack wasn't going to answer her question.

"I've never killed a man before," he murmured, his eyes never leaving the road, "not even in the war..."

Cassie waited, holding her breath.

"I've seen enough good people hurt by bad people, though, that I think I could do what I had to, to keep it from happening right in front of me. So, if it was going to be him or us... I guess it was going to be him."

This time it was Cassie's turn to pause before replying.

"Good," she said finally.

"Why don't you try to get some shut eye," Jack advised. "I was going to find a place to sleep in Phoenix, but I think we'd better put a few miles and a couple of turns between us and Mr. Wexler—"

"Who?"

"Mark Wexler," Jack replied, slipping the driver's license, the one he had taken from the wallet before throwing it away, from his pocket and handing it to her, "of Phoenix, Arizona. He must have just gotten back from a run, that would explain why his truck was empty," Jack smirked. "I took the liberty of mugging your assailant while we were waiting for you to bring the keys around." Jack smiled grimly. "I wanted him to know that *we* know who he is."

Cassie glanced at the license, and there was that narrow, pinched face, sneering into the camera. "Ugh!" she said, and handed the card back to Jack.

"I'm going to try to get us onto I-8," he said, "and then find a rest stop. I've been driving for better than twelve hours today, and I'd rather not nod off at the wheel."

"Okay," Cassie replied.

"I've got a tent in the back, and an extra sleeping bag. I'll pitch that for me and you can sleep here in the van with the doors locked. We'll try to get a few hours of sleep and then hit the road again at first light."

"Thanks Jack," Cassie replied, leaning her head against the dusty window, suddenly exhausted, "for everything."

"Goodnight kid."

Jack drove in silence for another two hours, cruising south through the featureless desert, Cassie sleeping in the seat next to him, drifting away comfortably to the endless hum of rubber and asphalt. Like two glowing eyes, the van's dusty headlights cut a bright path through the darkness, far down Interstate 10 until they reached the exit for Yuma and San Diego, then onto AZ-85, and finally to Interstate 8. When the high beams lit a sign reading *Sentinel Rest Stop Next Right*, Jack pulled into the near lane and took the long curving off-ramp into the parking lot.

A dozen empty parking spaces sat in front of a squat brick building housing a men's rest room to the left and a women's to the right. Two glowing soda machines stood, in heavy iron cages, next to a lit billboard covered with maps. Jack drove past the building, down to the last space on the lot and parked. His headlights came to rest on a wide circle of emerald lawn, backed by a thick, low hedge. As he turned off the engine, Cassie stirred in her seat.

"Okay," he said, gently shaking her, "we're home." Cassie yawned and stretched, blinking her eyes.

"Wow," she said, sleepily, "am I ever thirsty!"

"I'll grab us a couple of sodas on the way back. The tent's wrapped in that green tarp in the back," he reached beneath the driver's seat, "here's a hammer, do you know how to set up a tent?"

"Are you kidding," she yawned, "I was in Girl Scouts for six years. I can pitch a tent with my eyes closed."

"Good enough," Jack said, "what do you want to drink?"

"Something diet."

Jack rolled his eyes, muttering, "Never knew a woman who wasn't on a diet!"

"What was that?" Cassie asked sweetly, hefting the hammer.

"Ah…nothing," said Jack, making his retreat.

"Wait up," she called, suddenly, "I'll go with you. I need to…um…talk to a man about a horse, too."

Jack laughed as they crossed the lawn. Inside the low, block building, Cassie rinsed her face in cold water, running her fingers through her hair. She grimaced at her reflection in the scarred, graffitied, square of polished sheet metal bolted to the wall above the sink.

Digging in her pocket she pulled out a handful of coins and, walking back to the vending machines, popped in a couple of quarters for a diet cola. Jack met her by the machines and requested a root beer. Together they walked back to the van.

Jack pulled the tent and tarp from the back, thanking Cassie again for helping him set it up.

"This old back isn't what it used to be," he said, "and bending over to pound in tent stakes sure makes it squawk."

"I should be thanking you," she replied, "you're the one giving up your bed."

After her earlier ordeal, Cassie couldn't turn down the security of the locked van but she did insist that Jack let her pull the heavy mattress out from under the boxes and put it in the tent for him.

"My back," she replied to his arguing, "has a good thirty years on yours and I can sleep on the floor just fine."

Jack grumbled but conceded, rolling out his sleeping bag onto the thick twin-size mattress. He took a battered old Coleman lantern, and his root beer, over to the nearby picnic table and sat. Cassie joined him and Jack saluted her with his half-full aluminum can.

"To your health!" he said, and drank.

Cassie laughed, raising her own soda, "And to yours, sir!"

"So," Jack began, after setting down his drink, "what do your parents think about your little excursion?" Cassie averted her eyes, setting down her own pop. "Not much…" she replied vaguely.

"Is that a fact?" he murmured. "Please tell me I'm not harboring a fugitive. Do they do know you're out here?"

"I'm eighteen, so I wouldn't be a fugitive anyway, but it doesn't matter because I don't know my father and my mom…died a while back." Cassie stumbled over her words, which sounded strange and foreign coming from her mouth.

"I'm sorry."

Cassie shook her head quickly and smiled to brave off the tears.

"Boy," she said, "my mom would be throwing three kinds of fits if she knew what I was doing! She was quite the mother hen."

"You better be careful," Jack smiled, "you could get struck by lightning!"

Cassie took another sip of her pop.

"Why, Mr. Leland," she replied in a shocked voice, "does that constitute a belief in a higher power?" Jack's smile seemed forced, and his eyes had taken on that sardonic, self-mocking look once more. "I never said I didn't believe, I just said it never did much for me."

"So you do believe in God?" Cassie asked.

"You really need to learn to express yourself, Cassie Williams," he replied, sourly, "you're just too reserved."

Cassie said nothing, her eyes never leaving his. This was a trick she had learned from Guy Williams. When someone wanted you to take over the conversation, they would force a silence, hoping the listener would grow uncomfortable and speak. If you could hold out the longest, you usually won. In the silence, Cassie could hear trucks rushing past on the highway and the sound of crickets singing in a far-off field. The night air hung cool and motionless around them and only the faint hum of the vending machines disturbed the stillness.

Finally Jack sighed, "Let's just say that we have an understanding, God and I…"

"And that is?"

Jack finished his root beer in one long swallow, "…and that is, that He's better off without me." Cassie paused a moment to reposition her argument, "So do you—"

"Yeah," Jack interrupted her, "both of my parents passed on when I was about your age, too. 'Course, I was overseas at the time. Vietnam. Sweeping bird poop off an airstrip in Can Tho, serving my country," Jack said with a derisive snort.

"You were in the army?"

Jack winced, "Please, *Navy*!"

"Oh, sorry."

"Yeah," Jack continued, his voice a soft murmur above the night sounds, "I got a letter there at the airfield that they had died in a house fire. They both smoked cigarettes from dawn to dark, I figure that one of them fell asleep with a smoke smoldering in their hand and that, as they say, was that."

"I'm sorry," Cassie whispered.

"Oh, it's okay." Jack smiled, a little easier this time.

"That," he said, "is the one condolence that I can offer you now. Someday that hurt is going to fade and all that will be left are your memories of the good times and just a little bit of sadness."

Cassie said nothing, but watched as the moths flew in frantic circles around the burning globe of the lantern.

"The letter was three weeks old when it reached the base. By that time the funeral was two weeks past. I only had another couple of months of active duty, so I didn't see any point of coming all the way back home just to look at the headstones and then go right back to the war." Jack paused, crumpling the soda can in his fist before going on, "I stayed and finished my tour, so I didn't make it back until the next summer, by then the graves didn't even look new anymore. Three weeks after that I left for college."

Cassie wanted to ask him what college he had gone to, but her eyelids wouldn't stay open and her head was nodding. Jack noticed and stood, yawning himself. "Okay," he said, "enough ancient history for one night. It's almost midnight, and morning's going to come awful early."

Cassie began to turn away when Jack remembered something.

"Wait a second," he said, walking over to the van and rummaging briefly through the glove box. Coming back over to Cassie, he handed her a small bundle, wrapped in an oil-stained rag. Unwrapping the cloth revealed a heavy folding knife with the word *BUCK* imprinted on the wood inlaid sides. Cassie opened the gleaming, steel blade carefully, jumping slightly when it snapped into the locked position, and tested the edge with her thumb. The slightly curved bladed had been carefully honed to a razor sharpness, and ended in a needle pointed tip.

Open, the knife was roughly eight inches long and felt solid in her hand. Jack watched her eyes and nodded as she slowly pressed the lever on the handle that released the blade from its locked position.

"Good," he said, "you know how a lock-blade works. If someone grabs you again like our friend back there, you stick 'em as hard as you can and start screaming bloody murder; chances are they'll be doing the same! It probably won't kill them, but it'll sure slow them down in a chase. Could you do that?"

Cassie stood, hefting the heavy pocketknife in her hand, thinking back to the helpless fear that she had felt, being dragged back into the shadows.

"Yes," she said softly, "I think I could."

"Well," replied Jack, "you put that knife away in your bag until you're sure. A knife is no different from a gun; don't ever carry one for self-defense if you don't *know* that you could use it. Otherwise you're just providing your attacker with a weapon."

Cassie nodded hesitantly, her eyes still on the knife.

"I know it's an ugly thought," Jack continued, "maybe even wrong, but sometimes you have to weigh what's right with the way the world is and find a happy medium. Remember," Jack reached out and tapped her forehead with one thick finger, "the best thing you can do to keep yourself safe is to stay in safe places. Second-best is to scream your head off—"

Cassie nodded as she slipped the knife from one hand to the other.

"–and always yell *fire*," Jack went on, "never *help*. There are too many folks out there, sad to say, who'd rather not get involved, but everyone wants to see a good fire. Fighting is always your last option, when you've got no other way out."

She nodded again, a little more confidently this time, and slipped the Buck knife into the front pocket of her jeans.

"Just think about it is all I'm saying. Now get some sleep."

Cassie locked the swinging back door of the van behind her and twisted into the most comfortable position she could find on the hard metal floor.

She could feel the hard length of the knife pressing against her leg, and felt a little more reassured. Then, as she was trying to decide which boot to take off first, she fell asleep.

Chapter Six

Jack had been right, morning did come early, and Cassie felt as though she had just closed her eyes when there was a tap on the side window of the van. Cassie raised her head, groggily, and nodded to Jack, letting him know she was awake. Despite what she had said the night before, her back was stiff and sore from hours of lying on the hard floor. Also, she was cold; the soft gray light in the window told her the sun had yet to peak over the nearest hills to warm the desert. She shivered, pulling her jacket from the front seat and rummaging through her duffel bag until she found her toiletries bag.

Reaching up she unlocked the sliding door and, squirming out of her blankets, she stepped out into the cool morning air.

Jack was at the picnic table, his short white hair in wild disarray, and his shirttail flapping loosely in the slight morning breeze. He had a small tin coffeepot steaming over a single burner camp stove and, while the coffee percolated, Jack busied himself slicing apples and oranges. Cassie smiled as she passed him on her way to the restrooms.

"Morning Jack," she said.

Jack replied with an unintelligible grunt that may or may not have been good morning. Again, Cassie splashed her face with the icy water from the tap, brushed her hair and teeth and, beginning to feel somewhat presentable once more, started back to the campsite.

She found Jack still seated at the picnic table, a heavy mug full of steaming black coffee in his hand. He was staring absently into a patch of grass several feet ahead of him.

"Beautiful day!" Cassie grinned. Jack was obviously not a morning person, and her comment hung there for a while, as it slowly filtered into Jack's brain. He glanced up at Cassie with a sour expression, "The Japanese have a saying," he muttered. "*Never rely on the glory of the morning nor the smiles of your mother-in-law.* The only good morning is the one that you've missed when you wake up at noon!"

Cassie laughed and, nibbling on an apple slice, walked back to the tent.

While Jack slowly succumbed to the effects of sunlight and caffeine, Cassie broke down the tent and loaded it, and the mattress, back into the van. As she worked, the two semi trucks, which had pulled in during the night, fired up their engines and pulled out of the rest stop and back onto the highway. Except for a black pick-up at the opposite end of the parking lot, she and Jack had the rest stop to themselves. Jack nodded to the truckers as they rolled past.

"Wow," Cassie said, "they don't sleep long do they?"

"Probably sleeping in shifts," Jack replied. "When you're driving a big truck like that, you're only allowed so much time behind the wheel before you're required to rest for several hours. A lot of truckers get used to sleeping three or four hours at a time during those breaks so they don't lose any more time on the highway than they have to."

"Well, that makes sense, I guess," Cassie replied, "doesn't sound like much fun though."

"No," said Jack, gathering the stove and lamp. "I tried it for a while before I joined the Navy, just for a summer. I didn't care much for it."

"Oh?"

"No, some folks were meant to stay in one place, like they're born with roots already in the ground. I learned quick, that summer, that I could only be away from the smell of the ocean for so long before it started to wear me down."

"A homebody, then?" asked Cassie with a smile.

"Good a word as any, I suppose." Jack replied. "George Moore said that a person travels the world over in search of what he needs, and returns home to find it. I guess a few of us are born lucky enough to want to stay put to begin with."

"I don't know," Cassie said, plopping down at the table opposite Jack. "I couldn't wait to get out of Bowie! As much as I loved everyone, I just knew there was a whole world going on and we just caught the echo of it there. It was like standing outside the stadium listening to people cheering for a game you can't see."

"Now that you're in the game," he asked, "what do you think?"

"Well," Cassie grimaced, "I don't know that Sentinel, Arizona is exactly *in the game* either, but at least I feel like I'm moving in the right direction."

"So, let me get this straight," Jack grinned, "you're leaving a pitifully small town called Bowie, Arizona to go find the world in another pitifully small town called Long Beach, Washington?"

Cassie threw her orange peel at him.

"You can be a very disagreeable person," she said, haughtily, "do you know that?"

"It has been mentioned, yes."

Cassie tried to maintain her frown, but gave up and laughed.

"First, smarty," she retorted, "I'm not expecting to find *the world* in Long Beach, it's just a starting place. I thought that some time in a different small town might ease me into life at a city college."

"And what city would that be?" Jack asked.

"Portland," Cassie answered, "Portland State University. I'm enrolling there in the fall. The writing department requires a thesis at the end of each year, so I thought I'd get a head start on it while I still had some free time."

"So, you changed your mind?" Jack asked, smiling slyly.

Cassie looked at him blankly.

"Changed my mind about what?" she asked.

"I thought you had to hurry up and finish your book for *spring* term?"

Cassie's mouth grew dry and her stomach did a cold flip-flop as she groped for an answer. Jack saved her any further indignities, interrupting with a wave.

"Sounds like a good plan, either way," he said with a wink, standing and gathering the last of the items on the table, "and now, we should probably get a head start on the road!"

Cassie, her face flaming, retreated gratefully into the van; neither of them noticing as the black pick-up truck, with its dark, tinted windows, pulled onto the highway behind them.

❧

They followed Interstate 8 west through Yuma, and into California.

Reaching San Diego around noon, Jack pulled the van into a bumpy gravel parking lot, stopping in front of a small seedy-looking gas station and food mart. Sharing the parking lot with the fuel pumps was a worn Airstream travel trailer that some industrious soul had converted into a mobile lunch wagon. Cassie got the impression, looking at the rusty wheels and voluminous patch of weeds growing up all around it, that the aluminum trailer hadn't been *mobile* in some time. A brightly striped awning hung above the windowed counter of the trailer, and a giant sandwich board menu, all in Spanish, stood beside the road.

Jack eased from the driver's seat with a groan, as he stretched his back, twisting left and right, his hands on his hips. Yawning, he proceeded to fill the gas tank from the dusty nozzle hanging beside the pump.

Cassie wandered off to find a rest room and, finding it locked, went to the office, where she was handed the key, firmly chained to a long lead pipe. Jack snickered as she walked past, hefting the pipe with both hands. Cassie ignored him haughtily and returned to the back of the building to unlock the ladies room door.

After returning the key, she walked back to the van to find Jack holding a white paper bag in his lap. The smell rising from the bag made Cassie's stomach rumble loudly and her mouth began to water. Jack laughed.

"Well," he said, "I was going to ask if you were hungry yet, but I'll take that for a yes!"

Cassie grinned as he handed her an offering from the bag, warm and wrapped tight in foil.

"What is it?" she asked.

"A taco," he replied, unwrapping his own lunch, "and not your pasty, flavorless American versions of a taco either, these are the real thing!" With that, he took a huge bite of the steaming, tortilla-wrapped morsel, rolling his eyes in ecstasy as thick juice dribbled down his chin.

"Heaven!" he mumbled, his mouth full.

"Attractive!" Cassie laughed and handed him a napkin, then took a bite herself. Jack had been right; this was nothing like the offerings of the drive-through chains she was familiar with. The tortillas were fresh and warm and the chunks of stewed beef were delicious and spicy. Cassie chewed slowly, savoring the mouthful for perhaps a second and a half before her tongue burst into flames.

She emitted a muffled shriek; her eyes going wide as her taste buds burned and her lips grew numb.

"Water!" she croaked, flailing her free hand in Jack's direction. "WATER!"

Cassie could feel the surface of her tongue starting to crisp as Jack, laughing uncontrollably, handed her a bottle of water and several plain tortillas.

Cassie began to gulp the contents of the bottle.

"Eat the tortillas first," Jack advised, "they're going to do a lot more than that water. You could drink all day long and it's still going to burn!" Cassie, her face crimson and beginning to drip with perspiration, swallowed the offending bite of taco as she continued to pull from the water bottle, pausing just long enough to turn on Jack.

"You're gonna die!" she said between coughing fits. "If I live through this I'm going to kill you!"

Jack laughed even harder. "You must have gotten one of my tacos!" he gasped, his wide eyes the very picture of innocence, "the other two in there are mild. Besides, it's not really *that* hot." He took another bite.

"See? No problem," he said. "That's what you get for being raised on Twinkies and Wonder Bread."

Cassie gave him another dirty look as the fire finally began to fade from her mouth. He had been right; the tortillas had done more than the whole bottle of water. Slowly she reached into the bag and took out another taco.

"I swear, Jack," she warned, "if this is hot…"

"No," Jack snorted, still laughing, "that one should be fine, two of each." The food still seemed a little spicy to Cassie's smoldering palette, but it was edible and, what little she could still taste of it, was very, very good.

Wiping tears from his eyes, Jack dug into the remains of his own lunch. Cassie took a last, dainty sip from her bottle and smiled sweetly at him.

"Just remember, Jack," she said, "payback sucks."

This sent Jack into another gale of laughter, as he steered the van through the rocky parking lot and back onto the highway.

It was another five and a half hours up the coast to Pismo Beach. Jack tried to coax more information from Cassie about her home and family, but it was no use. Finally he conceded, at least for the moment.

"Ah," he murmured, smiling, "secret and self-contained and solitary as an oyster." He paused for a reaction, and got none.

"That's Dickens," he said.

"Yes," Cassie replied, "*A Christmas Carol*, page one."

Jack laughed.

The interstate scenery of Southern California grew monotonous and both Jack and Cassie soon lapsed into silence, lulled into a semi-conscious state by the hum of the tires and the sound of the wind rushing past the windows.

By the time they saw the exit for Pismo, Jack was stiff and sore from a long day in the driver's seat. After a brief conference, the two weary travelers decided to call it a day.

Parking along the boardwalk, they clambered out of the van and stood, stretching and rubbing their eyes for a moment as they took in the vastness of the Pacific Ocean.

Cassie had been to the beach several times while growing up in Bowie. Twice on school outings and once in a while with the Williams family; impromptu road trips in Guy's old VW Bus.

The enormity of the sea never failed to fascinate her, and she stood at the rail of the boardwalk for several minutes, breathing in the briny tang of the air and letting the cool coastal breeze flow over her. A tourist sign was posted to the rail a little way from where she stood and Cassie walked down to read it. Jack joined her a moment later.

"So," he said, "who killed whom here, and when?"

Cassie chose to ignore that, reading the sign aloud.

"This area originally gained fame as home for the Pismo Clam, a mollusk that used to thrive in the hundreds of thousands along the beaches here. However, over-harvesting has seriously depleted supply and now there's a limit of only 10 clams per day."

She finished and turned to Jack.

"And there is no greater disaster than greed," he quoted.

Cassie raised an eyebrow.

"Lao-tzu," Jack said. They stood a moment in silence, looking out over the water.

"They did the same thing back home," he went on, "the Chinooks harvested Olympia Oysters for thousands of years, maybe tens of thousands, out of Willapa Bay and all up and down the coast. Once the gold rush hit in California, it took the white man about thirty years to wipe 'em out. We had to import a whole new breed from Japan, Pacific Oysters, and that's still what we grow." He sighed. "Now we're doing the same thing to the salmon."

Cassie's gaze returned to the ocean, and she remained silent, unsure what to say.

"Well," Jack said at last, slapping his stomach with both hands, "on that note, let's go eat some seafood!"

Cassie rolled her eyes and followed Jack across the busy street and down the block to *The Oceanside*, a restaurant proclaiming *Gourmet Seafood* in glowing blue neon.

A polite waiter found them a seat near the window, pulling out a heavy, leather-cushioned captain's chair from the oak table for Cassie, and setting a menu and glass of water in front of each of them. The dining area was dim, a dark, low ceiling, the walls covered with fishing nets, glass floats, and starfish.

"I wouldn't drink that if I were you," Jack said, as she raised the glass to her lips. "I don't know how your water in Arizona is, but the stuff down here can have a mean streak."

Cassie set her glass back down, sliding it across the table and out of accidental reach, then browsed the menu long enough to find the hamburger section. Sipping at a bottle of water that Jack had requested from a passing waitress, Cassie waited to see what he would choose. The older man considered the menu for a several minutes and finally, with a nod of his head, closed his up as well.

"So, whatcha having?" Cassie asked immediately.

"I'm leaning towards the oyster kabobs," Jack said.

Cassie made a face, setting down her water. "Oysters?" she asked with ill-concealed disgust.

"God's most perfect food!" Jack replied, smacking his lips. "Ah, *Crassostrea gigas*, the Pacific Oyster. 'A beatific smile over his face! Man has tasted the oyster!' so sayeth Don Marquis."

Cassie groaned.

"And what," asked Jack, "did you decide on?"

"A cheeseburger and fries," Cassie answered defiantly.

Jack put one hand over his eyes and wearily shook his head. "I weep for the future," he muttered.

"But Oysters are so...*slimy*," Cassie replied, grimacing again, "ick!"

Jack harrumphed, sitting up straighter in his seat as the waiter returned to take their dinner order, bringing a diet cola for Cassie and a glass of root beer for Jack. As soon as the man had turned to hurry back to the kitchen, Jack pointed a long finger at Cassie.

"And just how many oysters have you eaten in your eighteen years?" he asked.

"Well," Cassie said, faltering as she realized she was being trapped, "none."

Slap! Jack's hand returned to his forehead, as he issued another groan.

"Well," Cassie said, feeling the battle being lost, "they *look* slimy..."

Jack didn't respond to this, but stared blankly across the table at her until Cassie felt herself beginning to squirm in her seat.

"Well..." Cassie began once more.

"Not," Jack said, "a very nonpartisan way to approach the subject, especially for a would-be journalist." That stung and, her shoulders drooping in defeat, Cassie nodded.

"Okay, I can't argue with that," she said with a disconsolate sigh, "the next place that has oysters, I'll order some."

"No need to wait that long," Jack replied, "you'll try some of mine right here!" He slapped his hand down in triumph.

"Greeaat!" said Cassie, thinking of how good her burger had sounded only moments before.

"Oh," Jack exclaimed, "that reminds me!" He suddenly began digging furiously through the pockets of his leather jacket, until he finally produced a battered paperback book. Cassie saw the words *Willapa Bay* on the cover as he handed it to her.

"That's a definitive history of Oysterville and Willapa Bay," he said, "and I'm not just saying that because I helped with it either! Now you can get started on your research; and you *will* be quizzed."

"Oh boy!" Cassie said with a groan, flipping through the pages of the narrow booklet as their dinner was served.

Jack's oysters, wrapped in strips of bacon and impaled on two long bamboo skewers, lay resting on a bed of fresh, green spinach. Each skewer held five or six of the fat bi-valves, pan fried to a golden-brown, interspersed with sautéed mushrooms, and chunks of toasted French bread dripping with garlic butter. The steam that rose from his plate was tangy with brine. As Jack removed the first oyster from the skewer with his fork, he offered it to Cassie without flair.

"I believe," he said, straight-faced, "that you were seeking to expand your horizons?" Cassie took the fork, trying to look anywhere except at the bacon-wrapped lump that she was about to eat.

Bad medicine is best taken quickly, Kathy Belanger had oft said and, with this thought in mind, Cassie popped the whole oyster in her mouth and chewed quickly. To her surprise, the taste wasn't bad, just unusual. In fact, she thought that maybe, just maybe, she liked it. As Cassie kept chewing, she found that she really did like it! The flavor was sharp, briny and pleasant, rich with butter and garlic, and the consistency was not at all what she expected. The oyster wasn't like anything she had ever tasted before, and she looked somewhat dubiously at the halves of the cheeseburger resting on her plate, a pile of French fries lying limply beside.

Much to her chagrin, the look on Jack's face showed plainly enough that he had seen her reaction. Wordlessly, he picked up the first of the two skewers and set it on Cassie's plate, taking half of her burger in trade.

"Thanks," Cassie said, a bit sheepishly.

"No worries," Jack replied, "I wouldn't have expected anything less from you. I take it as a sign of excellent breeding that you know good food when you taste it!"

Cassie studied him a moment, trying to decide if he was having her on.

Then she laughed and dug into her dinner, following Jack's suggestion and eating the burger first, "Lest she spoil the memory of the oysters." The burger was great as well, grilled thick and juicy, and served with slabs of beefsteak tomatoes, sweet Vidalia onions, and crisp lettuce.

Finally, Jack leaned back and sighed and, as he tossed his napkin onto his now empty plate, and drained the last of his soda, his eyes twinkled merrily.

"O Oysters, said the Carpenter, You've had a pleasant run! Shall we be trotting home again? But answer came there none. And this was scarcely odd, because they'd eaten every one!"

"Lewis Carroll!" Cassie exclaimed. "Finally, someone I recognize." Jack laughed.

"Not true," he said, "you knew Dickens. Tomorrow, we try out oyster shooters before dinner!"

"Oyster shooters?" Cassie looked at him quizzically.

"A raw oyster, in a shot glass with a spoonful of cocktail sauce!" Jack rolled his eyes and licked his lips euphorically.

"*Raw*?" Cassie asked, swallowing hard. Jack gave her a long look, and she raised her hands in surrender.

"Okay...okay, I'll try it! But you had better take me someplace you don't intend to eat at again, just in case I hurl!"

"Delightful," Jack grimaced, "the colloquialisms of youth."

Chapter Seven

Cassie insisted on paying for their dinner that night, having removed the cash from her boots that morning. She felt safer with Jack, even though she barely knew him. He still seemed a little strange though.

A couple of times on the long drive from Phoenix, she had noticed Jack watching her out of the corner of his eye with an odd look on his face. It was a sad look, almost haunted, and he would jerk his eyes quickly back to the road if she caught his gaze.

Jack had told Cassie that he'd never married and had no family, she wondered if he regretted this when he looked at her, and she felt bad, thinking that she might be causing him pain. He seemed like a nice enough guy, even though he tended to lapse into long, quiet, moody spells.

In just their day and a half together, Cassie had learned to recognize this look as it came, periodically, to Jack's face. His jaw would become tight and his perpetual scowl would deepen, in a subconscious reaction to his thoughts.

She had never met anyone like Jack Leland, and found he was an enigma. For someone who could laugh so easily, his moments of humor came like far-flung oasis in a desert of gloom.

It was as though the moment he finished laughing, a door slammed shut in his heart. Cassie thought about this as they walked back down the boardwalk.

Just before they reached the van, a flashing neon sign caught Jack's eye.

"You ever do any bowling?" he asked.

"The first and last time I went bowling," Cassie answered, grinning, "was at Megan Wilkinson's eighth birthday party. I broke a bone in my ankle with a bowling ball, and had to go to the hospital before they cut the cake!"

Jack stared at her for a moment, shaking his head.

"Surely," he said, his voice dripping incredulity, "you're not going to give in to that kind of defeat, are you?"

"You want to go bowling?" she asked.

"Did you have a previous commitment?"

"Well no," she replied, "I just...okay, let's go bowling!"

The bright-lit sign for Pismo Bowl led them just past the pier to the bowling alley. Walking through the double glass doors, Cassie felt her skin prickle in the cool, air-conditioned room. They passed the pro-shop, which was closed, and walked up to the counter. Behind her, Cassie could hear the low rumble of balls rolling along the polished lanes, the crash of pins, and the murmur of the players.

From somewhere off to her left came the electronic chatter of video games. The attendant, a bored teenager with long hair and bad skin, handed them their shoes and a transparent scorecard, then directed them down the concourse to lane twenty-two. Stepping down into the settee area, they searched the racks of scuffed house balls until each had found one that fit. Cassie's first roll hit the left gutter about halfway down the lane, as did the second ball, and the third.

"You're hooking!" Jack called from the plastic bench, his two strikes marked clearly on the overhead.

"I beg your pardon?" Cassie asked, frowning at the far-off pins, as she waited at the ball return.

"Hooking! Hooking!" Jack repeated. "You're hooking your arm before you release the ball. You want your hand to come straight up past your ear once you let go!"

Cassie hefted her bowling ball, lining up her sights with the arrows halfway down the lane, as Jack had shown her. She took three quick, mincing steps, allowing the ball to drop from its rest against her chest and swing down past her hip. When the ball was released, her right hand swung up and past her right ear and she watched, amazed, as the ball rolled rapidly down the polished lane and struck the pins. With a resounding crash, all the pins scattered, save one. The pin in the far right corner spun drunkenly before righting itself in the middle of the lane. Cassie spun, her arms raised in victory.

"You were robbed!" Jack roared. Cassie laughed.

For the next hour and a half Cassie worked on her form, under Jack's freely offered tutelage, and brought her overall score up to a record-breaking sixty-seven.

"Well," she said in her own defense, "it's record-breaking for me, my last score was zero, and a broken ankle!"

Jack's own tally hovered in the mid two-hundreds, causing him finally to admit, somewhat sheepishly, that he had bowled with a league every week for the last decade. Cassie decried this as a set-up and insisted that Jack pay penance at the ice-cream shop next door, which he did.

"Thanks! That was a lot of fun!" Cassie said, licking peppermint-candy ice-cream from her fingers. "You're really good at that, how often do you play?"

"Oh, maybe four or five nights a week."

"A *week*?" she asked, eyes widening. "Whoa!"

"Yeah," he said, sobering, "when you say it out loud like that, I guess it sounds pretty pathetic. What is it you youngsters say?"

"*Get a life*?" Cassie offered.

"That's the one."

"Well," she said, "I still had a great time, so thank you!"

"Yup," replied Jack, juggling his own double-scoop cone, "and to think, three straight games and you didn't break a single bone!"

As they walked back across the parking lot of the bowling alley, Cassie noticed a black pick-up in the far corner of the lot. Something seemed strange about the vehicle and she thought to tell Jack, who was deep in the middle of a monologue on the history and origins of bowling. By the time the sport had reached modern day, she had forgotten all about it.

⁂

They spent that night in a rented campsite at Pismo State Park. Cassie insisted that Jack take the van this time, and that she sleep in the tent. Jack turned in early, claiming exhaustion from their trip to the bowling alley.

After borrowing a towel, the one item that she had managed to overlook in her own packing, she walked through the moonlit park to the bathhouse and treated herself to a long, hot shower. The tile floor was cool to her bare feet, as Cassie stood before the mirror, brushing her wet, spiky hair. The cinder block building reminded her of the rest rooms and showers at the campground near Bowie where she and her mother had retreated to when the blistering heat of summer turned their trailer into an unbearable oven.

The ladies Belanger would pack up their meager camping supplies; a second-hand tent, two sleeping bags, a cooler and the pillows off their beds, and set up camp in the shade of the willows that lined the creek. Kathy would bring the monopoly board, and they would play long games of financial conquest, taking a break to toss a Frisbee or play Bocce.

When the heat became too much, the two would swim in the deep pool where a bend in the stream had been dammed. This was the same spot where, years before, Kathy had held her baby to be dedicated. Each night, they would walk across a meadow of short, brown grass to the shower house and wash away the sweat of the day. Then, sitting in the cool concrete building, her mother would comb the tangles from her hair as they made up scary stories together, and then raced back through the darkness to the lights of their camp.

Standing in front of the mirror, Cassie felt the ache of loss engulf her. Her mother wouldn't be waiting by the campfire when she got back, with two freshly cut sticks and a bag full of marshmallows. She wouldn't join Cassie in round after round of campfire songs about silly billboards and bears in tennis shoes, or lie with her on their backs and point out the constellations.

Her mother was gone. In her mind Cassie heard again squealing phantom tires, the dull thump of a steel bumper hitting flesh and then, worst of all, the broken cries for help echoing through the dark, quiet streets. Cries that no one heard.

She was alone now. As the tears rolled down her cheeks, Cassie fingered the folded scrap of paper in her pocket and felt the tiniest spark. If she could find him, track him down to wherever life had carried him in the last two decades; maybe he would be different than her mother had remembered.

Time, Cassie knew, could change people, sometimes mellowing and softening the hardest hearts. Why couldn't this be true for William Belanger?

Whoever he had been eighteen years ago, didn't mean that he had to be that same person now. Cassie shuddered as she remembered her mother's fevered voice,

"He's not someone you want to know, Cass."

Looking at her reflection in the harsh white lights of the shower room, Cassie heard once more the merciless screech of tires and her eyes narrowed.

Why should she give him a chance? Why should *he* be happy, after all the hurt he had inflicted on his wife and daughter? Maybe she *should* confront him, spitting the truth into his face without mercy, or maybe she should just forget about finding him and start building her own life.

But Cassie knew, even as she felt the anger and resentment churning in her stomach, that she had to find the truth. She wanted to start her own life clean, with no questions or doubts. She wanted to be rid of the hurt.

"Okay, Lord," Cassie whispered, leaning her forehead against the cool glass of the mirror, her hands clenched into white fists on either side of the steel sink, "please tell me what you want me to do. If you want me to find him, tell me what I should say. If you want me to forgive him, then show me how. I don't want to carry this around forever."

A sudden picture came to Cassie's mind as she spoke those words, the grim haunted look on Jack Leland's face, that expression of hopeless regret that made his jaw tighten and his eyes go flat.

Then, she saw herself in thirty years, her hair starting to gray, those same deep lines carving down from the corners of her eyes and mouth, that same look of bitter loss shadowing her face.

"Not me," she whispered fiercely to her reflection, "maybe I'll find him and maybe I won't, and even if I do and he's the same person he was, at least I can walk away knowing that I tried. I'm not going to spend my life wondering about what might have happened; I'm not going to end up like that!"

She spoke this oath to the empty walls, her voice echoing with the slow drip of water. Then, pulling on her boots, she gathered her dirty clothes and walked back to their campsite. Climbing into her tent, Cassie fell immediately to sleep.

Late that night, Cassie awoke to a strange sound outside the tent. Lying very still, she listened, and finally realized that it was coming from the van. Jack's voice escaped from inside, mumbling, rising and falling, silent then crying out loudly, deep in the clutches of a nightmare. The van squeaked on its springs with his violent thrashing.

Cassie untangled herself from her sleeping bag and, just as she found the tent zipper, Jack gave one last anguished cry and fell silent. By the time Cassie was standing, barefoot, in the cool moonlight beside the van, he was quiet once more.

❧

Jack was still snoring outrageously when Cassie rose and quietly rolled up the sleeping bag and tent. Behind her, the morning sun cast pale-pink spokes through the timbered campground. Rummaging through the plastic cargo box that Jack had left on the picnic table the night before, she lifted out the Coleman burner and the coffeepot. The latter she took over to the campsite's water faucet, a single gray pipe attached to a wooden post.

Cassie filled the pot, swirling the contents around and then, dumping the water onto the gravel-filled grave at the base of the pipe, she filled it again. This she carried back to the table and, lighting the stove with her Zippo, put the coffee on to heat. Cassie then filled the dented tin percolator from a baggie of coffee grounds. *Jack's special blend* he had called it the morning before, enlightening Cassie to the joy of specialty coffees. Cassie's own java experiences had been more in the arena of instant crystals, and Jack had rolled his eyes at this, commenting again on his concerns for the future of western civilization. Cassie had admitted, partially in hopes of avoiding further diatribes, that his personal recipe was *far* better than she was used to.

Once the coffee began gurgling over the tiny blue flame of the stove, Cassie dug into her duffel bag for the surprise. The day before, when they had stopped, briefly, for a rest room break, Cassie had remembered seeing an old skillet in the big camp box, and had bought a package of bacon and half a dozen big, brown farm eggs. These she had carefully stashed in her duffel bag before Jack returned to the van.

Sparrows had gathered, twittering, in the nearby oaks when she surmised the coffee had seeped long enough. Cassie removed the pot from the flame and replaced it with the iron skillet. Into this, she laid several thick strips of bacon, which sizzled and popped on the heated surface. While the bacon cooked, Cassie dug deeper into the supplies and pulled out two tin plates, a spatula, salt and pepper, and a bag full of plastic-ware. She turned the bacon with the point of the buck knife that Jack had given her, and was lining one of the tin plates with napkins when she heard the sliding door of the van creak open behind her.

"Now what in the world is all this nonsense?" Jack yawned, rubbing sleep from his eyes and blinking owlishly at her as he pulled on his shoes.

"I thought maybe," Cassie retorted, "just maybe, you wouldn't be such an old grouch in the mornings if you had a decent breakfast!"

She placed the crisp cooked bacon on the plate and cracked two eggs into the sizzling fat. These she dusted with salt and pepper before pouring a cup of the thick black coffee into a cup and handing it to Jack.

"One word," she warned, "about what a great little wife I'll make someday, and you're wearing breakfast!"

"I guess I'm not in much of a position to argue," Jack said, accepting the steaming mug and breathing in the aroma with a sigh of appreciation.

"You just make sure you don't put any soap in that skillet," he muttered, "it took me forever to get it seasoned just right!"

"What do you mean, *seasoned*?"

Jack sighed again.

"Cast iron," he began, "is porous. That means the surface of the metal is pitted with thousands and thousands of tiny holes. You have to heat oil in a new pan to fill all of these holes so food won't stick to the surface and the pan won't rust. This is called *seasoning* the iron."

"Okay," said Cassie, "that makes sense I suppose…"

"Thanks," Jack replied dryly, "now the reason you don't want to use soap on cast iron is that it will pull the oil out of all those little holes and leave soap behind. Then, not only does your food stick, and your pan rust, but until you season it again, your food is going to taste like the soap that's caught in the pores."

While Jack was teaching her the finer points of camp cookery, Cassie noticed a chunky squirrel, drawn by the smell of food, that had scampered down a nearby tree trunk and stood, nose twitching at the edge of their camp. Breaking off a small piece of the bacon, she tossed into onto the grass near the creature and watched, delighted, as he dashed over and stuffed the morsel into his cheeks, spinning and racing back up the tree with his treat.

"You haven't heard a word I've said," accused Jack, waving a finger in her direction, "have you?"

"I heard every word," she replied airily, "not that it matters anyway, I'm not the one who'll be doing the dishes." Jack had no response to that, but chuckled as Cassie handed him a plate.

"So," he said, chewing on the last of his bacon, "tell me something about Oysterville."

Cassie took a gulp of her coffee.

"Well," she began, "did you know that Oysterville was originally called Shoalwater Bay?"

"I'd heard that somewhere, yes," Jack replied.

"Hush," Cassie snapped, "I gave you coffee, be nice. Also, during the gold rush, that oyster you were talking about, Ost… Ostra…um…"

"Ostrea Lurida, the Olympic Oyster," Jack helped.

"Thank you," she continued, "Ostrea Lurida was about the size of your palm. During the gold rush, one oyster could cost as much as a dollar. That was a day's wages for most men back then!"

Jack laughed, taking a last swallow from his mug, "We'll make an oysterman out of you yet!"

They drove almost five hundred miles that day, heading north on Highway 101. Cassie picked up a disposable camera when they stopped for gas, and began taking pictures of the breathtaking views of the Pacific Ocean. Jack had been quite impressed with her cassette recorder, even submitting to her requests to say his name into the tiny microphone. As they followed the winding freeway, Cassie told him a little more about growing up in Bowie, and about her mother. Jack, in turn, told Cassie about his time in the war, and how he had gone to college afterward with his G.I. loan.

"Where did you go to college?" Cassie asked.

"Clear Creek Baptist Bible College, Pineville Kentucky."

"You went to a *Bible* college?"

"What?" he asked, his voice heavy with indignation, "are my horns showing again? Why couldn't I have gone to a Bible College?"

"I…uh…I don't know…" Cassie stammered, "you just didn't seem like the type."

"Well then," said Jack, his self-mocking grin returning, "this should, in the parlance of *my* generation, really blow your mind. In addition to graduating from Bible College, I spent a year as a missionary, and then another year as a pastor, as well."

"Okay," she said, "now I'm in shock! Where were you a missionary?"

"Lagos, Nigeria."

"Yeah, like I know where that is. Where were you a pastor?"

"*Assistant* Pastor," Jack corrected, "of Long Beach Community Church, Long Beach Washington." Cassie paused a moment, letting that sink in. "Why did you quit?"

There was a pause.

"Who said I quit?" Jack replied, his voice growing subdued.

"No one," said Cassie, recognizing the change in his tone.

"I guess I just thought…" Her voice trailed off into an uncomfortable silence.

"I left for personal reasons," Jack said in a tight voice, "I didn't feel like I should be in ministry until I worked out some things in my life. Unfortunately, it's been twenty years and I'm still working them out."

Cassie sat in silence, wishing that she hadn't brought the subject up to begin with.

They rode for a long while without speaking. Jack's face was a thundercloud, scowling through the windshield at the road ahead, his lips compressed in a thin, pale line. As the highway swung north, the temperature, already lower that what she was used to in Bowie, began to drop, and Cassie found herself shivering as evening progressed. Jack, finally glancing at her and seeing her huddled in her seat, reached behind him and pulled a thick wool blanket from the mattress.

"Here," he said gruffly, "take this. You should have told me you were getting cold, I would have turned on the heater an hour ago."

Cassie said nothing, huddling miserably beneath the blanket.

"Hey," Jack said, his voice softening, "I'm sorry if I barked at you back there. I'm not going to throw you out for asking a couple of questions." Cassie nodded as Jack turned the heater to high, repositioning the vents and directing them towards her.

"It's okay," she said.

"No, actually it's not," Jack replied, "I've made my mistakes, and I live with them, but I don't take them out on other people. So, like I said, I'm sorry."

Cassie looked up and caught Jack's eye.

"Okay," she said again, a bit more firmly.

"Good." Jack smiled humorlessly. "Now see? I warned you that I was a pain in the rear." Cassie smiled and they were fine again.

She didn't get a chance to try oysters that day, raw or otherwise, as the sun had long since set when they pulled into Fortuna, California. Jack drove into a nearby parking lot beneath a huge lit sign that advertised *Fortuna Super Eight, Best Rates in Town!*

Digging into the seemingly bottomless glove box again, he pulled out a battered coupon book, and licking a finger, he began to thumb through the dog-eared pages, peering through his reading glasses in the scant illumination of the dome light.

"Ah, here we go!" he said finally, tearing a page from the book and handing it to Cassie. "No sleeping bags and tents for us tonight, it's time to rejoin civilization. Besides," he winked at Cassie, "it's cold up here at night."

The coupon offered a free motel room rental with the purchase of a rental of equal or greater value.

"'Course," Jack went on, "You can always sleep out here in the parking lot if you really have your heart set on it."

Fifteen minutes later Cassie was standing beneath the steaming flow of the shower in the bathroom of room four.

Chapter Eight

She woke with the late morning sun slanting through the window of her room. Cassie yawned, stretching luxuriously in the soft twin bed, glancing around the sparsely decorated room as she rose and began to dress. She briefly considered turning on the television and seeing if she could find a news channel, then decided that she was enjoying the peace and quiet too much to disturb it with the prattle of world events. Jack bought a local newspaper each morning, and she had gotten in the habit of reading it when he was finished, usually on the first leg of each morning's drive.

The night before, Cassie had rinsed her laundry in the sink, and now she gathered her clean, if stiff, clothes from the shower curtain rod, and repacked. Checking the room one last time to make sure she hadn't missed anything, Cassie shouldered her duffel and closed the door behind her, walking to the lobby to meet Jack.

"Good morning!" she said to the motel clerk.

"Good morning yourself," the woman replied, glancing up from her soap opera digest with a smile. "Your dad said to tell you that he would be across the street at the Pancake House, if you ever got out of bed."

Cassie blinked at the woman, her shock at the mention of her father stopping her in her tracks. "Wha…excuse me?" she spluttered.

"Across the street at the restaurant honey. He said he'd meet you there."

"Oh!" Cassie exclaimed, realizing the woman was talking about Jack.

"Okay, thanks!"

"Sure thing, hon."

Cassie shook her head as she crossed the parking lot towards the restaurant. "Geez," she muttered to herself, "*good morning* Cassie!"

Walking through the front doors of the Pancake House gave her an eerie sense of deja vu. She could see Jack seated at a booth towards the back of the room, facing away from her, his short white hair showing over the top of the booth behind him. If she could have replaced the aroma of breakfast sausage with the smell of french fries, it would be the truck stop in Phoenix. This time, however, she approached him without apprehension.

"Well," he said, looking up from his paper, "I'd given up on breakfast, but I was hoping you would make it in time for lunch!"

"Very funny," she replied, sliding into the booth and picking up a menu, "how long have you been waiting?"

"Young lady," he growled, "I learned a long time ago, as a much younger man, there are two questions that a smart fella never answers."

"And those are?" Cassie asked, rolling her eyes, knowing he wouldn't go on until she asked.

"*How long have you been waiting*?" Jack answered with a flourish, "and *does this make me look fat*? Try the omelet, it's the talk of the town."

Cassie threw her napkin at him as she continued to scan the menu. The omelets did look good. "So," she asked, "will we make it to Long Beach today?"

Jack took a sip of his coffee, "Possible," he replied, "but unlikely. It would be a long drive to push all the way home. We'll probably hole up somewhere about halfway. I have to stop in Gold Beach for a book delivery. It's going to save me sixty bucks in postage, and a whole lot of worry, to pick them up myself."

"Where's Gold Beach?" Cassie asked absently, still scanning the menu and sipping from her water glass. Jack set down his newspaper and looked at her, his face serious but his eyes twinkling.

"I thought you were doing a book on coastal towns of the Pacific Northwest?"

Cassie nearly choked on her water, as she looked up at Jack and then back to her menu, her face a mask of guilt. "I've focused mainly on Long Beach and the Washington Coast," she replied lamely.

"Of course," Jack replied, picking up his newspaper, "I forgot."

As Cassie watched him make a great show of his reading, she had the sickening feeling that her story, as well-contrived as she'd thought it had been, wasn't fooling the older man for a second.

Later that morning, as Cassie sat dozing in the passenger's seat, they rolled into Oregon. Crossing over the Rogue River, Jack pointed down to the bank where a man stood, knee-deep in the current, lazily waving a long, supple fly fishing rod, back and forth, above his head. The sun cut the water in a curtain of sparkling diamonds, silhouetting the angler in a silvery nimbus of light, and glistened off the long slow curl of wet line. The scene reminded Cassie of Norman Maclean's vivid descriptions of his ill-fated brother Paul, plying the waters of the Big Blackfoot River.

Then they passed over the bridge and out of sight of the river.

"The charm of fishing," Jack quoted, *"is that it is the pursuit of what is elusive but attainable, a perpetual series of occasions for hope."*

Cassie nodded; she liked that one, being in pursuit of something elusive, but hopefully attainable, herself.

A short time later, they pulled off the highway into Gold Beach. Jack drove slowly through town as Cassie read the street directions that he had written on a napkin. Finally they pulled up to a quaint, shingled building sporting a hanging marquee that read *Spring Leaves Bookstore*.

"This is the place," Jack said, pulling into a parking space along the curb.

"Let's see if anyone's home!"

No one was.

A sign hung in the window telling them the proprietor would be back in an hour. Unfortunately, it *didn't* tell them what time the sign had been hung in the first place. Jack stood there, looking helplessly up and down the empty street, before sighing and climbing back into the van.

"I'll tell you what," he said, pulling away from the curb, "how about if I drop you off at the library while I track this guy down and get my books?"

"The library?"

"If you're planning to write a book, you had better get familiar with the local libraries. Those are the folks who know what there is to know about these towns and their histories. An hour in the local library can save you weeks' worth of research on your own."

"Oh," Cassie replied, "I guess I hadn't thought of that."

She was beginning to wonder if maybe she really would end up writing a book. Between the stories that Jack had told her, and the information she was likely to gather on the rest of their drive, she might as well. They followed the signs to the Curry Public Library, where Jack swung a quick, and probably illegal, u-turn in the middle of the street to drop her off at the curb.

"I'll be back in an hour," Jack promised, "whether I find him or not." Cassie waved him off and followed the winding gravel path to the door.

❧

As she walked through the double glass doors and into the foyer, Cassie found herself facing a low oak counter. A sign hung above the polished desk, with arrows pointing in various directions. To the left was the nonfiction section, the reference and research areas, and a doorway leading to a small room labeled *Videos*. To the right of the entryway she could see the fiction and children's sections, with another doorway marked *Research*. This caught Cassie's eye and she wandered over, through the hushed aisles between the shelves, to see what the room contained.

Against the far wall of this much smaller room sat a narrow folding table with two computers. A large humming machine, which Cassie didn't recognize, sat in another corner, and filing cabinets covered the rest of the available wall space. Just as she began to wonder if this might be an office of some kind, the librarian, a young man wearing black slacks and a white dress shirt, walked in to the room and asked if she had any questions.

He was tall and broad shouldered with closely cropped brown hair. Cassie cast an appreciative eye over him, then noticed the shiny gold ring on his left hand.

Oh well, she thought with a sigh, *I can't afford to get distracted anyway.*

"Can I help you?" he asked.

"I hope so," Cassie smiled, "I'm doing some research on my family..."

Her voice trailed off, unsure how to finish.

"Have you worked with the SSDI software before?" he asked.

"No," she replied, shaking her head. "What is it?"

"The Social Security Death Index," he replied. "We use it to look up the death certificates of deceased relatives, mostly for genealogy research." A thought stuck Cassie, and she turned quickly to peer at the glowing computer screen.

"Can you show me how it works?"

"Sure thing," he smiled, "have a seat. I'm Jay, nice to meet you." Cassie introduced herself, then sat and, at Jay's prompting, clicked the button of the mouse resting next to the keyboard. The blank screen disappeared and a window came up offering links to several web pages. Cassie clicked on the one that read *SSDI* and waited as the page loaded. The screen that appeared read *Social Security Death Index Interactive Search* and had boxes labeled for first, last and middle name, as well as social security number. The tag line below the page heading caught her eye.

"Sixty-seven million records?" she exclaimed in awe.

"And some change," Jay laughed, "but don't get too hopeful, there are a lot more than sixty-seven million dead people, and more are joining the list every day!"

"What a pleasant thought," she grimaced.

Cassie pulled the marriage certificate from her pocket and had a sudden moment of indecisiveness. What if she put in her father's information and found out that he'd been dead for ten years? What would she do then? As she brought her trembling fingers to the keyboard, Cassie told herself that it was better to know now, than to find out after who knew how many weeks of searching. Quickly, she entered the first and last name, as well as the social security number that was written on the page. She paused, agonizing for a moment, before clicking on the submit button and almost gasped with relief when the page came up that read *Nothing Found* in bold text.

"That happens a lot," Jay replied, "you might try taking out the middle name, or the social security number. Sometimes those get entered into the system wrong and mess up the whole process."

"Another thing you could try," he said, reaching over her for the mouse, "is putting the name in a general search engine, along with something else that might be connected to the person. Like a hobby, job, or school they attended, anything that they might have been associated with. There's a ton of information on the web, you just have to figure out how to find it."

Jay finished with the mouse as a small bell rung softly from the other room, he stood. "Duty calls!" he said. "Don't give up, I'll come back with some paper and a pen."

With that, Cassie was left alone at the computer. The search engine page came up and Cassie entered her father's name. This resulted in several hundred finds, most of them sites that had both Bill and Beckman on the same page but unconnected.

Cassie added Oysterville to the search, but the results were just as vague. On a whim, she erased her former entry and typed in William Beckman, Long Beach Washington. This time when the screen flashed that it had completed its search, the first result showed three of the five words in a single sentence.

"William Beckman of Long Beach."

Cassie held her breath as the browser searched and slowly brought up the page. It was a secondary screen for the Long Beach volunteer fire department.

She quickly scanned the article and found it was about a beach clean-up day following a local storm the year before. There, listed among the volunteers being thanked, was a Bill Beckman, age 51 from Long Beach.

Cassie stared at the screen for a long time, breathing in the faint dusty aroma of new carpet and old books, her heart beating loud in the tomb-like silence of the library.

The name *might* have been just an amazing coincidence, but the chances of there being two William Beckmans, of the same age, both from Long Beach, was a fluke that Cassie wasn't willing to accept. Her father was alive *and still in Washington*, or had been a little more than a year before. Resting on a low bookshelf was a hulking printer, with dusty cables running to both computers. Cassie took a chance and clicked the print button on the screen.

The old dot-matrix machine groaned to life and slowly filled two sheets of paper with text, as well as a grainy black and white reproduction of the antique fire engine shown on the web page. These she folded up with the marriage certificate and stuffed back into her pocket.

Cassie sat there several minutes longer, staring at the computer, hypnotized by the dark text, the cluster of black dots on the bright screen that spelled out her father's name.

Suddenly she was furious, clenching her fists to overcome the raging desire to fling the screen off the table, to smash the printer, to scream until the windows around her shattered. He was alive! Living here the whole time, and in eighteen years of his miserable, pathetic life he hadn't ever bothered to find them, to see her and talk to her and learn who she was! Suddenly the tiny spark that had been her wish for a relationship was snuffed; she slammed the lid down on her fantasies and nailed it closed with her fury.

She would find him all right, and when she did she would tell him exactly what she thought of him, and what her mother had thought of him and then *she* would leave *him*! She would walk away and never look back and he could live the rest of his worthless life alone with the knowledge of what he had given up.

Somewhere, in a far back corner of her mind, Pastor Guy's voice whispered something about grace and mercy, but Cassie tuned it out, slamming the door savagely on her too-persistent conscience.

The anger that seethed within her drowned any compassion she might have entertained, and she walked stiffly out of the library to wait for Jack, not even hearing when Jay said good-bye.

The sound of squealing tires brought her head up, and Cassie stiffened in surprise as the tail end of a black pick-up disappeared around the far corner of the building.

❧

She didn't have to wait long. When Jack pulled up to the curb, his expression spoke plainly that his mood wasn't much better than hers.

"So," he said, as he pulled back onto the road, "who put the burr under your saddle?"

Cassie came close to telling him the whole story right there, but for some inexplicable reason she could not. Even as her mouth formed the truth, she heard herself lie and say the librarian had been rude. Jack grunted, saying that he had more great news.

"The *pinhead* owner of the bookstore gave me the wrong date of delivery," he glowered, "not only that, he insists that he *told* me the books wouldn't be in until tomorrow. Here's the topping on the cake though," Jack said with a growl, "he says he's lost the invoice, so he can't be sure the books I need will be in the delivery!"

Outside the truck, a half-dozen seagulls battled over the tattered remains of some child's discarded hamburger, shrieking and screeching, feinting at one another with their yellow, hooked beaks.

"What are you going to do?" Cassie asked.

"Not much choice," Jack said, with a frustrated sigh.

"I have to be here when that delivery arrives. If I'm not, he can scoop the books I need and say that they weren't in with the rest. He must have found a buyer for them…" So saying, Jack muttered an oath that, had she not been in the clutches of such black thoughts herself, would have caused Cassie to blush. Instead she only nodded, thinking that with that one word, Jack had pretty much summed up the whole world.

"Now we have to stay and wait," Jack went on, "I booked us a couple of rooms at a cheapie motel up the highway. It's on me, since it's my deal that's keeping us here." Jack sighed. "That order is for about six hundred dollars worth of books, except for the two I really need. Those two are worth quite a bit more than that. I told *pinhead* before I left that if I wasn't there when the boxes were opened, I wasn't paying." Jack's frown deepened.

"He squawked a bit, but he doesn't really care. If I don't pay him for the rest of the books, he'll still more than break even just selling the two."

Cassie thought about this for a moment. "How will you know when the books arrive?"

"That's the simple part," he replied, "I'm going to hang around his shop, like the shadow of death, until the delivery arrives. I called UPS, and they estimated delivery between noon and four tomorrow, but I'm going to be there when his doors open and I'm not leaving until my books show up!"

"You're going to just sit there all day?" she asked.

"Well," Jack smiled sardonically, "it *is* a bookstore, I'm sure I'll find something to do with my time. Hey, are you getting hungry?"

"Starved!" Cassie nodded, her stomach rumbling in agreement.

"Let's find someplace that serves seafood around here," Jack laughed.

"Yeah, *that* should be a challenge!" Cassie snorted, "I suppose we're looking for oysters."

Jack looked shocked. "What else is there?" he asked.

Chapter Nine

They parked the van in front of a sprawling, single level eatery called *The Sand Dollar Inn*. Once seated near the door of the bustling little café, they sipped from their water glasses, waiting for menus to arrive.

"Oh my gosh!" Cassie exclaimed. "I almost forgot!"

"What's that?" Jack replied.

Cassie told him about the seeing the black truck with the tinted windows, pulling out of the library, and the same black truck in the parking lot of the Pismo Bowl.

"In fact," she went on, "wasn't there a black pickup at that rest area we camped at the first night?"

"I think there was," Jack said. He was scowling by now, his fingers drumming the table in nervous concern.

"Do you think," Cassie asked, "that it's the guy from the truck stop?"

"Mr. Wexler, from Phoenix?" Jack asked. "Could be, I suppose. It would be a long way to come for a little payback. Besides, if he wanted to jump us, he's had plenty of chances."

Cassie shuddered at the memory of the malodorous, tattooed truck driver. "What if he's following us to find out where we live?"

"Or waiting to see where I drop you off..." Jack muttered absently, then cursed himself under his breath as Cassie's face drained of color and her hands began to shake.

"Oh Cassie," he said, half rising from his seat, "I'm sorry, that was a stupid thing to say!" Jack's face grew as red as Cassie's was white, and he chewed his lip in frustration at his offhand comment.

"Don't worry," he assured her, "we'll get to the bottom of this before I drop you off anywhere."

"It's...it's okay," Cassie whispered, her heart pounding madly against her ribs. Suddenly the room seemed to be filled with the acrid stink of stale cigarette smoke.

Looking around, Jack noticed the pay phone in the entryway, just behind

Cassie's seat.

"Hang on a second," he said, "I'm going to make a quick phone call. I'll be right behind you." Jack hurried around to the back of the booth and Cassie heard the sound of change dropping.

ॐ

Sheriff Bryan Hallworth had just sat down at his desk, balancing a cup of black coffee and a bran muffin in one hand and a thick sheaf of Teletype pages in the other. For all the jokes about cops and doughnuts, Long Beach's head of law enforcement liked to keep himself in top condition. Hallworth prided himself on wearing the same size jeans that he had the day he graduated from college. He'd heard too many stories about potbellied cops ending up face down on the sidewalk after vapor locking during a footrace with a suspect.

No thank you.

Not much of that kind of thing in a small town like Long Beach. Still, Sheriff Hallworth might not be able to stop a bullet, if one should have his name on it, but he'd be darned if he was going to give some perp the pleasure of watching him buy the farm just because he couldn't keep his pipes clean.

So, bran muffins and black coffee, as well as five mornings a week at the gym, kept him in what his wife referred to as *fighting form*.

Still, Hallworth didn't try to fool himself, the bran muffins tasted like cardboard, fiber or no fiber.

He was on his second bite and scanning his third APB when Lisa, who had morning desk duty, poked her head around his office door and rapped shave-and-a-haircut on the glass.

"Call on line two, boss," she murmured as he looked up, "it's Jack Leland for you."

Sheriff Hallworth washed down his doughy lump of cardboard with a bitter swig of coffee and nodded.

"Got it."

Punching line two and the speakerphone button at the same time, he leaned back his chair, his eyes never leaving his paperwork.

"Hey Jack," he said, "what the heck can I do you for?"

"Bry?" Jack's voice sounded muffled and staticky.

Must be at a payphone, Hallworth thought, as Jack continued, "Hey, how's it going?"

"Oh, same old thing," the sheriff replied, "truth, justice and the American way. How are you?"

"Doing good," Jack said.

"Hey, we missed you at the tournament last weekend, it was quite a show."

"Really, how'd you do?"

"Not bad," Hallworth replied, "we took second. Chief Stuckey bowled like a madman and those turkeys at the fire department walked away with first but, like I told them, some of us have real work to do and can't practice all the time!"

"Nice!" Jack laughed, then his voice sobered and the sheriff reached for a pen out of unconscious habit.

"Hey, I need a favor Bry, fella by the name of Mark Wexler, Phoenix. I'd like to know a little more about him."

"Wexler, got it," Hallworth muttered, scribbling the name, "anything more?"

"Yeah, I have his license right here."

Sheriff Hallworth sighed. "Do I want to know why you have this man's driver's license, Jack?"

"No, probably not," Jack grimaced as he rattled off the number, "but I'll tell you anyway. A friend of mine had a little altercation with this guy. He wanted to give her a ride and wouldn't take no for an answer–"

"–And, I take it, you convinced him otherwise?" Hallworth finished dryly.

"Never mind that," Jack growled, "no one got hurt, no laws got broken. Well, okay, maybe I mugged the guy a little, but that's all!"

"I didn't hear that, Jack," Hallworth laughed and shook his head. Jack Leland had been an unofficial member of the Long Beach Sheriff's Bowling Team for nearly a decade, back when Paul Bradley had still been the big man. Paul had spent the last four years living out his *Old Man and the Sea* fantasies, drifting the Gulf Stream and fighting marlin. Before that he had recognized that Jack Leland was a guy who needed to be a part of something, anything, to keep him out of the bottle. He was also a heck of a bowler.

Over the years he had become something of a mascot for the department, and always had a hot cup of joe ready if one of them dropped by the bookstore.

"Gimme a minute," the sheriff said, "I've got an FBI buddy who'll run the number through the NCIC computer."

"NCIC?"

"National Crime Information Center."

"Great," Jack replied, "I can wait."

Bryan Hallworth finished the last of his tasteless muffin as he waited for the results to print out on the old Oki printer. Glancing at the two pages of small, single-spaced type, he gave a low whistle, his brow gathering in concern.

"Oh lord, Jackie," he muttered, "what have you gotten yourself into *this* time?"

&

Jack reached over the seat and gave Cassie a reassuring pat on the shoulder. A minute passed, then two, before Sheriff Hallworth came back on the line.

"Yeah, I'm here," Jack said. "Yeah? Yeah, that sounds like the guy. Uh-huh. Oh great! Does it say what he drives? Got it. Hey I've got to go. No, we're okay. I'll fill you in on Saturday, thanks Bry!" Jack hung up the phone and slid back into his seat with a sigh.

"Well?" Cassie asked, chewing nervously on a fingernail.

"Well," he replied, "I'm not going to lie to you, this Wexler guy is bad news. Drug charges, menacing charges, even a stint in prison for assault with a weapon. Also…" Jack sighed again and took a long drink from his water glass.

"Also?" Cassie prompted, as though that weren't enough.

"His motor vehicle file lists him driving a 1988 Toyota pickup. No color listed." Jack looked up at Cassie, whose face was pale as milk.

"Don't sweat it," he said, "the sheriff of Long Beach is a bowling buddy of mine; he's going fax a white paper to the police up and down the coast. They'll keep an eye out for Mark Wexler."

Cassie nodded, smiling tremulously. Finally, after draining her water glass, she started the conversation on another track.

"So," Cassie asked, taking a deep breath, "who in the world would pay six hundred dollars for a couple of books?"

Jack laughed.

"Well," he said, "that's what *I'm* paying for them, I plan to get a bit more than that back on my investment. You'd be surprised what folks will fork out for first editions, or those one or two books that complete their collections."

"What books are these?"

"Two very rare editions of *Ulysses*," Jack smiled, "both printed in 1935, for a private book club, and autographed by the illustrator. The gentleman who asked me to help him find them has offered $7,500 apiece. He's the great-grandson of the man who did the artwork."

"Whoa," Cassie exclaimed, "that's fifteen grand! I think I'd sit there all day too!"

"You said it." Jack grinned. "The rare book market is where the real money is. The woman who owned the bookstore before me dabbled in it, but she didn't have the energy or the time to do the research."

"Sounds like a lot of fun to me," Cassie said.

"It is," Jack agreed, "I can make as much selling a couple of dozen hard-to-find volumes, as I do in a year's worth of the tourist trade at the shop. The first book I tracked down was an out of print edition of *Moby Dick* for some friends of mine in Nahcotta. Took me six months to find the printing I was looking for," he grinned at the memory, "but it was a hoot."

"A bookstore can get a little boring as the years roll on, and searching for rare books was something interesting to do during the winter lull. After a few years, I started getting letters from people asking if I could find them such-and-such a book and telling me how much they were willing to pay for it. Well, it didn't take long to realize that I could do pretty well for myself, spending a couple of hours a day doing research and making phone calls. Now, with the internet, it's even easier."

The waiter arrived with their menus and Jack ordered another glass of ice water for himself and a diet cola for Cassie, along with six oyster shooters. The waiter smiled knowingly as Cassie's face blanched.

"I was afraid you were going to remember that," she said.

"Be brave!" Jack replied with mock seriousness, "and keep an open mind."

"I'm more worried about keeping my dinner down!"

Jack was still laughing at this when their appetizers arrived. Cassie studied the tiny glass in front of her, and its crimson contents, dubiously. Jack picked up one of shooters and, with a flourish, raised it to his lips and slurped the contents in a single, noisy swallow.

"Ah!" he sighed with pleasure. "Perfection!"

"Really?" Cassie asked.

"Hemmingway said that eating a raw oyster was like french-kissing a mermaid," Jack quoted, and suddenly blushed furiously, remembering his company. "Um… I mean…"

Cassie laughed and reached for her glass before she could have second thoughts or, being too late for that, maybe third thoughts.

The contents were icy cold as they slipped from the glass to her tongue and the sweet hot flavor of the sauce made her nose tingle. As she bit into the slippery body of the oyster, her mouth was filled with a sharp briny flavor, much more powerful than she had tasted with the oyster kabobs in Pismo.

As she swallowed her first raw oyster, Jack watching her intently, Cassie couldn't decide if she liked it or not. She didn't dislike it, but the experience was so unlike anything she had ever eaten that she couldn't categorize it.

"Well?" Jack asked finally.

"I…I'm not sure," Cassie responded. "I think I like it…"

Jack laughed. "If you think you like it," he said, "then you do. There's no middle ground here kid, you either love 'em or you heave them back up. In my experience it's about sixty-forty in favor of the oysters."

"Well then, I guess I must love them!" Cassie laughed in return, reaching for a second glass.

When the waiter returned with their drinks, he was grinning. "Well?" he asked in the same tone as Jack had.

"She loves them!" Jack replied.

"Excellent!" the waiter smiled, giving Cassie a wink. "Let me know when you're ready to order. The oysters, by the way, are fresh in from the bay this morning."

Jack ordered for both of them and, an hour later, their hunger finally abated, they lounged at the table awaiting their dessert. As Cassie studied the various watercolors adorning the restaurant's walls, Jack reached into his pocket and took out a small, heart shaped box of chocolates, which he placed on the table next to Cassie's plate.

"What's this?" Cassie asked, surprised.

"Well, didn't seem right to me that a pretty girl went without a valentine," Jack grinned, "just because she's on the road with a crabby old geezer like me."

Cassie smiled and picked up the small box of candy. "Thank you Jack, I wish I'd known, I'd have picked you up something."

"Ah, I'm probably better off without it," he said. "The doctors keep telling me I'm teetering on the brink of diabetes, so I try to keep the sweets few and far between."

Cassie was about to voice her concern over this when Jack suddenly looked at his watch and slapped the table, his face returning to a scowl.

"Shoot," he said. "I almost forgot, I need to make a phone call!" Jack stood and dug into his pocket for a handful of change. "I thought I saw a payphone out in front of the motel."

"Why don't you–" Cassie began, meaning to ask why he didn't just use the phone on the wall behind her, then she realized, this was a *personal* call.

Looking at the heart-shaped package in her hands, Cassie had a sudden insight and grinned at him, teasingly.

"Shame on you, Jack," she cried, "forgetting to call your girlfriend on Valentine's Day! You better read her some love poetry or something, before she finds another boy…"

The effect of her words on Jack were sudden and distressing, his eyes widening and his face going white for a breathless moment, then blushing red and finally, collapsing into a dark, angry scowl. More than the normal downward cast, it was a grimace of real anger. He stared at Cassie for a long moment, his eyes hard and unfriendly.

"I'll be right back," Jack said brusquely and walked quickly to the door and out.

Cassie's head was spinning as she sat alone at the table.

Whatever she had said obviously touched a raw nerve in Jack. Intuition filled in the blanks and she realized, to her own horror that Jack had, indeed, almost forgotten to call someone on Valentine's Day. Someone whom he cared about very much, but who would not, or could not, be his. She felt tears sting her eyes as she slipped the box of candy into her pocket. He had tried to do something sweet for her, and she had gone and ruined it, hurting him with a single, thoughtless remark.

She would have to try to apologize when he returned, but how? How could she have known the way he would react to her teasing?

By the time the *Widmer* clock above the bar had slipped from 7:00 to 7:30, Cassie had began to wonder if Jack would return, or if he had gone on to the motel. Then the door opened and he walked in. One glance at his haggard face and Cassie knew that whatever had happened in the last half hour hadn't gone far in improving his mood. Jack slumped into the chair across from her, looking tired. His shoulders sagged, and his eyes, usually aglitter with bitter humor, were dull and hooded. Cassie realized, to her shock and dismay, that for the first time since she had met him, Jack Leland looked old.

A long, silent moment passed, and Cassie fought the desperate urge to squirm in her seat.

"Jack," she faltered, "I'm really sorry. I didn't mean–"

Jack raised his hand to silence her, shaking his head.

"No," he said, "you don't have anything to be sorry for, you just caught me by surprise, and maybe you hit a little closer to home than I was ready to deal with. I have a friend; we've been close for, oh… a long time now. She's a lot like me, no real family or anything, so we've taken to spending time together, holidays and such, instead of being alone."

Jack looked down into his water glass, as though unable to meet her eyes. "Sometimes I think maybe she's waiting for me to do something, but I'm just not much of a romantic, 'fraid I'd mess up everything and then I wouldn't even have a friend, you know?"

Cassie nodded, though she had the feeling that Jack was talking more to himself than to her. Finally he looked up again and, catching her eye, his smile was bitter.

"Maybe I *should* have read her poetry," he murmured and then, draining the last of his water, he stood, "or maybe not." Jack paid the bill in silence and, as they walked across the parking lot to the motel, he handed Cassie her key.

"Here," he said, "you're in room eight, I'll be right across the hall in nine. You go on ahead, I'm going to drive around for a little while and try to clear my head."

"Jack," Cassie tried again, "I'm really sorry…"

"Enough said," Jack dismissed her again, "I told you it wasn't your fault. Go get some sleep; I'll see you in the morning." Then he turned his back and walked away.

Cassie felt miserable as she climbed the sagging wooden steps that led to her room. Unlocking her door, she barely noticed the shabby furnishings and faded wallpaper. A low bed, covered with a worn rose-colored comforter, took up most of the tiny space. A battered television rested on a dark chest of drawers, its surface scratched and scarred with cigarette burns.

The room smelled of stale smoke and old paint. She washed her face and hands and, too exhausted of mind and body to even pray, she collapsed onto the bed and was asleep.

❧

Jack sighed through clenched teeth as he pulled the old van out of the motel parking lot and back onto the highway, heading south. He shouldn't have snapped at Cassie. He knew, when he cooled down, that he'd be sorry and have to apologize. But right now he was mad, mad at himself for being so obvious, for being too gutless to tell Beth how he really felt, maybe before she *did* give up on him. Mad at life for beating him down until he was afraid to have anything for fear it would be taken away. Most of all, mad at Cassie for seeing through him so easily, for so thoughtlessly tearing the scab from the wound. As he glowered through the darkened windshield, Jack drove without considering his destination, on autopilot, his anger and frustration at the wheel.

A couple of miles further, the van seemed to pull itself into a potholed gravel parking lot in front of a low, dingy, brick building. Sickly yellow lighting washed the front of the tavern, pooling around the heavy wooden door and the single, blacked-out window with its glowing *Budweiser* sign. Jack sat behind the wheel for a long while, long enough for the engine to stop pinging and the interior of the van to cool.

Suddenly he was tromping up the three sagging wooden steps that led to the door.

The inside of the bar was a monument to the vision that every non-drinking American must have of a truly third-class watering hole. Somewhere across the smoky, smelly gloom, Jack could hear the whirl and ping of video games over the sad warble of Garth Brooks on the jukebox.

Dank and dingy, the place looked to be filled with men who wanted to get drunk in the darkness and maybe go a couple of rounds in the back alley if someone looked at them wrong. A couple of drink-spotted pool tables sat, untended against the back wall, and the only light came from a host of neon beer signs behind the bar.

Jack grimaced as he felt the soles of his shoes sticking to the grungy linoleum, and hoisted himself up onto a weathered barstool, its vinyl cushion crossed and recrossed with long, peeling strips of duct tape.

The bartender meandered his direction, laconically sponging at the filthy bar with an even filthier rag. He was average height, thin, but with ropy muscles showing beneath the rolled up sleeves of his tee shirt.

Most of the men in the bar probably had a hundred pounds on the guy. Jack was willing to bet there was a well-used Louisville Slugger, or maybe an old double-barrel smoke pole, under the counter if things got out of hand. The man glanced at Jack, his face set in the cold contempt that came from long association with the bottom of the barrel.

"What'cha having?" he grunted.

Jack was no stranger to his surroundings and, tossing several bills onto the beer-puddled bartop, he looked the smaller man in the eye and sighed, feeling his anger beginning to fade already, dissipating into a clinging cloud of familiar failure.

"Let's start with a tall bourbon and water," he muttered, "and go easy on the water, friend."

ঌ৫

When a fist pounded on the thin, motel-room door at three o'clock in the morning, Cassie had a sudden, dizzying moment of disorientation, unable to remember where she was or why. She stumbled from the bed towards the door and woke just enough to stop herself with her hand on the latch. Mark Wexler's face flashed through her mind and she was suddenly afraid.

"Who is it?" She asked.

"My name is Tom Barnhart," a deep voice replied. "I'm sorry to wake you Miss, but I have a man out here named Jack Leland who says that you know him."

Cassie opened the door a crack and peered out. Jack stood, leaning heavily on a stocky, younger man. The man had Jack's arm over his own broad shoulder, holding him up. Jack peered blurrily through the doorway at her, his eyes blinking and unfocused. Then, a bittersweet wave of whiskey breath hit Cassie like a fist, staggering her back a step from the door. The man, Tom *somebody*, pushed the door open with his foot and half led, half carried his burden to the bed, where Jack flopped on his back and lie, groaning.

The man held out his hand to Cassie. "I'm Tom," he said with a sheepish smile, "wish we were meeting under better conditions."

Cassie was fully awake now. "What happened?"

"I'm a member of AA here in Gold Beach," he said. "Every once in a while we'll get a call from one of the local bars that they have a member who's gone off the wagon and shouldn't drive."

Cassie looked at him curiously, her eyes narrowing.

"How would the bartender in Gold Beach know that Jack's in Alcoholics Anonymous?"

The man laughed. "When we drink, we talk. First thing we do, after ordering another drink of course, is tell the barkeep how long we've been dry." He smiled again. "Don't ask me why, but we all do it."

Cassie nodded, as he went on.

"So anyway," Tom said, "we take turns finding out who they are and where they're staying and trying to get them home before they hurt themselves or someone else." He nodded towards the bed.

"Jack here has spent the better part of the night in a real dive called *Chico's*, up on 101. When the bartender announced last call, they couldn't wake him up enough to ask if he wanted one more drink, so they called me."

Tom started moving towards the door. "I'll give a call to the group up in Long Beach," he said, "and let them know what's happened. Does he have his own room?"

Cassie blushed. "Yes! Across the hall."

"No offense," Tom offered, raising his hands in a gesture of peace, "I'm not here to judge anyone, I just want to make sure he has a place to sleep it off."

"His room is across the hall," Cassie repeated tightly. "You can leave him here though, I'll sleep over there."

Tom handed her a room key identical to her own. "The number wasn't clear and I didn't want to start trying doors in the middle of the night." Then he stepped out into the hall for a moment and returned with a white plastic bucket. "Better put this on the floor near his head." He said.

"You think he's going to throw up?"

"I always did."

"Good," Cassie replied, "I hope he's sick all night."

"Take it a little easy on him," Tom murmured, "everyone slips now and then."

"Yeah?" said Cassie, holding the door open. "Tell that to my mother!"

Tom looked at her, confused, then shook his head and walked out. Cassie slammed the door after him. The sound brought Jack momentarily out of his stupor and, groaning, he sat up on the edge of the bed, his head in his hands.

"Cassie," he started, his voiced slurred and pained, "I'm..."

"Don't," Cassie hissed, the anger in her voice bringing Jack's bloodshot eyes up to meet her own. "Don't tell me you're sorry!"

"What..." Jack started.

"Don't you dare tell me you're sorry, Jack," Cassie repeated as her voice broke and tears started down her cheeks.

She balled her fists in rage, fighting back the desire to leap at him, to lash out at the fog of confusion and the stink of alcohol that enveloped him.

Her own stomach heaved, and for a moment Cassie thought she might be the one who needed the bucket. In the sound of Jack's slurred voice she could hear, again, her mother's agonized cries for help and see the red taillights as they weaved away into the night. She could hear the driver's drunken voice from beyond the grave, calling in inebriated cadence…

"I'm sorry… I'm sorry… I'm sorry…"

Everything she had begun to admire and respect in Jack suddenly came crashing down around her in an avalanche of anger and disgust.

"Yes," she said, her voice low and hateful, "I'm sure you're very sorry, you'll be even sorrier the night you booze it up and kill somebody, if you don't luck out and do yourself in the process!"

Jack flinched, his cheeks flushing at her words, his eyes widening, "What are you talking about…"

Cassie picked up her bag from the floor and rummaged through it for her Bible. From between the book's pages she pulled a scrap of newsprint and flung it in his direction, as the tears overwhelmed her and she began to cry.

"Here," she cried, her voice cracking, "here's what I'm talking about, you…you stinking drunk!" As the clipping fluttered to the ground at Jack's feet, Cassie turned and ran, weeping, into the hall, slamming the door behind her.

Jack tried to stand, to follow her, but the spinning of the room brought him crashing back to the bed. He lie there for a moment, sheened in cold sweat, his stomach churning, and his eye fell on the piece of newspaper that Cassie had thrown at him. With trembling fingers, Jack reached down, and after three swipes, managed to catch hold of the clipping and bring it to his face.

With a great deal of effort, his eyes slowly focused on the scrap. Above the picture of a middle-aged woman was the headline "*Nurse run down by drunk driver*." Jack felt his stomach lurch at the words, his mouth was parched and dry as the first sentence burned though the alcoholic fog of his brain.

Katherine Anne Belanger, 40, of Bowie Arizona, was struck and killed by a drunk driver Tuesday evening in front of Bowie Adventist Medical Center.

The face in the picture swam before his eyes, his brain superimposing Cassie's face over it. The tiny, shabby motel room began to spin in earnest and Jack realized, as the paper slipped from his fingers, that he was suddenly stone-cold sober.

"Oh God," he whispered, "Oh my God…"

Without warning Jack Leland burst into tears and, curling up like a child on the faded comforter, he sobbed until the room spun into blackness around him.

❧

She is wandering in a dark, desolate place. A dank wind howls around her feet, bringing storms of dead leaves hissing along the flat ground. It feels like a graveyard, but there are no stones, none that she can see, marking the places of the dead. Cassie can hear, just above that mournful whisper, a voice far ahead, weeping and full of pain. She shivers with cold, drawing the thin, rose-colored blanket tightly around her. It is very cold and her bare toes are aching when she finally comes to the lip of a deep well. The voice drifts up from the bottom, someone is suffering, lost in the darkness below. A blood red moon suddenly rises over the edge of the featureless, shadowed horizon and, in a moment, it has reached its pinnacle, casting its bright crimson beams into the pit. Cassie leans as far as she dares, the fingers of the wind pulling her forward, clutching at her from the yawning chasm below.

At the bottom of the pit lays a man. The bloodlight strikes his face and it is Jack. Jack, ragged, bleeding and starved, his clothing is torn and ragged, caked with filth, gaunt ribs stretched with pale skin show through the rags he wears. Crisscrosses of raw, oozing lash marks cover his exposed back. Fresh bleeding wounds over a lifetime of scars. Jack's eyes are closed and his hands cover his ears. He is weeping.

"May the day of my birth perish," he cries, "and the night it was said, a boy is born! That day, may it turn to darkness; may God above not care about it; may no light shine upon it!"

The wind rises mournfully once more, as Jack repeats the words again and again, never opening his eyes, never unstopping his ears.

"May the day of my birth perish..."

Cassie calls to him, screams his name over the gale, but he can't hear her, his eyes are closed and can't see her.

"May God above not care..."

Over Jack's lament, she hears her mother's voice.

"You have to go down and get him, Cass," she whispers, "show him the way to get out..."

"May God above not care..."

Cassie woke up gasping, drenched in sweat and, over the painful hammering of her heart, the anguished words still echoed in her empty room.

"May God above not care..." she whispered.

Chapter Ten

The morning sun, streaming through the dusty motel window, finally roused Cassie from her fitful sleep. Her eyes still red and puffy, she winced at the headache that pounded beneath her temples from crying herself to sleep the night before, and glanced at the cheap clock radio on the bedside table; nine forty-five it read. If Jack had woken up from his stupor yet, he must have gone on without her.

"I hope he has the granddaddy of all hangovers!" she muttered to herself.

"Show him the way to get out..."

Cassie sat back on the bed as a wave of guilt and shame swept over her.

As mad as she was at Jack, and she *was* still mad, she knew the things she had said to him the night before had come from her own hurt and anger, and not from his drinking binge. Jack had let her tag along all the way back from Arizona, more than that, he had gone out of his way to become her friend and she had treated him like dirt the first time he disappointed her. Jack Leland hadn't killed her mother and, as much as her own pain made her spurn alcohol, she knew that whatever reasons Jack had for drinking were his own and wouldn't be resolved through bitterness and anger.

She might have had a chance of helping him, if last night hadn't gone the way it did. Jack had started to open up to her at the restaurant, who knew what might have come of that? Now though, he was most likely on his way home again, miles up the highway and glad to be rid of her.

Cassie gathered her belongings and repacked her duffel bag. She would hike up to the highway and see if she could thumb a ride north towards Washington.

As her hand reached for the knob of the motel door, she remembered...

...the books!

How could she be so dumb? Jack wouldn't have left town until the shipment of books arrived! Maybe she could still catch him and apologize. Though he wasn't likely to forgive her, at least she could try.

Cassie decided to check the café first, and if Jack wasn't there, she would walk down to the bookstore, where he'd said he would wait all day.

Breathlessly she left the motel and headed across the parking lot.

It was a bright morning, and the air was thick with the scent of the ocean.

Gulls soared and swooped overhead, calling raucously to one another in their endless search for food.

Jack was in the café. Seated, again toward the back, he had a cup of coffee and an unopened newspaper on the table before him, but seemed interested in neither. Instead, he sat watching the door, his eyes lost in thought. When his gaze caught Cassie's, the girl saw a flash of great relief and even greater embarrassment, as he raised his hand. Suddenly Cassie was mortified, wishing she were anywhere else in the world but here.

How could she explain herself to Jack, apologize for the way she had treated him? Her feet felt like great lead weights as she slowly made her way down the aisle to where Jack waited.

"Sit," Jack said softly, gesturing to the seat across from his own, "please."

Cassie sat, unsure what to do, and an agonizing minute passed. Jack cleared his throat twice, fumbling with his napkin and silverware, and Cassie was about to speak when the waitress sauntered over to their table to lay a menu in front of her.

"Here ya go, Hon," she said, smiling at Cassie. "I thought *this* one was going to take up roots here waiting for you." She gave Jack a withering look, her hands resting on ample hips. "How about you, Diamond Jim, a fresh cup of coffee or do you prefer it cold?"

Jack graced her with a sour smile. "Fresh coffee would be great, thank you." The waitress snorted and left with Jack's cup.

A long silence passed. Cassie glanced up, feeling Jack's gaze on her and he didn't look away, his face pale, his eyes wide and far-off. Cassie had to fight the urge to squirm, growing nervous and self-conscious beneath that relentless stare until, finally, Jack blinked, shaking like a man waking up from a dream and realizing that he wasn't asleep.

"Well," said Jack, "that was quite a soap opera we performed last night." Cassie, who couldn't think of a thing to say, only nodded.

He sighed. "I don't suppose that *sorry* begins to cover my behavior but, for what it's worth, I am."

His words took a moment to register in Cassie's brain. *He* was apologizing to *her*! Cassie blinked, and blinked again, trying to force out some response.

"I'll understand," Jack continued, his eyes on the table in front of him, "if you'd rather find your own way from here on out, but I'd like to at least buy you breakfast and part as friends." He sighed again. "I'm really very embarrassed and very sorry that you had to see me that way. It doesn't happen often and, even then, I usually have at least a shred of dignity and find my own way home. I guess...um..."

"Wait," Cassie interrupted in a rush, "please don't say you're sorry again. I came down here to apologize to you!"

"What?" Jack said.

"I let you wander off alone last night," she said, "when I knew you were hurt, and then I used your condition as an excuse to vent on you for stuff that you didn't have anything to do with." Cassie's lip began to tremble, "I thought we were friends, but I didn't act like one last night."

There was a long pause as they each, hesitantly, looked up from the table to catch the other's eye.

"Well," said Jack, "I guess we owed each other an apology, and, as that's been said," Jack took a deep breath, "I think we should put it behind us and get some breakfast."

"Really?" asked Cassie. "You mean it?"

"Sure," Jack replied, smiling, "unless you'd rather I keep apologizing all the way to Long Beach."

Cassie laughed with relief.

When they finished their meal, Jack set down his fork and looked up, he seemed nervous, glancing at her and then away.

"I've been thinking," he began.

"Yes?"

"Well," Jack said, "maybe I could give you a ride all the way to Portland, now that you've gotten some material for your book." Jack toyed with his silverware, barely making eye contact.

"That way," he went on, "you wouldn't have to spend any more money on a motel and if you had any questions or needed any material you could just call me and I could e-mail you what you needed. You could get in on the summer classes that way, instead of waiting until fall."

Cassie thought furiously, trying to come up with an answer.

"Um," she stammered, "I was hoping to get some pictures while I was there. Maybe talk to some people and get a feel for the place myself."

Jack nodded, stirring his coffee.

"Yeah, there's that." He seemed defeated, but pressed on, "I was just thinking that it might be nice to get an early start, and we could cut east at Tillamook this afternoon and have you there by nightfall."

"That's awfully nice of you, Jack, but I really need to spend some time on the Peninsula, I need to get it firsthand."

"Of course," Jack replied, chewing his lip, "of course you do. Oh, I thought you'd probably want this back."

Reaching into his jacket pocket, he pulled out a small paperback book, removing the newspaper clipping, and handing it to Cassie.

"I'm sorry about your mother," Jack said softly, and his voice seemed to quaver for a moment, "it must be very hard." Cassie looked up and, in the bright sunlight shining through the restaurant window, Jack's eyes glistened as though on the verge of tears.

"Well," he said suddenly, jumping to his feet, "we had better go see if the pinhead has gotten my books in yet or not."

Cassie had the uncomfortable feeling there was more to Jack's reaction than she was catching, and she frowned as she slipped the paperback into her Bible and followed Jack out to the van.

The rest of the afternoon was spent waiting in the Spring Leaves bookstore.

The shop was on the first floor of a very old building on the main street of town.

"Right between the kite store and taffy shop," Jack had commented wryly, "just like mine."

Two worn, concrete steps led up to the main door and into the small, cluttered shop. The front room was perfectly square, all four walls covered, floor to ceiling, with books. Several tables filled the open space, stacked high with works by local writers, cookbooks, and the latest best-selling novels.

Amid the tables were two overstuffed leather chairs, the one nearest the window had a sign taped to the high back that read: *Sebastian's Throne, sit at your own risk!*

Curled in the seat of the chair was Sebastian himself, a massive gold tomcat with piercing green eyes and white tufted ears. He lay contentedly, in sure authority of all he surveyed, his great ginger bulk filling the seat from arm to arm. Cassie felt sure, looking at him, that no one *ever* tried to move him from his throne.

In the very center of the room sat a small island with a cash register and a wheezing old monochrome computer monitor. Cassie's nose twitched at the smell of sage-scented incense burning in a copper dragon by the register. The pinhead, as Jack had referred to him, was a slight, balding man with round glasses and a pronounced lisp. Full of nervous energy, he spent the afternoon bustling about his shop and harrying the small handful of patrons that wandered in. Cassie watched him move the same stack of paperbacks three times in an hour.

The two men traded intermittent small talk, but their conversation was strained, and the owner seemed to be afraid of offending Jack in some way, possibly concerned about what the larger man might do if angered.

Jack, for his part, did nothing to encourage this perception, but nothing, Cassie noticed, to discourage it either.

After perusing the shelves, he had promptly relocated the cat from his throne to the floor and, taking a magazine from a nearby rack, began to read.

Sebastian had stalked from the room, not to be seen again that day.

Around two that afternoon, as Cassie returned to the shop after wandering down Main Street in search of an ice-cream cone, she found Jack standing at the cash register, scribbling out a check. The nervous little owner stood, with a pasted-on smile, gazing longingly into a box of perhaps twenty-five old books. Jack signed the check with a flourish and even shook the pinhead's hand as he turned to go, tucking the box safely under his arm. Cassie could tell by the excited flush of his cheeks the volumes he had wanted were there.

As they loaded the box in the van, Jack could no longer contain himself.

"They're perfect!" he exclaimed, clapping Cassie on the back. "*Much* better condition than I had hoped, the buyer is going to be ecstatic!"

"That's it, isn't it?" Cassie laughed. "It's not about making the sale; it's about finishing the quest. That's what you love, being able to find the one book that no one else can, and deliver it. It's your holy grail!"

Jack stared at her a moment and then, throwing back his head, roared with laughter,

"Of course that's it!" he cried. "Did you think it was the money? It's the hunt that matters." Jack laughed once more, rubbing his hands together like Ebenezer Scrooge at his counting table.

"Now, young lady," he said, "you and I are going to celebrate! The finest restaurant on the Oregon Coast is just up the road."

"Oysters?" Cassie laughed.

"That may be on the menu, yes!" Jack grinned, "The Queen Victoria makes *the* best *Oysters en Brochette.* You'll love it!"

The Queen Victoria Restaurant had once been an enormous farmhouse.

More than a century old, it had been renovated a decade earlier by a gourmet chef who had decided to retire from working in Paris and open a small restaurant in her hometown. Each of the dozen or so small tables scattered throughout the dining rooms were covered in creamy white alpine lace, and dinners were served on fine china with silver. Cassie glanced surreptitiously about the room, feeling a little underdressed in her jeans and hiking boots. Jack noticed and smiled.

"Don't worry about it," he chuckled, "this is the coast. Formal dining wear includes beach shorts and Birkenstocks."

Cassie grinned, feeling less conspicuous when she noticed that several other patrons looked as though they might have just walked up from a day on the beach.

Once again, Jack ordered for the both of them, including a soda for Cassie and water for himself. His first glass he drained at once, with several aspirin from a bottle he'd picked up earlier that morning.

"Head still hurt?" asked Cassie.

"Yup," Jack replied with a grimace. "This is the part you never remember when ordering that first drink."

Cassie nodded with as much sympathy as she could muster. Jack noticed and smirked.

"I've never met a woman who had much pity for a hangover," he smiled, "my friend Beth reminds me regularly that God invented liquor so we Irish wouldn't rule the world."

Cassie nodded again. "Sounds like a smart woman."

"Oh, she is," he nodded, "believe me."

Cassie laughed. "I'm looking forward to meeting her."

Jack's smile seemed to fade a little when she said this and he looked away quickly, fumbling with the long stem of his now-empty water glass. Cassie noticed and quickly changed the subject, hoping to avoid a repeat of the disastrous dinner the night before.

"So, what the heck am I eating?"

"*Oysters en Brochette*," Jack replied, relishing the words as though he could taste his meal already, "is oysters sautéed in butter with mushrooms, cherry tomatoes, and garlic, then spooned into a hollowed loaf of French bread and baked. Food of the gods, my dear!"

"Sounds like a heart attack on a plate to me."

Jack smiled. "*Part of the secret of success in life is to eat what you like and let the food fight it out inside*."

Cassie waited until she could stand it no longer.

"Well?" she demanded.

"Mark Twain," Jack laughed, "Samuel Clemmons if you prefer. A man wise enough to have two names." With this he winked at Cassie, who quickly looked elsewhere.

The meal was served, and proved to be every bit as decadent as Cassie had feared. Hot sweet garlic butter pooled on the plate beneath the bread. The meal was to be her best experiment with oysters yet, and she fell to it with gusto. Finally, pushing the remains of her dinner away, Cassie groaned.

"You're bad for my health, Jack," she said, rubbing her stomach, "I'll bet I've gained ten pounds since I met you!"

"Yes," Jack sighed, leaning back in his chair, "friendship can be broadening! Besides, you could use another pound or two; you're a twig."

Cassie snorted, rubbing her imaginary belly.

They sipped their drinks as the sun dipped to the horizon, sinking below the vast rim of the Pacific Ocean in umber glory. The blazing sunset slowly faded to twilight until, finally, the pounding waves became an invisible murmur in the darkness.

"Well," Jack said, breaking the silence with a vast yawn, "I don't know about you, but I didn't get much rest last night. I think I'm going to turn in early."

"Good idea," Cassie nodded, realizing suddenly that she was bone weary and very, very full. Once they had returned to the motel, each said goodnight and headed to their separate rooms.

A half hour later, Cassie was asleep, warm and comfortable.

An hour after that she was whimpering in her sleep.

&

The wind rattles against the windows, moaning across the desert in a cloud of dust and grit. The trailer rocks fitfully in the storm, the slam of a loose screen door wakes Cassie with a start.

Despite the chill of the night, she finds herself sweating as she reaches out to snap on the light. Nothing happens. The storm must have blown down a line somewhere between here and town.

"Cassssiiiiieeeeee...." A voice, barely audible above the wind, calls her name.

Her breath catches in her throat as she slips from her room and down the darkened hallway. "Momma?" she whispers. "Momma are you there?" The door to Kathy Belanger's tiny bedroom stands open. The room is empty, a thick layer of dust coats the closet shelves, and cobwebs hang from the naked light fixture.

"Cassssiiiiieeeeee...."

She whirls, this time the voice is closer, just outside, barely past the thin metal walls. A man's voice is calling her name.

Her hand cramps with fear and, looking down, Cassie realizes that she is holding a pistol, the huge revolver from her mother's dresser drawer. The trigger lock is missing now and she can see, in the reflection of the glinting streetlamp, the dull brass casings of the loaded gun.

The streetlamp. Its thin, yellow light seeps through the windows and across the faded carpet to her feet. No power lines have gone down, if they had, the lamp would be dark as well.

The gun is heavy, cold and frightening, as her chilled, bare feet lead her across the room to the front door. The living room is also empty of furniture, thick with the musty odor of abandonment. Glancing back into her own room she is hardly surprised that her bed is now gone.

The lamp that had refused to light moments before has disappeared as well, and her room, like the rest of the trailer, is an empty tomb.

And outside, through the filmy haze of the thin, tattered curtains, she can make out the form of a man standing in the amber spill of the streetlamp, a bottle held loosely in one hand.

Somewhere, a small voice whispers that this is wrong, that beds and blankets don't just disappear when you turn your back, that...

"Cassssiiiiieeeeee...."

The voice, more insistent now, rises with the howl of the storm and, unwillingly, she lays a hand on the cool metal of the doorknob. It turns and a shrieking gust of wind rips it from her grasp, slamming the door open. A cloud of dust swirls around her, pulling at the hem of the dress that she and her mother had bought just the week before.

"He's not someone you want to know, Cass," her mother's voice comes from behind her, and Cassie shivers, refusing to turn.

"You may be the only good thing that Bill Beckman's done in his whole life..."

Cassie begins to cry, fighting to keep from throwing down the gun and covering her ears to shut out the terrible, familiar, dispassionate voice.

Instead, she raises the pistol, gripping it with quaking, bloodless hands, as her father steps away from the lamppost and toward her.

"I've cleaned up after drunks before," Kathy Belanger whispers in her ear.

As she pulls the trigger, his head comes up and the pale electric light washes over Jack Leland's face.

The pistol belches flame and thunder, and Cassie screams–

–and sat bolt upright, alone in the darkness of the motel room. Her hair was matted to her sweat-slicked face as she stood shakily and felt her way to the small bathroom.

Finding the light and the sink, she splashed cold water on her face, looking up at the pale trembling figure in the mirror in front of her. The clock beside the bed reads 12:45.

She lay back down, staring at the ceiling for a long time.

Chapter Eleven

Sometime before the first light of morning crossed the eastern hills, Cassie fell back into a dreamless sleep, and when Jack finally pounded on her door at nine, she woke feeling more refreshed than she had in days.

Jack grunted through the door that he was going down to the café for breakfast and coffee. Cassie called back that she would meet him there and, after a quick shower, she repacked her bag and hurried to the restaurant, whistling as she blinked in the bright midmorning light. She found Jack hunched over his morning cup, staring absently at the menu in front of him.

"You look chipper this morning!" Cassie laughed.

Jack grunted and closed his menu, wrapping both hands protectively around his steaming coffee. By his third cup, he seemed to be able to focus his eyes and, pushing away the remains of their breakfast dishes, he and Cassie began discussing their plans for the day.

"Well," said Jack, "if we push through all day, we should make Astoria just after dark, that'll put us home around midnight."

Cassie nodded.

"I don't suppose," Jack looked away, "that you've changed your mind about going to Portland." It seemed to Cassie that he was nearly pleading with her, his hand clenching and unclenching his napkin as he spoke. "I could have you there by six tonight."

"No way," Cassie replied, her voice firm, "I want to see Nahcotta, Oysterville, the whole peninsula firsthand."

Jack's shoulders sagged in defeat, as he dropped his napkin on his plate and looked up.

"You're a stubborn one, you know that?"

"Yeah," she smiled, "I've considered that possibility!"

Jack laughed, and then pointed a finger, scowling in mock ferocity. "Fine," he said, glowering, "but get whatever you want here in town, and drink light, 'cause I ain't stopping!"

"Well, it's your van I suppose," Cassie replied, rolling her eyes, "but a potty-break here and there would be a lot cheaper than new upholstery."

Jack gave her a sour look. "You've got an answer for everything don't you?"

"That's what they tell me."

"Yeah," Jack said, giving up and laughing, "I'll just bet they do! Let's pay the bill and get out of here." Jack laid his wallet on the table next to his plate and stood, reaching for his coat. "Uh oh," he said.

"What's wrong?"

"Too much coffee," Jack grimaced, "Hang tight, I'll me back, I've gotta…"

"…talk to a man about a horse," she finished, "yes, I know."

Cassie rolled her eyes as Jack laughed, making his way to the other end of the restaurant. Sipping her water, she was watching the slow hum of weekday traffic up and down the highway, when she noticed that Jack had left his wallet on the table. The worn leather tri-fold had fallen open to series of plastic covered photographs.

"Cassie Belanger," she chided herself, "don't be a snoop!"

The first picture was of a beautiful woman in her late forties with dark, almost black hair. Her high cheekbones and chiseled feature hinted of Native American ancestry, and she had a slightly mischievous twinkle in her eye common among those who grew older but refused to grow old.

Cassie had a feeling that this was the woman Jack had called on Valentine's Day, *what was her name*?

"Beth," Cassie murmured.

The next shot was an old black and white, creased and dog-eared with age. In it, two boys, maybe ten or twelve years old, clad only in tattered jean cutoffs, stood at the bow of a small fishing boat. Piled high on the deck behind them were mountains of bleach-white oyster shells, and they stood, one with his arm around the other's tanned shoulders, barefoot and grinning on a cloudless summer day. The taller of the two boys had his tongue stuck out at the camera, and a devilish smirk on the other boy's face hinted of the man that Jack would one day be.

Cassie snickered and turned the page. The next photo was a grainy snapshot of a young Jack, late teens or early twenties, wearing fatigues, and hefting a large crate into the open door of a helicopter. Jack was looking at the camera with his familiar grin, his hair cropped close and a pair of aviator sunglasses perched low on his nose. Sweat stained the front of his shirt, and his face and arms were deeply tanned.

Must be the airstrip in Vietnam, she thought.

Cassie glanced up guiltily, scanning to room to make sure that Jack wasn't in sight before turning to the last photo.

Glancing down she froze, her jaw dropping as the blood drained from her face. For just a moment Cassie's vision was filled with small swirling black dots and she was sure she was going to slip from her chair to the floor in a wave of vertigo. Shaking her head, she brought the faded photograph closer to her face. There was no question the young woman in the photo, clad in a sleeveless white wedding dress and holding a small bouquet of wild flowers was a very young Katherine Belanger.

ൟ

With trembling fingers Cassie slipped the picture from its plastic sleeve. It had been torn in half, and only a hand around her mother's waist and a single black dress shoe were left of whoever had stood to her right.

Cassie took a deep hitching lungful of air, realizing that she had been holding her breath. The room seemed to have become very quiet, save for a faraway buzzing in her ears. Her mind spun, how could Jack Leland have this picture, and what did it mean? Suddenly she remembered her dream from the night before, the man standing beneath the street lamp, calling her name.

The man with Jack Leland's face.

Cassie heard the echo of Jack's voice, *"...names are like clothes, different suits for different occasions, that's what I say."*

"Jack?" she whispered. The twisted logic of it actually made frightening sense. He was from the same tiny village as her father or, at least, a very close neighbor. He was alone, the right age, even the drinking...

"I've cleaned up after drunks before."

It all added up, and Cassie felt a wave of nausea sweep over her at the thought that Jack Leland might be the man who had abandoned his wife and baby all those years before.

Quickly she put the photo back in Jack's wallet, fumbling twice with quaking hands before the picture slipped back into its plastic sheath. Cassie laid the wallet on the table and gulped the last of her water, suddenly parched. A moment later she heard Jack's footstep approaching, and stood quickly as he arrived and scooped up his wallet and jacket.

Jack turned to say something and stopped. Cassie's face was deathly pale and her eyes flitted nervously around the room avoiding his gaze.

"Hey," Jack asked, "you okay?"

"Yes!" Cassie replied, somewhat louder than she had meant to. She took a breath and tried again, "Yes, I'm fine...I...I..." her mind spun grasping quickly for something to say. "I thought I saw that truck again...but I was wrong."

Jack studied her face for several seconds, his brow furrowed, then scanned the room, his hand slipping unconsciously into the pocket of his jacket, "You sure?"

"Yeah," Cassie answered, fighting to control her voice, "but... uh...it wasn't him."

"Okay. You ready to roll?"

"Sure," she said, feeling anything but.

They rode in silence for a long while as the sky, which had seemed so bright and clear that morning, gradually clouded over. Dark, ominous, clouds blew in, threatening the rainstorm to come, and the sea turned iron gray, as high tide boiled and crashed ferociously against the beach.

"Storm coming in," Jack murmured.

"Hmm?" Cassie responded, distracted by her own thoughts.

"A storm," Jack repeated, "coming in from the ocean. There's a real humdinger blowing out there somewhere, you can tell by the color, and the way the tide's coming in. She'll always warn you, if you know what to look for."

Late that afternoon, despite Jack's declaration to the contrary, they pulled off Highway 101 and found a burger stand to stop at for lunch. Cassie excused herself almost before the van stopped rolling and hurried to the ladies room where, quickly locking the door behind her, she closed her eyes and, leaning wearily against the tiled wall, began to pray.

"Okay Lord," she whispered, "what am I supposed to do here? I was all ready to find my father and tell him what I thought of him, and now you throw this at me..."

Cassie pounded her fist against the wall, as her temper flared.

"What were you thinking?" she cried angrily, almost surprised at the silence that came in response.

"What am I supposed to say?" she shouted, near tears. "Hey, thanks for the ride, Jack, by the way I'm your daughter?" Cassie stopped, taking a deep, shuddering breath and leaning back against the wall. Arguing with God wasn't going to make the situation any easier.

"*Trust in the Lord with all your heart…*" she murmured, knuckling away tears. But God felt distant, turned away and unlistening, and Cassie felt alone.

Her plan, such as it had been, was out the window and, grabbing a handful of tissues, Cassie decided that she would have to confront Jack before they reached Long Beach. If he *was* William Beckman, they had a lot to talk about; if he wasn't, Cassie wanted his undivided attention while he explained why he had a picture of her dead mother in his wallet.

Taking a deep breath, she washed her face, raked her fingers through her hair, and walked back to the counter to order lunch.

❧

Overwhelmed by her own thoughts, Cassie didn't notice that Jack had become increasingly anxious himself, as the day wore on. Both spoke only the vaguest generalities during the meal, and then quickly resumed their silent drive north. Near dusk, the sky, which had been threatening rain all day, unleashed its fury all at once. In seconds the light drizzle became a roaring downpour, slowing their progress to a crawl, as the windshield wipers fought a brave but losing battle to keep the highway in view.

Traffic was nearly nonexistent as they passed Cannon Beach, Seaside, and finally Astoria, each town looking deserted and desolate in the storm.

They slipped out of Oregon and into Washington, crossing the Columbia River at low tide. Cassie could see long tracks of wet sand glistening under the bridge lights as they passed high above.

Across the wide, shallow mouth of the Columbia, the jagged heads of a thousand rotting pillars can be seen at low tide, pillars that once proudly supported the great wooden docks that stretched far out into the river. Once, steamships and sailing vessels had been emptied and reloaded, bound for Portland or San Francisco or beyond. From the bridge, it's two miles to the old stone tunnel. Cut through the skirt of the coastal mountains, the tunnel had been built for the now defunct railroad. The Ilwaco Railroad & Navigation Company had run the tracks, from the Columbia River's Baker bay to what was, at the time, called Shoalwater Bay. During the oyster boom, the great iron horses had rolled as far as Nahcotta.

The line closed for good nearly a century ago, and now the few remaining rails, the ones left unburied by time, are slowly rusting into oblivion in the salty air. In 1932 the tunnel was widened for auto traffic, and time caught up with Long Beach, as the first cars chugged towards Oysterville.

From there, Pacific Highway leads into Chinook, named for the tribe of Indians that occupied these shores for centuries, fishing and gathering from the river and tide. Long stretches of swampy forest parallel the road leading into Ilwaco, past Ft. Canby, its great iron doors frozen stiff and eaten through with rust, where the mighty guns of World War Two have been removed from their massive concrete bunkers without ever firing a wartime shot.

Past Sea View and Long Beach, past The Loose Caboose restaurant (the best breakfast in Long Beach) and Jack Leland's bookstore, nestled between 6th and 7th avenue. Into Ocean Park, the small hospital on the right, and the new Hill Top Bowl bowling alley on the facing hill. Next is Nahcotta, named in fading memory for the proud Tribal Chief, the highway now called Pacific Avenue turns west onto Sandridge Road, in sight of the Moby Dick Hotel, and heads towards Oysterville. Past the Oysterville store, where the locals, fisherman and artists, cattleman and cooks, have been buying their dry goods and soda pop since the 1920s. On into Oysterville, where Pacific County's First Baptist awaits its daily influx of Nikon-laden tourists. The church, built in 1872, ran regular services until 1930, and was placed, with great local pride, on the national historic register in '76.

Cassie knew none of this and, as Jack Leland's old blue van turned onto Pacific Highway, she had struggled for the last hundred miles to confront the man beside her.

Finally, she spoke up.

"Jack," she said, just loud enough to be heard over the staccato beat of rain on the roof, "I looked at the pictures in your wallet. You…you left it on the table this morning."

There was a long pause as Cassie, who couldn't force herself to look at him, continued to stare out the window at the deluged highway. A very long moment passed before Jack replied, "Did you?" he asked, his voice seeming weak and distant.

"Yes," Cassie said, and began to tremble, "I did. Jack, the picture of the woman in the wedding dress…who is she?"

Jack sighed, and this sound, wrought with concession to the inevitable, brought Cassie's gaze away from the road. Jack's shoulders were slumped and his hands, which had moments before clenched the wheel tightly, hung limp, barely giving enough pressure to maneuver the vehicle.

It seemed to Cassie that his face had taken on a new dimension, neither his sardonic grin, nor his deep, stone-carved scowl, instead, the creases had softened and gone lax as sadness, like gravity, pulled his features earthward.

"I think you're asking me questions that you already know the answer to, kid," Jack responded softly.

A long moment passed before Jack continued.

"But," he sighed, "if your last name isn't Williams, and we both know it's not, then my guess is that Kathy Beckman's your mother."

"Yes she is," Cassie said, then corrected, "she *was*."

Jack drew a quick, ragged breath, and Cassie felt anger begin to stir inside her once more. All the hurtful, spiteful things she had prepared herself to say crept back into her mind.

"Her name was *Belanger*," she said tightly, "not Beckman, and my name is Belanger too. Now tell me," Cassie's teeth were gritted in fury, "why is my mother's picture in your wallet, Jack?"

"Cassie," he said, "there's a lot we need to talk about, and this might not be the best time–"

Cassie interrupted, "No, this *is* the time, Jack, I've been waiting for eighteen years to talk about this–"

Jack rounded a steep shoulder of the highway and dropped onto the long, forested road leading toward Ilwaco. The diffused beams of his headlights barely caught a flash of brown, as the blacktail doe left the safety of the brushy shoulder and leaped into their path.

Cassie's statement was suddenly interrupted as Jack reacted instinctively, jerking the wheel to the left, and barely avoiding a collision with the startled animal. Several factors worked against him all at once. The pitch and grade of the road, and the flood of rainwater stole their traction as all four tires lost contact and the van began to spin, hydroplaning across the wet surface of the highway.

"Hold on!" Jack shouted, struggling to keep the wheel straight and fighting the urge to slam his foot down on the brake.

Cassie clung fearfully to the overhead handle, her seat belt biting into her shoulder. The van spun, its headlights sweeping both sides of the dripping forest before the back tires crossed the gravel shoulder and dropped into a deep ditch. The ride ended abruptly as the rear bumper slammed, with a sickening metallic crunch, into a thick fallen tree that filled the ditch from edge to edge. She shrieked once, as her grip was torn from the handle, flinging her first toward the drivers side of the van and then, just as quickly, whip-lashed back into her own door, banging her elbow and forehead painfully. The van came to a stop, its lights shining high into the tree line on the far side of the road.

Jack and Cassie sat, unspeaking, the suddenness of the accident leaving them numb. The world was filled the purr of the idling engine, the metallic thunder of rain of the roof, and the triphammering beat of their own hearts.

"You okay?" Jack asked finally.

"I think so…are you?"

"I'm fine," Jack let a great gasp of air escape, whistling, through his teeth, "bet I blew both back tires though. Maybe lost the axle too." Cassie stared, dazedly out into the storm, rubbing her forehead were it had bumped the door.

"Well," Jack said, after a moment, "bet you don't see *that* in Arizona very often!"

Cassie giggled despite herself. "Sure we do, but we use coyotes and sand drifts instead."

Jack snickered as he reached behind the seat and pulled out a long flashlight and a wrinkled plastic poncho, which he slipped over his head with a grunt.

"Better go survey the damage," he said, pushing the door open against the wind and pulling the flapping plastic hood down low over his face. He was back in a moment. "Well, it could be worse," he said, wiping rain from his streaming face, "the axle looks okay, but we sure enough lost both tires."

"Do you have spares?"

"Just the one," Jack replied, shaking his head, "but it wouldn't matter if we did have both. There's no way to put them on with the rear end in this ditch, and no way to pull her out without a winch."

"Oh."

"So," Jack said, reaching for the door handle again, "looks like it's hiking time." He tossed her the keys. "I want you to stay here with the van and keep the doors locked; it'll be quicker to walk to Ilwaco than to backtrack to Chinook at this point. If I can't find a tow truck, I'll ride back with Beth and pick you up."

"No way, Jack," Cassie said, shaking her head, "I'm coming with you!"

Jack's grip tightened on the steering wheel as he fought to control his temper.

"That storm's going to get worse before it gets better," he explained. "There's no point both of us getting wet, cold and sick. I know the way, and who to look up when I get there." Jack hopped out onto the shoulder. "That leaves you with the van, okay?"

"But, I–" Cassie began to protest.

"Just do as you're told!" Jack bellowed, slamming the door behind him in anger.

"Don't talk to me like you're my father!" Cassie shouted after him, her face flushing with anger. If Jack heard her he gave no sign as he turned and marched angrily off into the storm.

Chapter Twelve

Fuming, Cassie sat alone in the dark for perhaps a quarter hour, listening to the rain and thinking black thoughts about Jack. Finally, she reached for the door handle.

"You're not my boss!" she yelled, realizing how silly and childish the words sounded even as she shouted them at the walls of the empty van. Then she jumped out into the rain, slipping and sliding up the steep, oozing bank of the ditch and onto the road, coating both hands and knees with thick clinging red mud in the process.

"Dammit!" Cassie shrieked, finally past her own endurance. Wiping her hands savagely on the back of her pants, she started up the road at an angry jog.

Okay, Jack thought, pressing his hand tightly against his arm, *maybe I really did hurt myself.*

When he'd first stormed away from the van, the shock of the accident and his anger with Cassie had blanketed the pain in his side, which had taken a pretty heavy blow against the driver's door. Now though, it was a hot, spiking needle, shooting through his shoulder and down his arm with each jolting step.

"Breaking my arm," Jack grimaced, "would just make this the end of a perfect day." Then he gasped as another pain knifed through his shoulder.

Another mile up the highway, Jack knew, lay the outskirts of Ilwaco. A few miles past that was his shop and apartment, where he was sure Beth would be sitting up reading, waiting for him to pull up. Jack hoped that she had driven her shiny new Jeep instead of walking, as she often did in fair weather. The locals would have known this storm was coming for days, so the chances were good that she'd be prepared.

Rain and wind slammed into him, and Jack winced as the pain increased and his neck began to ache as well, he slowed his pace as he realized that he was dripping with perspiration. The pain in his arm grew more intense, and Jack lurched to the side of the road as another attack of nausea overwhelmed him.

"Oh no," he murmured, suddenly afraid, "Oh no…"

Then the pain came again, this time like a giant fist clamped tight around his sternum, squeezing his heart. Jack felt his knees buckle as he pitched forward, both hands to his chest, into the ditch, his face tearing a furrow through the mud and gravel and he slid down into the rushing drainage. By chance, he rolled onto his back before splashing to a halt, the change of position saving him from drowning in a six-inch river of muddy water.

He lay, paralyzed by the agony in his chest, his world reduced to a burning, exhausting effort for each constricted breath, the pain ebbing and flowing as his body convulsed uncontrollably. Frigid water rushed past his ears and he blinked as the fading twilight became unnaturally black.

As his eyes slipped shut, Jack felt himself drifting away.

ꟹ

Cassie had jogged until she was gasping for breath, stopping only to bend over and stretch out the stitch in her side.

For an old guy, she thought, *Jack could really cover some ground when he wanted to!*

She had left the van far behind, and was about halfway across a long flat stretch of dark road. As her eyes grew accustomed to the gloom, Cassie could make out about another quarter mile of straightaway before the road jogged to the left.

Jack must have *really* covered some ground, Cassie realized, too much ground. She had jogged and ran most of the way from the van, and Jack had only been walking when he left. She should have caught him by now, maybe even passed him up.

Passed him up?

Cassie felt the cold, copper taste of fear glaze her throat, as she turned to look back the way she had come. *Could she have missed him in the dark?* Unlikely. He could have stepped off the road into the trees to…to talk to a man about a horse, she supposed, but if not, then what? If he had fallen, surely she would have seen him. Hesitantly, Cassie began retracing her steps.

After a hundred yards in the downpour, she began to pray.

Another hundred yards and she heard a muffled cough ahead in the darkness.

Suddenly Cassie remembered that she was alone in the woods at night, and she got scared. The rain was easing and she listened intently for any other noise, but heard nothing.

Slipping a hand into her pocket, Cassie wrapped her fist around the cool weight of the buck knife, and continued to pray as she crept up on the side of the road. At last, the bottom of the ditch came into view and Cassie lost all thoughts of fear.

"You have to go down and get him, Cass," she whispers, "show him the way to get out..."

"Jack!" Cassie screamed, "Jack..." Flinging herself down into the gully, she slid to a stop at his side. His mud-splattered face was so pale and cold that Cassie was sure he was dead and her stomach cramped in fear.

"May the day of my birth perish..."

As she lifted his head from the clutching mud, she whispered another prayer. "Oh God," she wept, "please, please don't take him away from me, I just...I just found him..."

As if in answer, Jack coughed weakly. His unfocused eyes fluttered open, darting from side to side, and coming to rest at last, on her.

"Katie?" he mumbled thickly, his eyes widening. "Katie?"

Cassie began to sob as she realized that he was seeing her mother. "Jack..." she murmured.

"I'm sorry, Katie," Jack mumbled, shaking his head, "so sorry...all my fault..."

"Jack," Cassie whispered, wiping blood and dirt from his face, "don't talk, you'll be okay. Just lay quiet..."

"...she's so beautiful, Katie," Jack's shoulders shook lightly as he began to weep, "just like you, beautiful, and so smart..." Jack slumped back for a moment, then arched again, his fevered eyes blazing.

"Bill didn't deserve her," he murmured, and Cassie could barely understand the words. "He didn't deserve you..."

Jack's voice cracked and his body shuddered as another white-hot bolt of pain tore through his chest. He gazed up at Cassie through the rain, his eyes unfocused and distant. When he spoke again his voice was much weaker, fading even as his eyelids began to droop.

"I wish," he whispered, his voice thick, "I wish she was mine, I wish...I wish she was ours…"

"…so sorry…" and then his eyes were shut.

Cassie wept over Jack, his face muddied, and bloodied, and twisted with pain, crying out in his delirium to a woman who was, so recently, dead and cold in her grave.

The bright glare of headlights swept over them as someone came to a screeching halt on the road above. Cassie stuffed her soaked jacket beneath Jack's head to keep his face out of the water, and clambered up to the side of the road, drawing a breath to cry for help.

Suddenly, the words froze in her throat as the driver's door of the black Toyota pickup opened, the dark, tinted windows impossible to see through in the twilight. Then, just as suddenly, Cassie's fear turned to rage as some line, deep within her, was finally crossed. Her lips drew back; teeth bared in fury as she reached into her pocket and pulled out her knife, taking a step toward the truck, waiting for the stench of stale cigarette smoke to reach her. Her knuckles turned white around the wood grain handle, as she raised the blade.

"Cassie?" a voice questioned from the dark.

She stopped and blinked. She knew that voice! *Where did she know that voice from?*

"Cassie?" the voice repeated. "What in the world are you doing? Put that knife away!"

Guy! That was Pastor Guy's voice! Cassie was sure that her mind had finally snapped under the strain, as the tall, lean form of Guy Williams stepped around the front of the truck and into the headlights.

"What…" she stammered, "What are you…"

"Later," he said, looking past her, into the ditch. "Let's get him out of there and to a hospital." Cassie followed Guy back down into the gully as the storm let loose once more with sheet after sheet of driving rain.

Jack felt himself lifted and carried, his legs dragging on the ground behind him, up the embankment and onto the road. Finally, he managed to open his eyes, and could barely make out Cassie on his right. His vision blurred, and he couldn't see who was on his left; a man, he was sure by the feel of hard sinewy muscle beneath the arm of his jacket.

The blackness at the edges of his vision expanded, and then slowly became a burning white light, growing in brightness and intensity until he had to blink and raise a hand…

Chapter Thirteen

Long Beach, Washington
August, 1980

...to shield his eyes from the bright summer sun, as he stepped from the rumbling Greyhound bus and onto the busy sidewalk.

August in Long Beach, and the tourist season was in full swing. Jack Leland held his faded duffel bag close as he jostled his way through the crowd. Brightly colored balloons, flags, and kites hung from the storefronts, and the hot summer air was thick with the smell of caramel corn and hotdogs. Sunburned moms grimly drug sand-encrusted youngsters away from the candy shops and towards the public rest rooms.

Jack grinned; so much had changed since he was a boy. The sleepy little coastal village with its one gas station and two hotels was long gone, plowed under and rebuilt by a wave of summer money flowing west from Seattle. Someone had written him that the oyster cannery had finally shut down, and that, he supposed, was a harbinger of the final breath for industry on the peninsula. Now, it appeared, the boom in Ocean Park and Long Beach centered on art galleries and ice-cream shops.

Stepping into the shade of a candy-striped awning, Jack set his bag down on the sidewalk between his feet. Two pair of underwear, a small toiletries bag, jeans, his college diploma and his Bible; all of his earthly possessions, were packed inside.

Just turned thirty-one, with three hundred dollars in his pocket and the hope of a job at Long Beach Community Church, Jack paused to breathe the salty air of his hometown for the first time in seven years.

"Jackie!" a rough voice bellowed from across the street, "Hey Jackie! Over here!"

Bill Beckman was, if anything, leaner and darker than when Jack had last seen him. A faded tank top, stuffed into an even more faded pair of blue jeans, displayed Bill's bony shoulders and long wiry arms, tanned nut-brown. He was grinning, wide white teeth gleaming from a narrow face framed in shoulder-length dark hair. One arm was raised; waving in Jack's direction, while the other lay draped, casually but possessively, across the shoulder of a beautiful young woman in a faded flower print dress. Jack wracked his brain for a moment, having suddenly forgotten the name of his friend's young bride.

"Katherine..." he whispered suddenly, remembering, "Kathy..."

Then Bill was across the street and had those long wiry arms wrapped around Jack, lifting him from the ground in a spine popping bear hug.

"Okay, okay..." Jack gasped, laughing and wincing at the same time, "let me down...let me down!"

Bill dropped him, grinning, and offered a hand, which Jack shook.

"It's about time you got here; the tourists were starting to get to me..."

Bill sneered, glancing around him with a grimace of hard-pressed toleration. Jack looked to the young lady, and then back to Bill.

"Well?" he asked.

There was a pause as Bill glanced from Kathy to Jack questioningly, his grin starting to fade.

"Well, what?" he replied finally.

Jack shook his head and brushed past his old friend, extending his hand to Kathy.

"I see he still has all the manners of a stray dog," Jack laughed, "I'm Jack Leland, you must be Katherine, it's a pleasure to meet you."

The young woman grinned, her face lighting up like the sun, giving her husband a poke in the ribs.

"Yeah," she said, "we work on that! Nice to meet you Jack."

"Great," Bill said with a snort. "Just what she needs, reinforcements!"

The three laughed as Jack picked up his duffel and hoisted it onto his shoulder.

"Well," said Bill, "unless one of you has a hankering for some cotton candy, why don't we get the heck outta here!"

"Lead on!" Jack replied with a mock salute.

☙❧

Bill and Katherine Beckman lived in a rambling farmhouse far out Sandridge Road between Nahcotta and Oysterville. The house, better than a century old, had belonged to Jonathan Beckman, Bill's father, and to his father before him, who had built his home on a small rise facing Willapa Bay. Cancer had taken Florence Beckman while Bill was still in junior high school, and had finally come calling for her husband as well. By the time that Jack's own parents had lost their lives to fire, John Beckman was already a year into his long sleep beneath the pines at the Oysterville Cemetery.

At twenty years old, after securing a loan from the bank to buy his sister's half of their inheritance, Bill had found himself the sole owner and operator of the third largest private oyster farm on the Peninsula.

To Jack, the house looked much the same as it had when he and Bill had shot marbles across the wide front porch as boys. The tall, windswept oak in the front yard, from which Bill had once fallen and broken his ankle, still cast its protective shadow over the northern side of the house. The grounds, which John Beckman had kept scrupulously tidy did, in truth, look a bit seedier than Jack remembered. The weeds grew knee-high in places, and had enveloped the lower half of a rusting 1968 Camero that had found its rest in a far corner of the front yard.

The boat shed, which had stood behind the house at the end of the long gravel drive, had been torn down. The weathered lumber that had once housed the senior Beckman's trio of oyster boats, now lay in haphazard stacks amid the tall grass. As for the boats themselves, they were nowhere to be seen.

Inside the house, though, was just as Jack remembered, every stick of furniture stood exactly as it had two decades before. Both couches in the living room and the love seat in the den were covered with dark green blankets now, cloaking the wear of two lifetimes.

And it was in the sizable Beckman dining room that the three of them sat down to dinner. Fresh baked oyster pie, peas, and a green salad were served on Florence Beckman's blue willowware china and, as Jack dug in, he suddenly remembered that he had never been allowed to eat from these plates before. He, Bill, and Bill's younger sister, whom they called *The Snipe* when Mrs. Beckman was out of earshot, ate their meals from brightly colored plastic plates, bought at a nickel apiece from Jack's Market in Sea View.

After complimenting Kathy on the dinner, which was actually very good, Jack turned to Bill.

"So, tell me what I've missed," he said, "where's *The Snipe*?"

Bill chuckled around a mouthful of salad as Kathy rolled her eyes. "I think it's terrible that you two called her that!" she rebuked them.

"Hey," said Bill, "you're not the one who had to put up with her tagging along everywhere after you!"

"I'm telling Momma, I'm telling Momma..." Jack mimicked in a high singsong voice, and Bill laughed until he choked.

"Well," said Kathy haughtily, "I'm sure you gave her every reason to act like that! I know what older brothers are like!"

A shadow seemed to fall over the table and both Kathy and Bill became silent and stared down at their plates. Jack looked at his own meal for a moment, his gut twisting a little as he asked, "'Nam?"

"Yeah," Bill whispered.

Kathy said nothing, and Bill reached across the table and took her hand.

Then, as suddenly as the cloud had descended, it lifted, and Kathy, her eyes shining with unshed tears, looked up and smiled.

"So," she said to Jack, "Bill tells me you're a card player?"

Jack laughed at this. "If you mean that we played poker and he took all my money, then I guess so!"

"Well, let me get these dishes cleared away and maybe we can play some cards."

"Sounds good to me."

"Anyway," said Bill, "to answer your question, The Snipe..."

"*Curse her hide*!" both men intoned together, a quip picked up from the venerable Gary Cooper in an old western they had seen at the Bijou, and had immediately bestowed on Bill's less-than-welcome sibling. They roared with laughter, as Kathy shook her head, smiling in spite of herself.

"*The Snipe*," Bill continued, wiping his eyes, "is another man's torment now. She graduated high school a few years back, and started taking classes at Seattle community to be a teacher." Bill shook his head. "Instead, she fell head over heels for some flatlander upperclassman and *BAM*, they're married and moved back to Pittsburgh–"

"–Chicago..." Kathy corrected with a smile.

"Same difference," her husband replied, distastefully, "anyhow she was happy enough to get out of here. We get Christmas and birthday cards, and a phone call every month or so. Kathy talks to her more than me."

"Can you blame her?" Jack laughed, ducking the napkin that Bill threw in his direction. Kathy was laughing too, and Jack felt the mood lighten a little more.

Later, as Kathy was packing away the leftovers, Bill and Jack stood in the cool breeze of the porch. Bill produced a shiny Zippo lighter, lit the end of a small cigar and, puffing on his White Owl, he filled Jack in on the rest of the story.

"Anyway," Bill said, "I guess the two of them were pretty close, growing up."

"Oh, yeah?" replied Jack, leaning against the far rail trying to avoid the advancing gray-green cloud of cigar smoke.

"Yup. Parents got killed in a car accident with she was about eight, her brother maybe fourteen." Bill closed the lighter with a metallic *snick*. "They lived with one set of relatives and then another, getting shipped from here to there until Bobby turned twenty-one and joined the marines. From the time their folks died, he did most of the work raising her, then they ship him off to the war and his camp gets shelled his second night he's there. Four guys lived, out of the forty that were stationed there." Bill leaned forward and spit over the porch rail in disgust. "Four…Geez!"

Jack shook his head, looking out over the peaceful sunset and shadows of the bay. Beneath the whisper of the wind in the long grass, he could hear the screams of wounded boys being dragged from smoking, bullet-ridden helicopters. His nose twitched, remembering the cloying, overripe smell of the jungle, the chemical fires and acrid taste of gunpowder.

He closed his eyes for a moment; drawing a deep, welcome breath of the salt-sea air. Bill was watching him, his head cocked to one side, the cheap, machine-rolled cigar hanging from his lip.

"You see a lot of that?" he asked.

"Enough," Jack replied, watching a heron sweep low over the darkening bay. "More than enough."

"I'd have been there ya know," Bill muttered, his eyes downcast. "If they'd have let me go, I'd have been right there with ya."

Jack suddenly remembered the day, dark cool and overcast, that he and Bill had marched into the recruitment office together to enlist. Three weeks later, Jack was on a military plane to Mississippi and Bill was alone at his father's kitchen table with a 4-F letter in front of him. A two-inch steel pin in his right ankle had kept him far away from the horror in Southeast Asia.

"I know that, Billy," Jack said softly, reverting to his best friend's childhood name. "You know that I know that."

Bill pulled a flask from his hip pocket, still staring at the weathered boards beneath his feet. After taking a long draw he looked up and offered it to Jack. "Whiskey?"

"Nah," Jack shook his head, "gave it up when I started at Clear Creek, I guess I'm off it for good now."

"Oh yeah," Bill grinned, "I almost forgot, you're a full-blown preacher!"

"Hopefully, I'm a preacher," Jack replied. "Karl Ferguson hasn't promised me the assistant pastor's job at Long Beach Community. In fact, I should be bedding down before it gets too late; I have an interview with him at nine."

"You'll get the job," Bill nodded, flipping his cigar butt into a rusty coffee can at the foot of the steps. "Me and Kathy'll be there next Sunday, too," he said. "We've been going to the Baptist church here in town, but it's a little slow for us. I hear your church has a hot little band going."

"It's not my church yet," Jack laughed. "In fact, it won't be *my* church even if I do get the job. I'm just the assistant pastor, that means I preach twice a year and sweep twice a week. But now, I sure didn't figure you for church..."

"Oh sure," Bill grinned, "Kathy won't miss a week, and I'm right there with her. I got baptized and everything! As long as they don't ask me to pick up snakes or wash someone's feet, I guess there are worse ways to spend your Sunday mornings."

Jack took a long look at his old friend, concerned with the glib reply and lack of sincerity.

"Well," he said, "we'll have to sit down and talk about that sometime."

"Yeah, I s'pose we will," laughed Bill, taking another long slug from his flask before stowing it back in his pocket of his jeans.

"Hey," he whispered, "don't mention the hooch to Kathy, will ya? She has this thing about drinking, and you don't want to get her started."

"Bill..." Jack began to protest.

"Ah, just a little secret," Bill said, flinging his arm across Jack's shoulders and steering him back into the house, "let's go play some cards, Kathy's getting pretty good. Keep an eye on her, though, she's a bluffer!"

Jack let the subject of Bill's drinking pass, deciding that if asked, he would tell the truth, but he wouldn't volunteer any information until then. Somewhere in the back of his mind, a soft, guilty voice sang to him about compromise.

Kathy Beckman turned out to be a better card player than Bill had let on, and Jack wondered, briefly, if he was being had. Bill however, played as fast and wild as he had when they were kids. Every nickel that Jack lost to Kathy, he seemed to win back from her husband. Finally, Jack had his original stack of change in front of him, Kathy had a stack twice that size, and Bill's hands rested on an empty patch of table where his money had sat two hours before.

Just before midnight, Jack crawled into the old feather bed in the Beckman guestroom. He read his Bible until he couldn't keep the fine print from blurring on the page, then with a quick but heartfelt prayer for the morning, he fell asleep.

ờ๑ờ

Eight and a half hours later Jack was yawning and rubbing his eyes as he walked out of the coffee shop and down the street to the front door of the Long Beach Community Church.

A sandblasted wooded sign hung above the front lawn of the church, proudly displaying its name, Pastor Karl Ferguson's name, and the proclamation that LBCC was *A Spirit Filled Fellowship.* Jack smiled at this.

If the sign didn't give it away, the sound of amplified guitars and drums pouring out the open windows, every Sunday morning, would have made it clear to anyone passing within a block (or two) of the building.

Karl Ferguson shook Jack's hand with a wide grin and a twinkle in his eyes. It was no surprise to anyone that Pastor Ferguson had been elected to wear the Santa suit in the Christmas parade every year for the last decade. The vivid sky blue of his eyes did little to draw the on-lookers attention away from a large bulbous nose, bushy beard, and the unruly shock of white hair that framed both sides of his shiny, bald head. At sixty-one, a lifetime of sea winds and smiles had etched deep lines into his face, and the stocky, athletic build he had sported as a young soldier had softened and spread over the years. He still walked with the limp caused by German rifle fire on the beach at Normandy in June of 1944. World War II had lasted only a month for Karl Ferguson, but his eighteen hours on the French sands of Omaha Beach would be carried with him, like with the shrapnel in his knee, for the rest of his life.

The two men sat at the Pastor's worn, pinewood desk and covered the preliminaries over cups of strong black tea.

Jack told about his youth, growing up on the peninsula and working with his boyhood friends at the Beckman Oyster Farm.

Jack's mug was refilled from a steaming copper pot as he spoke briefly about his time in Vietnam, and finding God as a lonely, frightened soldier.

Karl Ferguson listened closely, interrupted occasionally, and nodded often and knowingly. Jack talked about his years at Bible College, covering the basics: grades, classes and the like. This led to a brief review of his year as a missionary in Africa, which led back to Long Beach.

After twenty minutes Jack ran out of words, having covered his personal biography from birth to their present meeting in less than half an hour.

The moment of silence stretched into two as Karl poured himself a second cup of tea and settled his girth back into his groaning chair. Blue eyes studied Jack from beneath an explosion of bushy white eyebrows, as the older man stirred his tea and formed the only question he would ask his applicant.

"Tell me, Jack," he asked finally, setting his cup down, "what is God's will for your life?"

Jack paused, taken aback by the directness of the question. *God's will for his life?* He had expected to be asked about his education, his philosophy of ministry, maybe even why he felt called to Long Beach Community Church. But, *God's will for his life?* How could he communicate that, did he even know the answer? Suddenly Jack realized that he was speaking, the words pouring out almost unconsciously.

"I know that God wants me to teach," he said, starting slowly and gaining speed. "I know that he has given me such a heart to teach others, and that even if I wasn't a Christian, I would still be teaching somebody somewhere, something. I think that many people have serious questions, fair questions about why the world is the way it is, and how God fits into it–"

"–And do you feel that you have answers to those questions?" Karl interrupted, leaning forward intently.

"No, not me," Jack smiled, relaxing a bit, "but I know where the answers are."

He reached forward and tapped the Bible that lay on the corner of Karl Ferguson's desk. "I've learned a little about how to find those answers, and how to teach other folks to find them for themselves. I guess that's God's calling on my life, to point people to where they can find the answers."

Another long silence filled the air as Karl lifted his cup to his lips and took a sip of the steaming liquid, a strangely dainty gesture for a man of his size.

"Well," he said at last, standing and extending his hand, "I don't think I can ask for a better answer than that. Let me show you your office…"

As quickly as that, Jack Leland became the Assistant Pastor of the Long Beach Community Church, *A Spirit Filled Fellowship*.

Chapter Fourteen

A week later, as the two men met for breakfast at The Loose Caboose Café, an old train-car turned restaurant, Jack raised the question he had been mulling over since returning to his hometown.

"Okay boss," he said, setting down his fork and taking a long sip from a heavy cup of coffee, "what do you think the chances of a revival in Long Beach are?" Karl snorted, choking on a mouthful of egg before wiping his mouth with his napkin and eyeing his young assistant.

"Bored, are we?" he asked.

"Seriously," Jack replied, "what do you think?"

"Well, first off," Karl said, "let me say that if God wants a revival in Long Beach, I'm all for it. I don't think it's beyond Christ's ability to sweep this town."

"But?" Jack asked.

Karl sighed. "Let me tell you a story, Jack. You grew up around here, so stop me if you've heard it."

Jack nodded.

"The first church in the area," Karl began, "out in Oysterville, opened its doors back in the middle eighteen hundreds. It's still there in fact." Jack nodded.

"Oysterville was a boomtown back then, oysters being almost worth their weight in gold. It was the second richest city on the West Coast, besides San Francisco, and most of the doors on the waterfront opened into alehouses.

The oystermen were a crusty group of sailors, here to make their fortunes on the bay. Working and drinking were their life."

Karl paused to nod at a passing waitress, who smiled and refilled his cup.

"The story goes that the day the church opened its doors for business, the whole kit and caboodle of tavern patrons got up and walked down Weather Beach Road and into the sanctuary. They each placed a single gold coin in the collection box. Then, without a word, they all walked back to the waterfront and got back to drinking. They never darkened the door of the church again."

Jack chuckled, nodding his head, "And the point?"

"The point," Karl replied, shaking his spoon in Jack's direction, "is that a lot of that attitude has hung on here over the years. They were making a statement. Organized religion was fine by them, as long as no one expected them to participate. A lot of folks still feel that way."

"So we just give in to that?"

"Not a matter of giving in or standing up," Karl said, picking up his fork again, "it's a fight we don't want to be a part of. Folks around here, especially nonchurch folks, are a stubborn and loyal lot. If they feel like you're gunning for them as a group, they're going to lock arms."

"Really?" Jack asked, sounding dubious.

"Really," Karl said. "Besides, revivals are overrated. I've seen my share of them and, often as not, they're all powder and no lead, a lot of emotion bandied around, under the big top. A night or two of that and then everyone goes back to the same old, same old."

"So what do we do?"

"Well, again," Karl said, "if God *wants* a revival in Long Beach, we're going to do as we're told. However, until he makes that clear, I think that personal relationship is the key. One heart at a time, saved, fed, discipled, and then turned loose. That one heart goes out and reproduces itself, and so on, and there's your *real* revival!"

"And we don't even have to rent a tent," Jack smirked.

"Exactly!" Karl said, laughing as he dug back into his breakfast.

❧

That first month was a blur, meeting the elders and the congregation, answering the same questions over, and over. Some of the older members of the church had known Jack's parents, and insisted that he come over for dinner. He didn't buy many groceries those first few weeks, spending most evenings seated around a table full of strangers, talking about Bible college, the war, the mission field, and what God wanted done in Long Beach.

It seemed to Jack that just about everyone in the church had a firm grasp on what God wanted done in Long Beach, and there were as many different destinies for the little town as there were dinner tables in the congregation. Jack learned to smile and nod, and then quickly reinforce the importance of prayer, and listening, and waiting on the Lord. Some of the families were happy with this answer, or if not happy, at least appeased; some were not.

Regardless of their response to his response, Jack felt sure that Pastor Ferguson got a full report from each.

He knew this, in fact, because many of the urgently phoned in reports became the highlight of Karl and Jack's morning doughnut break at the Coffee Clutch, the tiny coffee shop across the street from the church, or the Caboose, if the two were feeling peckish. Over tea and coffee, respectively, they would chuckle at Jack's observations of his hosts and theirs of him.

Mrs. Feldman, a matronly widow from the front pew, was horrified that Jack would eat Tom Pritchner's deviled eggs, everyone knowing that no *TRUE* Christian would touch Deviled eggs, deviled ham, or devil's food cake, and that Tom Pritchner, if not actually in cahoots with Satan himself, was most assuredly well down the path to becoming so. The Mack family, retired missionaries in their seventies, thought that Jack was wonderful but were quite upset with the rumor that he was often seen in the church building wearing jeans. While the Elders Mr. and Mrs. Peterson were concerned that their seventeen-year-old daughter, Aimee, had asked every night this week as to when the assistant pastor would be invited back. Jack, admittedly, found this last tidbit a little less humorous than did his pastor.

Karl had laughed until tears rolled down his ruddy cheeks, his santa-esque frame quaking with mirth as he told Jack the story over his apple fritter one morning in September.

Still, most of the sixty-one members of the church had found the young pastor to be, if not ideal, at least acceptable and soon Jack's schedule began to settle down and he found himself cooking his own dinners once more.

One of the first lessons that he learned was how his new pastor and mentor viewed the ministry. Besides the doe-eyed Aimee Peterson, there were almost a dozen youth in their mid to late teens who attended LBCC regularly.

Jack had gone to his boss, concerned that it was time to find a youth leader for a weekly Bible study with the teens. Pastor Ferguson had thought this was a wonderful idea, clapping a heavy hand warmly on Jack's shoulder and asking him what night he would want to use the church for his new ministry. Jack had tried to backpedal, but it was too late.

Karl Ferguson was a firm believer that preachers *preached* and *God* raised up ministers, if ministries were required.

"I'll ask you what I've asked every ministry leader here since the day I signed on as pastor." Karl laughed. "As it sounds like you have a heart for this ministry, when are you going to start it?"

The Long Beach Community Church youth group held its first study night on Wednesday, September 17th, Assistant Pastor Jack Leland presiding.

That first meeting took place in the basement of the church, Jack having spent the last week begging funds from the stewardship council for two dozen folding chairs and enough carpet scraps from the local hardware store to cover the cracked concrete floor. He was pleased with the turnout, eight young people, ranging from the thirteen-year-old Randy Brooks with his flaming red hair and braying, donkey laugh, to the ever-present Aimee Peterson who, at seventeen, was the oldest teen present. After an hour of teaching and discussion (Jack had chosen John's encouragements to Timothy as his subject for the evening), they had hiked the six blocks to the beach for a marshmallow roast that Bill and Kathy had set up.

The Beckmans, at Jack's request, made sure that they were seated to his left and right as they all sat around the fire telling corny jokes and singing camp songs. Jack, casting an occasional nervous eye towards young Miss Peterson, was relieved to have a buffer between him and his admirer. He was even more relieved when the Petersons' station wagon pulled up to the church an hour later to take Aimee home.

"Don't get me wrong," Jack had said, as he, Bill, and Kathy folded chairs and swept the new youth room, "she's a nice kid, and I think she's fairly serious about her relationship with God, it's...it's just..."

"It's just," Bill smirked, dropping the last of the chairs on the pile, "that she's like one of those paintings where the eyes follow you wherever you go."

"That's it exactly!" Jack cried, pointing a finger at Bill.

"You two are terrible," Kathy admonished, shaking her head. "Aimee Peterson is a sweet, intelligent girl, who loves the Lord and just so happens, for reasons I can't imagine, to have a hopeless crush on her skinny new youth pastor!"

"Ouch," Jack laughed, clutching his chest as though shot. "I think I have offended!"

"Hey, better you than me," Bill quipped, and Jack thought he saw a look of irritation pass momentarily across Kathy Beckman's face, before she shook her head and started up the basement steps.

"You two goofs can finish cleaning up," she called back, "I'm going to make sure all the lights are off."

Bill had been as good as his word; he and Kathy had attended every

Sunday since August, though it was obvious from the first that Kathy was much more enthusiastic about their weekly fellowship than her husband was.

If Bill had sung out loud or raised his hands during prayer or worship, Jack had yet to see it. Still, he got up every week, put on his best jeans and shirt, and warmed the pew next to his wife without fail. If his devotion wasn't all it could be, Jack thought, at least he was being exposed to the right stuff; seeds were being planted, to put it in the *Christianese*.

Jack had mentioned to them, over a plate full of spaghetti in the Beckman dining room, how his conversation with Pastor Ferguson, regarding a youth group, had gone. He had left the conversation hanging and held his breath waiting for their response.

"Well," Kathy had said, sipping from her water glass, "be sure to let Bill and I know if you need any help."

Jack had tried his best to adopt his pastor's philosophy as it related to ministries. Still, the prospect of starting a youth group, along with his other duties as assistant pastor, were daunting to say the least, and Kathy's response was close enough to leave him guilt free.

"Great," he had replied quickly, setting down his fork, "since you mentioned it…"

Bill groaned, having heard the clang of the trap shutting even as his young wife had volunteered their services.

"Lord, Katie…" he said, "you didn't see that coming?"

"See what coming?" Kathy asked, her eyes narrowing as she glanced back and forth between Jack and her husband.

"Now hang on," Jack had stammered, casting a dirty look in Bill's direction. "I was just thinking that I could use some help setting up the activities, and it might be nice for the girls to have someone of their own gender to talk to, since I don't have a wife…"

"Well," Bill said with an evil chuckle, "I hear the Peterson girl would be more that happy–"

"Hush!" Kathy launched a wooden salad spoon across the table, which Bill dodged.

"I think that's a smart idea," she told Jack, "I just hope I can answer their questions."

Since that night, Kathy and, more reluctantly, Bill, had helped him scout around for the chairs and carpeting, make space in the dusty church basement, and finally, set up the campfire on the beach.

Bill and his truck had been a Godsend in all of this, but Jack had grown more and more concerned about his friend over last several weeks. As Kathy disappeared upstairs and Jack heard the door close behind her, he turned to Bill.

"What was that about?" he asked.

Bill glanced up sheepishly and then returned his gaze to the broom in his hands. "Aw, nothing," he muttered, "we had a little tiff earlier and I guess she still ain't happy with me."

"Anything that's any of my business?" Jack asked.

"Nope," Bill replied, looking up and grinning, "but I'll tell you anyway."

Jack pulled two folding chairs back off the stack, handing one to Bill, as his friend went on. "First of all," he said, "it's all your fault, and I hope you feel bad!"

Jack laughed, settling himself into his own chair. "Go ahead man, don't hold back."

"Hang on a second," Bill raised his hands defensively, "this isn't a counseling session is it?"

"Nope," Jack said, "counseling sessions are done in the office only, specifically, in Pastor Ferguson's office only. I'm just the *assistant* pastor. Down here, with me, it's just yakking."

"Good," Bill replied, a little sourly, "though Katie would be just as happy as a clam if she thought I was getting counseling, the way she keeps jawing about it!"

Jack stayed silent, nodding for Bill to go on.

"Well, like I said," he sighed heavily, "it's your fault. Back when we were just going to church every Sunday, she seemed happy enough that I was there with her, and let it go at that. Now though," he muttered, "we're in *ministry*, and everything's different!" Bill was clenching and unclenching his fists, as his face began to flush.

Jack could see the man was working himself up, and allowed a momentary pause before probing.

"What's everything?"

"Me!" Bill growled. "I'm everything! No drinking, no cigars, no cussing, I'm a whole net full of bad influences on the poor innocent little church kids!"

This time the pause stretched to an uncomfortable length as Jack struggled with an answer. In his heart, he knew that he agreed with Kathy; if Bill was going to be involved in ministry, he needed to live a lifestyle that was a good witness to the teens. His witness had to be real, born out of the overflow of

Christ's love in him.

At the same time, Jack knew Bill, and if there was one thing that would turn the man to stone, impenetrable and unmovable, it was a sense that he was being ganged up on.

Jack remembered Bill's own mother used to say that if you paint a Beckman into a corner, he's likely to go through the roof. This was a fact for Jonathan Beckman and it was just as much a fact for his son. Jack knew he had to step carefully if he wanted to make Bill hear the truth.

The decision between ministering Christ to the youth of Long Beach, and protecting the feelings of his oldest friends, was a brutally short battle. The fact was, Bill wasn't going to like the truth no matter how Jack coated it and, in the end, the kids had to come first.

"Look Billy–" Jack started, pausing as Bill muttered a curse. "What was *that* for?"

"The only time you call me Billy is when you know you're about to make me mad…" Bill replied, crossing his arms.

"Fine, *Bill,*" Jack continued, trying to keep his cool, "no one expects you to be perfect, certainly not me. I'm a long way from perfect and you and I both know it."

"But?"

"But," Jack took another deep breath, "there are some things you need to work on, just like all of us, and the Bible is clear on how a leader is supposed to act."

"*The Bible…*" Bill snorted again, rolling his eyes.

"Yes!" Jack snapped, his own voice starting to rise. "The Bible! What do you think we're doing here, Bill? This isn't a game; we're trying to make a difference for these kids; we're trying to help them form a relationship with Christ!" Jack was speaking through clenched teeth now.

"This isn't a glee club," Jack said, jabbing a finger in Bill's direction, "this is serious. These kids need role models, and I'd prefer that their role models not show up smelling like Kentucky Bourbon!"

Jack stopped, as angry with himself for losing his temper, as he was with Bill's attitude. Locking eyes with his old friend, he could see the vein beneath Bill's left eye pulsing as his face reddened with anger. Bill stood slowly to his feet, and Jack did the same.

"Okay," Bill replied softly, his jaw clenched, "I won't show up again, problem solved."

With that, William Beckman walked across the room, up the stairs and out of the church. A moment later Jack heard his friend's truck roar to life and peel away in a clattering rain of gravel. Jack sighed, folding the two chairs back up and tossing them on the pile.

Boy did I blow that one! he thought.

Whatever Bill had needed to hear from him, he was pretty sure that wasn't it. Jack climbed the stairs, one heavy foot at a time, and switched off the basement light. Kathy was waiting in the hallway as he closed the door behind him.

"Where's Bill?" she asked, slinging her purse over her shoulder.

"My guess would be about halfway home by now," Jack said.

"What?"

"It looks like whatever disagreement you two had earlier, he and I just finished, sorry." Jack leaned against the whitewashed wall, closing his eyes.

"That doesn't sound good."

"It wasn't," he sighed, "Kathy, I feel like I'm betraying my best friend here, but keeping his secret isn't going to do him any favors. You know that he's been drinking?"

"Yes," Kathy replied, her shoulders slumping.

"A lot?"

"Yes, at least, I suspected."

"...and you understand," Jack went on, "why I can't have that in the youth group, around the kids?"

"Of course," she replied, her voice quavering, "that's what we were arguing about earlier. I think he used to be more careful about when and where he was drinking, and I believed him when he said he had quit. Now he comes staggering home and I can smell it on him before he's through the door."

Kathy paused, as tears started down her cheeks, and Jack struggled to think of what to say, what to do for his friend.

Suddenly, Kathy was in his arms, weeping into his shoulder.

"Jack," she cried, "I love him so much and I don't know what to do. Everything I say is wrong, I try to encourage him and end up making him more defensive!"

Jack patted her shoulder awkwardly, trying to think how to free himself from her embrace without hurting her worse.

"It's going to be okay," he murmured, "he'll cool off, let's go find him and–"

Neither of them had heard the truck pull up. As the front door swung open, bathing the half lit hallway in the amber light of the street lamp, Jack looked up to see Bill frozen in the doorway, his hand still clutching the latch.

Jack felt Kathy's body stiffen against his, just before she stepped away.

Bill's voice was low and rough, "I came back to get my wife..."

"We were just getting the place closed up..." Kathy stammered quickly, taking another step away from Jack, who closed his eyes in horror at how guilty her words sounded.

"All done here," Jack said, "look, maybe I'll walk back, I should finish a few things in the office before I go."

"Yeah," Bill murmured, taking Kathy's arm as she met him at the door, "why don't you do that."

Bill's face was still hidden in shadows but Jack winced at the chill in his voice. Anger was there, certainly, more anger than Jack had ever heard from his oldest friend, but worse than that was the note of suspicion, of betrayal.

As the door closed behind them, Jack slid down the wall until he was seated on the worn wood floor.

The emotional roller coaster of the day finally came to a crashing halt and left his head spinning. Jack struggled to decide which was worse, the accusation in Bill's voice, or the fact that he could still feel Kathy Beckman in his arms.

Chapter Fifteen

Jack hefted the last box of books into the back of Martin Peterson's old station wagon and swung the heavy door shut. He was amazed at how many belongings he had collected in just the two months he'd been home. Still, he could pack everything he owned in the back of a Ford Country Squire, with some room to spare. Karl had warned him to hold off before he spent any money on his new place, as the Ladies Ministry, headed by Martin's wife Bobbie, was collecting goods to help their impoverished, bachelor youth pastor furnish his new home.

"Look man," Bill said, coming up behind Jack as the wagons door slammed shut, "I said I was sorry, you said you were sorry, why can't we just leave it at that? I hate seeing ya go like this."

Jack turned, smiling to his friend.

"Billy," he said, "I appreciate your forgiveness, more than I can say, and I appreciate you accepting my apology, too, but I can't live here forever. This is your place; you and Kathy need your privacy, and I'm always going to feel like a third wheel."

"You're not–" Bill began

"Yes *I am*," Jack said, interrupting him, "or I will be eventually and I don't want that to happen. If you want me over, invite me over. I'm not going to turn down a home-cooked meal. But it's time I got my own place." He slugged Bill's arm playfully. "You should come over and see it, it's great, right on the bay!"

"I'd like to," Bill said, "but I got a meeting with the bank. They're squeezing me on the loan and you know what the harvest has been like this year."

Jack nodded in sympathy.

Beckman Farms was one of the last totally organic oyster producers on the peninsula. Most of Willapa Bay was owned by the Bjorklund family and Coastal Pacific Oyster. The rest, by a handful of small family operations like the Beckmans.

At low tide, Bill's own thirty acres, out past Nahcotta, looked like nothing more than a broad, muddy field of bristling iron rods. Closer inspection found that each of the three-foot high stakes, sunk deep in the floor of the bay, were clustered with layers of oyster shells. After swimming free in the high tide, the oyster seedlings, called spat, attached themselves to the vacant shells covering the stakes and grew there until they reached a size to harvest. When the tide came in, the stakes would be covered by eight to ten feet of water, allowing the oysters to feed.

During the gathering season, Bill, along with several high school boys that he hired part-time, would roll heavy plastic barrels out among the rows of stakes. At low tide, they'd collect fresh oysters from the clusters and from the tide flats surrounding them.

They used long flat-bladed oyster knives to pry the tough bi-valves from the clusters. Occasionally a shell would shatter under the weight of the knife and the worker would pause briefly to enjoy a quick snack. Few of the boys returned from the flats hungry.

Thick, black mud reached knee-high and sucked jealously at the men's rubber boots.

Often the only way they could free themselves was to lean forward on their buckets until their weight, working as a fulcrum, slowly pulled their legs from the squelching quagmire. By the end of the season both men and boys would have worked their calves into steel pillars of muscle. It was a hard way to make a living, and knee injuries were a common ailment among the oystermen.

Once filled, the barrels were left until the high tide floated them up off the mud and Bill, waiting in his battered aluminum boat, would then lasso each barrel and pull it to the dock. There the oysters would be washed, sorted by size, and bagged, with most going to local seafood stores and restaurants, or sold to tourists at the Beckman's tiny roadside stand, where Kathy sat reading her Bible most afternoons.

In good years, they could expect to harvest several hundred pounds of oysters a day. This season, however, Bill had been lucky to gather that many in a week. Already he had been forced to let go half of the boys that picked for him. Rumors were that chemicals used to fight the ever-spreading spartina grasses and the burrowing ghost shrimp populations might be affecting the mortality of the young oysters. Others claimed the dredging done by the larger companies was filling the shallower bay areas with silt and mud, suffocating the growing bi-valves.

Whatever the reasons behind the bay's dwindling oyster populations, the fact was the harvest numbers of earlier years, which had barely allowed Beckman Farms to remain solvent, were down by half this year. And the loan, which they had taken to cover expansion and new materials the previous winter, was becoming increasingly difficult to pay each month. The strain was starting to show on Bill, both in his temperament and in the frequency of his trips to the Surfside liquor store.

"We're praying for you guys," Jack said, his words sounding strained in his own ears.

"Well," Bill replied, "we'll take all the help we can get." He held the blue flame of his Zippo up to a fresh cigar, the fire dancing around the unlit tip in his trembling hands. "It's a good thing the house and flats are paid for, or we'd have been sunk by now." Bill shook his head, taking a deep breath, "Anyhow, you've heard all this before, best you get over to that new place and start settling in."

"Yeah, I'll do that," Jack said, extending his hand.

Bill paused a moment, shook, and then turned without another word and walked back into the house. Jack watched him go, grinding his teeth in frustration. There was a coldness, a detachment between them that had never been there before. They had never kept any secrets from each other, from their first boyhood crushes through the trials of adolescence...right up to the night that Bill had walked in on Kathy and Jack in the hallway of the church.

From that moment a wall had been erected, high and wide and ever thickening. Sure, they still talked and joked and teased each other like before, but it was more of a going-through-the-motions.

The spark of their friendship, if not smothered, had waned, and Jack felt helpless to bridge the gap that was forming between them.

❧

Jack's new home was a weathered, slightly sagging cabin, sheltered among the pines behind the Moby Dick Hotel, halfway between Nahcotta and Oysterville. Twenty yards past his front porch, Willapa Bay lapped the reed-swathed shore at high tide.

Two creaking Adirondack chairs rested beneath the covered porch and six split-log steps led down from the broad deck to the dirt path running from the bay, up past the cabin and hotel, and ending at Sandridge Road. The hotel, a great white box of a building, had welcomed travelers since its doors opened in 1929, and was a popular rest stop for returning tourists. It had served its country as well, housing the U.S. Coast Guard Horse Patrol during World War II.

The restaurant was known by both locals and visitors to serve the finest dinners to be had anywhere on the peninsula, especially when those dinners included oysters fresh from the hotel's own backyard farm. The current managers, Rolf and Tina Parker, had attended Long Beach Community Church since moving from San Francisco a decade before to take over the Moby. Rolf, the restaurant's much-acclaimed chef, was a painfully shy man with a slight potbelly and a receding chestnut hairline.

Shuffling up to Jack one Sunday morning after services, Rolf had, with much stuttering and wringing of hands, made his offer.

"The missus and I have an old cabin out back of the hotel," he said softly, his eyes wandering nervously, "it isn't much, but I've kept the roof tight and I can run an electric line out to it. You're welcome to stay there if you like, no charge," he added, hurriedly, "you could use the shower and toilet in the hotel, and maybe do a bit of the ground care in trade, if…if you'd like."

Jack told him he would like that very much, shaking his hand warmly, after which a much-relieved Rolf Parker fled to his car and headed back to the safety and sanctity of his kitchen.

True to his word, Rolf had run a power line and wired it into a small breaker box tacked to the wall of the tiny second room, where Jack set up his bed. He had no oven, but a wide hot plate rested on the counter. Beside it sat a wheezing refrigerator that had come from the appliance store in Astoria when Kennedy was still President. It kept the orange juice cold and the butter solid, so Jack found no reason to replace it with a newer model. His second day in the cabin, the Petersons' station wagon had pulled up to the hotel, hauling a small, covered trailer behind it.

Beneath that tarp Jack found enough flatware and dishes to serve half the church. Also, a small, overstuffed horsehair love seat, two table lamps, one floor lamp, towels and washcloths galore, a set of cookware, a fully stocked knife-block and lastly, a small color television set with a foil wrapped antenna. With the installation of bookshelves, consisting of six pine boards separated by cinder blocks and running the full-length of the main room, Jack's cabin was furnished in what Pastor Ferguson jokingly referred to as *Modern American Thrift Store*.

Karl's own contribution had astounded Jack. From the depths of the pastor's basement, Karl had dug out his grandfather's desk. Four thick, ornately carved legs held up the hinge-lidded writing table. At roughly three feet square, the desk fit nicely in the corner of Jack's living room, the oak top lifting to reveal a six-inch deep storage area. Karl identified the circular and rectangular cavities on the top of the desk as repositories for pencils and inkwells. Overjoyed with the antique, Jack insisted that it was too much.

"It's been taking up space in my basement for years," Karl insisted, "and it's way too small for me. I think someone should be using it!"

Running his hand lovingly along the polished surface, Jack couldn't force himself to argue. He accepted the gift thankfully, immediately placing it beneath the old wrought iron floor lamp and setting his Bible and a small, framed photograph of his parents on top.

That evening, Jack sat on the weathered deck of his new home, watching seagulls swoop low over the bay and great blue herons stalk the swampy, reed-lined shore. The Chinook Indians had called this area *Tsako-te-hahsh-eetl*, the place of the red-topped grass, and that made sense to Jack as he looked out over the crimson stalks, undulating in the ocean breeze. To the west, he could hear the throaty growl of oyster barges pulling into the old cannery, now a shelling station for the bay's harvest. From his seat, Jack could just make out the long, wooden pier, jutting out into the Willapa, with its great piles of oyster shells, rising like rocky, pallid mountains along the shore.

❧

Days turned into weeks, and then months, and soon the early winter storms were sweeping the coast in torrential rains. Jack had spent much of his free time bobbing around the bay in the Parker's rowboat, fishing, casting net traps for crabs, and gathering oysters at low tide. There were no longer any oyster beds open to the public but, besides his lawn care duties for the hotel, Jack had taken over the harvesting of the Moby's oyster beds just offshore from his cabin. The Parkers insisted that Jack keep a portion of his harvest and, eventually, he had been forced to haggle a used chest-freezer from the hardware store in Ocean Park. Now that winter was approaching and the weather grew increasing foul, Jack could relax in the knowledge that he had enough seafood, both frozen and smoked, to last him through the winter.

The youth group had been the highlight of Jack's autumn. For something that he had at first felt roped into, Jack found that watching the kids learn and grow, sharing in their hopes and fears, gave him a sense of accomplishment like nothing else he had ever done. A dozen teens had showed up on the last warm weekend of October, hosting a car wash in the church parking lot and splitting the profits between a weekend campout and a contribution to the missionaries in New Guinea that LBCC supported.

Both the elders and the parents had been pleasantly surprised when the kids had voted unanimously to donate the money. Jack had smiled at their reaction, and didn't mention that he had spent the last three weeks teaching on the missions and sharing his own experiences in Africa.

Kathy, along with the Petersons, had continued to show up faithfully every Wednesday night, and Jack decided that when the ministry grew large enough, he could create four small groups, two for the girls and two for the boys. Bill, however, hadn't been back to a youth meeting since their confrontation in September, and though he continued to attend Sunday services, his presence was becoming more and more occasional as the year progressed.

Jack worried about Bill and had spoken and prayed with his pastor on several occasions about his old friend.

"Jack," Karl had responded, leaning back against the rain splattered window of his office as the old wall heater chugged and hissed in the corner, "each of us makes his own choice. The invitation has been laid out for Bill Beckman. He can accept or reject the sacrifice Christ made for him. No one else, not you or I, or even Kathy, can decide for him."

Jack knew that this was the truth, but his concern gnawed at him, adding to his guilt over the one subject he had yet to broach with his pastor. As the weeks passed, Jack found it increasingly difficult to be near Kathy Beckman. His heart would start to race when she was near and he had dreamed, just once, that they were walking hand in hand along the beach together.

As the two worked on projects, or took part in events with the youth, Jack struggled to make sure that they were never alone together; there were always several youth between the two of them. On the odd occasion that they did brush arms or hands in passing, Jack would flinch back as though burned, as shame flooded through him.

Kathy didn't seem to notice his strange behavior, at least he hoped and prayed this was the case, as he knelt on the hardwood floor of his cabin, clutching his Bible and pleading with God to take away his traitorous feelings.

❧

"Ho Ho Ho!" Pastor Ferguson bellowed again, and Jack flinched as the cry passed through the thin wall between their offices.

"Yo, Saint Nick," he called, rapping on the wall with his knuckles. "You wanna hold it down, some of us are memorizing our lines!"

"What do you think *I'm* doing?" Karl shouted back. "HO HO HO!" he bellowed even louder.

Jack laughed, gathering his Bible and script. Time to flee to the sanctity of the coffee shop! As he turned to close his office door, a large, red, jovial figure stepped into the hallway, blocking his path.

"Look out Santa," he growled, "some of us have real lines to work on!"

Karl waggled a thick finger in his assistant's face.

"Watch it there, young feller," he warned, "or it's gonna be nothing but coal in *your* stocking!"

"As long as there's a paycheck in my stocking, I'll be fine!" Jack laughed, "Can I buy Saint Nick a cup of tea?"

"Nah," the old elf replied, "I have to get this jacket over to Myra Feldman so she can sew these buttons back on."

"You know," Jack called, getting a head start towards the door, "maybe if Santa cut back on the cookies and milk…"

"Why you…" Karl hurled a candy cane after him, which Jack dodged, "I'll have you know these buttons *fell* off!"

Jack was still snickering as he walked into the Coffee Clutch and straddled his usual stool facing the window. Here, between cups of coffee and pages of script, he could watch the world of Long Beach roll past through the squeaky-clean glass.

The play was a fun one and, after Sue the waitress brought him a steaming mug, he opened the cover page to read the entire work again. The youth group had brainstormed the script, which Jack had then painfully typed up on the church's moody old Smith-Corona, an aging electric beast that would occasionally add a few letters that you hadn't bothered to press the keys for. The plot was a modern telling of Dickens' *Christmas Carol.* The main character was a spoiled young girl named Rachel who, after complaining about the little orphan boy that her parents have taken in, is visited by an angel, late on Christmas Eve.

The angel, whose name is Michael (what else?), takes the young girl hither and yon through the city, showing her how the less fortunate are spending *their* Christmas Eve; in emergency rooms and back alleys. Finally, Rachel is shown the starving young orphan boy, as he would be if there had been no one willing to minister to him. The girl, of course, repents wholeheartedly and everyone lives happily ever after.

Not bad, Jack thought for the hundredth time, *not bad at all.* It had taken the kids three weeks to bring the script from seed to flower, and they had done a great job. No sets were needed, but Jack had half a dozen women in the church furiously fitting and sewing costumes, to be ready by dress rehearsal this Friday. Jack's only lines were narration and, though he could have just read them from the page, he felt he owed it to the kids to give the show his all, and memorize his part.

"Ladies and gentlemen," he murmured, hoping no one in the coffee shop noticed him talking to himself, "welcome to the night before Christmas…"

He had repeated this line a thousand times, it seemed, and he still fought the urge to say *Christmas Eve* instead of *The Night Before*. Sue passed by a moment later and swooped in to top off his cup.

"Remember," she stage-whispered with a grin, "the night before…"

"I know," Jack grumbled, waving her off, "I know!"

Sue returned to the kitchen, where he could hear her chuckling.

Jack continued to rehearse his lines all through the afternoon and by six o'clock that evening, when rehearsal started, he felt comfortable with the task.

❧

The run-through went smoothly, with only the expected theatrical disasters.

Aimee, who played the angel, spoke the wrong line in scene two, effectively rushing them directly to scene seven, ending the play in a record eight minutes. Howls and catcalls erupted from backstage when Jack yelled, "Cut!"

Aimee, whose pale cheeks blushed as bright as her auburn hair, started giggling and finally had to rush to the ladies room before something even more embarrassing happened. Kathy, the costume designer for the first annual Christmas play, was chuckling over this when she backed into the water cooler, which fell, dousing half of the freshly washed and pressed costumes with lime Gatorade. She, however, did not giggle, and Jack had to call a break and do some fast-talking to keep his costumer from bursting into tears. Bobbie Peterson saved the day for him by scooping up the whole stack and running them to the Suds-N-Duds in Sea View.

Finally, after two long, stumbling rehearsals, the last car full of kids pulled away from the doors of the church, leaving an exhausted Jack Leland, Kathy Beckman, and Peterson family collapsed across the front steps.

"Need a lift home, Kathy?" Martin asked. "Bobbie should be back pretty quick, you're right on the way."

"No," she said, "but thanks! Bill should be by anytime to pick me up."

"I'd better head out too," Jack said, a bit more quickly than he meant to, and stood to go. Kathy looked up at him, puzzled, and Martin stood and made a show of looking up the street for his returning wife.

"Jack?" Kathy asked. "Are you okay?"

"Yeah, sure," he said. "Just a little tired, it was a long day, ya know?"

"Okay," she said, seeming unconvinced, "you're sure I haven't done something…"

Jack felt his heart speed up and his tongue seemed suddenly thick and dry, clinging to the roof of his mouth and he feigned nonchalance.

"Not a thing," he smiled, "but if you do, you'll be the first person I'll tell." Jack tried to hide a grimace, certain that his smile looked as forced and fake as his words. "I'll see you Friday!"

With that he fled to the back of the church and retrieved his battered ten-speed, another relic that Karl had disentangled from the depth of his garage.

Pedaling furiously, Jack set off towards home. Praying all the way.

Chapter Sixteen

The play was an enormous success. The church was packed with family and friends, and Karl was euphoric, greeting each newcomer with a warm smile and a vigorous handshake. Jack, on the other hand, stood behind the hastily erected curtain, trying to calm his shaking hands and churning stomach.

His kids (and in three short months he had come to think of them as his) huddled around him, whispering, giggling, and trying to peek through the curtain at the audience. Jack's pants pockets drooped beneath the weight of the silver dollars they had given him. One of the youth, Trevor Rigby, who played Rachel's father, had real ambitions toward the acting profession. He had informed them that it was theater *tradition,* and this was spoken as though reading an ancient and sacred text, that each actor present the director with a coin before going onstage opening night. This was for *luck*, which was also spoken with the same unquestionable reverence. Jack had fought back a smile and nodded gravely. Trevor took the whole production very seriously, sometimes too seriously, but there was no doubt the imminent performance would be all the better for his dedication. Still, it had been difficult, as the boy had held forth on the *traditions of the theatre*, to take him completely seriously as his fake mustache waggled on his upper lip.

Finally, they heard Pastor Ferguson take the stage and, after welcoming everyone to the Christmas Eve service, and rushing through the announcements, he introduced the play as the houselights dimmed. Jack took his place in the dark and when the bright spotlight washed over him (a gracious loan by the Coaster Theater Playhouse in Cannon Beach), Jack paused a moment before speaking his first line.

"Ladies and gentlemen," his voice boomed through the sanctuary, "welcome to Christmas Eve..."

"Hey Jack," one of the teens called, shouting across the sanctuary and over the dull roar of people chatting and bundling up to head home.

"Yes, Trevor?"

"Welcome to the night before Christmas!" the boy called back gleefully, and then ran for the door. Somewhere across the room Jack could hear Randy Brooks' braying laughter.

He groaned, knowing he would never hear the end of the flubbed line; his kids had assured him of that in the short while since the play had ended. At least, Jack thought, his was the *only* glitch in the performance. The youth had performed flawlessly, getting a standing ovation as the houselights came back up. Jack saw Carrie, still clad in the pink bathrobe that was her costume as young Rachel, standing near her parents and giggling at him, as Trevor and Randy fled. Jack stuck his tongue out at her, and she responded by placing her thumbs in her ears and waggling her fingers back. Jack laughed, scooping up the two wrapped packages that lay on top of his jacket, and went in search of Kathy Beckman.

It seemed like everyone wanted to stop and shake his hand on the way out, patting him on the back and saying what a great job he had done. Jack murmured, repeatedly, that the kids had done all the work but thank you, glad you could make it, Merry Christmas. Finally, he glimpsed the back of Kathy's familiar black wool coat, just heading toward the front doors.

"Katie!" he called, waving his free hand.

She turned, searching the crowd until she found him and then smiled, gesturing that she would meet him out front. Jack pushed his way politely, but firmly, though the mass of humanity that filled the front hall, and out onto the lawn.

"Hey," he said, gasping breathlessly, "couldn't let you get away without your Christmas presents." He held out the two packages, both wrapped in the brightly colored pages of the Sunday comics.

"Oh Jack, thank you!" Kathy smiled, taking the packages. "Your present is at home under the tree; I was going to bring it tonight but I forgot."

They stood there for a moment, as the congregation passed around them, walking to their cars.

"So," Jack said, "tear it up!"

"Now?"

"Sure! I'm going to be at Karl's all day tomorrow, so this is my only chance to see you open it before Christmas."

"Okay!" Kathy laughed, grinning delightedly as she ripped open the larger of the two packages, her name emblazoned across the top in red felt pen.

"Oh, Jack…" she breathed, lifting the black, leather bound Bible from the wrapping, its gold-gilt edges glimmering in the foggy light of the streetlamp. He had sent away to Vermont for the Bible; a friend from college worked at the Lewiston Bible Bindery in Woodstock and had gotten him a good deal. The family owned and operated company made some of the finest Bibles to be had anywhere in the country, covering their work in flawless tanned calfskin. Kathy's was a Scofield Study Bible, with her initials embossed on the front cover.

She ran a loving hand over the smooth richness of the leather cover, slowly opening the flyleaf to read the inscription, written carefully in Jack's small, slightly slanting script.

"Trust in the Lord with all your heart and lean not unto thine own understanding, in all thy ways acknowledge Him, and He will direct your path. Proverbs 3:5-6"

A single tear coursed down the young woman's cheek as she read the words, and Jack overcame an involuntary, nearly overwhelming compulsion to reach out a finger and brush it away. Kathy looked up at him with a strange expression, tilting her head to one side and pursing her lips as though studying the man for the first time. Then, wiping the tear away herself, she tucked the beautiful Bible under her arm and nodded.

"Thank you Jack, it's very, very beautiful." She smiled. "I can't think of anything I would have wanted more."

Jack grinned and nodded. This was so typically Kathy. Most women he had known would have commented on the expense, or insisted that he shouldn't have, but not her. She had accepted the gift for what it was, a thoughtful expression of friendship on which value couldn't be placed. At least, that's how Jack *hoped* she took it. He had agonized over what to give his estranged friend's wife as a gift. Struggling with feelings he was barely willing to admit to, each gift seemed to take on some hidden motive or veiled meaning. Finally, as he had sat, studying his own tattered Bible and wondering if he should start looking for a replacement (the book of psalms was held in place with a paper clip) the solution had struck him.

What safer present than God's word?

Kathy would love it, of course, and it was a perfectly appropriate gift from a pastor to a friend. Breathing a sigh of relief, he had gone back to his study of Leviticus with an air of reprieve and anticipation the dry text had never before produced.

So, Jack had called Tom, his bowling buddy from college and found that he *did* still work at the bindery, and could get him a very good price, one that was only twice what the young pastor could afford. Jack decided he would go a month without root beer and ordered the Bible anyway.

Bill's gift had been much easier.

As boys, they had often perused the knife counter at the Chinook Hardware store with great avarice. They would stand, oohing and ahhing over the assortment of cutlery from companies like Shrade, Case and, of course, the best of all knives, the *Folding Hunter* by Buck. The model 110 had been the chosen knife of the oystermen of Long Beach since its inception in the early sixties. For the boys of the peninsula, there was no greater symbol of status than the ability to casually pull the *Hunter* from one's pocket and take care of the task at hand. Usually to the admiration and blinding jealously of one's friends.

A quick phone call to Kathy has assured him that Bill wasn't already the owner of such a knife. A slightly longer trip down to the hardware store had found that, indeed, the Hunter was still proudly displayed among its competitors against the red felt backing of the knife case. The price tag was a bit stiffer than he remembered it being in 1963, but still do-able, just another couple of weeks without soda. Both the knife and the Bible, which arrived just a few days earlier (soothing Jack's mounting panic) had been hastily wrapped in newspaper comics and slipped under his bed. Jack had chuckled to himself about this later. Why a man, living alone, had felt the need to *hide* Christmas presents, was beyond him, but that's where *his* parents had always stashed the gifts, so where else could you put them but under the bed?

Jack was pulled from his reverie as Kathy reached forward and squeezed his arm. The familiar rumble of Bill's pickup came from the curb.

"Thanks again, Jack," she said, "it really is a beautiful Bible. I'll swing by Karl's tomorrow and drop off your present."

Then she was gone, and Jack was again surrounded by the last stragglers from the church, still more congratulations, and the prospect of a long, cold bike ride back to the empty cabin. When Martin and Bobbie pulled alongside him and invited Jack home for hot chocolate and a movie, he had accepted gratefully, closing his eyes briefly to thank God, again, for his new friends.

ঌ৩

Christmas dinner at the Ferguson house was an event. Karl Ferguson, a widower for the past eight years, filled his home each December 25th with his two daughters, their husbands, and several rambunctious grandchildren ranging in years from three to ten. The overall din, when woven with the melodious crooning of Bing Crosby's *White Christmas* album, blaring scratchily from the old turntable, hovered somewhere just below deafening.

Karl sat in his overstuffed easy chair, quite obviously the king of all he surveyed. He bellowed orders to the kitchen staff and sneaked sweets to the children when he thought their mothers weren't looking, usually in reward to their sneaking Grandpa some sampling from the kitchen.

Jack spent most of his time bustling over the oven with Karl's daughters, Lisa and Jan. He had promised to cook the late Mrs. Leland's famous oyster dressing, to accompany the turkey, and so spent the afternoon elbow deep in ingredients, chopping onions and celery and occasionally dashing into the living room to catch a favorite scene from *It's a Wonderful Life*.

Capra's film, he learned, was an undisputable tradition in the Ferguson household. The daughters amused themselves, and Jack, by shouting out key lines in the dialog a moment before the actors spoke them; this was good for a chuckle from everyone but their father, who shouted dire threats from his padded throne.

One of the children, a small fellow with unruly blond hair and conspicuously missing incisors, entertained Jack with the same joke at least a dozen times over the course of the afternoon.

"What does a reindeer and a snowball have in common?" the child would ask gleefully, his breath whistling through the gap in his teeth.

"I don't know," Jack would cry, "what does a reindeer and a snowball have in common?"

"They're both brown," the boy would shriek, "except the snowball!"

With this the child would either run, screaming into the other room, or collapse to the floor, writhing in a breathless fit of mirth at his own wit. Jack had no idea what the joke meant, but laughed harder with each telling until, finally, one of the daughters excused herself from the kitchen to go have words with her father, regarding his excessive allotments of candy.

The other high point of humor came from Travis, the oldest grandchild who, at ten, had a slightly more advanced wit. He would occasionally call from the living room,

"Hey Mom, can I have a dog for Christmas?"

To which both mothers, and anyone else present, including Jack, would shout in response, "No, you can have turkey like everyone else!"

By the time said turkey was ready to enter the oven, Jack's head was ringing and he had to sneak into the bathroom and raid Karl's aspirin bottle.

The barely restrained pandemonium of Karl's home was a new experience for Jack. His own parents, though loving and supportive of their only child, wouldn't have thought to yell from the kitchen to the living room any more than they would have considered running naked down Main Street on Christmas morning.

Still, Jack was having a wonderful time.

Coming from the bustling camaraderie of his college dorm to living alone in his little cabin had been something of a shock. He hadn't realized how much he missed having people around, in a casual setting, until he had spent the day with his pastor's family.

❧

Soon the enticing smell of roast turkey and oyster dressing filled the house, mingling with the sweet-spiced aroma of pumpkin pies and buttery garlic potatoes. The children were herded from various rooms and closets, hands were washed, and everyone found a seat around the long, oval table in the Ferguson dining room.

A framed picture had been set on the polished ledge of the china cabinet, and Jack didn't need to ask who the smiling matron in the photo was. He watched as Karl, who sat at the head of the table, glanced at his wife's image, and then from one beloved face to the next, treasuring his gifts in the smiles of his children and grandchildren. He winked at Jack as their eyes met, his own glistening, and then stood, setting the long carving knife and fork beside the steaming turkey, and held out both hands. Wordlessly the family joined together and Jack found himself a part of their circle, a tiny, damp hand wiggling in his right, a strong, calloused one gripping his left.

"Let's pray," Karl murmured, and in unison the family lowered their heads.

"Father God," Karl Ferguson intoned, his voice warm, "bless our family and all its members and friends; bind us together by your love. Give us kindness and patience to support one another, and wisdom in all we do. Let the gift of your peace come into our hearts and remain with us. May we rejoice in your blessings for all our days."

Jack, peeking from beneath his eyelid, saw the words being whispered in unison by Karl's daughters, and realized that this was the family's traditional

Christmas prayer. He felt a surge of gratitude at being included.

Each voice at the table spoke up in conclusion, "Amen."

The chatter and laughter resumed immediately, as platters and bowls began their clockwise journey. As Jack spooned a second scoop of dressing onto his plate, the raucous squawk of the doorbell sounded over the general clamor. One of the children raced from the table, returning a moment later to tell Jack there was a lady at the door for him.

"And she's crying," the little girl informed him solemnly.

Jack and Karl exchanged a quick glance as they both rose. Halfway across the living room, Jack recognized the familiar idle of Bill's truck, and stepped in front of his boss to open the door.

The child hadn't been completely correct, Kathy Beckman wasn't actually crying at that moment, but it was clear from her reddened nose and swollen eyes that she had been in the not-so-distant past.

"Kathy," Jack asked, "are you okay?"

"I'm fine," she murmured, holding out a small envelope. "I just wanted to drop off your present."

"Come in for a minute," Karl said, his brow wrinkled with concern, "sit down and catch your breath." With this he shouldered Jack out of the way and placed a firm hand on the young woman's arm, leading her inside.

"I…I can't," Kathy whispered, tears starting in her eyes again, "Bill's in the truck…"

"Bill can wait," the older man said firmly, "or he can join us." Karl led her into the living room and sat her down in his easy chair.

"Jack," he said, without looking up, "why don't you go get Kathy a glass of cold water, and ask one of the girls to come in here."

Jack nodded. He was aware of Karl's philosophy on counseling women.

"Always have another woman in the room," he had counseled, *"and make sure that she's a married woman. Never give a woman a ride or accept a ride from them unless there's another person in the car."*

He'd made it clear to his assistant that these rules weren't from a lack of trust, and that Karl imposed this behavior on himself as well.

"Better," he had told Jack, *"to avoid any appearance of evil, even the possibility of wrongdoing, than to have to prove yourself innocent later."*

Jack came back from the kitchen with the glass of water, and Lisa, in tow. She immediately pulled a hassock up beside Kathy's chair and sat, resting a hand on the younger woman's arm.

Kathy glanced up at her and, as their eyes met, something unspoken seemed to pass between them.

Then Kathy gave vent to the tears she had struggled to keep back, pressing her face into Lisa's shoulder and letting Karl's daughter, a complete stranger, stroke her hair and whisper comfort to her. After a moment she raised her face, having regained some control. Karl handed her a tissue.

"So," he asked, "what's this all about?"

Kathy took a deep breath, wiping her eyes.

"It's not that big of a deal," she said, "Bill wasn't happy about Jack buying me a Bible, he wouldn't even open his gift, and he's been drinking all day."

"Do you need to stay here for the night?" Karl asked. "We could juggle things around and put you in one of the kid's rooms; there's plenty of space."

Kathy was shaking her head before Karl finished making the offer. "No," she said, "that would just make it worse. Bill's under so much pressure from the bank right now, every little thing sets him off."

"Kathy," Karl asked, "has Bill hit you?"

Kathy's eyes snapped up and caught Lisa's again. There was a long pause and Jack heard the tinny slam of the truck door outside. Whatever Karl was going to do, he had better do quickly. Pastor Ferguson, for his part, remained calm. He must have heard the heavy, uneven tread of boots coming up the wooden steps and across his porch, but his eyes never left Kathy's.

"No," she whispered finally, her eyes dropping.

Then Bill's heavy fist beat angrily on the door, rattling the windows. Jack began to rise, but Karl grabbed his arm first.

"You just stay put," he said, his voice making it clear that he would brook no nonsense on the subject, "whatever's going on, your two cents isn't going to help!" Then he stood and walked to the door.

His friend looked so different, standing in the pale light of the Ferguson porch, that Jack gasped out loud. Bill, who had always been whip-lean, now looked skeletal, his skin pulled tight across his cheekbones. His unshaven face was the color of paste, and deep purple hollows filled the space beneath his eyes like dark bruises. His hair, a thick mass of greasy coils, was pulled tight into his traditional ponytail and, even from across the room, Jack could smell the rank odor of alcohol and stale, unwashed sweat. He was also dead drunk, swaying slightly, with one hand resting on the doorframe to steady himself. Focusing his red-rimmed eyes on the cherubic old man in front of him, Bill took a belligerent step forward.

His voice a low growl, "I want–"

Karl stepped into the doorway, his bulk effectively blocking any hope of entrance, and placed a meaty hand in the middle of the younger man's chest, easing him back onto the porch.

"I didn't ask you what you wanted, son."

Karl Ferguson's voice was hard as nails; unlike anything Jack had ever heard from him before. "What you're going to *get*," he continued, backing Bill up another step, "is a night in jail, if you try to walk into *this* house uninvited…and drunk."

Bill stopped, blinking owlishly in confusion as the portly man took instant and unquestionable control of the moment. Thinking hard, swaying and covering Karl in bourbon fumes, Bill decided to try another tact. "Katie...honey, you in there?"

Karl snorted. "C'mon Bill," he said, "of course she's in here, you just saw her walk through the door two minutes ago, didn't you? If you'd ask *politely*, you could be in here too."

Bill thought about this, and then muttered, "'Kay, so can I come in?"

"Are you going to be nice?"

Another pause, "Yeah."

"Okay," Karl stepped back out of the doorway, "but no trouble, Bill, I mean it! I'll toss your rear right back out in the street and call Sheriff Bradley to haul you off. Understood?"

"Yeah."

He stumbled through the door and, for an awful moment, Jack was sure that Bill was going face down onto the hardwood. The unsteady eyes caught Kathy's and seemed to soften a bit, as he glanced shamefully around the room. Then he saw Jack.

Bill's face froze into a hard iron mask at the sight of his former friend. A hooded, dangerous look, that Jack had never seen before, fell over Bill's eyes as his lip curled into a snarl.

"So," he slurred, taking a lurching step in Jack's direction, only to have Karl's fist clamp firmly onto his narrow bicep, "you like to buy fancy presents for my wife, huh?"

"Be nice…" Karl murmured, his face impassive and unreadable.

But Bill was mad and here at last was the object of his anger, at least in his own besotted mind.

"I'm being nice, lemme go!" he cried, never looking away from Jack. "I can buy my own wife presents, buddy boy!" He turned back toward Karl, his voice rising, "Maybe you should tell your youth pastor there to be nice! Tell him to keep his lousy hands to hisself, and off my wife! I seen 'em together…"

Jack rose from the couch, his face flushing, "Now hang on!"

Bill twisted, trying to free himself and lunge at Jack, his features contorted in a mask of drunken fury, "You tell 'em Jack, you just tell 'em what I saw!"

Karl's free hand dropped to Bill's other bicep and, and he stood, an unmovable mountain of calm and, as he looked up at Jack, his voice was flat and emotionless.

"Jack, I want you to go into the kitchen."

Jack hesitated.

"Right now, I mean it."

Jack, stiff with anger, walked across the room and through the swinging wooden door, where he found both daughters' husbands standing, waiting to burst into the living room if Bill got out of hand. Wordlessly they pushed him to the end of the line, making it clear that both agreed with Karl; Jack wasn't welcome or needed in this confrontation.

From the living room, they heard a few more murmured words from both Bill and Karl, and then Jan went back to the table to reassure the children that everything was all right. After several moments, the front door opened and closed and they heard Karl flop into his chair with a heavy sigh.

"Okay," he called wearily, "the show's over, you can all come in now."

The three men hurried into the living room. Jack looked around quickly, realizing that Kathy was nowhere to be seen.

"You didn't let her leave with him did you?" he asked, aghast, not meaning to shout but doing so anyway.

Karl stood up and crossed the floor to face his assistant.

"With her husband, you mean?" he asked, frowning. "Of course I did. I asked her if she wanted to stay and she said no. What did you want me to do, Jack, kidnap her?"

The younger man said nothing, but stood fuming, knowing that Karl was right, but hating it all the same.

Karl turned to the rest of his family, "You guys go ahead and finish dinner; Jack and I will be in the study." With that, he turned and walked down the hallway, neither glancing back nor gesturing for Jack to follow.

Chapter Seventeen

Pastor Ferguson's study was the last small room at the end of the hall, chosen for the large picture window looking out onto the backyard, where Karl could watch his grandchildren at play while he worked. A floor-to-ceiling bookcase dominated the wall opposite the door, and a heavy oak desk sat in front of this, where the light of the morning sun would fall across his study area.

The narrow strips of exposed shelves in front of each row of books were taken up with all types of knickknacks and mementoes from a lifetime of ministry. Mostly these were figurines of preachers, ranging from an exquisitely painted porcelain Dutch minister in wooden shoes, to an African pastor forged in bronze. The three remaining walls were covered with pictures of Karl's children, grandchildren, and members of the congregation. Jack noticed little of this as his employer eased his girth behind the desk and gestured for Jack to close the door and sit, which he did.

Karl removed his glasses with a sigh, wiping them with a tissue and rubbing the bridge of his nose. He looked up at Jack with an expression of mixed sadness and resolve. A much-used study Bible lay on the desk before him and he flipped though this until he found the page he was looking for, and then spoke.

"Okay Jack," he said, "I'm only going to ask this once, and I'm not going to apologize for it, because it's my job. Have you had any inappropriate contact or conversation with Kathy Beckman?"

Jack felt his entire frame shaking, and struggled to steady his voice as he answered. "No, never."

Karl sighed again. "If it makes you feel any better, I was pretty certain of that, but the Word is clear on how this type of thing is handled, and I won't make any exceptions, not even fór you, Jack."

"I know."

"Good," he said, "and I believe you, but I'm still going to read this passage so we're completely clear on the subject." Karl slipped his glasses back on and peered at the page before him, finding the verse.

"Those who sin are to be rebuked publicly," he quoted, *"so that the others may take warning. I charge you, in the sight of God and Christ Jesus and the elect angels, to keep these instructions without partiality, and to do nothing out of favoritism.* That's First Timothy chapter five, verse twenty-one," Pastor Ferguson finished.

"I'm familiar with it," Jack said, "it was a popular verse in Bible college."

Pastor Ferguson's lip quirked upward. "I would imagine so," he said, "now, let's figure this mess out. Tell me why *you* think that Bill said what he said, besides the fact that he was about three sheets to the wind." Jack took a deep breath and told Karl exactly what had happened the night of the youth group meeting, in the hallway of the church. Karl nodded and then shook his head.

"I'm not going to coddle you, Jack," he warned, "I hope that you don't expect me to. If you want to be a pastor, this is the type of lesson you have to learn the first time because you might not survive it a second."

"So," he continued, "can you tell me why this situation is as much your fault as anyone else's, maybe more?"

That hit Jack hard, like a fist in the belly, and he nodded miserably, refusing to look down. "Because I didn't make sure there was someone else there with us. I allowed an opportunity for the appearance of wrong."

"Exactly," Karl nodded. "And now?"

"Now I'm stuck trying to prove myself innocent," he answered, miserably.

Karl nodded again.

"So," Jack sighed, "what can I do about it now?"

Karl leaned back in his chair, resting his hands on the worn leather arms.

"Well," he said, "the first thing that we'll need to do is explain to Kathy why she needs to step down, at least temporarily, from the youth ministry."

"What?" Jack cried, astonished. "Why should she have to quit the youth group? Isn't that just punishing Kathy for her husband's sin?"

Karl's hand went to the Bible once again, leafing through the thin, translucent pages.

"It's got nothing to do with punishment, Jack, it's about Kathy being a stepping-stone and not a stumbling block to her unbelieving husband. If Bill doesn't want her involved in youth ministry, even if it's only because he doesn't like *you*, then she needs to step down, immediately."

Jack shook his head. "I don't get it."

Pastor Ferguson found the verse he was looking for and read it aloud.

"For the unbelieving husband has been sanctified through his believing wife, and the unbelieving wife has been sanctified through her believing husband."

Karl's eyes rose to meet Jack's again.

"You and I," he said, "despite how much we may care for Katherine Beckman, or want her involved in ministry, can't be the reason that she refuses to submit to her husband. If she does that," Karl closed his Bible, "she steps out from under the authority that God has placed over her and then, no matter how noble her intentions may be, she's in rebellion. Her personal relationship with Christ, as well as Bill's, comes first before any ministry."

Jack's head was spinning. On one hand, he knew that Karl was right; Kathy would never help her husband come under the submission of Christ if she didn't stay in submission to him. Still, it seemed so unfair! Jack also knew how much Kathy loved working with the girls; loved being involved with all the youth. His frustration must have been obvious on his face, as Karl smiled.

"Try looking at it this way," he said, "Kathy's not being asked to step down from ministry, but to focus on her most important ministry, to her husband. That has to take priority over my wishes and yours, and hers."

Jack slumped in his chair. It made sense. He didn't like it, he probably never would, but then, it wasn't his place to pass judgment on God's design, was it? How often had they hammered *that* into his head at Clear Creek?

Knowing the answer and liking the answer were two very different things, and one wasn't nearly as important as the other.

He knew, like it or not, that he must do his part in allowing Kathy to minister to Bill.

"Look," Karl said, "I know it's a tough pill to swallow, but welcome to being a pastor. Much of what you're going to face in a lifetime of ministry is going to be like this. God hasn't called you to spread the gospel as *you* see fit, but as *He*'s ordained it. If you don't like that you'll have to take it up with God. You'll be wrong, of course, but He's always willing to listen."

There was a long pause and, finally, Jack smiled, realizing that Karl was teasing him...sort of. And suddenly he knew that he couldn't leave this room without telling his mentor the whole truth. Jack felt his stomach constrict and his mouth go dry as he spoke.

"Karl...uh...there's something more I need to tell you."

Karl nodded.

"I thought there might be." He sighed. "Do you have feelings, romantic feelings, for this woman?"

"Yes, I do," Jack said. "But I swear Karl, I've never–"

"Don't!' Karl interrupted sternly. "I'm not interested in a confession of your innocence. This is about a confession of your sin."

"Sin?"

Karl nodded, tapping the Bible with his finger. "Christ said it in the book of Matthew, and I'm sure that you're familiar with verse as well; *I tell you that anyone who looks at a woman lustfully... "*

"...has already committed adultery with her in his heart, " Jack finished.

He felt tears stinging the back of his eyes, as he looked at his pastor and friend. This was the guilt that had been eating away at him for the past months; the conviction that made him flinch away whenever his hand had brushed hers. For the first time in Jack's short career, he felt like an absolute failure.

"Good," Karl said, as Jack looked at him through swimming eyes, "now we're looking at it from the right direction. Now something can be done about it."

"What can I do?" Jack asked, his voice cracking.

Karl's instructions were hard, and there were times over the next months that Jack chafed beneath them, but he knew it was for the best.

First, the two men took hands, across the weathered desktop, and they prayed. Jack had wept, praying a prayer of confession and repentance and Karl followed that by asking for strength and healing for his young friend. Second, Pastor Ferguson had told him there would be no more contact, even socially, between Jack and Kathy; no further opportunities for the appearance of wrong. Karl made it clear that if Kathy had a heart for ministry, he could find her a place where she could do so.

Under no circumstances, however, was Jack to seek her out for help with any of his work.

"Don't tell her about our conversation," Karl warned, "knowing your feelings can only hurt her, as there's nothing she can do about them, so there's no point. I'll talk to Bill sometime soon and see if I can get them to come in together for counseling. I'll explain to her about stepping down from the youth ministry and keeping distance from you, for the sake of her husband."

Bill Beckman, Karl had gone on, would be assured that if he ever had any evidence that sin had been committed between Jack and Kathy, that he could come to Karl with it, who would deal with the situation without partiality.

However, if he continued to accuse without any proof, Karl would also treat *him* without partiality, like any other gossip. Lastly, he leveled a stern eye at his assistant pastor and made it clear that if any sin were to be committed, and Karl found out about it, Jack would be fired without hesitation.

"That's not a threat, you understand," Karl stressed, "I'm just making it as clear as I can, that I'm going to follow scripture, to the letter, on this. I'll do nothing out of favoritism."

Jack told him that he understood, and assured him that nothing like that would become necessary.

"It won't happen," Jack said firmly.

"Be careful, Jack," Karl warned him. "Anyone can stumble and fall into sin, *anyone*! It's only when we recognize that possibility that we can be watchful and guard against it."

Jack nodded.

With that, Karl heaved himself from his chair with a chuckle and started for the door. Suddenly he turned and, reaching into his pocket, removed a small white envelope with a red ribbon around it.

"I almost forgot," he said. "This is your Christmas present from the Beckmans. I'll tell her you said thank you."

Jack, mute, could only nod again.

"Now," Karl said, "I don't know about you, but I've got Christmas dinner waiting for me, if my grandchildren have left me any, that is!"

Jack laughed, but it was a polite, distracted laugh, his mind still focused on Karl's final warning. He had a feeling the things he'd been told in the last half hour might be more important than anything he had yet learned about being a pastor.

☙❧

The gift from Bill and Kathy turned out to be a twenty-dollar gift certificate to the Sand Castle Bookstore in Ocean Park.

A week later, Jack found the tiny shop just around the corner from the main thoroughfare, its display window crossed with a huge banner reading "After Christmas Sale." A tiny brass bell jingled merrily from the lintel as he walked through the door. The shop was larger inside than it appeared, and every wall was stuffed with books. A sign, taped to the cash register, read: *Specializing in Rare and Out Of Print.*

A small, thin woman, who looked to Jack to be somewhere between seventy and eighty, glanced up from the thick paperback she was reading as she sat behind the counter, and gave him a quick once-over. She wore a bright and eclectic collection of clothing, a deep purple skirt and top with a passion-red silk scarf that matched her lurid lipstick almost perfectly. A huge silver brooch twinkled from her blouse, and glittering faux diamond rings covered her gnarled fingers.

Best of all, Jack thought, were her glasses. Deep emerald lenses, perched on the tip of her thin nose and held in place with a gleaming silver chain, the frames were classic cat's-eyes from the fifties, in an *indescribable* shade of pink. Jack suddenly had the strangest urge to button his collar and make sure he'd combed his hair. The old woman smiled at his obvious discomfort.

"Welcome to the Sand Castle," she said, her voice surprisingly strong, and reminded Jack of the low, sultry voices of Hollywood starlets from the thirties and forties, and he fought back a grin.

"Can I help you find something?" she asked.

"No ma'am," Jack replied, "I just came in to look around; I have this gift certificate..."

"Ah!" the woman cried, rising from her chair and coming around the counter, "a *paying* customer! Well honey, *paying* customers get to call me Dottie! Now, what is your *genre préféré*?"

"Excuse me?"

"What do you like to read, sweetheart?"

Jack laughed at the woman's flamboyant style and, handing her the gift certificate, replied, "Well, let's talk about that..."

&

Months passed, and Jack found himself busy with his handful of youth as they dealt with the stresses of winter isolation, forced confinement with parents and siblings, and the rigors of their upcoming finals. Aimee Peterson wrecked her mother's Honda, missing a four-way stop in Sea View, and Trevor Rigby had been suspended from school for fighting, presumably over a girl.

Occasionally, as the weeks flew by, Jack would see Kathy seated across the sanctuary, or talking to one of the kids in the foyer. He would smile and nod, and then find something to attend to in another direction.

Prayer filled what few empty spaces he found in his schedule.

Prayer for the youth, their walk with Christ and their futures, prayer for the church and its influence on their community and, most of all, prayer for himself, that he would maintain the integrity that he had avowed himself to before his pastor and before God.

Bill, on the other hand, had been distinctly absent from Long Beach Community Church since Jack had last seen him in Karl's living room. Still, it was a small town, and most folk knew each other's business. It was no great secret that Bill could be found, most any night, warming a barstool down at Doc's Tavern in Long Beach, sharing his woes with whomever would listen.

Following that terrible night at the Ferguson's house, Jack hadn't dreamed of Kathy again, and though he knew that he wasn't completely free of his own misplaced desires, Jack found his thoughts drawn less and less to her.

This he took as an answer to the long hours spent on his knees, in heartfelt, and often tearful prayer, both in the sanctuary of the church and in his little cabin by the bay. Kathy, since her meeting with Karl and the Petersons in early January, had become an integral part of the church's work with the Missions board, and Sarah Mack's right hand in that ministry. Jack was relieved that she had found a place in the church where she could make a difference, though her presence among the teen girls was sorely missed.

By March, Jack and his kids, led once more by the theatrically gifted Trevor, were hard at work on an Easter performance. Pastor Karl, a big believer in putting one's money where one's mouth is, had included in his gushing praise of the Christmas performance, the announcement of a yearly youth drama budget of two hundred dollars. While not an overwhelming windfall, still, the youth were ecstatic, committing on the spot to match that amount in fund-raisers. Now, three months later, a script had been chosen and parts were cast.

"One nice thing," Jack told Karl, over breakfast at the Caboose, "about leading a small youth group is that nobody gets left out. Quite the opposite," he had laughed, "I have half the kids playing more than one part, and working as backstage crew as well!"

Besides the youth meeting and upcoming play, Jack still maintained the church building and kept up his weekly visits to those who hadn't been able to attend the Sunday service. It was a hectic, sometimes dizzying workload, but Jack found himself happier than he'd ever been.

Chapter Eighteen

Jack sat relaxing in a deep corner of the Sand Castle Bookstore's worn sofa, studying the script for his returning role of the narrator. He was surprised when Dottie came out of the backroom and told him, with an unabashed smirk, that he had a phone call on the office line.

Karl had come to refer to the little seaside bookshop as Jack's second office. In truth, a week did not often go by that he didn't find himself passing beneath the tinkling doorbell to peruse the shelves, or chew the fat with the shop's outlandish owner.

In the intervening months since he had cashed in his Christmas gift from the Beckmans, Jack had become a recognized piece of furniture at the shop. Dottie usually had a hot cup of coffee on the table beside his favorite seat moments after he walked through the door.

Jack had never known his own grandmother, but he liked to imagine that she was something like Dottie Westscott. A sweet old woman, barely five foot tall in heels; she would give you her last dime with a smile, but she had a twinkle in her eye that suggested it might be best to remain in her good favor. She was a woman who brooked no foolishness, not to her age, nor her gender. Dottie was famous, or infamous, throughout the peninsula, for having once faced down the hulking Sheriff Bradley as he stood at her counter, and rapping his knuckles smartly with a ruler when the officer had interrupted her. Glen Bradley, known far and near for his fearlessness and temper, had stammered an apology on the spot.

Dottie had taken an immediate shine to Jack Leland, and they quickly became confidants as well as sparring partners. The old woman had no truck with his *religious foolishness*, meaning the church, and she would tell Jack Leland that he could mind to his own corn, when he asked if she believed in God.

The first time that Jack had challenged her views on organized religion, she had sniffed and refused to reply.

However, when he came to the store the following day he found the *New*

Books table displayed every new age and evolution-related book that she could find on the shelves, with a hand lettered sign reading, *25% Off*. Jack had laughed until tears poured from his eyes, and bought a biography of Charles Darwin from the top of the stack.

"Doesn't sound good, honey," she whispered as she passed the cordless handset to Jack and then hurried away. "Hello?" Jack said. There was a pause and Jack thought he could hear a woman crying in the background.

"Jack," Karl Ferguson's familiar voice came back over the line, "I need you to come over to the church."

Jack stood and began stuffing his notes into his book bag. "What's up?"

He heard a pause and, with the sound of a door closing, the crying ceased, and Karl continued. "Just a little crisis with one of the families, and I need you to hold down the fort."

"I'm on my way."

"Good," Karl sighed, "I'll see you in a couple of minutes."

Jack hollered a thanks to Dottie as he set the phone down next to his coffee cup and, grabbing his bag and jacket, headed for the door. Ten minutes later his bike rolled into the gravel parking lot behind the church and he was up the back steps and inside. Many times, over the following years, Jack would wonder what might have happened if he had come through the front doors of the church instead, how much heartache might have been avoided.

However, it was the weathered back door, its paint peeling at the corners, that Jack tore open after vaulting the steps two at a time. Unfortunately, Karl Ferguson had just sent Kathy Beckman to that same door, promising to catch up to her in the parking lot, where the Petersons were to meet them momentarily. Karl then headed for the front foyer to meet Jack and get him into the office and away from the current storm that was brewing in the halls of Long Beach Community Church.

Jack lunged through the doorway and crashed into Kathy Beckman like a linebacker. Both went down in a jumble of arms, legs, and books.

"Katie!" Jack cried, leaping to his feet in dismay. "Oh man," he stammered, "I'm so sorry, are you okay?"

As Kathy rose shakily from the polished wood floor, Jack could see immediately that she was anything but okay. Much like the last time they had spoken, her eyes were red and swollen, and her cheeks damp with tears. This time, however, her right eye was a purple mass of bruised flesh, the upper and lower lids so swollen that Jack couldn't see the eye beneath. Kathy's knees buckled, forcing Jack to catch her around the waist before she could fall again, and, at that worst possible of moments, a furious Bill Beckman rounded the corner of the hallway, with Pastor Ferguson on his heels.

Bill skidded to a stop, his eyes widening at the sight of his wife, once again, in Jack's arms. With a roar, he started forward. This time, however, it wasn't embarrassment or shame that flooded Jack, as he lowered Kathy to the floor, it was rage.

Jack took two long strides and met Bill's charge with a thunderous pile driver, and the meaty *thunk* of his fist connecting with Bill's face reverberated down the hallway of the church. Bill's momentum carried him forward, and Jack's military training brought a knee up into the man's skinny midsection, driving the wind from his lungs and flipping him neatly over, crashing to the floor on his back.

Bill lay there, blood pouring down his face and he struggled to focus his eyes, his arms pin-wheeling drunkenly as he tried to rise.

"You *hit* her?" Jack bellowed, curling up his fists and starting forward again, he could hear Karl shouting as he ran towards them, but his words were lost in the crimson tinged fury that surrounded Jack like a thick fog.

As Bill made it, shakily, to his knees, Jack drew back his fist again, and then Karl Ferguson's bulk hit him like a freight train, driving him up against the hallway wall. Karl had some training as well and, when Jack's ears stopped ringing from the concussion, his pastor had both of his hands trapped behind his back and the younger man's feet spread wide enough to keep him off balance.

Jack felt blood trickling down his chin from where his lip had split when he hit the wall, and Karl's voice, shouting into his ear, began to form actual words as the haze around him dissipated.

"Calm down!" Karl bellowed. "Calm down, Jack, right now!"

Taking a deep breath, Jack slumped against the wall, wincing at Karl's grip on his wrists. "Okay," he said, "I'm okay Karl, you can let me go."

"Are you sure?"

"Yeah, I'm okay," Jack repeated.

The weight pinning him to the wall lifted, as Karl stepped back. The larger man kept his hands out in front of him, ready to grab Jack again if he tried to get at Bill, who had slipped back to the floor and lie groaning with both hands over his face.

In that first lucid moment after his rage had passed Jack realized that, as surreal as the moment seemed–

Wasn't I sipping coffee and reading the book of Mark just ten minutes ago?

–what made it even stranger was the silence, a shocked and deafening stillness as Kathy leaned against the wall where Jack had left her, staring at the bleeding figure of her husband, but offering no support or sympathy. She looked at Bill with a strangely distant, slightly disgusted look. As quickly as it had come, the tension seemed to melt from the room and Jack slumped back against the wall himself, panting and trembling. His right fist ached terribly as he flexed his fingers.

"Karl, I–" Jack started.

"Not now," Karl interrupted, wiping sweat from his gleaming forehead with one hand, as he waved off Jack's appeal with the other, "we'll talk about it later." Just then Martin and Bobbie Peterson opened the back door and froze in the entrance to the hallway.

"Good Lord!" Martin muttered, looking from Bill to Kathy to Karl. "Is everything okay?"

"Under control," Karl said, "but just barely. Let's get Kathy into your car and over to the hospital."

"Shouldn't we take Bill in, too?" Bobbie asked, grimacing at his swelling, blood-smeared face.

Karl glanced coldly over at Bill Beckman, who had given up trying to rise and simply lay, face down, on the floor. "Bill has his truck, let's get him into it and if he wants to get checked out, he can drive himself."

As the Petersons helped Bill and Kathy out of the hallway, and into the waiting cars, Karl caught Jack's elbow and pulled him into the office. Jack tried, again, to apologize for his actions, but Karl waved him off again.

"I'm not worried about that right now. If you hadn't given him that haymaker, I might have." Karl took a deep, shuddering, breath.

"Right now," he said, "my biggest concern is Kathy, I've tried to talk her into pressing charges, but she won't. She won't even admit that he hit her. She just keeps saying that everything will be okay."

Jack snorted in disgust, wiping blood from his lip with the back of his hand.

"Sorry about that," Karl said, nodding toward his bloodied chin, "I might have gotten a little carried away there."

"No," Jack said, "you did what you had to do," he shook his head ruefully, "I don't know what might have happened if I'd have gotten my hands on him again. I can't remember ever being that mad. Not in the war, not ever."

"We'll talk about that later," Karl repeated, and then turned to go. "Why don't you just lock up and head home, Jack?"

"Will do."

Once Karl had stumped wearily from the office, and after waiting to hear both cars pull out of the parking lot, Jack locked the doors to the old church and started for home. The sky was dark and ominous, thick with iron-gray storm clouds, and his heart was heavy as he pedaled toward Nahcotta, a lump of cold lead beneath his ribs.

Whatever chance he might have had at making amends with Bill had probably ended right there in the hallway. Jack felt an empty, hollow place in his heart where his oldest friend, his best friend, used to be. He knew it would never be the same after today.

It was nearly dusk, and rain was just beginning to patter across the cedar shingles of his roof, when Jack was startled from his reading by the brisk rapping of knuckles against his door. Crossing the cabin in his stocking feet, he peeked through the window to see Karl, a sad, exhausted smile on his face, peeking back.

Opening the door, he found his boss standing on the wide deck with a steaming pizza box in his hand. The smell of onions and sausage issuing from beneath the lid made Jack's stomach growl, as he ushered his guest in and took his coat, setting the pizza on the small dining table.

"Thought you might be hungry," Karl said, in lieu of a hello, "and I didn't feel like eating alone. You have any oysters?" Jack smiled as he pulled a couple of sodas and a plastic baggie of smoked oysters from the refrigerator.

The oysters he dumped in a pan and set on the hot plate to warm before adding them to the pizza. While they waited, Jack set out plates and napkins.

"Thanks Lord," he said simply, bowing his head, when the meal was ready.

Karl helped himself to a thick slice of pizza, took a long sip of his root beer and sighed.

"Well, they're keeping Kathy overnight," he said, "just to watch for a possible concussion…"

Jack felt the muscles in his neck tighten as blood rushed to his face; Karl noticed the set of his jaw and, reaching across the faded Formica, laid a steadying hand on his assistant's arm.

"Breathe, Jack. She's going to be okay."

"*This* time," Jack said with a grimace.

"Yes," he agreed, "this time. She still wouldn't make a statement, even after the doctor called Paul Bradley in," Karl chuckled humorlessly.

"Boy oh boy," he said, "you thought *you* were mad; you should have seen ol' Paul. If he could have gotten the truth from Kathy I think he would have tossed Bill into a cell about five minutes later, and I don't know that he would've opened a door first."

Jack smiled grimly, both at Karl's chuckle and at the thought of Bill Beckman's head bouncing off the bars a time or two. *Careful there*, he thought, *that attitude isn't going to solve anything.*

Karl must have been watching his face, or reading his mind.

"Prayer is what Bill Beckman needs," he murmured, "more than anything else, prayer." Karl sighed, "I know it's hard to think of what's best for Bill right now, but we have to."

Jack nodded, nibbling at his dinner, his appetite gone.

"Don't get me wrong," Karl continued, "I'd be just as happy to pray for Bill's salvation knowing that he's cooling his heels in jail, but that's up to Kathy, not me."

"Is she going to be all right?"

"I think so," he said. "As all right as she can be in this …situation. Hopefully one of them will come to their senses before she really gets hurt. If I had any proof, you can believe the good Sheriff would be knocking on Bill's door right about now. Ouch!"

Karl dropped the still molten pizza back on his plate and took a swallow of soda to cool his mouth. Jack took the opportunity to jump back into the conversation.

"So, is Bill going to be okay?"

"Oh, I'm sure he will be," Karl replied. "You popped him a good one, that's for sure, but he's tough," he grimaced, reaching for his dinner again, "and given his current attitude I'm sure you're not the first guy to slug him one recently. You learn that move in the war?"

"Yeah," Jack replied, remembering the long afternoons, sweltering in the Southeast Asian sun, practicing fighting forms on the blistering concrete runway at Can Tho. Karate, Tae Kwon Do, Kung Fu, torturous hours of exercise blanketing their minds from the horrors of the war around them.

"Never thought I'd need to do that again, that's for sure."

"Well," Karl chuckled, "I was pretty sure you didn't pick that up in Bible

College!"

Both men laughed at this, and then there was a moment of silence as Karl's smiled faded again.

"You realize," he said, "that this means that you're going to have to be even more careful around her? This is a small town, and word about what happened today will get around, I guarantee it. People are going to be watching you even more closely now." Karl shook his head, frowning. "It's unfair, you and I both know it, but what's fair and what's likely are worlds apart."

"I can live with that," Jack said with a grimace, "one point they did make clear in college was that, as pastors, we could expect to be under the microscope most of the time."

Karl breathed a long sigh.

"Boy isn't that the truth," he agreed, "but maybe it's for the best. There are a lot of temptations out there and sometimes it's easier to turn away when you know that somebody's probably watching," Karl smiled, shaking his head, "the irony being, of course, that God is always watching."

They talked some more as sunlight faded from the bay. The pizza cooled and, piece-by-piece, disappeared. Karl asked how the Easter performance was going, and Jack gave him the rundown, doing his best Trevor Rigby impression as he explained the *traditions* of the theatre. Karl roared with laughter. The two discussed the coming summer, plans for a second church camp-out, plans to paint the building, all the minutia of keeping the ministry rolling and bringing the souls of Long Beach to a saving knowledge of Christ.

Finally, Karl rose to his feet with a grunt, rubbing the small of his back and yawning hugely.

"About time for me to head home, Jack," he said, "any later and I'll be too sleepy to drive."

"Well," Jack replied with a straight face, "you can't sleep on my couch. I've heard you snoring at the office and I want to get some rest!"

"How did I ever end up with a smarty-pants like you, anyway?" Karl groaned, rolling his eyes beseechingly towards heaven, as though done some great, unwarranted, injustice.

"Just lucky!" Jack smirked, holding the door open for him. "You know what the Book says, the prayers of a righteous man…"

Karl laughed, turning to clap Jack on the shoulder. "It's going to be okay, Jack," he said. "Once we've had a chance to talk some sense to Kathy, I'm sure she'll do what's best. I don't think Bill's likely to give you a hard time again, at least until the swelling goes down and his nose stops smarting."

"I hope you're right, boss," Jack said, "I really do. You drive safe, I'll see you tomorrow."

"Will do!" Karl replied and then disappeared down the steps and around the side of the house. Jack could hear his heavy footsteps as he made his way back up the path through the rain to the parking lot of the hotel.

Karl had seen a lot in his four decades at the pulpit, some bad, a lot more of it good.

His experiences, coupled with his devotion to prayer and study of God's word, had built in him an above average wellspring of wisdom.

(Though Karl would have said it was God's wisdom and that he just listened as best he could.)

Still, if you received the pastor's counsel on something, you could pretty much take it to the bank.

This time, however, Karl Ferguson's optimism turned out to be, to the great misfortune of everyone concerned, about as wrong as wrong could be.

ॐ

After washing the plates and bagging the trash, Jack settled down to read a few more chapters in the new science fiction novel that Dottie had forced on him earlier in the week. Laser swords and androids weren't his usual cup of tea, but Jack found the underlying theme of good versus evil to be interesting. Sometime around eleven he found his eyes refusing to focus on the pages of the paperback and, slipping in a bookmark to save his place, Jack snapped off the light and settled back into his pillow.

He thanked God for the day, and asked for His guidance in the ones to follow, praying for Kathy and sincerely, if somewhat less fervently, for Bill. Moments later he was asleep.

Chapter Nineteen

When his eyes snapped open, in the cold, predawn hours of early morning, Jack lay still for a few seconds, trying to clear the cobwebs from his head, and determine what had woken him.

His question was answered when someone or something crashed along the deck and into the cabin's wall. Jack leaped to his feet and started across the darkened room as a heavy fist pounded on the door. Still groggy with sleep, the thought that he might be in danger came to Jack a split second before the locked door of the cabin burst inward, the frame littering the front room in a shower of splinters. Jack flipped on the overhead light, and this unconscious action saved his life.

In the sudden blinding glare, the first shot from the revolver went wide, the bullet punching through the door of the refrigerator a foot to his left. Bill Beckman weaved through the doorway, his face swollen and bruised, squinting and blinking painfully as he raised the gun for a second shot. Jack leaped forward, catching him in a tight embrace, his hand locking around Bill's wrist, forcing the weapon down and away. Bill shouted something, but his words were lost in the strident ringing in Jack's ears. The two men struggled back and forth across the room, overturning furniture as they went. As the deafening echo of the pistol's report began to fade, Jack could make out the steady stream of profanities, spewn into his face in a gale of fetid, boozy breath.

"Bill!" Jack bellowed. "What do you think you're doing?"

Bill grunted as Jack slammed him back into a wall of books, most of which came tumbling to the floor.

"You're dead, Jackie," he hissed, "you hear me? You've messed around with my wife for the last time!"

He brought a knee up into Jack's groin, connecting hard, and Jack gagged, barely able to keep his grip as waves of pain and nausea swept over him.

"You're crazy," Jack grunted, "you're out of your mind, Bill! Nothing's ever happened between me and Kathy; if you weren't drunk all the time–"

Bill tried to knee him again, but this time Jack was ready, waiting until his opponent had one foot in the air before dropping to the floor and sweeping Bill's supporting leg out from under him. Bill dropped on top of Jack, his elbow driving into Jack's ribs, bringing a dull crack like splitting branches and white-hot pain. The pistol skittered across the wood floor, coming to rest with a resounding *thump*, against the leg of Jack's writing table.

With another grunt, Jack drove the heel of his hand into Bill's broken nose, and the bigger man screamed. Jack threw him off and leaped towards the gun, only to come crashing back to the floor as knife blades of pain speared his side. Thick hot bile rose in his throat as he clutched at his cracked ribs, and hobbled across the room.

Bill had risen groggily, his head spinning as much from the liquor and the punishment it had received that day. Blood poured, anew, down his face as his eyes fell on the gun that Jack was crab-walking across the floor towards. He cursed as he launched himself across the room to get the pistol.

Again he dropped onto Jack, and Jack screamed as the sudden weight drove his injured ribs into the floor. The two men rolled together in a confusion of arms and legs, until Jack suddenly found himself on top, his knees pinning Bill's shoulders to the ground. He paused a moment trying to catch his breath as his side burned in agony. Bill stared up at him with dark, hate-filled eyes.

"I'll kill you," he panted through clenched teeth, "I'll kill you both before I'll let you have her!"

Jack looked into Bill's hate-crazed face and went cold.

That look, that mixture of unvented rage and unshakable resolve, was one that he had seen before. So many years before that it took Jack a long, sweaty moment to remember, and then the image of the Beckman's giant oak tree filled his mind. How old had they been, ten? Twelve? He couldn't remember for sure, but it had been summer, and both of them had been playing barefoot in the front yard. Having just returned with Bill's father from some errand in town.

The object that had kept them occupied for the last hour, and now focused their attention to the colossal old oak, was a little balsa-wood airplane. Just that morning, John Beckman, in a moment of uncharacteristic generosity, had laid a hard-earned quarter on the counter of Jack's Market for the toy.

The tiny aircraft, its thin wings striped with bright red ink, a squared-jawed pilot drawn into the cockpit, had made a number of daring flights from the Beckman porch already. Finally it was determined the real test would have to come from the high, dormered window of the attic. Moments after a much-regaled takeoff, the cool breezes off Willapa Bay proved to be their downfall as the little plane found itself hopelessly ensnared in the upper branches of the oak tree.

Jack had been disappointed, but Bill was livid. Toys were rare enough in his home that he wouldn't abandon this one so quickly and, after a long, jaw-grinding moment, he announced that he was going up to rescue the plane.

"Billy!" Jack had warned him, "your pop said to stay out of the tree. You're gonna get a whipping!"

"Maybe," Young Bill had growled, "but I'm getting my plane first."

With that he started barefoot up the tree and for several breathless moments it had appeared that he might make good on his oath. Then the inevitable occurred as, reaching for a branch just a little beyond his fingers, Bill had slipped, tumbling from the height of the second story bedroom window, to the ground below. Jack had winced at the audible snap of Bill's ankle as he landed, and rushed to him, as his friend turned pale, retching and crying out in pain. Jack had gotten a panicked arm under the injured boy and started toward the house and adult help, when Bill dragged him, hopping on his good foot, back to the oak.

Jack had tried to argue with him, but to no avail.

Billy Beckman, his pallid face awash with sweat and tears, started back up the tree. Something in his face caused Jack to step away, his protests dying in his throat. Something frightening.

Young Jack Leland watched his friend climb, hopping from one branch to the next, his broken ankle wobbling sickeningly behind him. Bone-crushing determination locked Bill's jaws so his screams of pain escaped muffled, through his teeth. It was a sight that he would never forget.

Moments later the cheap, store-bought toy had drifted to the ground, moments after that, Bill hopped from the last branch and onto the grassy lawn, where he fainted dead away into Jack's arms.

Suddenly it seemed as though some great valve was turned in Jack's soul as all the anger and adrenaline poured out of him.

He stared down into Bill face and realized he was looking at a stranger, someone who bore no resemblance to anyone he had ever known; a man who was going to kill him, or die himself, in the effort. Jack felt weak and sick, tired deep in his soul, as he drew his fist back and drove it into this stranger's snarling, maddened face. Once, twice, three times he brought his fist down with all the strength that was left in him, each time connecting and driving

Bill's head back into the floor with a reverberating thud.

Pain screamed at him from already bruised knuckles, joining with his fresh injuries in a throbbing duet somewhere in a far back corner of Jack's mind. The fourth time his fist came down, Bill's eyes rolled back in his head and his weakly struggling arms collapsed to the floor. Jack rolled off him with a groan, scooping up the pistol from beneath the desk, unconsciously setting the safety, and placing it on the lowest shelf of the one bookcase that was still standing.

As he lay, for a moment, exhausted and panting, beside the comatose body of his once-friend, Jack could feel blood trickling from his nose and down over his lips, but he was too tired to wipe it away.

His little cabin was a mess. Books and papers lay scattered near and far, furniture and pieces of furniture were knocked about, and a pathetic, wheezing sound was emanating from the hole that Bill's .38 had drilled through his refrigerator. Orange juice bled from the bottom of the door.

Jack was sweating, shaking; the pain in his hand and ribs returning in full force as he heaved himself from the floor. His chest screamed in protest as he bent, grabbing Bill by one limp arm and, gasping, drug him into the bedroom and up onto his bed.

Bill groaned when his head hit the pillow, and after thoughtfully studying his lean, battered face for a moment, Jack drew back and punched him one last time, making sure he was going to stay out until the police arrived.

"Sorry, Billy," Jack mumbled, then turned and staggered toward the door.

Out of the cabin and into the rain, he tripped on the almost-empty whiskey bottle that Bill had dropped while coming across the porch. A short ugly phrase, one that Jack thought was long since removed from his vocabulary, slipped from between bleeding lips, as he lurched into the porch rail, bringing a fresh shriek of pain from his ribs.

❧

Rolf Parker would tell Sheriff Bradley, late the next afternoon as he sat in the latter's office drumming nervous fingers on his knees, that the clock on his bedside table had read 3:45am when Jack had woke him, pounding on the wood front door of the Moby Dick Hotel. Rolf had answered bleary-eyed and confused, but woke up quick when Jack told him what had happened in the little cabin.

"I'm really sorry about waking you up at this hour," Jack said, shifting his weight from one barefoot to the other on the cold concrete step, "but I've got to use your phone."

"Sure, sure," Rolf had said, his eyes wide, "luckily we have no guests tonight–Hey, you all right Jack? You're moving pretty stiff."

Jack winced as he stepped across the threshold, one hand still pressed firmly against his side.

"Yeah," he said, "I might have cracked a rib or two in the scuffle. I think my refrigerator got the worst of it, though!"

Rolf looked confused, but didn't ask Jack to clarify, instead, ushering him into the small office behind the kitchen, he pulled out the desk chair for him, before turning back toward the door.

"I'd best let the Missus know that everything's all right," he said, "I'll be back in a minute."

Jack nodded absently as he dialed Karl Ferguson's number from memory.

Karl answered on the second ring, sounding surprisingly alert and awake. He listened as Jack, again, outlined the events of the last half hour.

"Have you called the police?" Karl asked, as soon as Jack paused.

"Not yet."

"Do that as soon as we hang up."

"Yeah, will do," Jack replied.

"Jack," Karl said, "I've got what might be some more bad news."

Jack waited.

"I got a call from the hospital about an hour ago," Karl went on, "Kathy checked herself out around one o'clock this morning. She told the nurse that she couldn't afford to stay the night and that she was fine. There was nothing the nurse could do but call me."

Jack felt cold. If Kathy had left the hospital at one, she would have been home thirty minutes later, which meant that she could have found Bill there before he came over to the cabin. Bill's words suddenly rung in his ears…

"I'll kill you both before I'll let you have her."

"Jack?" Karl's voice raised a notch over the telephone line.

"Yeah," he said, "I'm here. Karl, we have to get over to Kathy's and make sure she's okay!"

"I'll take care of that," Karl assured him, "you wait there for the police. They're going to need a statement from you and they'll have a lot of questions."

"No way, Karl," Jack replied, "I'm calling the police and then I'll meet you at the Beckman's." Karl started to argue and Jack took the most expedient route available to him and hung up the phone. He stood as Rolf walked back into the office, two steaming cups of coffee in his hands.

"Here," he said, holding one of the mugs out for Jack, "I don't think either of us are going to get any more sleep tonight."

Jack set the mug on the desk.

"Thanks Rolf," Jack said, "but I don't have time. I need you to do me a couple of big favors. First, I need you to call the police, tell them what's happened, and have them come pick up Bill." Rolf nodded, taking a small sip of coffee from the cup that shook in his thin hands.

"Second," Jack said, "I need to borrow your car. I have to meet Pastor Karl right away."

Rolf nodded wordlessly, as he reached above the desk and took a small ring of keys from a hook on the wall, tossing them to Jack.

"Take the pickup," he said. "The Datsun's low on gas." Jack nodded and was out the door and across the parking lot before Rolf had finished dialing the Sheriff's office.

Bill's big Ford was parked in the turn-around and Jack looked through the open driver's window and saw the keys dangling from the ignition. Without thinking about it, he pocketed them.

❧

Jack pushed Rolf's little Toyota pickup for all it was worth, barreling down Sandridge Road at roughly twice the posted speed limit. The nearly weightless back end of the compact truck fishtailed into the Beckman's long gravel driveway and, for a brief, sweaty moment, Jack was sure he was going to wrap it around the big oak tree in the front yard. He missed it, barely, and slid to a stop a few feet short of the walk.

Vaulting from the seat, the driver's door swinging half shut behind him, Jack raced up the sagging steps and across the wide porch. The front door stood open and Jack's heart leaped into his throat at the sight of that flat, yellow light pouring out into the darkness. He was calling Kathy's name as he crossed into the front room, his voice echoing hollowly through the quiet house. Everything seemed normal; couches and love seat were still beneath their dark green shrouds, photos hanging straight on the walls, the place was the picture of peaceful domesticity.

Jack rushed upstairs, shouting for her, his belly clenching with each room he entered, fearing the worst. Panic almost overtook him as he flung wide the door of the Beckmans' bedroom and saw what looked, at first, to be a woman's body draped across the back corner of the big oak bed.

Looked to be?

No way. For a dark and eternal two seconds, Jack had seen Kathy Beckman's corpse in the scant moonlight seeping through the bedroom window. He felt his stomach heave and a harsh, gasping, cry of shock tore from his throat. The world around him tilted, and when it righted itself, the shape on the bed was only a carelessly strewn pile of women's clothes, cascading across the comforter and down onto the hardwood floor.

Jack paused, sagging against the doorframe, certain that he was going to throw up. A couple of deep breaths later his stomach settled, and his legs, which had turned to jelly on him, quit their shaking and firmed up enough to continue his search. Coming back down the stairs, and rounding the corner into the dining room, Jack ran directly into a shadowed, hulking form coming out of the kitchen. This time Jack did scream and, blinded by fear, threw a quick fist out in front of him. Karl Ferguson blocked the punch smoothly and grabbed Jack's arm, spinning him out and away.

"You know," Karl growled, "for a pastor, you sure hit people a lot!"

For the second time in as many minutes, Jack's heart resumed beating and he looked at Karl for a long, frozen moment, as predawn silence descended over the house again. Suddenly he started laughing. The stresses and shocks of the last twenty-four hours came crashing down on Jack and his knees buckled, sending him to the floor in convulsions of silent, uncontrollable mirth.

Karl watched him, pulling a chair from the table and settling his big frame into it with a sigh. He chuckled, watching Jack slowly regain control and sit up, wiping tears from his eyes, as he held his aching ribs.

"Rolf told me you were hurt," Karl said.

"I'll be okay," Jack replied. "Kathy's gone, at least she's not anywhere I could find. There's a big pile of clothes on the bed upstairs but, besides that, everything looks normal."

Karl snorted. "It's a good thing you're a youth pastor instead of a detective," he said.

"Why's that?"

"The first thing I saw in here," Karl said, "was that one of the dining room chairs was overturned and there was a letter on the table in front of it."

He pursed his lips. "I don't think Kathy's dead, I think she left."

Jack pulled himself to his feet, grabbing the edge of the table for support.

"What's it say?"

"I don't know, it's got Bill's name on it."

"Yeah, and that's Kathy's handwriting, so open it."

"Isn't that against the law," Karl asked, "opening someone else's mail?"

Jack sighed, "It's only mail once it's been *mailed*, and you know it. Now, are you going to read it or do you want me to?"

Karl stared at him grimly. "I don't suppose telling you to leave it alone would do any good?"

"You told me not to come over here, didn't you?"

"Yes."

"And you can see how well that worked. So, why don't you just read the letter?"

Karl sighed again and picked up the envelope, as Jack eased himself into the chair opposite his boss. "Well?" he asked.

"It's empty."

"C'mon!"

"Seriously," Karl said, "it really is empty!"

He tossed the envelope across the table to Jack, and then stood looking around the room. "Aha!" he said, and hurried over to the china hutch on the far side of the dining room. Bending with a grunt, he scooped up a wadded ball of paper from the floor and walked back over to the table with it.

"I think Bill must have already gotten his mail, and he didn't like what he read." Quickly, Karl flattened the paper back out and read:

Bill,

I told you that if you ever hit me again I would leave. You are not the man I married anymore, and I'm afraid to stay here with you any longer. I know that what I am doing is sin and I will have to pay the consequences for it myself, but the risk has become too great.

I know what you think about Jack and I, and this is the last time that I'm going to tell you you're wrong. Stop drinking before it kills you. Jack has always been your friend and could help you if you'd only let him. I'll write when I'm settled, please don't try to follow me.

Kathy

The two men stared at each other in silence. Outside the old house, the storm resumed with full fury, sleet and hail peppering the windows and rattling off the shingled roof. A sudden clap of thunder, close by and shockingly loud, made them both jump in their seats. Finally, Karl folded the wrinkled letter and slipped it back into the envelope.

"We should go, Jack," Karl murmured. "The police will be waiting at the cabin."

Jack rose numbly and followed Karl out into the storm to their vehicles.

As they headed back toward Nahcotta, this time at a much more sensible speed, the storm began to dissipate. By the time the two trucks pulled off toward the gravel parking lot of the hotel, there was just a slight rain misting their windshields.

As soon as they rounded the corner into driveway, Jack knew that something was terribly wrong. A state police car was parked sideways across the entrance, and a trooper in a heavy black poncho stood, flashlight in hand, near the front bumper, waving them to a stop. Beyond him, in the wane light of the parking lot, Jack could see two more state police cars, Paul Bradley's suburban, and the boxy outline of an emergency rescue van. Each vehicle had its flashers going and the big, flat front of the hotel pulsed red and blue, as the first purple smudges of dawn began to ooze over the lip of the coastal range.

Karl spoke to the officer through the truck window, and the cruiser pulled forward allowing them to enter. As soon as the back bumper of the Toyota passed him, the trooper put the car in reverse, blocking the entrance again.

They parked and walked together toward the front doors, as troopers rushed back and forth around them, radios squawking, without a second glance. Jack figured that if they made it past the roadblock, everyone must assume that they had reason to be there. Coming up the walk, the two men could see the shattered remains of the hotel's big picture window that were spread, like a million tiny diamonds, across the stone path, and a great, gaping hole centered the frosted pane.

Inside the hotel was only slightly less chaotic.

Chapter Twenty

Jack and Karl identified themselves to the officer at the door, who ushered them into the dining room. There they found a very pale Rolf and Tina Parker, seated with Sheriff Bradley and two state troopers.

Rolf looked dazed, as he sat holding an ice pack to an ugly gash on his forehead. A paramedic stood behind him, just opening his med kit. The old innkeeper looked wearily up at Jack, recognized him, and began to weep, his wife taking his quaking hand in her own.

As all eyes turned to him, Jack's mind suddenly filled with a brilliant memory, almost a vision, of himself; rising slowly to his feet from the cabin floor and reaching over Bill's unconscious body to lay the loaded pistol on the bookshelf.

He felt something cold and hollow form in the pit of his stomach.

"Jack," the reticent little man wept, "I'm so sorry Jack, I tried to stop him..."

"My God," Karl breathed, "What's happened?"

One of the state troopers confirmed their identities again, and then briefed them on the events of the last hour, reading directly from the hastily written notes before him.

Apparently someone had hammered on the door of the hotel about ten minutes after Jack had pulled away in the borrowed Toyota. Rolf, thinking that it was the police that he had just called, opened the door to find Bill Beckman, his face covered in blood, the .38 in his hand pointed at Rolf's face. Bill was incoherent, screaming profanities and calling for Jack. He pushed Rolf out of his way and started into the hotel. The old man, fearing for himself and his wife, tried to grab the pistol from his hand, but Bill had shoved him off and then cracked him across the forehead with the side of the heavy revolver.

It might have been worse, much worse, if Tina Parker hadn't stepped out of the bedroom at that moment, her husband's pump action twelve-gauge shotgun at her shoulder (the Parkers prided themselves, each season, on fresh duck and goose from the hotel kitchen) the big barrel pointed at Bill.

He had taken a step toward her and Tina had twitched the gun to her right, firing a deafening shot through the window before jacking in a fresh round and leveling on Bill's head again.

She had told him, in a hard quavering voice, that the next shot wouldn't miss, and he must have believed her.

Months later, a friend asked her if she'd meant what she had said to Bill Beckman that night, and Tina had taken a long sip from her teacup before responding.

"I saw my Rolf there on the floor," she had murmured, "blood pouring down his face. Jesus himself as my witness, it was all I could do to put that first shot through the window instead of taking Bill Beckman's head off his shoulders."

Tina Parker had stood there, the weight of the big gun making her arms ache, as Bill lowered the pistol and staggered out through the door and back down the trail toward the cabin. Ten minutes later she had heard the gunshot over the raging wail of the storm. Paul Bradley had arrived five minutes after that, and called the state police after finding Bill's body lying in the shallows of the bay, the pistol and an empty whiskey bottle on the ground beside him.

Jack felt as though all the color had been sucked from his world. The black, cold well in his belly expanding to encompass him, and he heard his own voice speaking, as the room around him grew flat and monochrome. He couldn't feel his lips moving but, and though it felt like someone else asking, he knew it was his own words.

"Is he dead?"

Sheriff Bradley looked down at his paperwork for a moment, then back up at Jack with big, tired eyes.

"Bill shot himself in the head, point-blank, with a thirty-eight caliber revolver. By some…" the big officer glanced at Karl as he said the word, "…*miracle* he was alive when the ambulance got here. Miracle or not, I wouldn't believe my own mother if she told me he's still breathing when they get to the hospital."

Finally it was too much; the assaults on his mind and body in the last twenty-four hours rolled over him like a great black cloud. As the old hotel dining room began to spin, Jack gave himself over, and was enveloped by the encroaching oblivion with an almost grateful sigh.

ஃ

Kathy Beckman stepped from the wheezing Greyhound and into the arid, nearly deserted bus station. A sagging, dusty banner hung above the double glass doors, welcoming her to Bowie, Arizona. Reaching for her suitcase she pressed a gentle hand to her stomach, imagining that she could feel the life that had begun to quicken there. She shook her head.

"You haven't even outgrown your jeans," she muttered, "no one's moving around in there yet."

Lifting her suitcase, a cheap blue vinyl stuffed to bursting, Kathy stood looking around the room as the late afternoon sun glowed through the swirling dust.

So this is Bowie, she thought grimly. What in the world had Grace Ebretson found here that could have convinced her to stay? Kathy knew though. It was love; love for a gangly young Bible college student named Guy Williams.

Guy had wooed her childhood friend and then moved her out here to the edge of the desert, where the endless seas of sand baked in the noon sun and froze at night.

Love. The word burned in her brain, bitter oil on her lips, her year-long marriage having just ended in her flight to this infinitesimal town. She'd come here alone, pregnant and nearly penniless, based on the strength of a twenty-year-old friendship with a woman she hadn't seen in a decade. Behind her, far to the west, was the man she had fled. Her first three months as Mrs. Katherine Beckman had been a dream, but the dream had faded into a dark alcoholic nightmare as William Beckman slipped back into the life he had hidden so well during their courtship.

Once Bill had regained a firm grasp on the bottle, the fuse to his violent temper had become nonexistent and Kathy had found herself, more and more often, at the receiving end of his rages. A week before, she had come home from the doctor's office giddy with joy over her unexpected pregnancy, only to find her husband blind drunk and looking for trouble. Something had stayed her lips that night, and she had told herself to wait until Bill was in a better mood to give him the good news.

Then, just days later, she had walked into the living room with his breakfast and, from nowhere, a bony fist had connected with her eye. An explosion of bright, pain-filled sparklers, had driven her to the floor in a rain of milk and cornflakes. Light faded from the room and her ears had rung so loud that they drowned out her husband's drunken curses.

Eighteen hours later Kathy had found herself in Astoria.

The ticket she'd bought under a fictitious name clutched in her trembling hand, and her hat pulled low to hide the massive purple bruise that covered the right side of her face.

She had paced the worn linoleum floor of the tiny coastal bus station, trembling with fear that Bill would find her before she got away, that he would drag her back home, drag *them* back home. She couldn't let her child be born in that house; she wouldn't.

That had been two days before and, after her long ride from the West Coast, the bruises were just beginning to fade to a sickening yellow behind the cheap sunglasses she had picked up in Portland. Two long days of agony; the pain of her battered flesh overshadowed by the pain in her heart. She had loved her husband once, but now there was only fear. What would she do if Gracie couldn't help her; where would she go? And what must her friend think of her, after all this time, begging her to open their home to a stranger? A pregnant stranger? Kathy had huddled miserably, across all the miles, writhing in shame for what she had been reduced to, certain she had made a dreadful mistake.

One of the front doors squeaked open and a tall thin young couple stepped into the room. They paused, letting their eyes adjust to the relative dimness, before the woman caught sight of Kathy. Grace Williams crossed the wide concrete floor of the station and wordlessly enfolded her oldest friend in her arms, stroking her hair gently as Kathy began to sob.

Chapter Twenty-One

Long, yellowing fluorescent lights hung from the ceiling, washing down the stark white walls and across the lime-green tiled floors of the small hospital. Two doors opened, with a pneumatic wheeze, at the emergency entrance on the back wall of the building. Blue and white striped curtains attached to gleaming aluminum frames that hung from the ceiling, cordoning off each of the four tiny trauma rooms.

The waiting room was small as well, two couches with a long, low table between them, a couple of wooden chairs and an old console style television that gave a slightly greenish picture, though most folks don't seem to notice.

Their eyes may have been on the flickering jade sitcoms that filled the nighttime slots on KLTV, but their hearts and minds were usually elsewhere in the building.

Now though, there were no other patients and only one of the curtained exam rooms was occupied. The staff consisted of two nurses and one doctor, all three of whom were currently involved in the organized panic of station three, where their only patient lay. The waiting room, like the rest of the hospital, smelled strongly of bleach and some type of orange scented cleaner. A CB radio, for communication with emergency vehicles, crackled in the background.

Besides that and the low chatter from the television, the only sound was the rhythmic tick of a round wall clock, mounted above the main entrance.

It reminded Cassie of the clock in her high school cafeteria.

Guy, who had promised her that he would explain everything as soon as he got back, had headed out into the misty, predawn morning to find someplace, anyplace, that might have a cup of coffee. He had also promised to rescue the box of old books that Cassie had suddenly remembered were still sitting in the unlocked van.

Cassie sat slumped on the hard vinyl couch, her body exhausted, her mind awhirl. Jack's last words, before slipping into unconsciousness, kept repeating slowly and monotonously in her brain like a broken record.

"I wish she was mine, Kathy, I wish she had been ours..."

Over and over, the words ran through her mind. She had been so certain about Jack. The picture in his wallet, the handwriting in the Bible, how could it *not* be him? *Why couldn't it be him?* Was her father dead, then? Was he still alive, living somewhere close by? Now that she knew the man who had brought her halfway across the country wasn't her father, bitterness began to coil and writhe in her belly once more.

Jack, she could try to forgive and understand.

Now though, her father was again the faceless stranger who had abandoned her and her mother, and Cassie felt her heart hardening again. She ground her teeth in frustration. Everything that she thought she had learned on the long drive west, all the clues and hints, none of them meant anything!

Suddenly she was angry, no, she was *furious* with God.

How could he tease her like that, lead her along, and let her believe all that she had? She looked down at the Bible, resting beside her on the faded seat of the couch, and picked it up, ready to hurl it across the room and be done with it. Her mother's fading, gold initials caught her eye and, instead, she jammed the book savagely into her bag, and kicked it away from her.

Just then, the double doors *whooshed* open, and Guy Williams returned, carrying two steaming paper cups in one hand, and a white paper bag in the other. He saw the dark expression on Cassie's face and paused, then sat down on the couch opposite her, laying the fruits of his search between them.

"You look about ready to chew nails and spit staples," he said, offering her one of the white to-go cups, "settle for some cocoa, and a bear claw instead?"

Cassie took the hot paper cup from him, but shook her head slightly when he held out the bag.

"I'm not hungry," she said, taking a tiny sip of the scalding chocolate. It had the dusty, vacuum bag flavor of instant cocoa, and she set the cup on the table. Her anger at God was still seething, and here before her was someone on which to vent her spleen.

"So, that was you in the truck all along?" she asked, glowering across the table at him. "Do you have any idea how freaked out we were? I thought for sure that you were this truck driver that attacked me in Phoenix, hunting me down to finish the job!"

Guy set his coffee down, "You were attacked?"

Cassie waved a hand dismissively, "Jack rescued me, but when we realized we were being followed, Jack had the guy checked out and he was a bad character. We thought he was stalking us."

"Well," Guy said, leaning back with a frown of his own, "serves you right if you ask me. Last thing we knew, you were headed for Portland on a Greyhound, then we get a call from Eleanor Young, down at the bus station, who, by the way, had some fairly uncomplimentary things to say about you..."

Despite her dark mood, Cassie had to grin at the memory of the frustrated ticket agent. Guy raised an eyebrow at her response and went on.

"Eleanor plays Bunko with Grace," he said, "and she remembered your mom's accident. She called us to ask if we knew that you had cashed in your ticket, or where you were going." Guy's frown deepened, "Grace hasn't slept a night through since that phone call, you know."

Cassie looked guiltily at the worn tips of her hiking boots, her own anger beginning to fade into a gnawing shame, as Guy went on.

"Grace and I spent that night driving up and down I-10, looking for you. When we didn't find you, I figured that you must have caught a ride into Tucson or Phoenix."

"Wait," Cassie interrupted, "how did you know I was going to Phoenix?"

Guy sighed, "I'm not just some hick from the sticks, Cass. If someone wanted to hitch a ride west from Bowie, Phoenix is the most likely place to do it from. God answers prayers though, because I just happened to glance over and see you in Jack's van, pulling out of the truck stop as I was pulling in. I was just getting ready to turn around and head back home, too."

"Where did you get the truck?" she asked.

"I rented it in Benson, and left the car for Grace to pick up. Then we started our little cat and mouse game across the country. I thought you had me in Gold Beach, when I couldn't find the exit to that library lot."

Cassie laughed, and then frowned, "If you knew it was me, why didn't you just stop us?"

"What good would *that* have done?" he replied, sipping from the coffee and taking a huge bite of his doughnut.

"I suppose I could have hog-tied you and brought you back to Bowie in the bed of the truck, but you would have just taken off again. I can't spend the rest of my life tracking you down; the rental fees alone would break me."

Cassie smiled again, but sheepishly, still feeling guilty for the lies she had told and the trouble she had put Guy and Grace through.

"Besides," Guy went on, "I saw you and Jack together enough to feel like you were safe with him, so I thought I'd just tag along until you got to where you were going." He grinned suddenly. "I've known you your whole life,

Cassie, and your mother a long while, too. If I've learned any one thing, it's this: when one of you makes up her mind to do something, it's best to just stand aside and let you do it!"

Cassie laughed again, some of her anger with God and worry over Jack starting to dissipate. Guy was right; he had known her all of her life and he was the closest thing to father she had ever known. It was such a relief to have him near, to not be alone. The old photograph of Guy, waist deep in the river, baptizing Kathy Belanger and her baby daughter, sprung to Cassie's mind and her eyes filled with tears. They loved her so much, and she had treated them so badly.

"I'm sorry," she whispered, her voice quavering, "I'm so sorry that I worried you and Grace, I just didn't think."

Cassie broke down, burying her face in her hands to hide her tears. The next moment Guy was beside her, his familiar arms circling her, and she clung to him, desperate for his reassurance. She heard him murmuring prayers as he stroked her hair. Finally, the worst having passed, she sniffled and lifted her head. Guy smiled at her and kissed her forehead, slipping back over to the other couch. Cassie took a sip of her cocoa and then, slowly and methodically, gave Guy the step-by-step of her trip West. The hands on the big clock had made two revolutions by the time she had finished.

There was a long silence, punctuated by Cassie's occasional sniffle, and the squawk of the dispatch radio. Guy took her hand and said another quick prayer, thanking God for her safety, then sat back with a long sigh.

"That's a story and a half," he said, "but Jack sounds like a good guy. I can see why you thought that he might be your father. I wish I had a clue, but your mom never mentioned him, or your father, to us." Guy glanced at his watch. "Has the doctor said anything, yet?"

As if on cue, a nurse stepped into the room, smiling awkwardly. Cassie had the sudden impression that she had been waiting behind the half-closed door until Guy had finished his prayer. She looked to Cassie to be in her middle thirties, pretty, with dark red ringlets cascading over the shoulders of her crisp white uniform.

"Cassie Leland?" she asked, checking her clipboard.

Guy raised an eyebrow in Cassie's direction but said nothing. Cassie blushed to her roots under her pastor's gaze.

Names are like clothes, different suits for different occasions, that's what I say.

"Yes?"

The woman offered her hand, which Cassie shook.

"I'm Aimee Phillips," she said, "and I wanted to thank you for getting Jack here so quickly, he's a very old friend, and I think you may have saved his life tonight."

Cassie nodded, fighting back tears.

"I didn't know that Jack had a niece," Aimee went on, "but I sure *thought* you looked familiar, when you came in."

"Is Jack going to be okay?" Cassie asked, changing the subject.

"We're pretty sure he'll be fine," Aimee replied, checking her paperwork again. "He did have a heart attack, but luckily it was fairly mild. Too much fried food would be my guess. We'll keep him here a couple of days for observation, get him going on some blood pressure medication, but he should be home by the end of the week. We gave him enough morphine that he should sleep until tomorrow afternoon."

Cassie felt a knee-weakening wave of relief rush through her, as she squeezed Guy's hand. He squeezed right back.

"Just to let you know," Aimee said, "we sent a tow truck to pick up Jack's van. You can tell him that Wally has it in the shop, and he'll call in a couple of days for instructions."

Cassie thanked her, barely understanding what she was saying; *Jack was going to be okay!*

Aimee introduced herself to Guy, and asked if the two of them needed a place to stay for the night. "Not me," he replied, "I'm going to have to head back home tonight. I have to be back in Bowie day after tomorrow, I just wanted to make sure that Cassie got here safe."

"How about you?" he asked Cassie, and she smiled as he squeezed her hand again.

"I…I don't know. I need to find a hotel I guess…"

Aimee looked at her, puzzled. "A hotel?" she asked. "Aren't you going to stay with your uncle? Jack's place is only a few miles up the road."

"Oh," Cassie said. In the panic of the last several hours, she hadn't given a thought of where she'd be sleeping tonight.

"I'll tell you what," the nurse replied, "I'm off shift in about twenty minutes, how about if I give you a lift to Jack's apartment? Since you're a relative, I can give you his keys and things; at least you won't have to try to find a hotel at this time of night." Cassie agreed wearily. By now she was so exhausted that she would have agreed to a cot in the local jailhouse if it meant she could close her eyes and get some sleep. Aimee told her to wait there and she would meet her when the shift ended, leaving Cassie and Guy a few minutes to say good-bye.

"Is Grace going to kill you for not bringing me back?"

"Nah," Guy smiled, "she wanted me to make sure you were safe, that's all. It sounds like Jack's going to be okay, and you have a place to stay, Grace will be fine with that."

Guy paused a moment, thinking, then continued, "Well, maybe I'll give her a call tomorrow and let her know what's going on before I get home–"

"–and she can kill you." Cassie finished, laughing.

"Exactly!"

Guy and Cassie took hands and said a quick prayer, then he hugged her fiercely and she was surprised to see tears in his eyes.

"You take care of yourself, Kiddo," he murmured, "call Grace tomorrow and let her know you're all right. And you call us if you need anything…*anything*, you understand?" Cassie nodded and squeezed his hand one last time. Guy turned to go.

"Hey!" she called, as he reached the door.

"Yeah?" Guy said, turning.

"Don't lose your banana comb!" Cassie smiled.

Guy grinned and waggled a finger at her, "Don't you go pulling a knife on anyone!" he laughed. Then he was gone.

❧

Aimee and Cassie headed north in the nurse's Honda, the streets gleaming wetly beneath the blue-white glow of streetlights. They made some small talk about the weather, but it was clear that Aimee was tired from a long shift and Cassie from her lack of sleep. The conversation lapsed into a comfortable silence and the lull of the windshield wipers, skimming the morning mist from the glass, soothed Cassie to sleep. When she awoke, they were pulling up to a curb just off the main street.

"Here we are," Aimee said, shutting of the engine and lights.

Cassie looked around dazedly for a moment, expecting to see an apartment complex. Instead, what she saw was a looming, two story building, covered with heavy wooden shingles and painted a flat gray. It took her a moment to realize that she was looking at Jack's bookstore. A solid set of wood steps led up to a second-story landing and a single door. A dim light gleamed through the door's small window. Aimee had parked her little car behind a gleaming red Jeep with a black leather ragtop.

"Oh good," she said, coming around to meet Cassie on the sidewalk, "Beth's here."

Cassie grabbed her bag from the backseat and followed Aimee up the stairs. They knocked and a moment later came the sound of light footsteps, and the door opened.

A tall, willowy woman stood in the doorway. Her nearly black hair, just starting to gray at the temples, was pulled back and held in place with a leather barrette. High cheekbones and long raven lashes accentuated her bright, coral-blue eyes. She glanced from Aimee to Cassie, and when her gaze fell on the younger girl, something seemed to surprise her, her azure eyes widening and her hand starting to rise toward her mouth. There was a long pause as she stared at Cassie Belanger, her face gone slightly pale. Then she blinked, as though shaking herself from a daze, and turned her eyes from Cassie's face.

"Aimee," she said, taking the woman's hands in her own, "thank you for calling, I was just starting to worry. I still think I should have come down to the hospital. You're certain he's going to be okay?"

"He'll be fine," Aimee smiled, "and he wouldn't have even known you were there, with all the drugs we pumped into him. Better that you keep the home fires burning tonight; you can visit Jack tomorrow afternoon when he's awake. Until then you both need your rest." She smiled. "He's a tough old goat, and too stubborn to let a measly heart attack beat him."

The dark haired woman rolled her eyes.

"Don't I know it!" She sighed, and then seemed to remember that they were standing on the dark, cold landing at just after five in the morning, "Come in, both of you, come in!" She ushered them into the small apartment, closing the door behind them.

From the stunted hallway, a small living area gave the illusion of space beneath a high, vaulted ceiling. Beyond this, Cassie could see a tidy dining area and a door that she presumed led into the kitchen. One corner of the living room was taken with a small, antique writing table, the two adjoining walls with a leather sofa and love seat the color of warm caramel. All four walls were covered, from floor to ceiling, with books. The carpet was a deep, shag brown, and at least as old as Cassie, but clean and not too worn. The one space on the wall that was free of books stood above the writing table; this housed a stereo and three deep shelves of records and compact discs.

Cassie could see the corner of an old, upright piano, its top littered with picture frames, through the entrance to the dining area. It took her a long minute to realize what seemed out of place in the room: there was no television! She wondered, for an instant, if Jack kept a TV in his bedroom, but decided that he probably didn't. Who had time for the idiot box (as her mother had called it) when there were hundreds of books here to be read, and probably thousands more in the shop below?

"Can I get you something to drink," the woman asked, breaking Cassie's reverie, "some water, perhaps, or orange juice?"

"No, thank you," Cassie answered, feeling suddenly, strangely shy, "I'm fine, Ms…?"

The woman laughed, a high, silvery tinkle, and extended a hand towards her. "I'm getting too old to remember my manners," she smiled, "I'm Elizabeth Marshall, but please, call me Beth. I look after the store when Jack is gone."

Cassie might have been a young woman, but she *was* a woman, and she didn't miss the way Elizabeth Marshall's voice softened when she spoke Jack's name. Or the sad determination that crossed her face for a moment and then was gone.

The younger woman realized, in that moment, that Beth was very much in love with crusty old Jack Leland, and probably had been for some time.

Cassie felt a warm rush of empathy for her, and a sudden surge of irritation with Jack that made her jaw clench.

Beth smiled knowingly, still holding her hand, and murmured, "Careful honey, don't close the cover until you've read the whole book." Cassie blushed, embarrassed at being read so easily and, finally, Aimee broke the uncomfortable silence of the moment.

"Well," she said, a little louder than she meant to, "I'm going to head home. I've got a husband to feed and send off to work, a hot bath, and a warm bed waiting for me!"

Elizabeth laughed again and walked the young nurse to the door, giving her a quick hug and thanking her once more.

"Sounds like quite a schedule," she said, then bid the younger lady a goodnight and closed the door behind her.

The two women looked at each other, and Cassie felt that shyness again, beneath the older woman's strange, questioning gaze. Finally, Beth smiled.

"Well," she said, "I'm going to brew us a nice cup of tea to put us to sleep, then I'll make up the couch for you." She started toward the kitchen, calling back, "Why don't you put your bag down and have a look around?"

Cassie thanked her, dropping the duffel bag by the door and walking around the living room, studying the odd collection of books and knickknacks that lined the shelves. The books themselves ranged from huge, leather bound collections that looked to be hundreds of years old, some in foreign languages, to modern western and science fiction paperbacks. She brushed her fingers over the silky surface of the writing table and peered at the titles of the discs above. Mostly jazz, she noted, and no one she had ever heard of. Cassie stepped into the dining room, where a small oval table rested on the off-white linoleum.

The apartment must have been bigger than she had at first thought, Cassie realized, as she noticed the entrance to a second hallway.

A picture, resting on top of the piano, caught her eye and she crossed the room to it. It was an old, square, colored photo, similar in vintage to her baptism picture. That, however, wasn't the only common factor.

Three young people, with the beach and ocean behind them, stood, arm in arm, smiling at the camera.

Kathy Belanger was in the center.

Her hair hung in long, dark braids, her face broken in a carefree grin, and Cassie's breath caught in her throat, seeing her mother at a time before the sadness and fear had come to her eyes.

She was wearing a t-shirt that read LBCC Youth, and a pair of white cutoffs that showed her long, shapely legs all the way down to her bare feet. On her right was Jack, twenty years younger than the man who lay sleeping in the Ocean Park Hospital, medications slowly dripping into a needle in his wrist. No, this was Jack soon after the picture in his wallet was taken, the one of him in Vietnam. He, too, was grinning, and giving the camera a cheesy thumbs-up with one hand as the other was draped across Kathy's shoulder, his hand resting on the shoulder of the man opposite him. To Kathy Belanger's left, with a slight smirk on his lips, was a man that Cassie had never seen before, but a chill went through her all the same. Tall and lean, his bare chest and arms tanned, and his long black hair shining in the hot summer sun, was William Beckman, her father. He stood with his arm protectively around his young wife, one dark hand resting on her light-skinned waist.

Cassie slowly lifted the small photo from its place on the piano and gazed at it, so lost in thought that she didn't hear a door open and close softly from the hallway behind her. Shakily, her fingers traced the fading images of her mother, her father, and Jack. There was a faint ringing in her ears and everything seemed suddenly very bright. The small room began to spin.

"I'm going to faint," Cassie whispered matter-of-factly.

She might well have fainted, too, dropping the photo and slipping bonelessly to the cool, white floor, if a man's voice, sleepy and confused, hadn't, at just that moment, spoken up right behind her.

"Beth?" the voice asked, softly and slightly slurred.

Cassie spun with a blood-chilling shriek, dropping the picture after all, and lurching backwards into the piano. The man stood in the entrance to the hallway, clad in a gray t-shirt and matching sweatpants, shifting his weight from one barefoot to the other. He was tall, and looked to be going slightly to fat in his middle age. His hair was short and peppered with gray and a long pink scar ran down the left side of his face, from temple to jaw-line. His right eye seemed to bulge and be slightly off center. The man looked at Cassie with confused, slightly dull eyes, his lips wet and slack and his big hands clutching a worn stuffed rabbit nervously.

In another, less terrified, setting, the sight of the grown man with the toy bunny might have struck Cassie as humorous. Instead, as she stared at the man's face, her mouth gaped open and her breath came in a choked whistling gasp.

He was older, certainly, and had put on some pounds, but the man in the gray pajamas, one side of his fleshy face oddly skewed, was unmistakably her father.

Bill's reaction to Cassie's shriek was a shrill cry of his own; bringing the stuffed animal up to be clutched protectively to his chest. For just a moment, Cassie Belanger thought for sure that he was going to burst into tears. All of this happened in a heartbeat. Then, just as suddenly, the walls began to warp and close in, the pictures, the furniture, even Bill himself loomed in on her from where he stood, filling her vision, suffocating her.

Cassie whirled, she couldn't breathe!

She heard, over the roaring in her ears, the sound of Beth calling her name, faintly and from far away. Then she was out the door and down the wooden steps, barely catching her balance and saving herself from a nasty tumble to the concrete sidewalk below.

In the cold darkness the streetlights were ablaze and bolted to the one sitting on the nearest corner was a large sign, bathed in yellow light, that read: "Public Beach, 3 Blocks," a huge white arrow pointing the way. Cassie didn't hesitate, even at the sound of the older woman's voice calling to her from the landing, but ran, gasping the cold morning air as tears streamed down her pale cheeks.

Beth Marshall, formerly Elizabeth Beckman, once known to her older brother and a certain sandy haired friend, as the snipe, stepped back from the door and into the kitchen, where William Beckman stood clutching Pete, his stuffed rabbit, fearfully.

"It's okay, Billy," she murmured, taking his hand and rubbing his back, comfortingly, with the palm of one hand, "it's all right, I think you scared her as much as she scared you. She's a friend of Jack's, that's all."

Bill sniffled, brushing tears from his eyes with the back of one hand. "Heard a noise, sissy, thought it was you…"

"I know," she whispered, "but it's still early, you need to go back to sleep. When you wake up, I'll make us all French toast, okay?"

Bill forgot his fears at the mention of his favorite breakfast, "Promise?" he asked.

"Promise," Beth replied and led the big man back down the hall to his room.

After tucking her brother in, and switching on the little Looney Tunes night-light by the door, Beth walked back out into the dining room with a frown.

"Now what in the world was *that* all about?" she muttered to the empty room. Who was this strange girl that Jack had, more or less, brought home, and what, exactly, was wrong with her? She bent to pick up the picture frame, which had landed face down on the floor. The glass had cracked in the fall and, as Elizabeth Marshall, aka Beckman, aka *The Snipe*, set the photo back on top on the old piano, she glanced at the picture and froze.

"Oh my god," she whispered, her hands beginning to shake, "Oh sweet Jesus…"

Now she realized why Cassie's face had stopped her and sent her mind racing furiously for a connection. Hadn't she seen those same faces peering out at her from this picture for so many years? The faintest mixture of her brother's face into that of the young woman he had married, but Beth had never met.

"Oh Lord," she prayed again, her knuckles turning white around the edges of the frame, "Cassie…"

Elizabeth turned, the picture still in her hand and, pausing to grab the blanket that covered the back of the couch, she rushed out into the cold morning, the door of Jack's apartment slamming closed behind her.

Chapter Twenty-Two

August 1982

Outside the stuffy confines of Long Beach Community Church, tourist season was in full swing. For the last four months the music of the carousel, the roar of go-carts, and the smell of popcorn had wafted, dawn to dusk, through the small window of Pastor Karl Ferguson's office. Those, and the goose-like burble of the crowded sidewalks, which rose and fell like the surf, went unnoticed by the two men seated across the wide, cluttered desk from each other.

Jack felt old, like he had aged five decades in as many months. Deep, gray circles bruised the flesh beneath his eyes, and the hand that held a tepid can of soda trembled slightly.

"So," Karl asked, "how's Bill?"

Jack took a deep breath, rubbing his free hand across the tight, stress-corded muscles at the back of his neck.

"He has another surgery next month," Jack replied, "they're hoping it's the last one. The plate they put in seems to have been accepted okay, no infection or anything." Jack sighed, "It looks like he'll just have the scar, maybe lose some sight in the one eye."

He waved a hand down the left side of his own face and Karl nodded. He'd seen the devastation that Bill Beckman caused himself when he pulled the trigger.

Sometimes, more often than he would have wanted Jack to know, Karl wondered if it might have been better for everyone in general, and his young assistant especially, if Bill *hadn't* flinched as the pistol went off, the bullet creasing his frontal lobe and exiting above his left temple to leave a ravaged mess of ruined flesh and bone chips in its wake.

Despite all the sheriff's certainties, Bill had, indeed, been breathing when the EMTs had wheeled his blood-soaked gurney through the emergency room doors of Ocean Park Hospital.

Maybe it would have been better if Paul Bradley had been right. Karl knew that his thoughts went beyond being uncharitable, denying a man the chance to accept his salvation, condemning him to everlasting torment, just for the convenience of those around him.

Jack wasn't the only one who felt older. Bill's attempted suicide had shaken the church, and there was a whispered undercurrent of questions, accusations and gossip that would flow, like a dark, noxious river, through Karl's beloved congregation for years to come.

"What about…" Karl continued, "…what about the other thing?"

Jack set the can down on the corner of the desk with a sigh.

"His brain?" Jack asked. "Doctor Blanchette keeps saying that it's a miracle he ever regained consciousness, much less his eyesight and speech. He said we should consider it a gift from God that Bill isn't a vegetable, but that we shouldn't hope that he'll ever have more than a six or seven-year-old's mentality."

Karl had glanced up at the sound of raw bitterness in Jack's voice when the younger man spoke of a gift from God.

He knew, better than anyone, how Jack blamed himself for Bill's actions. The young pastor had tearfully insisted that Bill had somehow known, somehow *sensed*, Jack's own feelings for Kathy, and had been driven to his terrible deed that stormy night in March, because of that knowledge.

And, of course, there was the gun. The pistol that Jack had inadvertently left on the bookcase shelf, that Bill had found, after waking up alone in the tiny cabin, and carried with him down to the shores of Willapa Bay. Karl knew that Jack blamed himself for all of this, and more. The younger man was plagued with unanswerable questions about Kathy Beckman as well. In the months that had passed, no word had come, no one at the bus station, train station, or taxicab offices had remembered her, or recognized her picture.

The young woman had simply disappeared into the storms, and the uncertainty of her fate was slowly consuming Jack Leland's soul in an agony of self-loathing and guilt.

Karl's voice softened, "Are you sure you want to do this, Jack?"

For a moment Jack thought his pastor was referring to his decision to accept guardianship of William Beckman, and he closed his eyes, too tired to go another round in *that* particular fight.

He had told Karl, again and again in the last two months, that if someone didn't take responsibility for Bill, he would end up in an institution somewhere. Some state funded hellhole of an asylum where he would be locked away, only his most basic needs seen to, maybe. A prison for the incompetent, the embarrassing, and the unwanted. Jack knew, somewhere deep inside himself, that the knowledge of Bill, existing in a place like that because of *him*, would quickly drive him mad with guilt.

Bill had no other family. His sister, Beth, would have liked to help, offered to in fact, when she and her husband Bob had come down to see Bill in the hospital. Jack had seen in one brief glimpse into Robert Marshall's eyes, that Bill wouldn't long be welcome in that home.

Jack had thanked her, thanked them both, but told them it was important for Bill to be in familiar surroundings for his recovery and rehabilitation.

And what could be more familiar than the town, and the house, that he had grown up in?

Beth had cried, asking him again and again, if he was sure, if he was *certain*, that he wanted to do this? Jack had told her he was very certain and had put her and her much-relieved husband back on the train, heading east.

Jack had sat down, in his long hours at the hospital in Seattle, and again here at Long Beach, and worked it out.

Between the social security that Bill would receive from now on, and the modest income to be had from the oyster farm, they should be able to get by.

Jack had helped with the sale of a little less than a third of the acreage in June, to pay off the bank, and this year's harvest was beginning to show a decent return.

Once the paperwork was complete, he'd move his belongings back up the highway and into the Beckman homestead again. This saved him the pittance of rent he had insisted on paying the Rolf's, since he no longer had time to look after the grounds.

He had toyed with the idea of cleaning up the old house. Getting it in a condition to sell as one of those bed and breakfasts that were popping up all over the peninsula the last few years. The plan only left one problem, there was just one more spinning plate than Jack could handle. That, he realized, as Karl Ferguson leaned forward and tapped the letter sitting in the middle of the desk, was what his pastor's question had been about after all.

"Are you sure, Jack?" Karl asked again, touching the single sheet of typing paper that held Assistant Pastor Jack Leland's carefully written letter of resignation.

"Yes," Jack said, around a surprising lump that rose suddenly in his throat, "I'm sure."

"I can keep the oyster farm going and take care of Bill, but I can't afford to hire someone to run the farm while I work here, and I can't ask you to pay me what the farm would, to keep my position."

Jack looked down at the scuffed, wood floor.

"A year, maybe two, and I'll have the house ready to sell. If my job's still available then, you better believe I'll come knocking. Until then I'll be as involved as I can, you know that."

Karl smiled and nodded, but his big heart was heavy.

The haunted look in Jack's eyes, the bitterness in his voice, and a lifetime of ministry told Karl that Jack might, indeed, return someday, but it wouldn't be in a year or even two. Jack would have a formidable host of personal demons to contend with before he would be ready to accept God's mantle again. What hurt Pastor Ferguson, turning like a knife in his faithful, if weary, soul, was the knowledge that he couldn't do a thing to help his young friend.

Well, that isn't completely true, he thought, *I can pray.*

He could and did, bending his knee and folding his hands each day, speaking grace and mercy into his young friend's life. He would be faithful in his daily supplications over Jack Leland's soul, for a long and rocky decade until he, himself, would at last be called home.

The two men stood, finally, and shook hands, neither recognizing that Jack's tenure with the church ended almost exactly as it had begun, with a handshake across the big, oak desk on a warm August morning. The bang of the heavy front door echoed down the hallway, sounding to Karl like the closing of a tomb. Jack didn't even notice it as he walked away.

❧

Bill's paperwork was completed in short order. The gentlemen from the state seemed more than happy, eager even, to let Jack take responsibility for William Beckman. Jack spent his first night back in the old house as the leaves on the big oak tree were turning a deep burnt-umber and making their slow, fluttering migration to the weed-choked lawn. In the early hours of the morning Jack thrashed and moaned in his new bedroom, dreaming.

He was walking across a wide, hot desert. His mouth caked and dry, his legs trembled with exhaustion. The heat of the midday sun burned against his face and sweat poured from beneath the heavy pack on his back. He trudged on and on, one heavy foot falling in a cloud of alkali dust, wearily followed by the next. There was nothing in sight but the desert, no water, not one shred of merciful shade, only the heat and pain and terrible thirst. Slowly, in the manner of dreams, Jack became convinced that he heard liquid sloshing in the unbearably heavy pack that rubbed at his raw shoulders. Staggering to a halt, nearly swooning in the baking glare of the sun, Jack slipped the pack to the ground. Being a dream, it didn't strike him strange that, though the pack now rested in the burning white sand at his feet, he still felt the unmerciful weight of it bearing down on him.

Again he heard the tempting, teasing sound of water, coming distinctly from the depths of the pack as, licking cracked and bleeding lips with his parched tongue, Jack noticed buzzards beginning to circle overhead. His fingers fumbled thickly with the knots that held the flap shut and an eternity passed before it was free. Swallowing painfully, he tore open the top of the pack and gagged.

There, folded impossibly and stuffed into the pack was the body of Bill Beckman. One side of his face was gone, a pulped mass of flesh and bone, crawling with great green and black flies. Blood dribbled from a black hole in his right temple, running a thin rivulet down his cheek and dripping into the depths of the pack. As the maddening buzz of flies filled Jack's ears, he took a horrified step backwards and Bill's eyes opened to stare at him, the left eye bulging grotesquely from the massive internal pressure of the passing bullet. Those staring, distended eyes imprinted themselves on Jack's mind like a boot track in the mud. Slowly, the white heat of the desert overwhelmed him, driving him to his knees, and Bill's head swiveled an impossible two hundred and sixty degrees to follow him to the ground.

Then that horrible, bulging eye closed slowly, in a ghastly, knowing wink, and Jack woke himself screaming.

Four weeks later, Bill Beckman came home.

Jack had moved him into the small bedroom behind the kitchen, as Bill still had some trouble with his balance and the long flight of stairs to the master bedroom could have proven disastrous.

Along with a small bag of clothing, and a few toiletries, Jack lugged in a heavy bag full of plastic letters, numbers, children's reading books, and several other physical and mental therapy tools. These he scattered across the floor of the living room until he could build a box to keep them in, which he never did. Bill would wander through the room and pick up the ones that caught his fancy and he and Jack would work with those.

Of the Bill that Jack had known, good and bad, there was no longer any real resemblance. Oh, certainly, the features were the same, give or take the odd bulge or scar, but the hard, wary look was gone. That sharp, intelligent glint was absent in his eyes, and his face had settled into a soft, questioning expression, hanging from his skull, thick and rubbery, ready to laugh or cry.

In his face you could see what Bill had become, a six-foot, two-inch child.

He was weak, at first, on his right side, but that passed soon enough, though Bill would favor that side and use his left hand (though he'd been right-handed before the accident) for the rest of his life. The doctors had warned Jack that Bill could suffer from seizures, but he'd had yet to have one and the danger of them lessened as the weeks went by.

The bullet had passed within millimeters of his optic nerve but, amazingly, there was no visual impairment.

There had been some residual damage to the muscle tissue around the eye, which caused the eyeball to bulge slightly in its socket, and gave that eye a tendency to wander.

Jack would sit with him, most evenings, amid the educational clutter of the living room floor, and they would sound out the alphabet together, or count painstakingly from one to one hundred. By winter, Bill was speaking in full sentences, albeit the faltering and wandering sentences of a youngster, and helping Jack work on the house, scraping paint and clearing the weed-covered grounds.

Still, Bill was a full-grown man, and could be a dangerous responsibility on those rare times that he threw a tantrum.

After replacing a second window in a month, Jack and Bill took the bus to Seattle and came home with a new prescription in hand. The tantrums ceased almost immediately.

❧

One evening, during that first winter, after an especially long and difficult day with Bill, Jack had finally gotten him to bed and was cleaning up the mess the former had made of his dinner, having spread it across the far reaches of the dining room.

Exhausted, defeated and angry, Jack gathered the dishes and flung them in the general direction of the kitchen sink, taking some perverse satisfaction in the sound of shattering china from that direction. He knew he'd have a bigger mess to deal with later, but he didn't really care. Flopping onto the couch, he sat fuming for an hour, reading the same paragraph of the same book over and over, until he finally rose and started searching the house for some gloves to clean up his *own* tantrum.

Gloves, he mused darkly, were one of those many household items that seem to be in every drawer. They were always in the way, when searching for a pen, or scissors, or something else, but just you try to find one pair of gloves when you need them.

Finally, he stumped down the creaking stairs into the dank, cobwebbed cavern of the cellar. A waist-high workbench sat against one long wall, the width of the house. It was a relic of grandfather Beckman's workshop, and liable to outlive this house and the one to follow. The legs were built from huge, black railroad ties and two-by-fours covered in thick plywood made up the much-pitted surface.

Great, heavy drawers were built into the table at knee level, and it was here that Jack went searching.

What he found, instead, there in the moldering gloom, was Bill Beckman's hidden treasure. The one thing that young William had found worthy to invest his hard earned and much needed income on. After prying open the last of the deep, creaking drawers, Jack found that half of the three-foot by six-foot interior had been filled with dusty, unopened whiskey bottles.

There must have been fifty bottles in there, all with the same familiar black label, all filled to the narrow neck with the same dark amber liquid.

Jack held the first bottle in his hand a long while, gazing down at it as he stood in the dim light of the naked bulb, surrounded by the forgotten, rotting treasures of the dead.

In his mind's eye, he could see Bill, on his increasingly frequent trips to the liquor store, buying two bottles at a time.

Always two.

The first for his instant gratification, the second to store up against the threat of the unknown; against that day when there might not be even a handful of wrinkled dollars, smelling of sweat and brine, to buy relief for the dry, screeching demon in his throat.

Minutes passed, five, then ten, and still Jack stood there, unblinking, a great thousand-yard stare on his face as he gazed into the tawny depths of the bottle. Then, with a defiant, agonized growl, he ripped the plastic cap from the bottle.

Ramming it to his lips hard enough to draw blood and crack painfully against his teeth, Jack tipped it back and took a long, gurgling swallow. Thick, wet fire tracked a snail trail down the back of his throat. Swallow after swallow, choking, the bitter bourbon sloshing from his mouth and over his chin, a baptism of anger and rebellion.

That evening he slept, and had no dreams.

Dawn found him, nearly unconscious, clinging miserably to the cool porcelain of the toilet bowl; finally reduced to muscle wrenching dry heaves, his head throbbing like a mouthful of infected teeth.

Two nights later, Jack revisited his dank, basement altar, returning to the kitchen with a fresh bottle.

By spring he had exhausted Bill's rainy day supplies, and walked through the swinging doors of the Surfside Liquor store for the first time in his life.

He'd glanced around guiltily like a young boy taking a peek at a dirty magazine. By summer he was a regular, receiving a nod from Bob, the owner, each time he walked in.

By September, the dreams were back, and no amount of Tennessee whiskey would wash them away again.

⁂

A year stretched into two, then three, and Pastor Karl's unhappy prediction proved true, as the church body of Long Beach Community saw less and less of their former friend and youth pastor. Karl knew that guilt and bitterness had kept Jack away, ashamed to show his face to those he felt he'd failed.

Jack always claimed that it was work on oyster beds, or Bill's condition, which kept him home, and it was some time before his former employer learned just how far his young friend had slipped. Jack had all but disappeared from their lives, but in a small town, secrets are hard to keep, and what small town folks see, they talk about. Jack's late night drives to Surfside were soon grist for the church rumor mill, and far be it from the congregation to keep their pastor in ignorance. Karl came by the house on occasion and once, over a cup of coffee on the wide front porch, he asked Jack about his drinking.

It was a Sunday, Jack remembered, and the church service he'd missed had been over long enough for Karl to close up the building and make the drive down Pacific Avenue to Nahcotta.

Jack had been sitting on the porch, wearing the same rumpled jeans and stained chambray that he had slept in the night before. A steaming cup of coffee rested on the porch-rail, his second that morning and not yet touching his hangover. He was just considering lacing the caffeine with a little hair of the dog when Karl's old Chevy had chugged up the gravel driveway and groaned to a stop.

"Morning Jack," Karl had smiled, climbing the three wide steps up to the porch, "or afternoon, I guess. We missed you this morning."

Jack nodded, reaching for the chipped coffee cup and thinking what Karl had left unspoken.

We've missed you the last six *Sunday mornings...*

"Yeah," the younger man grimaced, "been feeling a little under the weather lately."

Karl eased himself into the old wicker chair opposite Jack and stared at him wordlessly for several moments. Jack suddenly wished that he had combed his hair this morning, maybe put on a fresh shirt as well.

"Hmmmm," Karl intoned finally, "so, just how much did you have to drink last night, Jack?"

Jack sighed. There it was, out in the open now. Trust Karl not to beat around the bush. If only he could have gotten a couple of more cups of coffee in him first, he wouldn't have felt so off guard—

(guilty)

—and been a bit more ready to face the tongue-lashing that was about to begin. How much *had* he drunk last night? Jack couldn't say. Fuzzily, he seemed to remember an empty bottle, one more dead soldier, laying on the floor beside his bed this morning and, even more fuzzily, the recollection that he'd stopped at a liquor store yesterday afternoon.

"That much, huh?" Karl had asked, interrupting the thick molasses flow of his thoughts, and Jack had felt the warmth of blood rushing to his face.

He rubbed a hand across his eyes as the headache that had plagued him all morning began to return in earnest, like a rusty, frozen spike piercing his forehead.

"Look Karl," he started, "it's not a big deal. I had a couple of drinks to help me get to sleep, that's all. I might have had a little more than was good for me last night, but it's under control."

Karl nodded, letting the conversation lapse back into silence as he picked imaginary lint from the knees of his slacks. Jack sat there, the cup cooling in his hands, and began to wish that he'd stayed in bed this morning, pretending not to hear when Karl knocked.

"*It's under control*," Karl repeated to him softly. "I guess I don't need to tell you that's what they all say, huh?"

The warmth in his cheeks had turned hot, and Jack had sat with his burning face pointed at the weathered planks of the old porch. He felt as though Karl were seeing into the dark, hidden corners of his soul, and he found himself desperately embarrassed at what his pastor was finding there.

"I know," he muttered, looking away across the wide expanse of the bay, where sparrows flitted across the mudflats, picking at sand fleas. He was too ashamed to look his former employer in the eye. "It really is under control. I just need some time to get a handle on this..."

"You're not going to find any answers in that bottle, Jack. You and I both know it." Karl nudged Jack's foot with a black loafer. "You have friends here that can help you through this, if you'll let them."

Suddenly, unexpectedly, Jack felt tears start to form, and he fought them off savagely.

"I know," he said again, "and when the time comes–"

"What time?" Karl interrupted, exasperated, "what time are you waiting for? This...this, *life* you're living isn't going to get you any closer to what you need. You pick up a bottle and go down that road and you're just following in Bill Beckman's footsteps, and we saw where that got him, didn't we?"

Jack's head snapped up so fast that the bones in his neck cracked like pistol shots, his lip curled and his face pale with anger, his fingers clutching the armrests of his chair until the tired wicker creaked. The coffee cup, which had rested precariously on his knee, slipped and crashed to the porch in a splash of cold coffee and glass shards. Jack started to rise, paused, and then slumped back into his seat, the clear fury that had risen at Karl's words dissipating as the cloud of guilt and hopelessness returned.

Yes, he had certainly seen where Bill's footsteps had led him, hadn't he?

After all, Jack was the one to put him back on that path. Hadn't his own weakness and sin driven Bill on, hadn't his betrayal been the impetus that had put Bill's finger on the trigger?

Karl watched these conflicting emotions flicker across Jack's face until his features settled, once more, into a mask of bitter apathy. He had stood, reaching into his pocket for his keys, trying not to show the disappointment that flooded his heart.

"Look," Jack muttered without glancing up, "I'm going to have to head out to the farm pretty soon..."

"Yes."

The conversation, such as it had been, was over. Karl descended the steps and, as he reached the gravel walk, he turned back. "You know where I am, Jack, if you need to talk."

"I do," Jack replied, "and thanks. That means a lot, Karl, really."

"It'll mean a lot if you call me."

"I will."

Pastor Ferguson climbed back into to his listing Malibu, and rolled down his window, as Jack started back into the house.

"Jack?" he called.

Jack turned. "Yeah?"

Karl's face was set and impassive.

"You're giving up on Him, Jack," he said, "but *He* isn't giving up on you."

The old preacher raised a hand, and then backed out of the driveway and was gone, leaving Jack standing there, biting back tears. It was the last time he had been available when Karl dropped by.

❧

By the fall of 1987, Jack had only the most tenuous grasp of what was happening with the oyster beds, having long since turned the day-to-day details over to one of the young men he hired to work the fields. Under sober management, the small farm prospered as it never had under Bill's leadership, and the income it produced, along with Bill's monthly check, was more than enough to cover the meager lifestyle the two men lived.

The beauty of oyster farming, as Jonathan Beckman (a man not unfamiliar with that demon rum, himself) had been fond of saying, was that you could leave the cows in the pasture, as it were. And, many a morning, Jack found the cows were doing just fine and he had more urgent concerns at home.

Glass in hand, he would begin to deal with those concerns as soon as the breakfast dishes left the table.

In fact, most days found Jack a fair way through his bottle by midafternoon and passed out, often as not, by nightfall. The only day that he refused the temptation of the black label was Saturday, for their trip to the Sandcastle Bookstore to see Dottie Westscott, which had become a weekly ritual.

Having given himself over to debauchery, some small spark of self-respect still flickered in him, and Jack wouldn't have the outspoken old woman see him in that condition.

In an alcoholic blur, he rode this unending carousel round and round as the seasons changed and life went on about them. Each year, as summer pressed on toward fall, Jack would ease himself out of the fog enough to get oyster beds ready for another season, while the weather was at its best.

Two long weeks of sweating, shaking and mostly trying not to vomit as he repaired old stakes and buried new ones, washed and patched the equipment, and repainted the little roadside building where Bill sat, selling oysters and waving to passing cars.

Laboriously, the two men had gone over the rudimentary math skills involved in making change on a five-dollar bag of oysters, until Jack was comfortable that he wasn't losing *too* much money to the tourists.

By mid-autumn the operation would be up and running itself again, usually with a four-member crew of high schoolers and one supervisor.

Then, as the leaves began to turn color once more, he would begin the long winter descent back into drunken oblivion. This was the pattern of Jack Leland's life.

The last letter had come during the winter of 1984 and, like the five previous correspondences, Jack returned it, marked as undeliverable.

The address was that of a law firm in Texas, and Jack was pretty sure that Kathy's letters to Bill were being forwarded from a real address that she preferred to keep anonymous. Jack understood this, as he also understood that if she knew what had happened to her husband, Kathy would feel as responsible as himself for Bill's current condition and insist on taking care of him. Even in the depths of his own descent, Jack couldn't allow that to happen. Wherever Kathy was, she had made a life for herself, hopefully a good life, and Jack wouldn't let himself to destroy it again, allowing her to spend the rest of her years caring for her childlike husband.

Worried that Kathy would recognize his own handwriting; Jack took each letter back to the post office with a red line through Bill Beckman's name and address and stamped with the words "Undeliverable".

"Sorry, Katie," he whispered, as he slipped the last letter across the counter.

Finally the letters stopped coming, and Jack tried to convince himself that Kathy must have decided to get on with her new life.

Chapter Twenty-Three

In the winter of 1988, Long Beach Community Church burned to the ground. A freak winter ice storm brought down the power lines that ignited the roof of the building. With the slick roads and high winds, the fire department couldn't reach the blaze, and by the time they got control, there was little left that they could do. The church, which had stood for almost ninety years, burned to its foundation.

Late one night, nearly a week after the fire, Jack drove Bill's pickup down to the Sunshine Market. Parking just across the street from the charred remains he'd stood, heedless of the bone-chilling winds that whipped around him.

Tears had wet his cheeks as he stared at the pitiful blackened hole that remained. At dawn he'd returned, shivering, to the truck and drove slowly down Main Street towards home. He'd fallen into bed too saddened, sickened, and exhausted to even stop by the kitchen for a bottle.

The next great shock came in 1991. That spring Karl Ferguson was found by his daughter, slumped in his easy chair with his worn Bible open across his lap. His eyes were closed, as though in sleep, and his wide face relaxed and content. He was buried in the Chinook Cemetery.

Jack watched his former pastor's interment to the grave from the window of the truck, parked on the far side of the graveyard on that rainy April morning, and pulled away from the curb as the service ended. He went home, boiled a pot of water, and sat in his study, looking out on the Willapa Bay from the attic window and sipping his tea. Karl's passing brought a deep regret for the days and years that had been lost between them, but no tears, for a man who had surely been welcomed into victory with open arms, there was no need for tears. The teacup grew cold in Jack's hands as he watched rain sweep the wide gray surface of the bay, sitting alone with his envious thoughts.

If there was a bright light in the lives of the men who shared the rambling confines of the old Beckman estate, it was Dottie Westscott. She had, over the years of his self-imposed isolation, become Jack's last friend and only confidant.

The first winter following his resignation from the church, the old woman had invited him and Bill to come over for Christmas dinner. Jack had declined politely. The next year she had invited him again, and again he graciously turned her down.

In November of 1983, Dottie had informed him, as he lounged in the bookstore's easy chair one Saturday afternoon, that if he didn't come over for Christmas dinner that year, he could find another bookstore to sit his sorry, loitering rear in.

"No arguments!" she'd said with a growl, wagging a stern finger in Jack's face.

Jack had graciously accepted the invitation to dinner, and that December the twenty-fifth was a brief voyage to the past, to a time of laughter and warmth.

Dottie had opened the door to her small apartment clad in a crimson evening gown, glittering with thousands of bright sequins. A silver tiara encrusted with deep green-glass emeralds atop her head, shod in a faded pair of pink Converse high-tops and, of course, wearing her lime lensed glasses.

"You look lovely," Jack had said, grinning and smoothly kissing the back of her outstretched hand.

"You are too kind, sir," she returned. "I don't believe a word of it, but don't ever stop!" She waved them into the small apartment that was permeated with the mouth-watering aromas of roasted turkey and garlic stuffing.

After eating what was, by general consensus, far more than they should have, the three retired to the living room to drink eggnog and watch Christmas specials on Dottie's TV. Bill gazed in rapt and joyous attention as the misfit toys cavorted across the screen, and Tiny Tim proclaimed his seasonable, "God bless us, every one!"

Laughing together, in the blinking rainbow glow of Dottie's little plastic Christmas tree, they exchanged gifts.

The week before, Jack and Bill had driven down to Lincoln City and browsed the shopping mall. Bill had insisted on an outrageous pair of electric-blue fuzzy slippers. (Which, in retrospect, Jack had to agree were a perfect gift for Dottie.)

He, himself had picked up a more restrained, purple silk scarf, hand painted with bright tulips. Her gift to Bill was a small portable radio and cassette player with headphones. He had looked at the device with some confusion until Jack had popped open the tape player and explained that Bill could take his music, a handful of *boom-twang* country cassettes, anywhere he wanted now.

As far as Bill was concerned, he had won the lottery, and he spent the rest of the evening blissfully lost in the wonderfulness of his new toy.

With great excitement he showed them, again and again, how the little door popped open and how to adjust the headphones, grinning from ear to ear all the while.

Dottie handed Jack a heavy rectangle wrapped in white tissue. Tearing open the paper revealed a red, tooled-leather case holding a matching hardbound volume of Tolkien's *The Lord of the Rings*. The edges were gleaming gold and, opening the front cover, he saw that it was a first edition, printed in 1974. Jack took a deep breath, running his hand over the warm, textured surface.

"Dottie," he whispered, "this is too much…"

"Nonsense," she replied, "I've had that copy forever. No one will pay what I'm asking for it and I'll be darned if I'll lower the price!"

Jack thanked her, his gaze never leaving the crisp, unread pages of Middle Earth, and Dottie smiled, satisfied with his reaction. After Bill had fallen asleep on the couch, Jack and Dottie sat up late, nibbling on sugar cookies and sharing memories of Christmases past.

From that year on, the invitation was open and by the holiday season of 1985, the custom had expanded to include Thanksgiving and Christmas both, usually held at the Beckman house, with the much larger kitchen and dining room.

Before long, Jack and Bill became the outrageous old woman's unofficial dates to the tourist events and music festivals that toured the coast each season.

She would walk, arm in arm with *her men*, flattering Jack shamelessly and buying sweets for Bill whenever his protective guardian's back was turned.

When he was with Dottie, something about the irrepressible old woman was infectious, and Jack found himself, for a few brief hours, setting aside the pain which, by now, seemed as much a part of him as his beating heart.

He could almost forget those things in life that had been denied him, his mistakes and regrets, casting off the shadow of his guilt and living again.

Soon enough, the day would end, though, and Jack would lead Bill back across the old porch and into their home, with its lonely, empty rooms and gray future.

ꕥ

The years of abuse were starting to take their toll, and over the winter of 1991, Jack was hospitalized twice for an irregular heartbeat. The doctors gave him the same choices both times, stop drinking or die.

Bill remained much as he had been since the accident, much as he would forever remain, a child in an aging man's body. Both men grew a bit thicker at the waist and thinner at the hairline, though in contrast to the lines that began to etch Jack's face, Bill's appeared to remain untouched by time. Life seemed as though it would continue, unchanging and unchangeable, until time claimed one or both of them, as it had Karl Ferguson. This was Jack's only real concern during those dark years, when his mind was lucent enough to worry: who would take care of Bill, when his guardian finally drank himself to death?

One cool June morning, a Saturday, Jack rose at first light.

After scrambling up some eggs and oysters, a dish known to the locals as *Hangtown Fry*, he bustled around the house, preparing for their weekly visit to the bookstore.

Dottie had assured him the latest John Grisham legal thriller would be in that week, and Jack was excited to get the book in his hands.

After showering, hunting up some clean clothes, and making himself as presentable as possible, Jack loaded Bill into the pickup and they headed into town. First stop was the Coffee Clutch (now owned by some big, nationwide company, but Jack refused to call his little java brewery by any other name) for their weekly mocha. Then they briefly admired the new house of worship that had risen, phoenix-like from the ashes of his former church.

Though the pastor's name, etched into the hanging wooden sign, was unfamiliar, the building itself was still "Long Beach Community Church". There was, Jack knew, a marble plaque above the double doors of the new fellowship hall that proclaimed it to be dedicated to the memory of Karl Michael Ferguson.

Knowing that always seemed to start his Saturday off a little brighter.

As the pickup rounded the corner onto the sixth street, Jack noticed a police car parked near the staircase leading up to Dottie's little apartment.

One of the new Long Beach deputies stood beside the cruiser filling out paperwork as they parked. He saw Jack and waved, more than a cursory acknowledgment, but a '*well there you are, get over here*' gesture. The windows of the shop were dark, and the front door's small cardboard sign, which should have been flipped an hour before, still read *closed.*

Jack stepped from the truck and up onto the curb, trying to remember the young officer's name. Brett? Brent? Something like that. The gold nametag above the pressed pocket of his uniform shirt was no help, reading *B. Hallworth.*

"Hey Jack!" Officer Hallworth greeted him, shaking his hand warmly, "Sheriff Bradley just sent me to go find you. Must be ESP or something! I sure wish you'd get a phone out there!"

Jack considered, briefly, telling him that it wasn't anything as esoteric as ESP; Saturdays were just the only mornings that he wasn't too drunk to drive. He dismissed the urge, deciding the humor might be lost on the eager-beaver young cop. Besides, he liked the kid, whatever his name was.

"That a fact?" he asked, turning and giving Bill a reassuring nod, but motioning for him to stay in the truck.

"Jack," he said, the grin slipping from his face, "I'm afraid I have some bad news."

Jack looked up at the tiny, unlit window of the apartment. It didn't take a genius to figure out what the young officer was going to say. Dottie was creeping up on her nineties now, and had never opened the doors of her shop a minute past eight in the morning in all the years that he had known her. The last few months she had seemed to be slowing down a bit. She had asked Jack to help her pick up deliveries with his truck a time or two, and place a few orders on the computer when her eyes hurt. Still, being able to take care of herself and a business, at her age, had lent an air of immortality to the cantankerous old woman, and Jack had never thought of her actually being gone someday. She had waggled a disapproving finger at him, the last time he had asked her about retirement plans, glaring at him over her hipster glasses.

"You can just pack that talk right back in your ditty-bag, Mister!" she had said, her mouth wrinkling down into a contemptuous frown of disapproval.

"Some of us still have work to do," she'd glowered, "and I'll tell you this, the only way they're going to get Dottie Westscott out of here is to carry her out, feet first!"

Standing on the sidewalk with Officer B. Hallworth, Jack felt a sudden flood of sad relief that he hadn't shown up an hour earlier to see that very thing.

"When?" he asked softly.

"Well, barring an autopsy," Hallworth replied, "the guess is around midnight, maybe one o'clock. I'm sorry, Jack."

There was a long silence, and the young policeman shifted uncomfortably from one foot to the other. Jack felt tears fill his eyes, but he blinked them back, scowling and biting the inside of his cheek until the wave of emotion passed. Dottie was no Karl Ferguson, and her reception into eternity was a much more questionable thing. One more weight, one more burden of guilt, as Jack thought of all the hours he had spent in this little building, talking, laughing, and arguing with her. Maybe he should have been more concerned with Dottie's soul than with her opinion of him.

Had he ever asked her?

Even back in those first weeks when he was still a pastor, when he had still felt worthy of raising the subject of salvation with another human being? Had he? He didn't think so, and the burden for the old woman's destiny slowly settled on his tired, but obliging shoulders.

Officer Hallworth cleared his throat, and the sound brought Jack back to the moment.

"One of her customers came by to pick up a book that Ms. Westscott was holding for her," Hallworth said, "when the woman couldn't get an answer from the shop, or at the apartment, she got worried and called us. We found Dottie in her bed; looks like she went peacefully, in her sleep."

"Well," Jack said, "thank God for that much, I suppose. What did Bradley want me for?"

"For this," a voice like a bag of broken glass spoke from the upper landing, deep and gravely from a lifetime of cigarettes. "We found this on her desk; it has your name on it."

Sheriff Paul Bradley descended the staircase, each wooden step creaking beneath his six-foot-six frame, and his broad shoulders brushing the side of the building. The years, if they had any effect at all, had only touched the big man's close-cropped auburn hair and mustache, peppering them with gray. As he reached the sidewalk he held out a large, mustard colored manila envelope. Jack took it and saw that his name was written plainly in the center, in Dottie Westscott's firm block script. In the upper corner was stapled a white business card with the name and number of a Vancouver law firm, and the name of an Alan Jarrell, Attorney at Law.

"What's this?" Jack asked, looking from one cop to the other.

"Dunno," Bradley replied shortly, "envelope's sealed, your name's on it, so I thought it'd be best if you were the one to open it."

Jack felt somewhat unnerved as he gazed at the envelope, then a thought struck him. "You don't think that I…"

Sheriff Bradley uttered a short, unpleasant bark of a laugh.

"Please Jack," he grimaced, "Dottie Westscott was ninety-three years old, and everyone knows that you were the only soul on the planet that she said more than '*morning*' to. I just thought that if she wanted you to have it, it might be important to get it to you before her belongings were dealt with.

It's probably a little out of line with police procedure, but you're one of us here and, as long as you dry yourself out before you climb behind the wheel, we'll try to watch out for each other."

Jack saw Hallworth's eyes widen at his boss's bluntness, but Jack just nodded. Bradley was doing him a favor, in his own way, and, after all, Jack *was* the town drunk. No offense taken.

"Thanks Paul," he murmured, slipping his thumb beneath the sealed flap and tearing it open. Inside was a single sheet of paper, an ostentatious gold and black masthead named the same law firm that was listed on the business card.

Jack was surprised to see the letter was addressed to him. It requested that he call the firm, at his earliest convenience, to begin proceedings to transfer title and ownership of the Sand Castle Bookstore, the contents thereof, and the estate of Dorothia Jean Westscott into his name.

Jack stared at the paper blankly. "I don't…I don't understand…" he stuttered.

Bradley, who had shamelessly read the letter over Jack's shoulder, grinned. "Well," he said, "I'm no lawyer, but I'd say that you just inherited yourself a bookstore."

Two nights later, Jack found himself in room 107 of the Budget Inn of Vancouver, gazing down out of his single occupancy window onto the dark flowing expanse of the Columbia River. Bill was safely ensconced in his own room, back in Long Beach, by now. As soon as Dottie's service ended, Jack had pressed the farm supervisor into spending a couple of days baby-sitting (at time and a half), and had left a tearful Bill waving from the porch as he pulled away. Jack realized, on the long drive up the river, that this would be the first night in a decade that he had slept somewhere other than in his own small bedroom in the Beckman farmhouse.

He stood, chewing ice from his plastic water glass, and thumbing through the first pages of the Tom Clancy novel he had picked up at the bookstore across the street from the motel.

He realized, with some sense of irony, as he paid for the mass-market paperback of Jack Ryan's latest cold-war adventure, that by this time tomorrow he would very likely own a half-dozen copies of the book. Still, that was tomorrow, and this was tonight, and he needed a thick best-seller to keep his mind off the rows of tiny bottles lined up in the mini-fridge beside the room's desk. He hadn't even dared to open the refrigerator door, but he could sense them, little vials of sweet oblivion to cool the burning itch that was already forming in his throat.

Jack swallowed two tiny red Benadryl tablets with the last of his water, hoping the allergy pills would help knock him out. Then he walked across the room and lay down across the double bed, holding the paperback before his eyes, trying to banish the siren song of the mini-bar.

Jack had an 8:00am appointment with Alan Jarrell, at the Smith, Jarrell, and Weinstein offices on Mill Plain Boulevard. Mill Plain, the smiling bookstore manager had assured him, scribbling a map on the back of Jack's receipt, would be easy to find. Jack wanted to be clear-eyed and coherent for that meeting, which might just be the most important of his recent life. A hangover was the last thing he needed.

Finally, somewhere in the middle of Clancy's all-inclusive description of Red Square, Jack slipped off to sleep.

Once again, he trudged across the burning desert. His parched lips crying out for water, his legs trembling with exhaustion. Pain hammered through his brain like the ringing of an anvil, and he could feel the black, burned skin of his forehead peeling back beneath the brutal heat of the merciless sun, as sweat poured down his back. On and on, one heavy foot achingly following the next until, far ahead, he could see a single shape breaking the wide, monochrome monotony of the wasteland.

The tree had once been a great spreading oak, but now its branches were withered, blackened and charred by some great fire. It grew in his vision as he plodded onward and soon he began to realize the enormity of the thing, its dark, skeletal branches reaching up and up until they grew blurred and indistinct, disappearing into the pale blue sky. The terrible thirst gnawed at his throat. The tree cast no shadow, despite the blazing sun, and the words of T.S. Eliot sang mockingly in his tortured brain.

A heap of broken images, where the sun beats,

And the dead tree gives no shelter, the cricket no relief,

He wondered briefly, his face burning in the place where the oak's shadow should have fallen, if this great and terrifying monolith of death had been in the poet's eye when he penned The Waste Land.

Then the pack bore down on his bleeding shoulders, driving him to his knees in the white, lifeless sand, and he thought he heard, far away, a thin, piping voice calling his name.

Jack raised his weary head, blinking against the assault of light and heat, and saw, far up in the dead branches, a small boy, calling his name and waving his hand over his head. His tiny fist clutching something that Jack couldn't, at first, make out.

Then he knew. It was a balsawood airplane, with bright red stripes down each wing and the blue, painted face of a pilot where the cockpit would be. How high was the boy? Two hundred feet? Three? Bill waved triumphantly, and Jack tried to cry out, to warn him, but he had no voice, just a dry, broken croak of desiccated vocal chords disappearing into the desert wind. He tried to wave his arms but they were too heavy; the pack on his back had doubled, then tripled in weight, flopping him forward onto the blistering sand. The muscles in his back pulled and tore as he strained to rise, to get to his feet before...

He heard the gunshot, a sharp, metallic crack echoing through the thin hot air, and he screamed, rolling over and looking up into the high branches again. He watched the limp lifeless body of the boy tumbling over and over as it plummeted to the desert floor.

In his dream, he saw Bill falling for a long, long time, and the sound of the small body, striking the unyielding sand beside him, woke Jack, sweating and gasping.

Sitting on the edge of the bed, listening to the pounding of his heart in the quiet blackness of the hotel room, Jack could feel his hands shaking.

Tremors ran along his arms and legs, and his thoughts began to wander, once more, to the contents of the little refrigerator. Forcing his mind to find an off-ramp from that dangerous road, Jack switched on the table lamp, blasting the room in harsh white light. Blinking painfully, he opened the bedside table drawer and lifted out the Bible. *Bless the faithfulness of the*

Gideons, he thought, holding the drab little hardbound New Testament in his lap. A long moment passed, then two, and finally, with a sigh, Jack slipped the book back into the drawer.

You're giving up on Him, Jack, but He isn't giving up on you.

Whatever answers he was looking for, he still wasn't ready to look there.

God had once trusted him, and Jack Leland had dropped the ball, he didn't deserve the grace offered in those diaphanous pages.

The tremors in his arms and legs grew steadily worse, and yet, for the first time since he could remember, Jack refused to answer his body's supplications for alcohol. In a few hours he would meet with a man who might, finally, shine some small light into the monotonous gloom of his life.

Jack thought about the bottles, all the whiskey bottles, lined up in that deep wooden drawer in the Beckman cellar. The thousand or more he'd emptied since. And he was sickened by the truth of it, the truth that he had gone down those creaking shadowed steps into the mildewed twilight beneath William Beckman's house and he had never come back up again.

Now though, sitting in a cheap motel room, a folded sheet of paper from a law firm he had never heard of tucked safely into his jacket pocket, something had woken him at last.

Deep in his tired spirit, something sparked, so unfamiliar that he couldn't even put words to it, and yet he could feel it. Like a faint light in an endless darkness it called to him, leading him on, pulling him back up the cellar steps, to stumble into the world once more.

Hope.

For the first time in so many years, a breath of hope wafted through the stagnant cell of his life and Jack clutched for it, breathing it in desperately.

"Maybe it's time," he murmured, staring at the beige walls as the hollow, sucking need grew in his chest. A pad of paper and a pen, both bearing the logo of the motel, sat on the cheap, pressboard desk. Shakily, Jack stepped over to take a seat and jotted a quick note to himself, just four words really, *Call Martin Peterson – AA*. Then he sat there, in the hard wooden chair, the note grasped in his trembling hand.

Martin was a recovering alcoholic. Jack knew, from hearing the man's testimony so many years before, that he had been where Jack sat now, and he attended his Alcoholics Anonymous meetings with the same weekly dedication as he did his church. Maybe, just maybe, Martin could help him take a first step.

Finally, Jack rose and, after drinking three glasses of tepid water from the bathroom tap, he dressed quickly. Jack left his room to wander the motel lobby with his novel, plopping down in one of the overstuffed chairs, and reading until morning.

He was, if not safely away, at least further removed from temptation, with the note tucked securely into his wallet.

Ten hours later Jack was back in the pickup, headed west, and hoping to be home by nightfall. His head was spinning from the day's events as he squinted through the rain splattered windshield and the scintillating headlights of the oncoming cars.

The Sandcastle Bookstore was his. At least the *contents* of the bookstore were, the lease was paid for a full year and, as Mr. Alan Jarrell assured him in his most serious tones (Jack had tried desperately to banish the image of *Deputy Dog*, as the man's drooping cheeks waggled back and forth) that if Jack were interested in selling the store at that time, there would be no difficulties in finding an eager buyer.

Jack, however, was about as likely to sell The Sand Castle as he was to run for president, and had signed each of the forms placed before him until he had lost count and his fingers ached.

He would show great patience by waiting nearly an entire week before contacting Ocean View Realty and putting the Beckman house and oyster beds up for sale.

The apartment, all the furniture, and Dottie's somewhat eclectic collection of artwork was his as well. He was pretty sure the local libraries would be happy to accept some of the more sedate watercolors, since most of them were painted by local artists.

As the truck passed under the amber wash of a streetlight, Jack noticed his hands, as they clutched the wheel before him. Hard and calloused, his palms and fingers were nicked and scarred by the razored edges of unknown thousands of oyster shells, the stripping of thick wet ropes on icy mornings, and too many accidental slips of the oyster knife. They looked, in the wane light, like an old man's hands, gnarled and spider webbed from a lifetime of hard work.

Jack thought that maybe, just maybe, those hands had seen their fair share of sand and saltwater. Maybe it was time to slip behind a desk and relax in the warmth of an office, sheltered from the fury of the weather; his most backbreaking responsibilities being unloading an occasional box of paperbacks from the bed of the pickup.

It was more than the work, though, Jack knew, more than ownership and security.

It was the worn leather recliner across from the sales counter, the coffee from the stained pot in the cluttered office. The bookstore was the home he had never found in the decade he had slept within the walls of the Beckman house. The little apartment above the store had echoed nearly every happy moment, every bit of laughter that he had experienced over the last ten years.

The road before him blurred again, as much from the tears that welled and slipped down his cheeks, as from the pounding rain outside.

Most of all, he knew, it was Dottie; that sharp-tongued, eccentric old woman who had been his only real friend for longer than he wanted to think about.

The bookstore would remain, he would see to that, and the little apartment would always keep some small part of Dottie Westscott's spirit for as long as Jack lived there.

But he would never again knock on that thin wooden door and have her yell from the kitchen that, for Pete's sake *he knew* where the key was. He'd never again barbecue hamburgers on the tiny landing in the freezing dead of winter, never again have her reach over and squeeze his hand with all of her surprising strength, her eyes glittering through emerald lenses. Thanking him wordlessly for keeping the loneliness, that slavering hound of the old and forgotten, from her door.

Jack saw a rest stop ahead and pulled the truck into the slow lane, slipping beneath the dripping pines, to stop between the faded yellow lines at the farthest edge of the parking lot. There he turned off the engine and buried his face in his hands. His shoulders shook as great silent sobs wracked his frame, the windows of the cab slowly fogging over from the heat of his grief. He wept for all that the eccentric old woman had become to him, and for all the things that he had never told her.

At forty-two years old, Jack Leland, former pastor, part-time oysterman, and full-blown alcoholic, felt like an orphan once again.

Chapter Twenty-Four

A chilly north wind whipped fine sand, in creeping fog-like tendrils, up the moonlit beach. The storm clouds had finally parted to allow the wane rays of the moon to blanket the wet shoreline.

Cassie huddled in the lee of a huge driftwood stump, its gray web of weathered roots casting long, thin shadows across the sand, like a thousand gnarled fingers. She was cold. The sweating, sobbing race down to the beach had warmed her, but now the icy teeth of the coast wind bit deep. She shivered miserably, wrapping her arms around her knees and leaned deeper into the scant protection of the tidal refuse.

She had no idea how long she had sat there, the cold creeping into her bones, the sickness slowly ebbing from her belly. She felt faded and thin, diminished, like evening sunlight through a dusty pane of glass. Looking out over the crashing waves, Cassie wiped the last of her tears from the sand gritted corners of her eyes.

She had found her father, and she knew, finally, that all the ranting and raging and spite-filled words that she might spit in his face, would profit her nothing. Whatever small, mean part of her that had yearned toward revenge, for her, and for her dead mother, would never have the satisfaction of seeing her pain and hopelessness reflected in the eyes of the man who had fathered her. Cassie sighed, remembering the dull expression, the blank, uncomprehending eyes, and the fading pink scar running from his temple.

She understood that whatever reprisal she had hoped for had been stolen by the devastating injury that had snatched away William Beckman and left that frightened, rambling child in his place. Cassie felt cheated. Cheated, robbed and, more than anything, ashamed.

She could hear Guy Williams' reproachful voice, far in the back of her mind, reminding her that, as Paul had told the Romans, vengeance was the Lord's. All the lessons she had learned, in church and at home, about grace and mercy and forgiveness, she had set them all aside in hopes of wounding her father the way he had wounded them. Instead, she had hurt people that she loved, and put her own life in danger, for the chance to dole out the judgment that God, in His grace, did not dole out on her.

"I'm sorry," she whispered to the shadowed waves, to Jack, and Guy, her mother and, mostly, to God. "I'm so sorry."

"Well," a voice spoke up just behind her, "sorry or not, you better take this blanket or you're going to freeze to death out here!"

Cassie was too cold, too emotionally exhausted to shriek, a quick hiccup of surprise was the best she could manage as she turned to see Elizabeth Marshall silhouetted in the moonlight.

Cassie hung her head in embarrassment.

"Sorry if I freaked you out," she said, "I didn't mean to dash like that, my feet just wouldn't stop."

The dark outline stood for a long still moment, as though considering her apology. Then she stepped around the snarl of roots and sat down beside Cassie in the sand, shifting her weight until she found a comfortable seat, and spreading a thick wool blanket over the both of them.

"Please, call me Beth," she replied, "I've had a panic attack a time or two myself," Elizabeth smiled, "there's not a lot you can do about it. I'm just glad we didn't find you in a heap at the bottom of the stairs!"

The older woman placed an arm protectively around the young woman's thin shoulders. Cassie could feel her warmth and, shivering even harder, leaned into it gratefully. She should have felt awkward, accepting such an embrace from a stranger, but she didn't. Elizabeth's touch seemed, instead, somehow familiar, and Cassie had a sudden overwhelming memory of snuggling under her mother's arm as they sat together on the couch in their little trailer. After a moment she realized that this was the first memory of her mother, since that terrible tinny knock on the trailer door, that hadn't brought tears or grief. Instead she felt a warm regret, a sad longing for her mother that she supposed she would carry always.

"That's the one condolence that I can offer you now," Jack had said. *"Someday that hurt is going to fade and all that will be left are your memories of the good times and just a little bit of sadness."*

Cassie let out a deep, wistful sigh and felt, for the first time, that maybe he was right.

"Jack told me about your mother," Elizabeth spoke into the darkness, "I'm very sorry, Cassie, she was a wonderful, special woman."

"How did Jack know my mother, Beth?" Cassie asked before she could stop herself, the words passing her lips in a rush. She tensed slightly and felt the older woman's body do the same.

"That's a long story, dear," the older woman replied, "and I don't think it's mine tell, at least not all of it, but I'll tell you what I can." She drew a deep breath. "First though, I need to know that *you know* who Bill is, though I'm pretty sure by your earlier reaction that you do."

"Bill is my father." Cassie spoke the words without emotion, just a jumble of syllables released from a small iron box in her heart, her own voice sounding foreign to her. "Isn't he?"

"Your father's name was William Beckman?" Beth asked.

Cassie nodded.

"And your mother was Katherine Belanger?"

Cassie nodded again.

"Then yes," Beth murmured, "Bill's your father. Though I have to tell you, and I'm so sorry for it, but the Bill you met tonight isn't really that man anymore." She sighed, "I don't think he ever knew about you, I know that Jack didn't, but I do know that he has no memory of your mother. It's taken years for him to pull together even the haziest recollections of me."

There was a long pause and, finally, Cassie clutched the edge of the rough blanket tightly in her fist and asked, "Who are *you*, Beth?"

Cassie felt a hand gently lower her head to the older woman's shoulder, and once more she was overswept with that warm familiarity, as Elizabeth took a deep breath.

"My name is Elizabeth Marshall. Before I was married, it was Elizabeth Beckman, I'm Billy's little sister. I guess that makes me your Auntie Beth, Cassia Belanger."

Cassie squeezed her eyes shut, wrapping her free arm around Elizabeth and clutching her tightly. Something swelled and swelled within her and after a dizzying moment, a dark, suffocating weight was lifted from her soul and she felt her heart flood with warm relief. The two women held each other for a time, rocking and weeping softly together as the chilly wind sprinkled sand about them.

Finally, they dried their eyes on the rough wool and sat quietly, warm and safe beneath the heavy blanket. Elizabeth told her niece all that she knew about the three lives that had intertwined to bring them to this night.

"So," she finished, "when my husband Robert died, I decided that I didn't want to spend the rest of my years rambling around that big house, reminded of his death every time I turned a corner. I called Jack and he helped me look around for a house to buy. I ended up with The Morning Tide and decided to refinish it and start a Bed and Breakfast, so that's what I did. That was eight years ago.

"I watch Bill fairly often," she said, "Jack refused to let me take him after I moved back, but he's grateful for my help from time to time, so he can find his books."

When Beth finished, Cassie told her about growing up in Bowie, the Williams family, and of Katherine's death. She gave a brief overview of her trip westward with Jack and then fell silent.

"Poor sweet Kathy," Beth murmured. "Nothing ever came easy to her, and she deserved so much more."

"Yes," Cassie said, "yes, she did. That's what I came all the way out here to tell him, that she was dead, and that he would never see me again. I wasn't even going to tell him how she died, I didn't want to give him even that much."

There was a pause and the only sound was the sad whisper of the wind along the shoreline, and the muffled crash of the surf.

"So much anger," Beth whispered, "so much hate. That's an awful lot for a girl to carry around." She sighed. "I'm sorry Cassie, I'm sorry Bill did this to you. I don't know what turned my brother into the man he became, but I'm so sorry that you and Kathy had to pay for it."

Cassie nodded, unable to speak, staring instead into the darkness and listening to the ceaseless pounding of the waves.

"He really is gone you know," Elizabeth said, breaking the long silence, "the Bill Beckman that my brother was is as dead as if that bullet had killed him. There's no one left to hate, you know that, right?"

"Yes," Cassie whispered, her cheeks burning with shame and unspent anger, "I know."

"That doesn't make the feelings go away though does it?" Elizabeth continued. "You can't just turn off that kind of emotion because life throws a twist at you." She squeezed the young woman's hand in her own. "It's okay to still be angry, Cass, keep that in mind. It's going to take time to work it out, and that's okay too."

Cassie nodded. Her eyes were puffy and dry, her tear-soaked skin felt chapped and raw in the cold wind; she had no more tears to cry. Elizabeth was right, the anger was still there, pressing heavy on her heart, aimless with no target any longer, but this, like the pain of her mother's death, would begin to pass. Cassie had faith in that, clinging to it as she clung to Beth's hand.

Suddenly another question leaped to the front of her troubled mind, slipping her from one train of thought to another with hardly a bump between.

"Aunt Beth?" she asked, tentatively using the title for the first time.

"Yes?" Elizabeth replied, and Cassie could hear the smile in her voice, and felt a hand squeeze her shoulder. Cassie hesitated, feeling awkward and more than a little embarrassed.

"Did Jack call you from Gold Beach on Monday night?"

Elizabeth paused a moment, thrown by the change in course.

"Um…yes, I think he did," she said, "wasn't that Valentine's Day?"

Cassie grinned in spite of herself. "Yes, yes it was."

"What are you smiling about, young lady?" Beth asked, elbowing her lightly in the ribs.

"Nothing," Cassie responded, giggling helplessly.

"Cassie…?" Elizabeth intoned threateningly, jabbing with her elbow again.

"Aunt Beth, are you in love with Jack?" The words rushed out before Cassie could stop them, and she started in shock at her own brazenness.

There was a long pause and, in the darkness, Cassie could feel her aunt tense and prepare to stand. She suddenly had a terrible thought…what if Elizabeth didn't have feelings for Jack, what if that was the reason that Jack seemed reluctant to talk about it? What could she have possibly asked that would have ruined the moment any more effectively?

Finally, Beth spoke.

"I don't think I'm ready to discuss that with you here," the older woman said, her voice flat and strained.

Cassie felt sick. How could she be so stupid? When would she ever learn to think before she opened her mouth? The girl scolded herself silently, wishing that the sandy beach would open and swallow her whole, as her mind struggled to find a suitable apology.

"Beth, I'm–" she started.

"However," Elizabeth interrupted, grinning as the first gray streaks of dawn touched the far horizon, "if you want to come back to the apartment, we can heat up that tea. I'll break out some cookies, and tell you *all* about it there!"

Cassie jumped to her feet, barely noticing the twinge of her stiff, cold muscles, and helped her Aunt fold the blanket.

"It's a deal!" she laughed.

❧

He staggers on and on, miles and years, across the burning, featureless landscape. One blistered bare foot falling, wearily followed by the next, leaving faint bloodied prints, which the desert sand sucks up greedily. Heat and pain and thirst, his back screams in protest beneath his terrible burden. Jack hears water sloshing in the heavy pack that grinds away at his shoulders. He stops, the wasteland's desolate horizon shimmering and spinning sickeningly beneath the baking sun. Jack slips the pack to the ground. The skin of his hands is burned crimson and peeling, his fingernails are cracked and caked with filth as he struggles to loosen the knots of rope that hold the bag closed.

Again he hears the tempting, teasing sound of water, coming distinctly from the depths of the pack. Licking his cracked and bleeding lips, Jack sees the buzzards have landed around him. Slowly, they stalk forward though the sand, their hideous naked heads stretching hungrily towards him.

Swallowing painfully, he tears open the top of the pack.

Despite the blistering heat of the desert, a frigid bolt of terror, like frozen lightening, rips through his body. He shrieks, trying to lurch backwards and away, but his legs are locked in horror as he stares into the pack...his own body impossibly crushed within.

Bill's bullet wound bleeds from Jack's ruined temple as he looks into his own blood-filled eyes.

He screams again and suddenly the heat and light are gone.

Jack found himself fumbling in sweaty terror with the controls of the hospital bed, his trembling fingers cold and numb, searching for the button that would light the shadowed corners of his room.

He stared, eyes wide open, still unable to pull themselves from the fading images of his nightmare, and of his own face peering back at him.

Alone in his hospital room, Jack Leland began to weep.

❧

The storms that had lashed the shores of Long Beach through the night blew themselves out by dawn. Damp, glittering calm settled over the peninsula as the sun rose to wash Main Street in sharp, golden light.

Cassie awoke with what was becoming a familiar moment of

disorientation. A week and more of strange beds had changed that first blurry morning thought from *where am I?* to *where am I now?* It took her several sleepy seconds to recognize the library-like environs of Jack's apartment, from her spot on the quilt draped couch. Cassie's eyes felt sandy, and she rubbed them as she succumbed to a jaw-cracking yawn. She and Elizabeth hadn't stayed up too long after returning home, but Cassie had found, once she was safely tucked in, that she couldn't sleep. The welter of emotions and confusion left her wide-eyed and reeling and she had sat up for a long while with her mother's Bible in her lap, reading the comfortingly familiar words.

Even after turning out the light, she had spent the rest of the night drifting in and out of a thin, anxious, doze.

She could hear Elizabeth, *Aunt Beth* she reminded herself, enjoying again the warmth that suffused her at the thought, she could hear her bustling around the kitchen, preparing the promised French toast.

Beth carried on a murmuring conversation with her brother, almost certainly about Cassie. The younger woman lay, for a long moment, savoring the homey comfort of her borrowed bed and the delicious aromas calling to her from beneath the kitchen door.

Finally she arose and, slipping on the faded bathrobe draped over an arm of the couch, she took a deep breath and walked into the kitchen.

"Well!" Elizabeth exclaimed without turning from the stove, "it's about time, sleepyhead. Billy and I were about to start without you!"

Cassie smiled and mumbled an apology, accepting a steaming cup of tea from her aunt and slipping into the kitchen chair opposite the table from her father. Bill stared at her owlishly with equal parts apprehension and curiosity, as he sipped at his own mug. The silence grew uncomfortably long as Elizabeth clattered pots and pans across the range top, and Cassie realized the older woman was waiting for her to make the first move with Bill. Cassie squared her shoulders and met Bill's eyes, offering one hand across the table.

"Hi Bill," she said, "I'm Cassie."

Bill looked first to his sister, his eyes growing even wider, then, as she nodded in affirmation, he tentatively took Cassie's hand in his own and gave it a brief, slightly limp shake.

"Hullo," he said shyly, his eyes returning immediately to his study of the contents of the mug before him. Silence filled the room once more.

Finally, Beth took pity on her niece and, turning from the stove, sat herself at the third and final chair at the table.

"I was just telling Billy that you're an old friend of Jack's," she said, "and that you'd be staying with us for a while."

Beth nodded to Cassie, making sure the girl caught the relevance of her statement. Cassie did. There would be no great revelations around the kitchen table this morning, at least not in front of Bill.

Bill nodded, a shy smile at the corner of his lips, as his slightly bulging eye drifted around the room aimlessly.

"Sorry that I scared ya," he murmured.

Cassie smiled. "That's all right, Billy," she said. "I was the stranger in your dining room, I probably scared you just as bad." Bill Beckman grinned back at her, a small drip of maple syrup clinging to his chin, and suddenly everything was all right.

"Boy howdy, didja!" he exclaimed. "I thought you was a burgalist!"

"A burglar," his sister corrected gently.

"Yeah!" Bill agreed.

All three at the table laughed, and just that quickly, Cassie realized, Bill had accepted her presence and forgotten his concern.

Soon the older man was babbling merrily to her about his new disc-man, visiting Jack in the hospital today, and the book that Bill had bought to take to him. Cassie smiled and nodded, losing the occasional word beneath a mouthful of waffle, but maintaining the gist of Bill's wandering monolog. A happy hour passed before Elizabeth stood and, gathering the breakfast dishes, shook her finger at her older brother.

"Okay Billy," she said, "that's enough, you've already talked one of her ears off, how about you leave her the other?" She shook her head. "I swear mister, your tongue–"

"–is hinged in the middle an' loose on both ends!" Bill shouted, grinning hugely as he completed the sentence. This said, he threw back his head and howled in red-faced laughter, stomping his feet and slapping the tabletop until neither Cassie nor her aunt could hold back any longer and joined him.

Chapter Twenty-Five

An hour later Cassie and Bill sat on the bottom steps of the staircase, waiting for Elizabeth to emerge so the three of them could make the short drive to the hospital.

Cassie wore her freshly laundered jeans and a PSU sweatshirt (a gift from Grace). Her hair, washed and damp, was pulled back into a ponytail and her feet felt strange inside a pair of borrowed white tennis shoes, after wearing her clunky hiking boots for so long.

Bill was dressed up for the occasion as well, in dark slacks and a pressed white dress shirt. Her father could have passed for any other business man on the street, save for the outlandish, multicolored Christmas tie he wore.

The black background of the tie was splashed with neon red and green Christmas trees surmounted by a golden sleigh piloted by a snarling Tasmanian Devil in a Santa suit and hat. Bill seemed fascinated by the tie and was careful to straighten and smooth it whenever he moved. Cassie found herself grinning at the older man's obvious pride in his riotous neckwear.

"That's some tie, Billy." She smiled.

Bill, grinning, smoothed the tie carefully again with one wide hand. "It was a Christmas present from Kim at school. I go to school two days a week."

"Really?" she replied. "I'm hoping to start school in September, myself."

"Neat!" Bill said. "'Course it's not really from Kim, I don't think she can buy stuff on her own, so her mom musta picked it out, but it's still my favorite."

"That's a pretty great tie, all right," Cassie agreed, and Bill's grin grew even wider, then faded a little as he leaned closer, glancing around as though he were about to impart a secret for Cassie's ears only.

"My momma's gone to Heaven with Jesus," he said. "She caught a cancer. Jack told me so." Bill's smile slipped away. "Sometimes we look at her picture in the family book, but I don't really remember her good."

Cassie's throat tightened as Bill lowered his head, his eyes going to his shoes as though ashamed.

"Jack says it's cause of the ax'cident, that I don't remember anyone in the pictures, 'cept Sissy of course," he sighed, "my momma looked a lot like Sissy though, so that helps me remember a little."

Bill Beckman's voice trailed off, and Cassie watched him watching his shoes.

"So," Bill asked, brightening, "do you look like your momma?"

Cassie stiffened in spite of herself, looking away down the street where cotton ball clouds, all that remained of yesterday's storm, scuttled over the roofs of the main street shops, following the Pacific breeze. Her voice was little more than a tight whisper. "People tell me I look a lot like my mother."

Another pause and then Bill whispered back sadly, "Your momma's with Jesus too, isn't she?"

Cassie bit her lip until she was afraid it would bleed, her hands forming white-knuckled fists in her lap as she continued to watch the clouds.

"Yes she is."

Bill nodded sadly. "Did she… catch a cancer?"

He said this in a hushed, fearful tone, as though cancer might be a fanged monster waiting in the shadows to leap on you, and you didn't dare speak its name too loud, lest you draw its attention. Cassie felt her head begin to pound from the strain, her body trembled and she felt tears trying to escape the corners of her eyes, she bit down even harder, crushing her tears with the force of her will.

I wasn't even going to tell him how she died, I didn't want to give him even that much.

"No," she said through gritted teeth, "it wasn't cancer, she was in an accident."

"Oh," Bill exclaimed, "an *ax'cident.*" He nodded knowingly as though that single world explained everything bad that could befall a person. Cassie watched the last of the clouds scuttle from view, her jaw still clenched against impending tears. Bill let out a great deep sigh, his brows knit together in commiseration, and patted her shoulder with one heavy hand.

"Jack says that sometime ax'cidents just happen and you can't do nothing about 'em. Beth says it's God's plan." Bill sighed. "I'm…I'm sorry your momma died." He gave her a final pat and then rested his hand comfortingly on her shoulder.

I'm sorry.

The words seemed to come from very far away as they repeated themselves in Cassie's mind, over and over. The tears that had threatened just seconds before were suddenly gone; the tension in her neck and jaw eased as though some groaning internal spring had been released. Apprehension seemed to flood from her, replaced by a warmth and relief that she hadn't felt in all the long days since her mother's death. Hearing the words *I'm sorry* from the lips of her father allowed the last of her anger to fall away and she felt suddenly light-headed in its absence.

From across time, came the memory of her mother's voice reading from the Old Testament, *"To the Lord our God belongs compassion and forgiveness, for we have rebelled against Him."*

Finally she leaned across the step and rested her head on Bill's shoulder, feeling him tense slightly in surprise and then relax.

"My mom was coming home from work," Cassie murmured, "she worked the night shift at the hospital, and she was hit by a drunk driver." She closed her eyes at the sound of phantom tires, screeching along imaginary asphalt.

"It was late and there was no one around, and by the time someone saw her she was already gone."

She had done it. The focus of her burning anger, the hunger for vindication that had carried her across all the miles from Bowie to Long Beach, had been forsaken. Broken and sacrificed. Cassie could feel the pain, that wrenching, emotional agony beginning to fade. Not that she believed it would ever go entirely, but she hoped that time might help it fade until only the scar remained, like a jagged tattoo on her heart. It was enough for now. She had given up on God, but He had remained faithful, waiting for her exactly where she had left Him, forgiving her unforgiveness, accepting when she had not, and now, finally, she could feel His presence once more.

Bill continued to pat her shoulder, and they sat silently, as Cassie's lips moved in a silent prayer of repentance and gratitude.

"It's okay," Bill murmured in his slightly slurred child-voice. "It's okay. Your momma lives with Jesus now, just like mine."

Cassie smiled, giving the big man one last squeeze before sitting up, "I know, Bill, I know." She turned, hearing a slight sound behind her and found Elizabeth standing at the top of the steps. She smiled at Cassie, her face wet with tears.

"Aunt Beth," Cassie asked, "can you let me into the bookstore for a minute? I have to get something for Jack."

Bill stood beside her and, reaching into his pocket, pulled out a thick paperback, the latest Tom Clancy thriller.

"I got him a book already," Bill said, showing the cover to Cassie.

"I know," she said, "but this is different, this is a surprise."

Elizabeth gave her a questioning look but unlocked the front door and keyed in the alarm code for her. Cassie disappeared into the unlit twilight of the shop, returning from the stacks a few minutes later with a slight, secret smile on her face. Her aunt reset the alarm and locked the door behind them as they stepped back out onto the sidewalk.

"What are you up to, young lady?"

Cassie just smiled and shook her head as she walked around the corner to where the Jeep was parked.

&

A slow, steady beeping woke Jack from his drug-induced slumber. Light poured into the tiny hospital room through the huge picture window to his right.

He lay there for a long moment, as a wave of dizziness passed. He listened to the soft alarm that told him the IV bottle, the one that had been feeding him medication through the night, had finally run dry. Soon, he knew, one of the nurses would knock softly on the door before coming in to change it. He hoped they brought breakfast with them.

Now that it appeared that he wasn't going to die after all, Jack realized he was famished. He glanced away from his window and towards the door and emitted a shriek on finding Cassie Belanger seated in the chair beside his bed, her eyes intent on the Bible in her lap. She looked up and smiled.

"You know," he growled, "a poor guy has a heart attack the night before and what do you do? Try to finish him off the next morning!"

"Oh hush!" Cassie laughed. "Couldn't they give you something to improve your personality?"

"No medicine for that, kid." Jack smiled, his words still a little mealy from painkillers. "Were you here all night?"

Cassie looked at him, as the wall clock ticked one long revolution; his eyes watery and his white hair tousled from sleep. "No," she said, "Aunt Beth set me up on your couch." A long pause descended on the room, and Jack pursed his lips thoughtfully, nodding at Cassie before he spoke.

"So," he said, with a slow nod, "she told you the whole story, then?"

"Yeah," Cassie said, "pretty much."

"Well, she's smarter than me," Jack replied, "and that's no surprise. I didn't realize who you were until the night I saw your mother's obituary."

Jack took a deep, quavering breath, and Cassie saw his eyes start to glisten before he went on.

"The first time I saw you, there in the restaurant, my heart about stopped," Jack sighed. "You look so much like her, you know. I just looked up and there was Katie, standing in front of me. I was going to tell you, in fact I'd started to when–"

"I know," Cassie nodded.

"I'm…I'm sorry, Cassie," Jack said, "more than you can know, for everything…"

Jack went on to tell a similar, if somewhat slanted version of what she had heard from Beth the night before. In Jack's memory, much more of the blame was laid on his shoulders. Her father's suspicions, her mother's flight, the gun that Bill had used. The culpability for everything seemed to fall at Jack's feet, and he kept his gazed fixed firmly on his lap, unable to look into her eyes. Finally, Cassie stopped him.

"Jack," she said, "I know what happened, Beth told me all of this last night." She swallowed hard. "You've blamed yourself all of these years, but it wasn't your fault.

"My father," she said, chewing the words slowly, "chose to do what he did and you did everything you could to keep it from happening."

"No Cassie, I–"

"No," she interrupted, "I know what you *think* you did, but you've blamed yourself all this time, punished yourself for something that wasn't your fault! You loved my mother, and you knew it was wrong, but you never acted on it, you never said or did anything out of line." She felt tears threatening, and fought them back. "She never even knew."

Jack sighed, and Cassie continued.

"I resented her you know, my mom, for keeping my father a secret from me, but I can see now that she was protecting me, just like you were protecting her."

Cassie paused and took a sip of water, her throat suddenly dry. "Jack, I want you to think about this. I grew up in a home filled with love, surrounded by people who cared about me, who supported me." Her voice began to quaver.

"What kind of home might I have grown up in with Bill, the old Bill?"

Jack raised his eyes slowly; his face looked haunted, lined with guilt and self-loathing, but there was something else there as well, something like the first faint light of dawn after a long, long night. A tiny predawn glimmer of hope.

"Don't you see, Jack?" Cassie said. "We've made the same trip, you and I, because of our anger and our unwillingness to forgive. I couldn't forgive my father for leaving us, and you couldn't forgive yourself for what happened. I thought I had to hurt him the way he hurt us, and you had to hurt yourself the way you thought you had hurt everyone around you." Cassie moved to sit at the edge of the bed.

"I realized this morning, when I sat and talked and laughed with the same man that I swore I would never forgive. I finally remembered; Jesus reminded me," Cassie swallowed hard, "that I didn't have the right, that it wasn't my place to hold back forgiveness. That's what you've done, Jack, you've taken away God's right to forgive and claimed it for yourself. Are you qualified to do that, do you know better than God?"

Jack lay silently, his jaw clenched, the edge of the thin cotton sheet balled up in his fist. Cassie could see tears shining in his eyes.

"You don't understand–" he started.

Cassie's voice rose in sudden anger. "Don't tell me I don't understand, Jack!"

"I understand," she grated, "that I had more reason to hate my father than you have to hate yourself! I thought he abandoned us. I thought that we were so unimportant to him that he never even tried to find us. My mother lived most of her life sad and scared because of Bill Beckman.

"You, on the other hand, have spent the last twenty years with your life on hold, taking care of him, pretending like it was your finger that pulled the trigger. And making sure that you always had him near so you could use him as an excuse to hate yourself!"

Jack's head snapped up at this, his cheeks flushing and his eyes flashing with sudden anger.

"Well look at that," she said, her voice dripping sarcasm, "he's alive after all!"

"Show him the way to get out..."

Cassie took a deep breath, trying to calm herself.

"Listen to me, Jack," she went on, "I wouldn't say these things if I didn't care about you. I've spent the last couple of days convinced that you were my father and trying to decide if I loved you or hated you." Cassie's eyes locked with his.

"Now I know who you are, who you've been to my family and I know that you're the closest thing to a real father I'll ever have, maybe you're even the man who should have been my father…"

Tears began to course down Jack's cheeks as the flush of anger faded from his face. His lips trembled as he groped one hand blindly toward the edge of the bed and Cassie took it in her own, clutching it desperately, so tightly the older man's fingers began to go white, but neither noticed.

"Jack," she said, and she was weeping herself, now, "this isn't God's will for your life..."

Tell me Jack, what is God's will for your life?

"It happened so fast, Cassie," he whispered, "she was just gone and I never got to say I'm sorry. I never saw her again, never spoke to her or even read her letters. If she had anything to say to me, I never got to hear it."

Cassie lowered her head and stared at the gleaming white tiles beneath her feet. Suddenly her eyes widened and she reached into her jacket, retrieving the tiny dictation machine. From another pocket she pulled a small cassette decorated with a red heart.

"Jack," she whispered, looking up into his grief-reddened eyes, "this is what she would say to you if she were here…"

Cassie pressed the play button.

"*Trust in the Lord with all of your heart and lean not unto your own understanding. In all your ways acknowledge him, and he will direct your path…*"

"…He's forgiven you," Cassie whispered, "I forgive you, *she* forgives you…"

The cry came from the depths of Jack's soul, rumbling up like an earthquake, a geyser of pain bursting from his heart, his lungs, demanding escape. He couldn't contain it; in truth, he was hardly aware as the sound of his voice echoed off the thin, white walls of the hospital room. Faces seemed to float through his wavering, tear-filled vision. Katherine Beckman, Pastor Karl, Dottie Westscott, all the people that have loved him, the last people that he had allowed himself to love. Then Cassie was in his arms and he was shaking, convulsing with sobs.

The first of the pain, the self-loathing, the waste of his life was vomited up, spewn from him like poison.

He said things and was hardly aware of the words he spoke.

Crying out for forgiveness, from whom? From Cassie? From Katherine? From God? Each of them, all of them.

You're giving up on Him, Jack, but He *isn't giving up on you.*

"I'm sorry," he whispered, "oh God, I'm sorry…" over and over again, and each time the words left his lips, the burden, the great weight that he had carried so long, seemed to lighten. Half a lifetime of bitterness and guilt, festering in the darkness of his self-inflicted prison, buried deep where no one could touch it, was being dragged into the light.

No one?

"I will take it away, Jack."

He felt the voice in his soul, so familiar and so close, a voice that he had silenced so long ago.

The voice of Christ spoke to him as He once had, and faintly Jack could hear the sound of voices raised in worship. He felt the touch of a holy hand on his head as he felt and remembered the hardwood floor beneath his knees, and smells the oil and pulp, of pews and Bibles.

A thousand memories raced through his mind, each perfectly clear and laced with longing.

Jack opened the heavy door and took his first tentative step in twenty years, back towards light, towards home.

When Cassie at last stepped away, Jack was exhausted. Drained, and wrung out, he collapsed back into the lumpy pillows, breathing heavily. But there was a light in his face, sparkling from his eyes, a glow of rediscovered hope.

Cassie smiled and closed the Bible that had been lying open on the seat behind her, she recognized that light, hadn't it just begun to shine from her again, as well?

"Well," Cassie said, after a moment, "that was a good start."

Jack emitted a sound that was half laugh and half groan.

"It was a start," he admitted, "but it's going to be a long, hard road."

Cassie smiled, and murmured, *"Trust in the Lord with all your heart..."*

He looked up at her, his eyes red from weeping, his face pale from the trauma of the last day and the emotional exertions of the morning.

Cassie lifted the worn leather Bible from her lap and rested it on the edge of the bed. Jack looked at it and squeezed his eyes shut, his lips forming a painfully white line, as he reached for the book.

"That's good advice, you know," Cassie said, "someone very special gave that advice to my mom a long time ago, and she gave it to me more times than I can remember."

As Jack picked up the battered Bible, a small scrap of paper slipped from it to fall, face down, onto his chest; it was an old photograph, its scalloped edges faded and worn. Jack turned it over and sighed, seeing the young woman with long dark hair, standing in the river, the small, pink wrapped bundle in her arms.

"It's funny," Cassie said, "how the Lord works. He knew what was waiting for me here, and the whole time I thought it was just that I needed to confront my father, to tell him off." She grimaced. "All because of that silly marriage certificate."

"Marriage certificate?" Jack asked, shaking his head.

Cassie reached over and pulled the folded page from the back of the Bible, opening it and handing the much-worn paper to Jack.

"Yup," Jack said, "that's a marriage certificate, what's the question?"

"The question," Cassie replied, giving him a dirty look, "is that Bill wrote his place of birth as *Just Past Oysterville*, but there isn't anything past Oysterville; I looked. It's at the end of the peninsula, so what the heck did he mean?"

Jack had begun to laugh before she had finished asking, deep belly laughs to rival the power of his earlier tears. He tried to speak but couldn't, his entire frame was quaking and the heavy bed squeaked in time beneath him. His face turned crimson as tears squirted from the corners of his eyes. Cassie sat, her frown deepening, until Jack's mirth had run its course and he lay, gasping once more, the certificate still clutched in his hand.

"Well," Cassie said, "I'm glad that amused you. Are you going to let me in on the joke, or what?" Jack snorted one last time, wiping his eyes.

"Sorry," he said, "I couldn't help myself, I'll tell you, I'll tell you…"

Cassie waited, her fingers drumming the edge of the bedside table.

"It's a family joke," Jack said, his voice still quavering with laughter, "you see, your grandfather, John Beckman, was an oysterman, and he ran boats offshore during the harvest. Your grandmother used to go out with him and help, even after she was pregnant with Bill."

Cassie nodded, handing Jack a tissue to wipe his eyes.

"So," he went on, "one day, when your grandmother was about eight and a half months along with your dad, they were out in rough water and she went into labor."

Jack chuckled again as Cassie's jaw dropped.

"You can imagine," Jack said, "with nothing but a handful of dirty, smelly oystermen on board, your grandma was more than a little anxious to get back to shore and to the hospital. John pretty near burned those old Iveco twin diesels up, trying to get back, but they didn't quite make it, and your dad was born right there in the wheelhouse, in sight of land. So, quite literally, he was born—"

"—just past Oysterville," Cassie groaned.

"That was one of his favorite jokes," Jack sighed, smiling, "whenever anyone asked him his place of birth, that's what he'd tell them. I'd completely forgotten that story..."

"Well," Cassie said, "I guess that's typically ironic."

"What's that?"

"I came all the way out here based on a joke."

"I don't know about that," Jack said, "more likely God used that joke to provoke you into coming here, so you would find your family."

Cassie nodded, then smiled.

"Why, Jack Leland!" she said. "You almost sounded like a pastor there!"

Jack grinned a little fearfully. "Let's not get ahead of ourselves, okay?"

"Okay, for now," she laughed, "but I'm going to keep hounding you, you know that?"

"Why does that not surprise me?" he groaned.

"Oh, by the way," she poked his bare arm with one finger, "thanks for trying to ditch me in Gold Beach. What was up with that?"

"What are you talking about?" Jack asked, sheepishly.

"I'm talking about you trying to hard sell me on going straight to Portland," she said, poking him again, "you knew who I was and you tried to ditch me!"

"Ow!" Jack replied. "Go easy on the heart attack victim, okay? I had a plan in Gold Beach, thank you very much, and if you hadn't been so obstinate–"

"*Obstinate*?" Cassie objected loudly.

"Sorry," Jack replied, "stubborn, headstrong and inflexible. Anyway, I was going to drop you off and then come back up there with Beth, so we could break it to you gently."

"Yeah, sure. I think you were trying to ditch me."

"I'm not saying that's a bad idea…"

Poke.

Jack laughed, holding the Bible out to her.

"Why don't you keep it, Jack," Cassie said. "Mom would have wanted you to have it, the picture too."

"I can't take your Bible, Cassie," Jack argued, shaking his head.

"Fine," she smiled, "a loan then, until you can get home and get your own. No arguments!" She waggled a stern finger at Jack, who looked surprised for a moment, and then burst out laughing, once more.

"What's so funny?" Cassie asked.

"Nothing!" Jack said.

"No way," Cassie said, "tell me…"

"You just reminded me of someone for a minute there."

"Who?"

Jack smiled, still chuckling, "The most cantankerous, stubborn old woman I've ever known."

Cassie rolled her eyes, "Gee, thanks Jack, that's just what every girl wants to hear."

Jack laughed even harder and, despite herself, Cassie joined him.

"Speaking of what every girl wants to hear…" Cassie took a deep breath, as she reached into her pocket and produced a small, hardbound book.

"Here," she said, "I brought this for you." Jack picked up the thin tome, holding it at arm's length to read the feathery inscription on the faded cover.

"*Shakespeare's Love Sonnets, Volume One*." He looked curiously at Cassie. "And why in the world would I want these?"

Cassie shook her head. "You're hopeless," she said. "You know that don't you?"

Jack nodded, "I've considered that possibility, yes."

Cassie ignored that. "They're love poems, you goof, remember, you were going to read her love poetry?" Jack dropped the book like it was suddenly burning his fingers. "Oh Cassie," he said, "I don't know—"

Cassie scowled, "You don't know *what*?"

Jack looked at her pathetically.

"It's been a really long week," he said, "I don't know if I'm up for this right now." Cassie's scowl deepened, and as Jack saw that he was going to get no sympathy for his condition, he switched tactics, his face darkening in a glowering scowl of his own. "Now, you listen here young lady—"

Cassie shook her head, interrupting again.

"Uh uh," she said, "nice try, but I'm not buying it. You've been shutting her out for years, you said so yourself. Now that *that's* behind you, *this* would be a good second step in the right direction. You love my Aunt Beth, and she loves you—"

"How do you know that?"

Another rolling of the eyes, "Maybe I'm not doing her such a favor here…"

"Hey!"

Cassie continued. "Beth and Bill are down in the coffee shop," she said, "they probably think I've forgotten them by now, but Beth promised not to come up here until I came and got her." Cassie smiled her sweet smile. "So you'd better start reading because I'm going to go get her now."

"Now wait a minute…"
Cassie kissed him on the cheek and walked from the room.

Epilogue

Summer was beginning to wane. The crowded boardwalk of Main Street was seeing fewer visitors with each passing day, though still plenty enough to keep the carousel at the midway running from dawn to dusk. Even in the tiny, enclosed office of the Sand Castle Bookstore, Cassie could still faintly catch the summer smells: hot oil, popcorn and the sweet-hot scent of fresh waffle cones. She smiled, her fingers flying over the ten-key machine as she tallied the month's sales, a task that Jack had always dreaded, and had happily passed on to her. It had been a good spring and summer, on many levels, starting with Jack's return home from the hospital.

"He'll live," the doctor had replied dryly, "keep him off the deep-fried foods and the ice-cream, and he might still be a pain in our rear in another forty years!"

Jack and Doctor Ottman had formed a grudging acceptance of each other over the last several months, not a friendship, per se, but at least they weren't shouting at each other any longer. Cassie was staying with her aunt, who had taken a small bedroom in her Bed & Breakfast out of availability, and moved Cassie into it, refusing to consider any arguments on her niece's part. This would be "home" for her on her weekends and holidays for the next four years.

Guy and Grace had come up for one wonderful week in June and, as Cassie had suspected, they had become an almost instant addition to the Long Beach family. Guy insisted, however, that he would never allow Jack to take him deep-sea fishing again.

"I'm a desert-boy, I guess," he had said, still more than a little green around the edges when Jack had brought him back from their day trip. "That was my first time out on the ocean and, if it's all the same to everyone, I think I'll stay on dry land from now on."

Later, after poor Guy had been mercifully sent to bed, Jack had laughed in sympathy with the others. "I felt so awful for him," he chuckled, "I don't think he got an hour of fishing in the whole day, by afternoon I was waiting for the poor fella's boots to come up!"

Despite the less than successful angling experience, all parties had shed some tears when the Williams family had been dropped off at the Portland Airport for their flight home. Promises had been made for a trip to Bowie the following year.

"We'll catch us a big 'ol bass down there," Guy had laughed, slapping Jack on the shoulder, "and from the dock!"

Cassie was teaching her father to read again. It was slow going, and more than one person had told her it couldn't be done, but she persisted. Jack, however, had encouraged her.

"Don't listen to them, Cass," he had told her firmly, as they were returning home from Sunday services one late spring afternoon, "and don't believe 'em. Love can accomplish anything, we know that, don't we?"

Cassie smiled, remembering his words. *Love can accomplish anything*, and the changes that it had worked in Jack Leland since February were miracles in themselves. Jack, she knew, was teetering on the brink of becoming an elder at Long Beach Community, a title he was considering with great trepidation.

"You can say no," Pastor Edelstien had told him, more than once, "the title only officiates what you're already doing. You *are* an elder, Jack, to any number of the young couples. A title, or lack of one, isn't going to change that."

Still, Jack struggled with the idea, but it was prayerful struggle and that, their pastor had assured them, was the best kind. That wasn't the only issue on Jack's heart, either. Cassie happened to know there was a small velvet box hidden deep in the top drawer of his dresser, beneath a jumble of mismatched socks. The box, of course, contained a diamond-studded band of gold, just the right size to slip onto the finger of a certain relative of hers.

Cassie had about lost patience with Jack, and had told him, a day or two before, that steps had better be taken *before* she left for school in September.

"Why couldn't you have taken summer courses?" Jack had grumbled.

Cassie had laughed, hiding her regret that she hadn't, in fact, been able to get her loan in time to start school in June. Still, she had enjoyed a wonderful summer, and had earned enough to attend fall classes with only a part-time job to supplement the small loan she had already been approved for. She was awakened abruptly, from her thoughts of school, as Jack and Beth came through the door and into the office.

"Hey guys!" she said, hitting a final button on the ten-key, "looks like we had a better summer than any of us thought, unless I added when I should have subtracted!"

Jack laughed.

"Why do you think I have *you* on the books?" he said. "That's what *I* kept doing!"

Cassie handed him the small roll of paper from the old adding machine and smiled as his eyes widened and he whistled appreciatively. "Not bad…"

Elizabeth winked at her niece. "That's what happens when you staff the front desk with a pretty young girl instead of a grouchy old man!" She laughed at Jack's wounded expression and kissed him lightly on the cheek.

"Cass," Beth said, taking Jack's hand in her own, "we have something we need to tell you."

Cassie's gaze immediately shifted to the third finger of her aunt's left hand, but it was still bare. She glanced at Jack in time to catch the barely perceivable shake of his head. She frowned at him as he shrugged sheepishly.

"What's up?" she asked.

Elizabeth took a seat on the edge of the desk, Jack standing behind her.

He was already grinning, unable to contain himself, as his soon-to-be fiancée handed the young woman a thick manila envelope. Cassie took it suspiciously, glancing back and forth between the two of them.

"What's this?" she asked, slipping open the flap.

"Well," Jack said, "consider it an early inheritance."

Cassie removed the first thing that her fingers touched and it was a small, plastic checkbook. Check-register, actually, and she found that her name was written boldly on the outside. Her hands begin to shake and, without knowing why, Cassie was suddenly desperately thirsty. She opened the register and read the amount of the first and only deposit into the account that was in her name.

She read the line again, and a third time, just to be sure her eyes weren't deceiving her. The amount, written in blue ink in the first small box beneath the *deposits* column read One-Hundred-Forty-Three Thousand Dollars and Zero cents.

"Guys," she whispered, when she could breathe again, "what did you do?"

"Oh don't panic," Jack laughed, "I didn't sell the store, and Beth didn't sell her house. That's your inheritance, literally. It's Bill's half of the money that I got for selling his parents' house. The rest is what I've added as his weekly salary since I opened the store. He gets his social security, so that money has barely been touched. Beth invested it several years ago and, apparently, made some very good choices!"

Cassie gazed wide-eyed at the number once more, then looked to her aunt.

"It's money we put away for Bill," she said, "just in case something happened to us. Now that you're here, we know that you would take care of him in that very unlikely event."

Cassie nodded dumbly, of course she would.

"So," Jack grinned, "looks like you'll have plenty of time to hit the books this fall, without having to worry about flipping burgers or delivering pizzas, or any of that nonsense."

"We called last week and canceled your loan," Beth said. "I hope that was all right?"

"Guys..." Cassie said again, unable to find any other words.

"Hey," Jack said, "don't think that it comes without strings; I expect a big fat thank you in the acknowledgments of your first book!"

Cassie laughed a bit distractedly, her mind spinning, "You betcha," she said, "and...and if it's okay, I'd like to send some of it to Guy and Grace...for Mom's headstone. I promised."

"Of course," Beth smiled, putting her arms around the younger woman.

Cassie clung to her aunt, her eyes swimming.

"It's your money," Jack agreed, "you can spend it however you like. I'll tell you this though, if you don't have a degree and the better part of a book written in four years," he shook his finger at her, growling, "I'm dragging you back here and making you work it off in this office with me!"

"Ugh," Cassie rolled her eyes, "anything but that! I think you just guaranteed my grade point average."

Jack laughed as she reached out and pulled him into a three-way embrace, feeling two pairs of arms squeezing her tight.

❧

Later, as she locked up the office and prepared to close the shop, Cassie found her father seated on the store's worn leather couch. His brow was furrowed as he painfully attempted to sound out the sentences in the colorful children's Bible that his daughter had given him.

As she smiled, sitting on the floor beside him and pointing out the words,